The St George's Angling Club
First Edition. 2010
Self-Published
All Rights Reserved.
Printed in the U.S. of A.
Version: 20110303

Reach Caleb at:

calebgarling@gmail.com

www.calebgarling.com

A short, but important note to YOU

The copy of the book in your hand has been edited by some very close friends, family and the author. It has not passed under the raptor gaze of a professional fiction editor or benefited from the staff and tools of a formal publishing house. While each page has been scoured roughly eleventy billion times and most of the fat fingerings trimmed, you will find an error, a typo or two. This book has been published because of technology's advances and while the curve has not enveloped copyediting, we can give it a little bump. If you spot an error and feel so inclined, there is a portal at **www.calebgarling.com** where you can register it. In a dorky/fun e-bounty, you will receive credit for your catch in the next revision of the book. Call it WikiEditing.

Otherwise, thank you for reading. Believe it or not, you're the reason this book was written in the first place. True story.

- Caleb

WikiEditors:

- S. Neil Larsen -
- Mitchell Schneider -
- Nick Jocelyn -
- Chad Mohling –
- Kim Howland -
- Lee Jester -
- Keith Lane -
- Whit Garling -
- Brett Garling -
- Grandma Dale -
- Mom -

**Giving Thanks,
drops from an ocean...**

*Adam: for creating a cover, a face of such mammoth magnitudes of awesome.
I am so proud to call you my friend.*

*Captain Lane: for giving the righteous feedback that only an old fishing buddy can.
HU-RAH.*

Alden and Kate: for reminding that you can find a gem any time in life.

Darryl and Laurel: for boundless kindness and generosity.

Brett: for distilling a brother's voice.

Whit: for being a brother's voice.

Dad: for showing, not telling.

Mom: KB says 'tank you.

El: I love you.

To Grandpa Joe,
For teaching me to fish.

I

~ 1 ~

I'M A FISHERMAN, so you'll find this story easiest to digest if you don't question the details. Now, the pencil outlines are true, it's just that a fisherman's mind has a funny way of taking license with the bits and pieces that paint the colors. Sure, Paul and David Ambrose came to St George's valley, started an angling club and got into a mess of adventure, laughter and tears, but I wasn't there for every conversation; I didn't hear the wind whistle through the trees every afternoon; I won't remember the weather every day and I'm not going to try to either. I'll take that license and have fun instead. I guess that's why I'm telling this story in the first place. And I suppose that's the plight of fishermen anyway: We're never fishing for fish; we're fishing for a story. And good weather.

Though brothers, the fickle nature of genetics had adorned Paul and David with vastly different frames. David had been bestowed a short and wiry build and fire from their father, passed down from the roving and warring British Isle clans that abandoned dialogue for the fists. And maybe in a subconscious homage, he let his hair grow long when he got older, hanging it low on his freckled neck. Paul, however, had taken on his mother's eastern European heft and broad and tan features through the waist and shoulders, all crowned with a strong jaw and cheekbones. Though he always kept his hair short, draped from his great height was a pair of thick hands, bestowed from ancestors that evolved them into the sockets of creation. The only hint that the two brothers were related was in their eyes—the way they focused. Though Paul's were green and David's a light blue, you could see they were examining, always, even if guided by different motivation. If both Paul and David were given a quick glance into a crowded gathering of people and asked for the first thoughts to their head, David would tell you whether or not it seemed fun, Paul would theorize the reason it was being held.

I'll tell one quick story from well before their time in the sprawling lengths of St George's Valley. When Paul was ten and David was eight, two of their aunts came by their home near Boston to take them to the beach. They pulled into the short winter-cracked driveway that fed a garage that didn't work anymore. The grey paint curled and fell into the patches of grass that indicated what was once a lawn. The windows were spotted and off-kilter from their sill; and if you looked closely at the front door, you'd notice that the screen had been torn from the hinges.

Paul would later remember how their cousins had stayed in the car because his father was home. He heard cautious voices from the driveway. "No," Aunt Dee had said firmly to her children, "stay here. Uncle Richard is here and I don't want you—well—"

"He's sick," Aunt Aubrey had cut in quickly. "That's why we're going to the beach with Paul and David."

"Yes," Dee said just as quickly. "We'll be right back."

From his room, Paul had heard the car doors slam shut with extra force, like a warning shot and then a tentative knock at the front door. It had opened quietly and a moment after, Aunt Dee was knocking at his room and cooing him from his covers. He could hear Aubrey doing the same with David across the hall.

"Paul, sweetie," Dee had said softly, settling at his bedside. "You want to come to the beach today…and maybe sleep over later with your cousins?"

Paul pulled down the covers and tears welled in his eyes, but he sucked them back. He nodded his head as resolutely as he could. "Yes," he said quietly.

"Good, sweetie. David's going to come too. I'll talk with your mom and maybe you can spend the whole weekend with us until your dad leaves or, well—would you like that, hon?"

"Yes."

He had wandered down the hallway steps, a shaft of sunlight bursting into the stale air of their tattered home and sharpening in the standing cloud of cigarette smoke like cream swirling in cheap coffee. As he approached the door, he tiptoed through the stale smell of sticky bourbon and shards of a broken glass; David walked behind him, matching the placement of his feet between the sharp pieces. They didn't see their parents, but Paul could feel them; he knew they were in the house, smoldering like two volcanoes around the kitchen table.

He stepped into the summer sun and tipped his head back into the heat, letting it warm his face as his aunts sealed the door behind him.

When they'd all arrived at the shore, Aunt Dee procured an old green fishing rod from her trunk. Cobwebs strung like dead bridge cables from one guide to the next and the reel hung lamely in its rusting seat at the base. She'd sheepishly handed it to Paul, knowing that it was useful, but trapped because she didn't know how—counting on her tall, smart nephew to figure it out. Paul had looked it over and chewed the inside of his cheek in thought.

They walked from the parking lot to the beach and as the cousins built castles made of sand and hit wiffle balls into the wind, their aunts' attention diluted, focusing on their own children and magazines filled with pictures. Paul wandered away, over to a couple black rocks around a tidal pool, drawn by some void he didn't understand and bent over the salty waters. David crept up behind him, trying to follow quietly.

"I hear you," Paul said.

David ran forward, released from hiding, and looked around the pool with him. "What's that?" he asked quickly, then stepped backwards, his face fragmented in fear. Gulls had dropped clams on a rock to shatter their shells and the destruction and sparse remains of the exposed meat lay scattered in the hot sun.

Paul picked through the pieces and found a chunk of clam under one glinting shard. "I'm going to use it...for bait," he said and fed the rusty hook through the softest part, letting the line dangle in front of him; and Paul saw why a fish might be tricked into eating it. He continued down the beach, away from their aunts, holding David's hand, until they came to a jetty.

Sitting along the line of rocks, men in wide straw hats cast into the waves and drank. Paul eyed their quick swigs and their overzealous laughs with wary eyes; but his dark dream vanished when these men spoke in quick tongues that he didn't understand. He forgot about their drinking and watched them as they whipped their lines into the ocean.

"Come on," he said to David, as he climbed onto the first rock towards the fishermen.

David cocked his head and looked back at Dee and Aubrey.

"Come on, David. Let's go."

David crawled up the rock, inserting his little fingers in the crags and holes smashed by the tides, and followed his brother out over the ocean. The whitecaps unfurled and beat on either side and lapped up onto their feet, leaving salt between their toes as it dried. Just short of the men with hats, Paul stopped and watched again.

David sat down. A wave crashed behind him on the jetty and sucked out to sea like a hunting paw coming up short of its prey.

Paul watched the men for a moment longer and then, before he knew what was happening, he'd cast the rusty old rod. His motion was awkward and stilted but somehow the hook and clam plopped a short distance away and sank out of sight, a lame coil of line extending into the spidery floor of the waters below. He looked at the other men, sat down and waited. The sea breeze blew over them and whipped little droplets off the white caps; they spattered and stung them and dried.

After a minute David said, "Paul, I want to go back." His eyes searched for the familiar women back on shore. "I don't feel good." He stood, but Paul clasped his wrist.

"Wait a second—please David."

David chewed the back of his knuckle and looked at the rusty fishing rod his brother held between his hands. He plopped down. As he did, the tip of Paul's rod bent forward and shook. Paul's hands, unfamiliar and untrained, clamped the handle as it waved from side to side and the line disappeared into the huge, unknown depths of the ocean. David took a step back and his face became tight with fear as the dark sucked away line. Another wave thundered behind him.

But Paul stood and held the rod tighter. He looked over at the men, who'd taken a mild interest in his whining line. He fastened his lower lip to the top of his jaw, hard and set, and turned back to the ocean. He started to turn the reel, and for the first time, could feel the fish actually pull back on the line itself. His eyes hardened and he kept reeling, the rusty and cracked gears of the crank clunking as they brought in the fish, each turn coming in a circular spasm. Soon little darts and flashes of white appeared among the rocks and through the lapping waves. Paul lifted his rod and a little porgie, no longer than his fists laid side by side, popped onto the rocks around them, flopping and searching for air with gasps of its thin white mouth.

David looked at his big brother and down at the fish, his eyes wide in terror—he had never been around a live fish—but before he could stumble backwards, a great cheer came from the men next to them. They clapped and held up their thumbs and whistled with joyous loops at the end of each blast. David looked over to them, taking in the kind applause and yelps. A void in his heart, smacked open by drunken hands, filled with the foreign men's support. He couldn't understand what they said, but he could feel it. They laughed and their eyes told him that he was standing amongst something very wonderful, something to take pride in. An accomplishment had occurred and an addictive warmth flourished in his chest.

He wheeled back around to his big brother.

Paul beamed at the flopping fish, his face drawn in a wide grin, his chest broadening and swelling. David's eyes darkened and he reached for the rod. "My turn," he said defiantly, having lost all interest in the flopping fish between them.

Paul pulled the rod away from him. "No it's not," he said letting his words trail and lay empty with no justification other than a similar desire to make the men proud. "No it's not," he said again, putting himself between the rod and his brother.

"Paul, yes it is. My turn." David lunged this time.

But before they could fight, the panicked voices of Dee and Aubrey filled their heads, stumbling and huffing out onto the rocks and thanking God that they were okay. The rod was confiscated and they walked back to their towels and sandcastles.

David still focused on his brother's applause and the

warmth the men's support had put in his heart. "It isn't fair that you got to catch one and I didn't," he said in an undirected whisper when they were alone again. "It was my turn."

Paul didn't hear him. He looked back at the waves crashing against the dark rocks of the jetty, chewed on the inside of his cheek and thought about what he'd just wrought from the waters of the ocean.

~

From there, fishing infected the Ambrose brothers and flourished in their hearts. They snuck out of the house and pedaled their bikes to the estuaries near Beverley and Marblehead, teasing baby bass from the marsh grasses. As they got older, they learned the bus systems around Boston and moved on to the shadows of the tall docks and abandoned piers between Hingham and Quincy and learned the tricks for the bigger fish beneath. Eventually, by high school, they worked charter trips in the summers between high school around Boston harbor and on Cape Cod, helping doctors and lawyers catch bluefish, striped bass, tuna, marlin and even shark. They knew the world of fishing; they knew the world *as* fishing and they planned to make it their life forever. Someday, they agreed, they'd start Ambrose Brothers' Charters.

But over those young years, a benign fissure had been growing between the two brothers. While fishing served them as a reason and a means to get out of the house, Paul's angle on the sport developed a different shade than David's. He didn't just learn the tide charts; he set down the tables and found books on the lunar orbit, eclipses, planetary motion and the history of the Moon Race. He didn't just learn the shifting focus of fishes prey over the course of the summer, but learned about the cycles within the entire food chain in which bait and game, plants and ocean currents participated. His stock was not of powerful, innate intelligence and he quietly reasoned this; yet it only drove him to work harder to learn.

Quietly and slowly, this began to drive David away. He'd look on with distant jealousy when Paul would answer a question and then tie the answer into a far greater picture than what had originally been asked. Paul never did it with hot air, always casually, as if he simply explained the interworkings of a great network with no singular piece more impressive or less interesting than the next. When Paul left for college on a partial academic scholarship, David watched him go with veiled support and encouragement. He also knew that he didn't come from a stock of powerful minds, but in his own manifestation of the insecurity, it drove him farther from knowledge. He rejected because it had already rejected him. He would have been content fishing the same waters each day and spending each night discussing the Red Sox and siphoning talking points from local headlines. Yet, when he finished high school with no college in sight, he did not stick to his young visions of starting a local charter company, or a local replication of them. He moved away. He worked bartending and construction jobs in Baltimore, Philadelphia and Washington DC. As soon as he'd feel the footing of one city coming firm, he'd pick up and go somewhere else.

He and Paul kept in vague contact; they would catch up every month or so with brief conversations that touched the extremities of life. Paul spent his college days studying economics, philosophy and science so there was little common ground other than their health and perceived happiness. Yet, curiously, when he graduated, Paul returned to Boston, taking a job at a market research firm, working long days and nights, navigating the moments of stress by gazing from the office window to the islands of Boston harbor, known to hold striped bass.

~

Life has its strange way of throwing wrinkles at us. One of the benefits of being a fisherman is that you have a lot of time to think, so I've tried to understand why—why it can't just leave us alone, why it won't just let us be by ourselves. But I suppose that's just simple. To think the breeze won't affect us somehow is a tad naïve. Every breath and bump of our world, layered together with our proclivities and psychologies are folded together like a rat's nest of line, as much as we'd like to cut our way out of it.

So in one of those curious twists it took their father's passing to bring the two brothers back together. After the wake—one of those dark moments where the void of grief is the true tragedy—Paul and David had loosened their ties, shared a few beers and reminisced about young days fishing. They rehashed their favorite spots in the marshes and around the docks and eventually, started looking to the future. They wound the conversation to the idea of taking a trip. As the empty glasses stacked up, they agreed they would get out of New England. They needed to see the West. They would learn freshwater fly fishing and try their hand at trout. The science of the sport would be for Paul, the adventure for David. Their glasses rang in cheers and they quickly flicked their eyes to the heavens, shaking their heads—then looked west, out the window to the blood-red sun settling into a horizon of shivering oaks and tall sycamores.

THE CRESCENT RANGE, running north to south with sharp and layered ridges, like the back of a great oyster shell, sits in the west. St George's Valley is one of the westward watersheds that drain these craggy peaks. Like all the great valleys, it is formed by forces only visible with an eye that spans the millennia. Years ago, lava poured through the shells of the earth and settled atop the planet's crust, still deep beneath the soil, poking and pouring through dark crevices like tectonic cement. It cooled, hardened and became rock and as the years past, the earth weathered away and seismic pressures shoved these great masses toward the light where they became mountains. Then the ice came. Settling in the valleys and shrugging glacial shoulders, it pushed the walls apart and smoothed everything beneath it. These frozen barges filled the depths of the Crescents in an icy blanket, suffocating life under its blue and white cracked hulls. But as abruptly as it came, the ice melted and left the St George's Valley in its current form — smooth, deep and wide.

And through the valley runs the Elizabeth River, the sparkling green ribbon of division. She comes to life in the deep recesses of the Crescents as small trickles of rain, springs and melted snow. Outlining fall lines and slopes, these baby currents bind and shuffle forming light falls throughout the creases and dark places. As they drop with the elevation, they build and crash, braiding in and out and forming larger cataracts until they appear in the fields lining the head of the valley as creeks and streams. The speed of the current slows but the force builds. Controlled and constant, they push their way to the center of the valley where they braid with their brethren and form one pulse of water.

That's when she can be first recognized as a river—the Elizabeth—shallow, with a gravely floor of browns, grays and black. The sun glitters off her riffles, the delicate water laughing on her surface. As she winds down the valley, she cuts deeper swaths from the banks with each turn, eventually forming dark pools, big enough to mirror the sky—her great bends moving like the hardened lava that collected her. Grasses and low brush come gently to her edges and the animals bow their heads as they sip from her waters. She is central to the valley, the life force silently flowing with peaceful precision, always unyielding. As the valley ends at the western slope and the walls lower, the shelves of earth drop from beneath her in staggered tiers that mark the western border of the Crescents. The Elizabeth spills over and around them to make light falls and rapids where she weaves down to the flat, hot plains of the lowlands and runs to the ocean, and disappears.

On one of the northern ridgelines of the St George's valley, on a tight alpine road unscarred by recent tires, a white truck rumbled through the shade, bouncing over rocks and swerving around loose branches. It was dark and there was little to see except nearby trees and the occasional foraging squirrel. The truck turned a sloping corner and hit the brakes, sliding and coming to a stop before a fallen pine. The remains of the tree looked like it had been torn in half, from top to bottom, and then ripped in half by its width. One half jutted at an angle into the road, leaving only a few feet between it and the steep pitch on the other side. The charred innards flickered in the threads of sunlight—black keys of carbon humming a fading tune of the last storm.

Paul stepped out of the driver-side door; the chassis of the truck rocked as it discarded his large frame. He lobbed a long, thoughtful gaze into the treetops, and then to a couple boulders off the road where a couple squirrels played, and then back to the road where the shattered remnant of life obstructed their way. He bent down, then nodded. "Lightning," he said, impressed.

"How do you know?" David asked, cocking his head and pushing back his long hair as he opened the door. The truck barely noticed him exit. His eyes darted about the forest like BBs, then to his brother.

"The burn marks down the center. Blew this thing apart." Paul picked up a dead branch and tossed it into the dark woods.

"You sure?" David asked with a sibling's reflexive skepticism. "Nothing else burned." He kicked his boots through the bark and sent a black cloud into the air.

Paul gazed at the still standing tree trunks and rolled his shoulders as if a great beam were flexing within his broad frame. "Pretty saturated up here," he said taking a breath and letting it out. "Too much water to get anything going—any fire."

"Well, let's get it out of the way. You think you can lift it?"

"Maybe. I'd rather use the rope."

"Getting it from under the gear will take too long."

Paul closed one eye and lazily turned the open one to his brother. "You going to help me—or should I put on a saddle too?"

"Aren't late twenties supposed to be your prime?" David smiled, "Kidding. Of course I'll help."

A shaft of sunlight cut through the trees and highlighted the dust, still hanging in the thin air. The woods were quiet. Paul bent a pair of arboreal thighs next to the top of the severed tree and slid his hands against the exposed coals. He straightened his back and settled into coiled haunches, waiting for his brother. David stepped to the other side and bent down to pull. He nodded and leaned back, jerking and yanking at the stump. Paul leaned forward and drove his hips and thighs against the wood as he pushed with the full force of his broad chest and arms. His energy was straight and concentrated into a point on the log, the end of a piston, exactly where the force was best applied.

The log began to roll.

"Keep pulling," Paul said through gritted teeth.

The log shifted further and completed a half turn. The stump of a branch where David held, rotated downwards and dug into the earth, putting finality in their effort like a doorstop.

David stood. "I think we can *just* get by now," he said walking around his brother. "Barely."

Paul leaned against the log for a moment longer, catching his breath and then stood and rubbed his lower back, wincing and stretching. "I don't know. If we slip onto that pitch, we're screwed."

"We can make it—just need to move fast."

"No. Let's just get the rope and finish the job. It won't take long."

David jumped into the driver's side and fired up the engine, motioning his brother out of the way. Paul didn't move.

"Come on," David said, rolling down the window. "I'll get us past."

Paul shook his head disdainfully, stepping to the side. "If you screw this up, you realize how far we are from anything, right?"

David shut the window. A breath of exploding gas filled the woods as the tires ground in place and launched the truck forward; it approached the barrier and turned, the driver side door inches from the log, as the tires on the passenger side came closer and closer to the steep slope. David rose up in his seat to see both edges, keeping one hand on the wheel. The truck came to the end of the tree and the tires on the passenger side began to slide down the pitch. He gunned the engine and turned into the log. The door scraped and screamed against the tree as the truck came away from the slope and fishtailed dust, returning all four wheels to the road.

It stopped; a pregnant calm descended in the high woods; the forest waited.

David hopped out. "How bad is—yikes..."

Paul shook his head in disgust. "You're paying for this when we get back."

"I got us around without slipping didn't I?"

Paul ran his thumb through a divot of exposed metal and flecks of white paint collected on his nail. "I'm not sure how to answer that." He knocked his knuckle on the silver wound. "Let's just get into the valley and find a campsite."

The door clunked with the dents as it opened and shut. Paul tried to think about fishing as they drove down the remainder of the old logging road into St George's Valley.

~

Down in the valley, next to one of the wide bends of the Elizabeth, stood an old man with a wide brimmed hat, a cigar and a thin white beard. He was fishing. He balanced on a rock in the Elizabeth and cast his line to a pool of trout feeding on the surface. One took and he fought it to shore, scooped it with his weathered hands and knocked it cold on a rock. That would be his dinner. He saw a white truck making its way down the switchbacks under a cloud of dust and walked upstream to get a better view. The truck sped along the mountain road sinking lower into the valley. The old man leaned against a tree and watched until the trees blocked his view and all that was left was the dust. He grunted and went back to fishing, shaking his head with a little, experienced smile in the corner of his mouth.

The Ambrose brothers hit the valley floor and drove along the old service road that parallels the Elizabeth, stopping sporadically to check the pools and bends, mentally marking spots for later. Finally Paul got out, reached into the bed of the truck and rummaged through their gear, fishing rods, waders, boxes of tools, boxes of flies and spools of line, leader and tippet, all in plastic boxes.

"What are you doing?" David asked, but he knew the answer.

"I just want to know. This will take two seconds." Paul pulled a seine from his fishing vest and jogged to the river.

Usually consisting of only a piece of mesh or netting supported by two dowels, a seine may be the most important piece of gear that isn't used in the actual motion of casting and fly fishing. Larger seines can be used to catch fish, but in fly fishing, they are used to catch bait—for examination. A fisherman lowers the seine into the water and collects the passing aquatic life. While most of the contents will be flecks, algae, leaves and other detritus, there will be a precious collection of insects at their various stages. This evidence solves the mystery of what fly to select from the box when fishing. We call them "flies" but they can be any insect—or any bait—in any stage of life.

David walked over to his brother, kneeling on a rock in the Elizabeth. As he stepped onto a different rock, he lost his balance for a moment, but regained himself.

"Careful," Paul said not looking up.

"This river all it's hyped up to be?" David asked as casually as he could.

Paul held the seine in the current a moment longer and then withdrew, procuring a mess of writhing insects, black and glimmering in the sunlight. "Whoa," he said solemnly.

"Look at this. Caddis, drakes, stoneflies—even a grasshopper. They're all here." Paul poked through the specimens and laughed to himself, shaking his head. David started to hurry his brother along but stopped short.

Paul set the seine back into the black currents of the Elizabeth. She clasped his submerged hands with icy fingers and scooped away the contents. Downriver, a couple shadows slid out from under a rock and darted towards the freed insects and debris. The white insides of a trout's mouth opened and slammed shut. They glided and twirled like pink-striped submarines under the froth and bubbles of the silent eddy.

"Let's get on the water for an evening hatch," Paul said shaking the water from his hands.

David noticed the strong shadows and Paul watched the realization, then elation, wash over his face. The subtle shifts in David's facial muscles, the angle of his head, the tightness of his shoulders, the folds around his eyes, were all returning to Paul. They weren't forgotten but pushed to an old closet and the hinges had rusted.

~ 3 ~

THERE IS VERY REAL HISTORY to the idea of strength in numbers. A while ago living creatures figured out that the game of life was shaping around one basic idea: the strong feeding on the weak. After years of trial and error, many species decided that the key to surviving the contest was in playing the odds. If the end goal was to get a set of genes across the finish line to the next generation, the best solution was to have as many players on the field as possible. Some animals decreased their gestation time so they could have offspring faster and populate the world more often. Others increased the size of their litters from a couple to many. Deer, elk and other grazing animals decided to migrate and feed in herds, rather than as individuals. Predators in the shadows may kill prey, but they won't kill lineage.

The phenomenon is not restricted to the forest and the grasslands either. Aquatic insects make use of numbers to survive the hungry mouths of fish. Since these bugs live submerged adult lives but must mate in the air above, at some point along the evolutionary highway, nymphs—the pre-mayfly form of the insect—agreed that The Collective was better off making a break for the surface than The Individual. Trout are the stream's ultimate hunter—quick, aware and unforgiving. You can't out-power or out-maneuver them, so *everyone* has to out-work them.

It is in these instances that fishermen take notice. These

are hatches. But like most of life's beautiful and important events, as much as we hold them to the sun in gratitude, those that study these things don't totally understand them. To start, the actual signal for "charge!" that governs the surface exodus is not well understood. Environmental factors like air pressure, temperature, acidity, water volume, cloud cover and time of day, along with a host of more debatable notions, play a part in firing the starter's gun. But they aren't the whole story. Most fishermen will agree that your odds of experiencing a hatch are best in the early morning or late evening, with water in the low fifties and a mostly cloudy sky; yet they can also give you countless cases where any of those rules are broken—badly. So it is in this respect that a hatch of insects resonates with innate curiosity: recognition of organization, ignorance of structure.

The events before and after the hatch are not simple either. After a short time fertilized eggs turn to nymphs. It is in this form, not as a flying insect, that the bug spends most of its life—scuttling about the rocks underwater, over pebbles and in the sand of the riverbed or lake, feeding on algae and a host of imperceptible prey. While they are good swimmers and clingers of riverbeds, it is in the nymph's best interest to stay out of sight. There is a lot of safety under rocks. At some point, after spending life peeking at that murky blue world above, they get the silent "charge!" signal and whether they are ready or not, they crawl or swim to the surface in great numbers. They avoid the trout they'd seen cruise overhead from time to time; they brave the swirling currents and powerful whirlpools that suck them back to the depths; they dodge a litany of destructive debris. And if that wasn't bad enough, when they hit the surface, the moment for emergence is worse. Now the frantic nymph must shuck its heavy husk (its body armor and wet suit), spread unused wings (and keep them dry) and escape the surface tension into the open air. Depending on your perspective, water is an incredibly cumbersome and sticky liquid. We may rub it between our fingers, but to an almost-weightless insect, emerging from a body of water, while shucking husks and learning how to fly, is like trying to get out of a bubbling tar pit while changing your pants. And all of that stress compounds when they watch a friend pop to the surface, wave hello and disappear into the mouth of an opportunistic trout.

But those that emerge successfully take flight and fill the air like confetti. This is the most palpable stage of the hatch and now they enjoy that one ultimate act that every creature secretly lives for, whether they know, acknowledge or care to admit: sex. The air fills with fornication. Docking with every partner showing vacancy, they are living the dream. Over the river, on the ground, near rocks, on branches and even in the bushes, mayflies are dancing in a synchronized orgy. A happy and free buzz throbs in the air during a good hatch. If you look closely, you might even see little smiles. This can go for a while, but as with most matters concerning procreation, the fun is fleeting.

Together and in rat-tat-tat fashion the moms swoop to the water and deposit their newly fertilized eggs into the current. They are wary of the waiting mouths below, but pushed by the silent, unyielding drive to propagate. The successful mother gets her eggs into the water and watches her children fall and disappear into the darkness below. She doesn't know it, but her offspring will settle safely and start the process anew.

Finished with their only true quest, the adult mayflies find their way onto the water in a sleepy daze and if a fish hadn't caught them as a nymph, emerger, mayfly dun, or even while mating, it gets them now. But they don't care. They are exhausted. Life is over. Complete. They lay their big, fragile wings on the surface, close their eyes and die— their bodies rotating in the river. They are a spinner, the final stage of life. The spinner may ride the current for miles, but at some point, that big mouth comes from the depths and takes them away.

~

A few days after their arrival, the Ambrose brothers sat by the river sipping beers. A hatch was winding down and the buzz was dissipating into the breeze. Two medium-sized rainbows and a brown trout lay on the bank next to them; their expired eyes looked into the grey sky as empty pinholes. Paul wrote in his small black notebook, jotting down numbers, fly types and various observations about the conditions and successful fly patterns. The pages were starting to dog-ear and the cover boasted visible scars from rocks or abrasive gear in the truck. The rainbows had been the most fun, hitting the surface with primal tenacity at each offering laid in front of their snouts. Paul kept laughing about the bright pink spots on their cheeks, just above the gill plates, as if a child had tried to color them with red marker and not stayed between the lines. While the browns lacked pulsing colors, they made powerful, long runs through the deep pools and riffles, staying lower in the water column and hitting nymph patterns weighted deeper in the current. As the hatch subsided and the splashing of tails and clapping of mouths in the river slowed, the brothers retired to the bank and enjoyed the waning light by the riverside. A few remaining duns circled in the air around them, readying to lie down on the water.

"How many fish did you say you'd had?" David said from the corner of his mouth before taking a sip of beer. "Eight?"

"Ten," Paul said firmly without looking up from his notebook.

After a minute David said, "Only saw you land six."

Paul rolled his neck and leaned back on the riverbank, watching the Elizabeth flow past. He wrote one more note and slipped the book in his vest pocket. The birds gossiped about the coming darkness in the trees above them. "I wasn't with you the whole time."

"So you caught four fish in the time we were apart— which was all of fifteen minutes?"

"I caught three while we were apart. You must have missed one while we were together." Paul took a sip of beer and shifted his shoulders, settling into the bank like a blanket.

"Well, I took eight fish and you saw every one of them," David said abruptly and finished his beer.

Paul watched the waters of the Elizabeth skip past them and the remaining light sprinkled on her surface. About thirty yards away near the far bank, a trout sipped a mayfly in the film, then flipped back to the unseen. "Pretty different than going for bluefin and stripers, huh?" he said casually.

A *baetis* dun alighted on Paul's chest. It seemed determined to avoid the river. The soulless eyes peered toward infinity; the wings stood tall, shuddering in the breeze; and the ringed thorax extended and curved toward the sky, sending its two pronged tail high into the elements. It weighed no more than a whisper, yet held firm, standing up to the evening wind rushing about it.

David nodded curtly. "Which do you like better?"

Paul shrugged. "They're the same. Stripers and bluefin run in currents, hide in ocean shadows and make runs at the surface just like trout. You just need a boat instead of a good pair of boots and waders to get them."

"I know," David said impatiently. "They're not the same though. A bluefin would eat ten of these trout without thinking about it."

"Just like a trout would eat ten of these." Paul motioned to his chest.

"You're being difficult on purpose."

"I just don't see a reason to pick favorites."

"Fine. If you could only do one for the rest of your life, which would it be?"

"That's the same question."

David waved him away, "You're annoying." Then a sly smile crept to his face and he set bait in his voice. "How about this, deep-sea fishing or your job?"

Paul sighed. "*Oh*—my job, of course," he said sardonically.

"Thought so," David said. He pressed on, "Okay, you've explained it a couple times, I know, but tell me what you do again."

"I'm not going to play this game," Paul said coolly.

"I really don't understand. You're good at explaining."

"Then you should remember"—A bolt of memory passed through Paul's face— "and take it easy with the old *invisible eyes* routine."

"What—invisible eyes?"

"You know what I'm talking about."

"I don't."

"Invisible eyes!" Paul said in a high, childish tone.

David shrugged exaggeratedly.

"You don't remember me saying 'invisible eyes!' when you'd think you had me cornered or when you were doing something heroic?"

"No," David said weakly.

Paul continued, "You'd play yourself up for an invisible audience and act overly funny or dramatic, even if it was just the two of us."

David's face condensed quickly around a furrowed brow—then relaxed. "I don't remember that—come on, tell me about your job again."

"You do—and no."

"Come on."

"No."

"I have a question—I just can't remember a term you

used once."

Paul shook his head and spoke quickly, without invested emotion, racing against an expiring timer. "We look at the entirety of a particular market and devise reports that examine saturation, customer base, competitive advantages of participators—"

A snore blared; David's head lolled back; his tongue flopped out to the side. He hung lifelessly.

"Exactly," Paul said rolling his eyes, but smiling. "Glad we went through that."

"Sorry," David said, pretending to shake awake. "I don't know what happened. I passed out. Keep going."

Paul laughed a little, then turned the coin over. "Tell me a little about your work again. You enjoy the stimulation of deciding how much tonic to put with someone's gin?"

"I do," David said quickly, ready for the counter. Though, his eyes darkened a little at the slight. "You know why? Because I'm not given a set of bottles to take home with me." He gestured back in the direction of their camp. "Did you make sure to put your laptop and that weird looking adaptor away before we left this morning?"

"Fair enough," Paul said slowly. He could have continued down the path of salary comparisons, but the point lost out to serenity.

David stood and stretched in the waning light. "Speaking of—let's head back and cook up some dinner. I'm hungry."

"Give me fifteen. I just got comfortable." Paul tipped down the brim of his ball cap. A breeze blew over him and the rich smells of pine and wildflowers filled his nose.

"Fine. I'm going to go see what's downstream from here. I'll be back in fifteen. Oh yeah—I still don't believe you had ten fish," he said over his shoulder.

"Mm," Paul muttered indifferently and he watched his brother go. There was a glide that he hadn't noticed a few days prior. David moved from bank, to rock, to shallow pool with a fluid impact embedded in each step as if it was part of the next three steps, a point on a curve—not a transfer from one place, then to the next, then to the next, then to the next. Paul pulled his hat over his eyes and closed them, and listened to David's footsteps over the gurgling drone of the river, the thump and light splashes of his wading boots growing dimmer as he made his way along the bank. The games he and David had just played, in their so many forms, brought an old ease to his mind. As the reach of sleep began to dim his senses, a fire appeared in a brown space with no dimensions, no sound. It burnt brightly. He had a match in his hand and it had just gone out; people were suddenly around the fire; they were on the beach. The world had sound and dimension. The cool ocean breeze flickered over the fire and perturbed a little sand around their bare feet and sprinkled it between their toes. He could see the blond form of his old girlfriend, his high school sweetheart, Gretchen Wilde, moving around the fire. Other people laughed and through it, she smiled at him; the warmth of the fire flourished in his heart—

—the hollow whistle of the wind snatched him awake.

It was almost completely dark. The sky was a thick grey and white pinpricks of light dotted the eastern horizon as the first stars sharpened in the night. The moon was near full, but still gibbous, like a watchful eye. The Elizabeth flowed by his feet, unchanged, and Paul was alone. The wind swept down the valley and over the top of the water, through his thin cotton shirt and to his core. He shivered, looked up and saw three fluttering forms weaving over the river—bats.

Paul rubbed his arms and jumped to his feet. He grabbed the dead fish and his fly rod and looked around, setting his bearings. David was bull-headed but rarely late or not in keeping with his plans. If he said he'd be back in fifteen minutes, he'd usually be back in fourteen.

"David," Paul said into the woods, trying not to yell but wanting to be heard in the stillness. He walked along the border of the forest and the river. There was only the gurgle of the Elizabeth and the black shadows of rocks around his feet. Paul turned and walked into the woods, away from the river, and pulled out a thin flashlight from a vest pocket to make his way under the dark trees. "David!" He yelled this time. A mixture of annoyance and fear filled Paul and he picked up his pace, peering into the woods around him. It was familiar, wrought decades prior from defending his brother on the playground, the playing field and elsewhere: he was frantic to find him, but aggravated he had to. "David!" The woods sealed off the noises of the river and his voice seemed to die only yards away. He trotted towards their camp, trying to find the road, but the darkness kept moving behind him. He turned over his shoulder to see it with his light, but it slithered away. Finally, he came upon the road and he called on bravery to allow the undetectable to follow as he searched.

"*David*," he yelled again.

"Hey! Paul! Here!"

Paul wheeled around. The fear vanished and only the aggravation for having to find David remained. A flashlight approached in the forest, bouncing in the dark. It moved through the trees, turning the branches white and grey, and lowered into Paul's face. He shielded his eyes with his arm that held the fish. A second silhouette walked next to David and a little smoke burned from the red coal of a cigar.

"Over here," David said calmly. "Meet the local mountain man."

Paul heard the silhouette chuckle and walked towards the light. "Aww, I ain't local—no such thing," the silhouette said. "Only camping for a bit."

The two approached and Paul stood tall, still unsure of

the stranger. He'd heard and read enough stories about crazies in the wilderness. "Hi," Paul said evenly.

"Z," the old man said with a voice as gentle as a firefly. Paul unclenched his fist and shook his hand. The calluses of Z's hand were tough like gravel, but under his broad brimmed hat peeked a pair of soft green irises wrapped tightly by a white beard.

"Nice to meet you, Z. Paul Ambrose."

"Yeah," David said. "I walked a little way downstream and noticed a fly line casting from behind a rock and there he was—he's been here a ton over the years and wants to show us the river tomorrow, outside of our little area right by camp."

Paul held up the three trout, each hooked by the gills to one of his big fingers and displayed them proudly. "We're going to cook up some food. Want to join?"

Paul and David had found a campsite midway down the valley in a little meadow on the north side of the river, across the old logging road they'd driven down. The meadow, in the daylight, was filled with blond mountain grasses and scattered rocks covered with slivers of moss and aqua lichen. Over the treetops, the ridgelines and peaks of the Crescents loomed, watching from their great height.

When they returned that evening, David reached into the truck and flipped on the headlights while they prepared dinner. The bright bulbs cast long, planks of shadow across a camp that gave off the feeling they'd been the victims of a mild ransacking. Laid out in the clearing was a tent pegged without a tarp and the flap still open, a couple dirty plates scattered across the ground amongst utensils and empty tin cans and a used frying pan on a rock next to a firepit that still smoked slightly. A mess of torn paper and plastic behind the firepit was peppered with little tracks and scratch marks.

"Nice work," Paul said to his brother, editing some annoyance in front of Z. "You left the bread and peanut butter out and something got into it."

"I'll clean it up," David said carelessly and grabbed a piece of plastic.

"Raccoons," Z said softly. He took a long pull from his cigar and held it between two fingers as he blew the smoke towards the light's boundary. "You know what *those* tracks are?" he asked nodding towards the edge of the shadows. He leaned onto the hood of the truck and pointed the red coal.

Paul set the fish near the firering and walked over. He bent to one knee and flipped on a flashlight, looking at the prints more closely.

"A dog or something." His tone was between a question and a statement.

"Mountain lion," Z said rubbing his beard.

The muscles on Paul's cheekbones came taught. David looked up from the mess of plastic.

"I've seen her a couple times," Z said with a disarming ease. "Good sized cat. She doesn't want any part of you—or anyone. I'm a little surprised she came this close to your camp."

"How big is it—the mountain lion?" Paul asked.

"About a hundred-twenty pounds. Like a big dog."

"A big dog that can tear your face off, right?" David interjected.

Z nodded slowly and walked over to the firering and knelt, looking at the coals.

"So should we be worried?" Paul asked as David resumed cleaning.

"Well," Z said, not looking up, "that's up to you."

He scooped pine needles and kindling, stacking them in a neat teepee in the center of the ring. He grabbed a couple of medium width sticks and broke them in half cleanly, folding them and growing the structure higher. Before David had finished gathering the plastic, Z had put a match to the base and stoked the fire. "There you go," he said. "My contribution. Now you don't have to worry about mountain lions anymore."

"Thanks," Paul said somewhat absently. "Can I get you a drink? A beer?"

"Whiskey." Z sat down in a chair and leaned back.

"Good eye," Paul said with a grin and picked up a square bottle nested in between a backpack and a cooler by the fire. The amber liquid bent and flickered in the growing flames as he poured.

"Cheers," they said at once and knocked glasses.

"So what brings you boys down here?" Z asked easing deeper into his chair.

"Fishing," they both said in harmony. "Yeah, fishing," they both said again, but staggered.

"Good for you. No easy place to get to."

"Well," Paul said nodding to the dented and mangled side of the truck. "We almost didn't make it."

"I'll get it fixed," David said darkly.

Z just looked down and smiled, lit another cigar and blew the smoke into the air above him. It billowed and wove with the smoke of the fire—a tributary to a grey river into the night sky. "So, why aren't you fishing together more?"

The odd directness stopped them both, then David tried to shrug casually. "Hadn't seen each other much, I guess."

"Seems more than that," the old man said calmly.

"I went away to college and we just lost touch really," Paul said throwing the fish on the fire but avoiding eye contact.

Z puffed on his cigar as the coal breathed red and faded. Even in the open air and with fish sizzling on the grill, both brothers could smell the richness of the wrapped tobacco. Z leaned forward and spoke. "I saw the way you two fished earlier during that hatch," he said tapping a little ash from the end of the coal. "I watched for a little while before heading downstream—when I let you find me." He nodded slowly, letting them in on a secret. "You boys have the same cast. The *exact* same cast. But you fight and release very differently."

He pointed the cigar coal at Paul and spoke slowly.

"You ease the fish to the bank, gently, and even though you've got a set of bear paws for hands, you scoop that fish like it was a newborn, keeping it in the water, resuscitating and getting air back in the gills, like you were reviving your own soul, sometimes holding on too long, longer than that fish wants you to. Then you examine it, look it over with an interest and curiosity of a child."

He shifted the red coal to David and spoke with more pace.

"You horse your fish like you held that mountain lion's tail and the only way to be free is to rip it to shore and get it off your line. As soon as you hook up, you don't want anything to do with it. You get that fish in your net and back in the water like it was made of fire."

He put the cigar back in his mouth. "But your cast is the same. Both are smooth and powerful and emanate a bit of aggression as the line shoots over the water—as if you *demand* that fly to go farther than you know it can. You grew up fishing together. So when you tell me that you haven't fished together in a long time, and I see the way you fish now—starting the same, but ending so differently—I smell something heavy falling between you. Something divided you after you'd been by each other's side for a while. And now you're trying to make up for it."

Z continued, "But you're wise to keep moving like you are." He flicked one finger in a small arc. Both brothers followed it until it rested again. "Life is movement. That's all it is—any time you're sitting still, you're no different than dead."

The reaching branches nodded while the night breeze sifted through the long grasses of the meadow. An owl hooted in the dark woods as the brothers looked into the fire, then back to Z.

~ 4 ~

AN OLD BOOK lay open on Paul's lap. He thumbed through the creased pages—the spine heavily taped—in the dust of a sunrise. Roughly 80 years before the Ambrose brothers arrived in St George's, a Denver publishing company, Black Saddle Press, released an all-encompassing book for the outdoorsman. The guide was ghostwritten by two trappers that didn't want publicity, but did want to share their knowledge of survival and life among the mountains. They'd helped and rescued enough stranded adventurers and inexperienced explorers to know that even though they would leave the planet without much of a name in the history books, they might as well do their best to keep future generations safe in the woods. That was their home and being thinkers—having had so much time to do so—they wanted others to love and hold the outdoors with as much respect as they did. The only way to foster that love was to educate. Some might have called them progressive. They called the book *The Hunter's Guide.*

Unfortunately Black Saddle went bankrupt seven years later, both trappers died shortly after, and the book was never republished. New York publishing houses bought and traded for the rights to Black Saddle's small list of books, but *The Hunter's Guide* was too antiquated, they said, too raw and irrelevant to the modern outdoorsman. People wanted to read about cowboys, outlaws, gunfights and Indians.

When people did decide to brave the outdoors, they said, people drove their new automobiles to Camp Something-or-Other where they lounged under towering canvas tents set by the staff and rode horseback to picnics in nearby meadows. They didn't need to know how to start fires without matches and collect rainwater with bouquets of leaves. People didn't need to build shelters out of fallen timber or create tourniquets and slings from clothing. They didn't want to know how to set traps of thin branches or even how to fend off packs of wolves. People had guns and cars! The outdoors would be harnessed soon anyway. The world had changed, they said, it was time to look forward and acknowledge the gifts of technology and progress, not worry about building a lean-to under a tree in the middle of nowhere.

Forty years later when fabrics evolved away from heavy canvas and the portable tent hit the camping scene, bringing about a new wave of outdoor exploration, publishing houses looked to the military and other said-experts on how to educate the public and write their guidebooks. The remaining inventory of *The Hunter's Guide* was either destroyed or relegated to dusty attics and garage sales. With everyone looking forward, the names of the two trappers were lost in the ether of history and the book forgotten. So, that Paul spotted a copy in the backroom of Lee's Used Books was quite a stroke of cosmic interference.

Now, in the dust of the sunrise, as the heavy beams lay through the trees and gilded the whispering grasses, Paul read his book. He had lumbered out of the tent and noticed a mule deer at the other end of the meadow—head up and alert brown eyes staring back at him under a new set of felt antlers—and was now enthralled with what the two trappers had to say about deer, their habits, their meat and how to hunt them.

"You ready to hit the river soon?" David said from behind him.

Paul jumped, knocked from his concentration and turned. "Let me finish this section," he said regaining his composure, then looked back to the book.

"When did Z say he'd be by?" David asked walking to the firering.

"About an hour."

David looked at the book and his eyes darkened a bit. "Haven't you read that whole thing?"

"No. not even a quarter. There are more drawings and techniques and information than I'd know what to do with. You should read it too." He went back to a diagram on skinning a buck.

"What's it say about fly fishing?"

"Nothing. They only talk about hand lines, nets and natural bait. There are some pretty cool ways to spear a fish with sharpened branches too."

David nodded indifferently, picked up a frying pan and headed for the coolers to make breakfast

"I'm going to take a quick dip in the river," Paul said snapping the book shut, standing and stretching. This had become a morning tradition for him; the cold waters shocked his system for each new day. "Want to come?"

David averted his gaze. "I'm good; I'll start some coffee and some breakfast and wait for Z."

"He won't be here for an hour. Come on," Paul said with an element of teasing in his voice.

"I just don't feel like it."

The teasing took over. "It's just a little water. It's not *that* cold."

"Enough," David said. "I just don't *feel* like it…but I may come down and fish for a minute."

"Well, you're missing out. The sun shower doesn't have anything on the river. The real refreshment is in the temperature, not the cleaning."

"Thanks for the insight, Paul."

"Don't get testy; I'm just trying to help out. It's for your own good."

"I can take care of myself," David hissed. "Just take your *damn swim*."

Paul looked at his brother and flashes of a young David's anger came back. He watched his fists curl up into the bullwhips that had cut across his face when they were kids. David had never had the size advantage, so he'd made up for it with quick hands; Paul's move had always been to smother him and take the punches out of play. Yet, the disparity in their sizes had always prevented Paul from punching back too hard.

"Hey, just kidding," Paul said calmly, but David had been provoked.

"How about this?" he said quickly. The tenseness in his fists dissipated as his fingers snatched his fly rod. "You take your swim and I have to fish nearby. If I catch a fish in the time it takes you to clean off—make it five minutes—you do dishes for the rest of our time here. If not, I will."

"Just take it easy, hotshot—" Paul quietly prided himself on a control over his own intensity. If only by steadiness, like extra money in his pocket, he had gained an aloof satisfaction that he had control over his brother's as well. Yet even though he'd provoked David, he wasn't going to shy from a challenge either. "—but, game on."

A few minutes later, Paul ambled to a big pool in his shorts and sat down on the bank. David, in full fishing gear—boots, waders and vest—peered into the Elizabeth, at her deep green and black pools and her frothy riffles, and eventually nodded to a rock about forty yards downstream from Paul's swimming hole. Tall pines cast their grey morning shadow from the south bank of the river.

David looked at his watch and splayed his fingers and counted down. The first time he'd gone swimming, Paul had tried wading gingerly. The frigid preview crept up his legs and raised the hairs as flags on a mountain range of goose-bumps, sending him back to shore shivering.

David's countdown hit zero. Now, Paul dove. The crisp waters coursed through his hair and cooled his scalp, and when he surfaced the morning air sucked into his lungs; life exploded within him. He fell back into the water again and held, completely submerged, for a moment. Soon, the cold began to grow heavy on his lungs and, he could stand it no more and got out, eyes bright and alert. Only a couple minutes had passed.

"How much time?" Paul yelled.

But David kept casting. He was focused, straining to get his line to the farthest point from his rock. A dark black pool held just out of reach. He snapped his shoulder forward as a tight, horizontal, U-loop formed in the morning air. The U-loop slid through the tracks of its motion and came forward as David, again, stopped his arm, this time over the river. The whole rig—line, leader, tippet and fly—unfurled over the current and settled gently on the water. The fly sat lazily on the corner of the dark pool.

Paul dried off and watched his brother's shoulders—so free and loose during his casting—come tight against his body in a tense, expectant pressure, as he worked the fly on the current. A few more seconds passed and the current became too much, yanking the line and fly out of the pool and downstream. The fly briefly dipped underwater as David collected the slack and unloaded his energy, all of it, a funneled explosion, into the handle of the rod. This time the U-loop unfurled, reaching the head of the pool and the fly settled on a delicate crease between the flat water and the main current.

A shadow snapped to the surface; a large mouth emerged, engulfed the fly; it disappeared. Only smooth ripples remained.

Paul stopped drying himself.

David raised the rod with his right hand and removed the slack line with his left. The line came true, taught and humming, fastened to the black pool.

There was a short, quiet pause. Then the explosion.

"Yeah, baby." Paul clapped his hands and put two fingers in his mouth and blasted a looping whistle.

A black flashing mass detonated the pool. Tremors shook through the line, rod and reel, grounding themselves in David's hands. The once flat eddy was a mess of bubbles and frothing water. A face emerged, the fly delicately hooked in the corner of the mouth, and violently shook its head. The line bounced once more and the dark shape smashed into the roiling current; the fish pointed downstream and ran with the flow, right at David.

Having totally forgotten their bet, Paul blasted another looping whistle.

The point where the line punctured the surface passed David, the fish deep in the current. The guides of his rod nodded erratically as the big trout moved in and out, and up and down the water column. Farther down river, the fish broke from the mainline current and curled around a tall rock, sitting like an epitaph at the head of a downstream pool. David's eyes narrowed as he jumped off his rock, into the shallow water by the bank. He moved with a heavy sense of purpose: as one boot released from the river bottom, the Elizabeth grabbed his waders and shot them forward where he'd fight to plant again. A dramatic grimace forced across David's face with each step.

On the bank, now strolling behind his brother, Paul smiled a little and shook his head. "Invisible eyes!" he taunted playfully, but David didn't hear.

Paul didn't see any eyes however; he only saw the river menacingly crouched around his brother. As David waded deeper in pursuit of his fish, the blue and white froth of the pounding current encased his hips and lapped up his back, threatening to pour over his waders and fill them. Slipping into roiling current and swimming with filled waders is worse than swimming with pockets of concrete.

Paul walked to where he was even with his brother on the bank, speaking sarcastically, yet with a tense readiness in his muscles. "You, ah, need some help landing that fish, buddy?" he said as David staggered downstream.

David had no sense of his brother's concern and only heard the sarcasm. He signaled with a middle finger against his ear and a vague smile. "What's that?"

Paul tossed a rock into the shallow water near the bank. "Just checking on you, little brother. I'm happy to land that fish, if you're having trouble." He smiled provokingly.

David's eyes narrowed. "I'll let you know."

Soon, he reached the tall rock with his fish on the other side. With the current too deep on the river side, he centered himself and rose as high as he could in an effort to lift the line over the crest, but it caught on a craggy edge. David sagged back in the water—the Elizabeth growing louder around him. He regrouped and tried again, but the line caught. He collected his thoughts while the fish beat rhythmically through the handle of his rod.

Before he could organize a strategy, he heard Paul cry out from the other side of the rock. His fly line tightened and slackened like a loose fire hose. Then there was a second cry, this time as a holler and Paul's looping whistle.

"What the hell is going on—*Paul*?" David craned his neck and took a step back, but before Paul could answer, his reel began to scream line; and then the line rose in the air. Against the shadows of the late evening, at first, he could only make out flapping wings. Then the eyes pierced like yellow arrowheads through the dim light and David realized he stared back at the menacing gaze of an eagle. Their fierceness made him avert his gaze and in looking away he saw his fish writhing in her curled talons. They punctured through the spine like coils in a notebook.

David watched for a brief moment of splendor, then jolted from his trance. In a feeble effort to reclaim his trophy, he dampened the speed of the whirling reel with his palm and pulled back on the rod. His line, ending at the fly in the corner of the dying trout's agape mouth, came taught. There was a flinch in the eagle's ascent and she looked at him with daggers. Her beak cracked and she released a sharp cry of warning. She pounded her wings upwards with great *whooshes* and the line snapped and fell back onto the water. She turned into the sky, and in a few more powerful strokes was over the tall trees and gliding down the woods on the south side of the river. She caught an updraft and was gone, the trout trailing in her crooked claws.

The Elizabeth continued flowing, unimpressed. David stood in the water looking at the tree tops, his mouth slightly agape. Paul's frame reappeared on the bank against the trees in the dim light. "Holy *shit!* Did you see that?" he yelled, then looked back at the trees and laughed.

"When it was off the water." David gazed absently at his reel.

"I've never seen anything hit so hard. I was just watching the fish run back and forth in the pool and then a shadow passed over and then BAM!—the water just *exploded*." He plumed his hands in the air. "I think I screamed like a little girl."

"Yeah, you did. I can't believe it would come that close to you," David said, trudging back to shore and reeling in his line.

"I was under a tree. I didn't want to get too close to the bank, in case I'd spook your lunker downstream." He paused, gauging whether to make the next statement. "I don't know if you saw, but that was a gorgeous rainbow." He waved at the tall rock. "Here at...here at Epitaph Rock."

David stepped onto the bank. "I did see it—as it flew

away." He examined his broken line and shook his head, then a reality hit his eyes. "I hooked up in less than five minutes," he said defiantly.

Paul looked at him, perplexed. "What?"

"I hooked that fish in under five minutes."

"*Oh.* You sure?"

"Positive. I looked at my watch when I set the hook."

"You said 'catch a fish.' You didn't land it...."

"I would have," David said, his voice rising dramatically. "If I hadn't been robbed by that goddamn bird."

Paul stopped him with a hand. "You know—fine. I'd do dishes for a year to have seen that up close. You win."

The sudden, peaceful void left a moment of self-reflection for David. "Well, I'll help you," he said, pulling back. "Call it a draw."

"Fine," Paul said, as the Elizabeth flowed behind them with little gurgling protests along the rocks.

~

They returned to camp and after some oatmeal and toast, Z materialized from the woods on the other end of the meadow. He walked lightly through the brown grasses, rocks and lichen and stood by as the brothers finished getting their gear together for the day. As they left camp and walked down the logging road, they told him the story of the eagle. He just chuckled: "You *were* leaving it out there for her." The trees threw their lattice shadows over the road as the three continued side by side. Z would occasionally point out a knot in a tall tree with his bamboo fly rod: "Something ran into her when she was a sapling. The young branch never healed right and that's why she's got that funny little flare at the base of the second branch. She made it though." Or motion to a set of tracks: "Mother fox and her four pups. They were pretty thirsty. Look at the tracks on that sandbar—all them pups yearning for a drink." Or just inhale deeply: "I can't keep my mouth open for ten seconds before it's drier than the dust of this road—about time for some rain...to keep things moving."

After about two miles, the Elizabeth opened into a wide bending meadow and thinned to gravely shallows. Shadows glided in the corners. Her tense currents dissipated into a smooth expansive pool among the waving brown grasses and low scraggy bushes. Z pointed to a few sections of the bank with undercuts as they surveyed the waters and walked to the lower end of the pool. As the river curved and condensed again, it picked up intensity. A grove of dark trees on the south bank and a high rock wall on the north punctuated the end of the peaceful pool. The path of quick-ening water wove between them as it continued down the valley, around the bend. Just before the turn, a black log angled from the bank into the river. Its branches had long since broken off, save one, which stood straight up from the rushing water like a thick, gnarled snake.

David stared at it and started walking away. "I bet that twisted log holds a *helluva* brown trout."

"Careful," Paul said. "Looks like the current gets pretty strong."

David waved off his brother's words dramatically. "See you guys in a bit," he said over his shoulder and stepped into the Elizabeth. She objected to his presence and rushed about his boots. He waded onto a short gravel bar that bi-sected her middle and began casting.

"This pool have a name?" Paul asked.

Z kept his eyes fixed on the smooth waters. "Not to my knowledge."

Paul scratched his chin and began nodding his head. "I'd call it The Flats," he said and part of his tone was asking for permission.

"Sure," Z responded indifferently. "He'll tear it apart, won't he?" Z said nodding back to David, as he and Paul walked upstream to find their own stretch.

"Yeah. He bites down and doesn't let go, like a dog," Paul said, half-laughing. "When we were in high school, during sports, he was always the one who would take a shot after the whistle. If he loses at something; he just comes back again, and again, until he thinks he's won." He trailed off and put his thumbs under his vest, letting out a little heat.

"You must have been quite the pair: You, this quiet sequoia and he, a mound of fire ants."

Paul laughed. "We used to fight a lot, rolling around punching each other. I used to get him going by quizzing him about something that I knew he didn't know, then he'd get mad and come after me. Though when it was over, we were back to normal; we just had to get it out of our systems. Once we bet who could name more guys that had played for the Red Sox and I beat him so badly that when I wasn't looking, he chucked a baseball as hard as he could and hit me in the eye—seven stitches." He rubbed his left eyebrow. "But then, like clockwork, after that, he was cool again. Just had to get his shot and feel even."

Z chuckled a little as they meandered through the long grasses by the river. "Sounds about right."

Paul continued, lost in the folds of memory. "Though, I hit my growth spurt and we grew out of the fighting. We used to really get after it—though it was usually me just trying to subdue him—but he would never quit until he felt even." Paul looked around, a bit surprised, and his face indicated he was a little ashamed of how far he'd drifted within the folds. "But Z—we've had an awesome trip together. It's really been good to hang with him again."

Paul could only see the top of Z's wide hat as he walked behind him, but heard his soft voice, "Yup…gotta keep moving."

This made Paul smile. "You've got a funny way of reading people, Z," he said lightly.

"Well," he said with a little chuckle, "there are always signs; with people they're just more subtle. That's all."

"Speaking of which," Paul said snapping back to business. "Go ahead and fish here. I'll head up a few more—"

David's yell came tearing from around the bend of trees. "Paul! Pa—" It was frantic with fear, then smothered.

Before Z could turn, Paul had dropped his rod and was in full sprint. He crashed through branches, bushes and shrubs like a locomotive in the rain and returned to where his brother had entered the pool. "David!" he shouted into the surrounding forest as he trudged through the water. "David!" He looked downstream as the current condensed at the black log that was supposed to hold a *helluva* brown trout. It sat peacefully in the Elizabeth; her rushing waters flowed innocently around the rotting wood.

Paul sloshed back to shore and ran downstream, into the trees and high rocks around the bend in the Elizabeth, searching for his brother.

~

David inhaled water in the swirling black. He spun in the Elizabeth; his legs draped over his head. Churning branches. Something—his knee?—smacked him in the face. Air on his cheeks, his eyes flew open. Water projected from his mouth. He couldn't hear his exhale. Water rushed around him—white, blue, green, frothy turmoil. An invisible rope came taught around his waist. Under again. He grasped at the surface of the river, but it slid through his fingers. His lungs folded, tearing from his chest. Under her surface, the Elizabeth was calmer, quieter, a digestion, but he could only feel the compression in his chest. Hear it. His boot glanced off a rock; he pushed off. Skin against air and the tension from his chest shouted from his mouth. The rope came tight again and he was under; his chest was screaming soundlessly. He jerked at the buckles that would release his waders. He opened his eyes and screamed underwater, tearing at the harness.

Thick greens and blacks with wide stripes of pink waved and bent in the current and then became shadows. And disappeared downriver.

~

Paul bounded, slipped on rocks and algae and he scanned the current and banks for signs of his brother. His felt-sole boots tried to grip the bank to make up for his erratic steps, but failed. One leg plunged into the river. The wall of rocks that lined the river to his right had moved in quickly as he left The Flats. He wrapped his fingers around craggy edges; they cut his skin and palms as he swung downriver. He didn't flinch. *David* had become a frantic mantra under his breath.

"DAVID!"

Quiet.

Only the Elizabeth running next to him. Calm. And menacing. It knew something precious that Paul did not. He kept running downstream. The branches and leaning trees reached farther and farther over the river until what had once been open sky over the river became a large tunnel of flora. The river slowed too, becoming narrow and deep, coated in a stagnant veneer, only broken by occasional swirls and gentle dimples of infinite origin. Patterns that resembled a frothy paisley left wispy tails in their wake. Paul continued shouting his brother's name until the rock wall on his side of the river moved too close and he could go no further without swimming.

"DAVID!"

A few birds chirped back and forth.

He threw off his vest and tore off his shirt. He bent over to remove his boots and fumbled with the laces. He pulled the tag ends and they condensed into a knotted glob and some water wrung out. He tried to get the boot off without untying but it wouldn't budge; he went back to the laces and yelled in frustration. Every time he pulled one section, another knot tightened. Paul wrenched the boot off his foot. He couldn't focus enough to scream at the pain of his compressing ankle and the boot came off with a *pop!* He removed the other boot without issue, tore off his waders and socks, stripped to his shorts and jumped into the Elizabeth.

Before he resurfaced, he was around a bend of trees, his waders, clothes and hat on a rock out of sight. Despite the calm veneer, the strength of the Elizabeth was still powerful and swift. He set his bearings and in a few broad strokes, using the current to his advantage, reached the other side.

The air was damp and heavy; moss and lichen covered everything and emitted a thick sash of moisture in the dense shade. Paul didn't notice a deer grazing nearby on the thick grasses under the trees. The big animal looked at him with empty eyes, sensed his tension and in a few bounds, disappeared into the woods. The movement startled Paul out of his trance.

"DAVID!"

As he yelled, he noticed David's fly rod tangled in a submerged branch. He ran past and yelled again. A rock cut through the bottom of his foot and yanked open the skin, but his face didn't register, even when dirt ground in the wound. It was hard and directed like the barrel of a gun.

"DAVID!"

As brittle as fallen leaves, his brother's voice: "*yeah.*"

Paul crashed out onto a log and saw his brother lying in an alcove behind a branch. He jumped down and grabbed him under the shoulders, sat back and pulled him out of the river; their bodies fell into the riverbank mud. David's waders extended, inside out from his boots into the water. "I'm okay," he said thinly and coughed. "Just give me a minute." He rubbed a swollen mark on his face that burped a little blood.

With his arms still under his brother's, Paul felt him breathe. The still air of the forest settled around them. They lay there for a while in the dark air—two brothers in the cool mud.

"Managed to get these undone and mostly off," David said after a while and nodded to the waders, "before they could fill and really pull me under." He coughed and spat out some watery phlegm.

Paul pressed his lips together and sucked back tears in a sharp breath. He exhaled carefully, but irregularly.

David sprung forward as if Paul had taken on unexpected heat. "I'm okay, man. Just shaken up." He pulled his waders and boots off and stood up, then took off his shirt and wrung it out. As the water seeped from the twists of fabric, his knuckles turned red and white in the creases. Paul saw the movement of life under the skin. David coughed and rubbed the bump on his head—ripe with healthy, but clotting blood.

"You scared me, little bro," Paul said quietly.

David dismissed him with a dramatic wave. "Come on, Paul. Remember when I used to beat you when we'd race at Durgin's Pond? You know I can handle myself." He flexed his arms dramatically and grinned. He'd never beaten his brother during those races.

Paul tried to match his levity. "Not bad for a guy who was scared to swim in the river a few days ago." David started to defend himself, but Paul continued, "It's weird," he said rubbing his neck and shaking his head. "When I was running down here, all I could think about was how sad Mom was going to be."

David absorbed the weight of his older brother's words, then grimaced darkly and shook his head. "Well," he said, "better than worrying about how pissed Dad would have been."

Paul nodded distantly, and lobbed his thoughtful gaze into the treetops.

David followed. "Like a jungle or something in here. I can barely see the sky." The flora on the forest floor was exhaling too. A mist covered a ground of leaves and moist needles. Thick trunks of pine, firs and spruce launched high above, their canopies weaving and overlapping in a strange lattice. Sprawling and crawling up their trunks were thick symbiotic vines that braided and filled the crevices between the bark. A heavy musk filled their noses and coated their skin; the valley breathed over them.

"Well, we should head back," Paul said and stood, wiping some mud from his arms. "Z is probably wondering what happened to us. I lost him a ways back." His eyes drifted to the river—and narrowed.

David was organizing his waders. "How long of a walk is it? I don't know how far downstream I—"

"*Shhhh.*" Paul put a finger to his lips and pointed.

Near the bank, waving calmly in the current was a huge rainbow trout—bigger than anything they'd caught or seen so far. It hung at the surface, seeming to acknowledge them, unperturbed by their presence or sudden motions. A second rainbow pulled up beside the first, just as big, and they undulated together. Their long pink bands illuminated the water around them and the dots on their sides were as big around as tackheads. The air was completely still. There was no chirping or buzzing or any chatter and the wind was gone.

A small mayfly alighted on the current, its wings beating as its hair-thin forelegs and tail tangled in the surface tension; its abdomen vibrated in the film like a guitar string. The second trout looked casually to the surface and with a smooth wave of the tail, raised her head and enveloped the trapped insect. Her wide shoulders and head breached the surface breaking the even veneer and left oval ripples across the flat river.

"Paul," David said, speaking quickly enough that his brother couldn't silence him, but not taking his eyes off the two behemoths. "Tell me—" He coughed into his hand, muffling the noise "—you saw my rod."

~

In his own camp, Z squatted over a smoking fire as the flames picked up in the waning light. His bamboo fly rod leaned against a tree. He looked sideways at the two dripping brothers as they approached, then turned back to his fire. A slight smile crept across his lips and around the cigar clenched in his teeth. He blew gently on the flames and shot a glance to David. "How are you not lodged in the river bottom?"

"Because he's a lucky piece of shit, that's how," Paul said and forced a nervous laugh.

"Not luck," David said without looking at his brother. "I fought out of my waders, held my breath at the right times, swam my ass off and eventually made it to shore. That's how."

"Looks like you've got a nice shiner to show for it too," Z said. David pushed back his hair and rubbed the swollen cut on his face. Z continued, "So what's with the shit-eating grins. You find a saloon downstream?"

"Better," David said. "Trout the size of your thigh."

Z paused and shifted to face the brothers; a knowing intrigue passed across his eyes. He tipped up his hat as the smoke drifted in front of his face and then flattened against the brim. "Yeah, where's that?" Z said carefully.

"The Grove," David said proudly.

"*The Grove,*" Z said with a little fatigue in his voice. He stood and looked at their hands. "If you boys found such an amazing spot, how come you're not carrying any fish—you take a trip to the store or the museum?"

"It wouldn't have been right—" Paul said.

"Paul wouldn't let us keep any," David cut in. "We didn't even get a picture."

"Why is that?" Paul asked sarcastically. "Maybe next time bring a waterproof camera." Then to Z with a second searching confirmation, "It wouldn't have been right."

Z pursed his lips in thought. "The Grove, huh—that's what you're calling it...The Grove." He leaned forward and stoked his fire, then looked Paul right in the eye, locking in with only him. "I'm glad you let those fish be."

~ 5 ~

A COUPLE DAYS PASSED. But Paul and David didn't return to The Grove. They fished the stretches by their meadow, learning sections farther upstream and farther downstream until they could mention a rock or a pool and the other would nod quickly and comment on the riffles or the shade or the size of the trout holding in the area. Z would come and go during the day in his ethereal way, always with a guiding ease. Not returning to The Grove was not due to lack of effort on David's part. Each morning, he'd lobby with his brother, but Paul always talked him out of it, finding a new place nearby.

Finally David confronted him, "Why not?" he asked with a hot note of annoyance. The morning light beamed over his shoulder as the sun rose over the trees in the east; their meadow shivered in the new breeze.

Paul kept his focus on organizing a fly box full of large nymphs and streamers that looked like miniature tropical bird tails. "I'd rather stick closer to camp." He picked up two Muddler Minnows and his fingers stayed suspended over a couple compartments. His gaze remained downward; the silence continued.

David sat back in his chair. "We won't keep any fish. I swear I won't even bring it up. Just pictures."

Paul's fingers continued their decision for another moment and then dropped into the left-hand compartment.

"It's not that," he said slowly. "I just need some time away from that place, another day or two. I need it to clear out of my head. When we left and walked back along that tight rock wall, I felt like I was going...well, to puke."

A bolt of shock ran through David's eyes and he said, "*Oh*," under his breath, then louder, "I didn't think about it that way." Then, with his eyes still riding that bolt, their focus rose over the trees, out of the valley and fastened to the tall northern ridgeline above their camp, "Let's get off the river for a day. What about a hike? I bet we can get to that ridgeline...maybe to that peak."

The energy transferred to Paul and he took in the high peaks. "We could," he said. He glanced down at this fly box and closed it tightly. "Yeah, let's get off the river for a day."

David looked over the ridgeline one more time and said, "Maybe Z knows the way up."

Paul was already setting his rod aside and grabbing his hiking boots.

They drove down to Z's camp; the dust in the road plumed around the cab like a brown spinnaker. Z stood by his firering and was eating a couple biscuits; a pan with used grease and a couple flecks of bacon sat as a lid on the flames. He looked up as they hopped out of their truck. David explained what they wanted to do that day. "Want to come with us?" he asked and there was an aggressive excitement in his voice, as if it were almost a challenge. The dust was still settling around the tires of the truck.

Z thought for a moment, looking to the blue horizon. The cirrus patterns spread west, sharply and sporadically, like the sky had been dashed with acid. "No, have fun though. It takes a lot to get me up one of those long ridges these days," He waved over the trees at the near walls of the valley. "You'll have to drive until you hit a little creek and hike from there. There isn't a trail—you'll have to get creative."

"You sure? You're sturdier than either of us," David said shifting on his feet.

"Naw, a guy once told me that 'a mountain is the best medicine for the troubled mind.'" He glanced at the brothers and smiled to himself. "Anyway, what are you bringing with you? A camera this time, I hope."

"I have my notebook, a lunch, a windbreaker as well..." Paul said trailing off and in his face he knew he was forgetting something.

"No first aid kit?" Z asked. "You're heading into ankle-twisting, rock-slide, branch-to-the-face territory. There are no trails."

"We'll be fine. We're not idiots," David said as he started back to the truck, past his brother. "We'll catch you later, Z."

Z grunted, then went over to his pack and took out a small first aid kit with an old red cross that faded into the black tanned leather. He handed it to Paul. "Keep an eye on your brother."

Paul's nod was well rehearsed.

"Here." Z rummaged in the bottom of the pack and soon handed him an old foldable knife in its case. "I don't need it anymore."

Paul took the knife and pulled the blade from the handle; it locked into place, two strips of metal coming flush with menacing agreement. He drew the edge on the back of his thumbnail, leaving a threatening white line in its wake. "You don't need this?" he asked with his focus still on his nail.

"Naw, at one time I did, but you can have it now."

"Where'd you get it?"

Z peered into the tree tops and let a little laugh whistle through his teeth. "Long time ago."

Paul snapped the blade shut. "How'd you keep it so sharp?"

"Didn't use it, I guess."

Paul nodded, thanked Z and got into the truck with his brother.

As they drove away, David opened the blade. It snapped open with a sharp click. "*Badass,*" he said to himself and ran his fingers over the smooth, ivory groves. "Is the handle made of bone?"

"Long bone—probably deer."

"We should hunt something with this—like a deer."

"Oh yeah?" Paul cocked a skeptical eye sideways. "How would we do that?"

"Wait in a tree—for one to walk underneath. They're everywhere in this valley. Once it passes, drop down and—" He sliced the knife through the air. "We could probably live off one deer for a month, right?"

"If we were staying that long. So to clarify David, your plan is to wait for a deer to pass under a tree, drop on it and then kill it with that knife." Paul looked out the window carefully at the approaching stream.

"Well, I'm half kidding."

"You sounded pretty serious."

"Well, I think it would be pretty badass."

"If we were in a *movie.*"

David avoided his brother's eyes. "This would be cooler. I'm sure there's something like that in your survival book."

Paul had stopped listening to him. "I think this is the spot that Z meant for parking."

David put the knife case on his belt, cinching it tightly.

They parked, grabbed their packs from the truck bed and started their hike. David stepped with heavy feet through the dead leaves and the grasses; Paul walked in front of him carefully, smoothing a path. They followed the little stream as it opened to a thin glade lined by ponderosa pines, sprinkled with purple and yellow wildflowers and moss covered rocks. A squirrel watched them approach, batted its paws and ran up a nearby tree, spooking a couple finches that took flight to the next available bough amid protests.

After they passed the clearing, Paul peered down into the stream and stopped. "Hold on a second."

David tried to see the peaks through the trees. "We're not going to make it to the ridgeline if we stop a lot."

"Just take it easy." Paul stepped onto an almost-submerged rock and reached into the water. He pulled out a smooth stone with both hands and held it like an ancient oracle. The sun reflected brightly off the surface, enough to make him squint. He turned it over and examined the bottom, covered with little black, brown and grey larva, amongst which crawled a few small nymphs. "Covered in life. Even in this little tributary. Gorgeous *baetis* right here, a couple early *trichoptera*—that's caddis."

"What flies do those match up to?" David asked impatiently looking upstream.

"I'll show you later when I have my boxes." Paul caught his brother's eye. "I'm going to stop telling you the real names."

"Paul—we've talked about this. It's not called fly *lecturing*. Speaking Greek doesn't catch fish."

"It's Latin. Do you even have a sense of *why* there is so much life to begin with? Does that question even come into your mind?"

"We're in the mountains and there is no one around and no towns. Of course there is going to be tons of nature life around here. There aren't people."

"That's a sort-of-correct answer."

"It's true."

"In some ways, but you're missing the bigger picture. That's like saying you have long hair because you haven't had a haircut. The better answer is that you have long hair because your body has grown it all. We're about to hike this ridgeline with all the rocks and dirt and minerals coming out of these big, old peaks, right?"

"Yeah...."

"So what does that mean?"

"I don't know, Paul," David said with a cornered tension in his voice.

"Where does all that stuff go when it rains or snows?"

"Downhill."

"That's the point. The rain washes the minerals off. All the eroded debris and dust flows into the streams and eventually to the Elizabeth, feeding the algae and plant life along the way. And what feeds on *that*?"

"Don't talk down to me—Latin bugs." David said rolling his eyes, but interest was waging war with a forced apathy.

"Exactly. Bugs—everything we try to mimic as we fish. And with lots of bugs, we get lots of healthy fish. It's good to know what's what, so you can be smarter about catching them." A flash of provocation went across Paul's face. "Then you don't have to look so lost when there's a hatch."

David rolled his eyes. "Whatever. I just look for the fly in my box that looks like what's buzzing in the air. I catch as many fish as you do."

"Pretty sure I netted more fish during that caddis hatch last night."

"*Bullshit* you did! I took seven; you took seven." David kicked some rocks and a piece of the bank at his brother.

Paul batted a clump of soil from the air as it sailed towards him. "Don't do that," he said calmly. "I took five in that first stretch near camp and then four downstream from there. We'll settle this when we get back tonight."

"Think you're so damn smart," David said looking back to the peaks ahead.

"I don't, David. There is nothing smart about being curious."

Paul set the rock back in the river and they continued hiking. Soon, as the peaks loomed closer, the creek whittled away until only a thin laminate of water remained. The pitch began to bend upward and they finally came to the base of the true slope.

"What do you think?" Paul said sipping water and adjusting his hat. "Time for some rock hopping, or at least hiking with a hand on the ground."

David pointed upwards and drew a vertical line with his finger. "I think if we follow this drainage until about *there*." He focused on V-shaped division in the ridgeline. "We can make it up to that first landing, about a mile or so up. Then figure it out."

Paul nodded. "Z wasn't kidding when he said there weren't any trails."

They ate their lunches in the heavy grasses at the base of the slope and then continued up the drainage. They pushed upwards, until the rocks started to shrink and turned to gravel. They kept going until the pace was sloppier and their feet slid in the loose scree. The trees that once sheltered them thinned, replaced by small shrubs, fallen branches and occasional patches of grass and wildflower. Each step kicked a plume of dust that settled in the creases of their skin.

Finally, Paul had good footing and turned around to get his bearings.

"David. *Stop*."

"What?"

"Turn around."

David crawled up a few more paces before he found some taller grasses with deeper roots to provide support. He took his hands off the ground and turned.

"Whoa."

The valley sprawled below. Greens, browns and golds of trees, grasses and underbrush melted around the Elizabeth, the serpentine division. The southern wall of St George's cast a toothy shadow through the length of the floor. The brothers looked up and eye to eye with the opposite row of peaks, the towering ramparts of time, and then beyond, southward, down the Crescents and to a jagged blue horizon. The clouds gathered and loomed above—great white ships moored in a celestial harbor.

"How high do you think we are?" David asked, his wayward hair snapping in the wind. They weren't enjoying coincidental breezes but standing in throughways of the planet's weather systems.

"A few thousand feet off the valley. Maybe a little more."

A moment passed. Birds and rodents played in the shrubs around them; hawks and eagles circled in the valley below.

"Even from here, you can see The Elizabeth sparkle." An awe—a respect—crept into David's voice.

Paul continued, "And you can see the little streams that feed her—more than I'd realized, especially at the head." He pointed to the east and around the beginnings of the Elizabeth, then turned west and looked towards the end of the valley. "And you can see where the river covers up in the high trees and behind that rocky hill. That must be The Grove. Also, I never realized how the valley runs to those drop-offs at the end; the whole river comes apart over that pitch."

"Yeah, I think Z mentioned those once," David said, shifting his feet in the loose gravel and putting down a hand to steady himself.

"They look like giant steps," Paul said, then repeated, "The Giant Steps." The wind whistled across their faces. "Can you imagine living in this valley?" Paul asked.

David spoke before his brother was done with his question. "I've been thinking about that," he said almost defensively.

Paul sensed his abrupt intensity. "I guess I don't mean *actually* living, but trying to stay here for a while. I mean, we have jobs."

"Well, if we really sat down and thought about the logistics, we could figure out how to make it work. And Paul, you hate your job — as much as you won't admit it."

"I only vent about the bad parts."

"Right. And why would you ever want to focus on the good parts? That's not in your nature at all," David said sarcastically. "Anyway — we could set a *permanent* camp here."

Paul enjoyed the idea. "We'd need to get better tents for when it rained."

"Or a cabin."

Paul laughed, then tightened when he saw David wasn't joking. "What — build one?"

"Why not?"

"Well—"

"Since when do you shy from hard work?"

"I'm not. Just seems like…a lot."

David looked back out over the valley. "Not if we did it right," he said as squinted back towards the bending section of river near their little meadow. The faint glimmer of their nylon tents blinked back at him. In his mind, he replaced them with a tiny cabin with smoke coming from a chimney.

Paul lost interest in his brother's reverie. "Hey, do you have any water? I'm out."

David responded slowly, extracting his focus from the vision. "I'm almost out too."

"How thirsty are you?" Paul asked.

"Not that thirsty, I guess." David didn't make eye contact.

"Well, let's get back."

"Wait a sec — I want to get up to that peak. I bet we can see the next valley and to the north and get a way better view than this."

"Maybe. But we don't have any more water and I'm sweating my ass off."

"I'm not sweating that much." David said not looking him in the eye again, and started to turn.

"Yes, you are. It's evaporating so you don't feel it. You have salt crusted all over your cheeks."

"Well, whatever. I'm going to reach that ridgeline. You can come with me or not. I've been looking at it all week and I'm not turning around now." David began climbing again as his brother followed.

"David, don't be stupid. We can come back with more water, or a purifier, and do it again." Paul reached out to stop him but David pulled away. They climbed another twenty yards with Paul following. "David, *wait—*" Paul started to yell, then cut short; his eyes widened.

A menacing grumble emanated from the nearby shrubs; the hackles on their necks straightened. It grew to a deep growl and exploded in a scream from the shadows; tremors ran through the branches and leaves; the thunder smoothed to a slow rumble; then tore apart the air in a piercing roar. A mountain lion crept out from the darkness. She looked down at the two brothers flashing her long teeth and searing them with two green-gem eyes.

David shuddered and slipped backwards.

~

If there is royalty in the North American Wilderness then, without question, the king's crown belongs to the grizzly bear. He is the most powerful force roaming the continent. Standing over eight feet tall and weighing over three-quarter ton, his shimmering brown coat can withstand the blade of a hunting knife; his claws can shred a truck's door into ribbons; his long incisors would dwarf the thumbs of a carpenter. He can shove down young trees that harbor prey and chase down sprinting deer in an open field. He can wade into whitewater and snatch trout and salmon with his powerful jaws, as his four thick limbs anchor him like bridge pylons. Save man aiming a high-powered rifle at his heart, no creature stands a chance against nature's greatest man-of-war.

But if the grizzly is king, then the mountain lion is the stealthy and delicate queen. While she goes by many names—cougar, puma, panther, catamount—she is rarely seen. The nickname "ghost cat" seems most appropriate. She shares a diet similar to her lumbering brown counterpart but hunts in contrast. She lies low. She blends into grasses, melts onto branches and peers from behind rocks. She tracks her prey methodically, exhibiting iron patience and a guile that weaves her into the fabric of the woods and unseen places. When she strikes, the shadows spawn snuffing paws, appear in a flash of lightning and leave only the echo of a rumbling purr behind. And because she is so quick, she wastes little energy, saving that strength to defend herself and, if need be, her cubs.

So here, in her fierce, but rarely used defense, the Ambrose brothers stumbled upon the queen of the wild, startled by their argument as she crept from her cave to hunt. She screamed, batted a paw in the air and stepped toward them. Her black and green, tear-drop eyes had been reduced to violent slits, underscored by her sharp white whiskers and tight wrinkles above her wide, pink nose. She took another step and stopped, as if loading a catapult—ears laid flat against her head, muscles in her haunches wavering like fields in the wind, incisors and carnassials glinting in the sun.

Paul first:

—Don't look in the eyes.

—*My back foot is slipping.*

—Don't move. I'm behind you.

—K.

—Link arms, flail; make all the noise you can. Ready?

—*Mhm.*

And they did. A man's yell to save his life is no more replicable on paper than a lonesome aria; the waves transcend sterilized communication and speak from a mouth we can only feel. They harnessed their fear, and blasted and tore into the wind with it. The cat scowled at this new creature with two heads and limbs in every direction, bellowing sounds of strength; the tremors rumbled over her white and gold fur.

She hissed.

They kept yelling.

The cat batted its paws and hissed again, narrowing her eyes farther.

David threw a handful of dirt; it caught the wind and spread harmlessly in the air.

The cat took a step forward, pawed the air and screamed like lightning.

They kept yelling; Paul hurled a rock. The mountain lion side-stepped, but the stone caught her hip. The cat hissed, took a step backwards, tucking its ears lower, batting its claws in the air; the razors gleamed in the sun. Then a flash of knowing calm passed over her face and she stepped back, around some boulders and was gone. They yelled for a few more beats, then ran.

They bounded down the mountain, sliding on the rock and dirt and scree. Dust and gravel sprayed into their faces and mouths as they descended back into the valley, holding the last shred of control over the physical forces around them, like cowboys on a bronco, just maintaining balance. Fear crippled and propelled them at the same time. With every step they expected crushing paws on their shoulder as their neck crumpled under the force of her jagged jaws. They bounded over rocks, around trees, through shrubs until they could scarcely breathe. Just before the dense trees, Paul yelled to slow down, but the words came out as just grunts and vowels and wheezing and spittle. He stopped and took one huge breath and put his hands on his knees and focused on his vocal chords. "We're okay." He took a gulp of air.

David bounded to another rock, barely making the gap.

Paul caught his wind. "*SLOW DOWN, DAVID!*"

David jumped again. His name cleared a path to his brain. "No!" he yelled over his shoulder and kept bounding.

"It's not hunting us." Paul gasped and shook his head. He hacked dirt from the back of his throat. "It wanted us out of there. That's all." He spit and brown mucus hit the ground, leaving trails across his chin as he doubled over. He looked up, watching his brother close on the thick trees below.

David jumped to another rock, almost falling, and then made the gap to another. He stopped for a brief moment, looked back to his brother and shouted, "How do *you* know what it wanted?"

"I read—"

"I don't give a shit what you *read*." David took off again; he was almost to the trees.

"She didn't want anything to do with us either. Don't think about it like a person."

David was into the trees and gone.

~

Paul tried to enjoy his walk along the stream again, stopping to look at bugs, animal tracks and the trees. But he couldn't shake his anxiety. Every noise in the forest, even from the smallest twitch of a branch made him jump. A bird swooped low through the trees and he cowered in fear. He regained his composure and pretended nothing had happened; he willed himself to be comfortable. But after a couple scares from harmless rodents, he decided it would be best to jog.

The truck stood where he'd left it and David sat inside on the passenger side, staring ahead. Paul got in without saying anything. Outside, the birds chirped merrily, the insects buzzed and the trees waved in the wind. The sun beat down and warmed the cab. Paul cracked the window and leaned his head back against the seat. "See, I'm alive."

David looked like he might say something, stopped and then continued with a different thought. He shook his head and laughed weakly. "How did that not scare you?"

"What are you talking about? I almost shit my pants."

"Yeah, but you just strolled through the woods, taking forever to get back here—to make a point, I think."

"Because I read enough about mountain lions to know that they don't want to mess with humans. They don't. She just wanted us out of her space. And when I stopped, we were a ways from her. It seemed way more dangerous to be bounding down a mountain at that point."

David looked out the window a while longer, took a deep breath and emerged from his trance. Again he started with one train of thought, paused and then continued with another. "Well, you're here, I guess." He smiled weakly. "Let's get back to camp and do some evening fishing. We need to settle our discussion from earlier on who catches more—"

Paul put up a hand. "What were you about to say?"

"Nothing—it's nothing."

"What?"

"It's dumb."

Paul smiled a little, "I'm sure it is, but go ahead anyway."

David shook his head and shrugged one shoulder. "I've been sitting here, pissed at you—"

"Well, I'm here—"

"Let me finish. You asked." David cleared his throat.

"This will seem random; but do you remember how we could always tell when Dad would come home drunk?"

Paul took a second to adjust to the change of topic. "Of course, he'd wrestle with the lock on the front door, as if it hadn't been locked the last million times—"

"And we'd always run to bed as he fumbled for his keys." He turned to his brother. "Do you remember the night I'm thinking about?"

"No." Paul did, but wanted his brother to continue on his own.

"That night Dad walked in and we were in the living room watching TV. We'd both heard him shake the handle and had looked at one another. But we didn't move—well, I should say, *you* didn't move and you told *me* to stay put." David scraped at some dirt on the dashboard and flicked it away. "So Dad came into the door way—you really don't remember this, Paul?—and the room was dark, only the TV was on, and stood there looking at us on the couch. And I remember he looked at *you*. He looked at you *hard*; he really stared you down." David pursed his lips and shook his head. "And that was it. He never messed with either of us again. But Paul—do you know why he didn't take a run at you or me again? Because he was *scared* of you. That's why. And I remember feeling safe, but in that same instance, jealous that you could do that—and I *couldn't*. If you hadn't been there, he'd have taken me to task. But he realized he'd pushed his luck far enough and you were probably going to fight back one of these days." He leaned onto his knees and knocked on the dashboard, looking at where the dirt had been a minute before. "So while I've sat here waiting for you, wondering if you'd been nailed by a mountain lion, I've been thinking about that...I don't know why." His voice trailed off and he looked out the window.

Paul's face searched for words but only nodded, chewing his cheek. He began to speak, then stopped himself and his eyes developed a frustration at their edges. "I think that—" he started then cut short, shaking his head at his lack of available words for his brother and a little anger went through his brow. David continued looking out the window. Paul regained his composure and reached over the seat and put a hand on his brother's shoulder with a lighthearted provoking note in his voice, "Maybe we should settle our little competition from earlier."

"Yeah," David said, coughing and nodding.

The emotion in the cab of the truck slowly dissipated out the windows. They drove back to camp in silence as the old road rumbled under their tires and the silver scar on the driver side door glinted in the sun.

~

They fished the evening hatch in the shallows upstream from their camp with a celebratory pull of whisky for each trout. When the score was roughly six to six, they lost count but continued fishing, acting as if they hadn't. Around the campfire with a couple victory filets on the grill, the fear and flight of the day had faded in their minds—the adrenaline gone—only its residue, and two brothers around a growing campfire remained.

Paul started the game this time, tapping a pen in his notebook, "I'm pretty sure you didn't have ten fish. And you can't count those two that you lost behind that flat rock shaped like a candy bar. That was the same fish."

David rolled his eyes. "We fished near each other for four, I went upstream and caught two, then I came back down past you and caught three more, then I walked up behind you, cast into your riffle and caught my last." He burped and inhaled quickly.

Paul laughed. "That *was* impressive." He tossed his notebook aside and cracked a beer. "Okay, you can win."

"Don't give me that. I beat you." He covered his mouth

and burped again.

Paul leaned forward onto his thick knees and turned the fish over on the fire. He put his hands up and felt the pulsing heat against his tender palms. He closed his eyes wistfully.

During his high school years, Paul had always been a proponent of moving the clandestine festivities to the beach and starting a bonfire in one of the deserted sections of sand nestled in the layered shorelines of Cape Cod. The first to arrive, two loads of wood pinned to his chest, he'd carefully lay them in the pit as he constructed his sacrificial wooden teepee—the structure that would start the blaze. He filled the center with newspaper and kindling in the same patterns, careful not to let them blow away in the sea breeze before he could apply the first match. He always wanted to light his fire in one match. At some point he'd challenged himself and had done so ever since out of habit. It was pointless but he quietly relished when he succeeded and quietly seethed when he didn't. One evening at the end of high school, he'd struck match number one as a sharp gale blew in from the Gulf Stream, snuffing the flame before it had burnt all the phosphorus off the tip. He swore loudly, a rare crack in the lid he kept over anger, and Gretchen Wilde heard the sharp words and the intensity. It drew her to him. Later, when the party had slowed and dissolved in pairs to the dark dunes, he'd stayed wrapped around her next to his fire, staring into the embers and listening to the hum of the ocean through her blond hair.

Paul opened his eyes; the heat was burning his tender palms and he drew them back, slowly; something about the pain was pleasurable. The flames had grown and swirling bursts rose above the wood, popping and snapping. He looked up to his brother and noticed his face was in the same taught expression from their earlier discussion in the cab of the truck.

David felt his brother's gaze and turned. "Do you think we could have taken that mountain lion if it had attacked us?" he asked solemnly.

"Maybe," Paul said after a minute and dusted the dirt from his knees. "Those things are pretty gnarly. They say you should fight back if they attack. Did you see those claws? I'm not sure what we would have done about those, let alone the teeth."

"How much do you think it weighed?"

"One-thirty or so."

"One-thirty? You're almost twice that." David replayed the crouching mountain lion in his head. "It was bigger than one-thirty. At least one-fifty, right? Paul, I bet...I bet if we each had a knife and a big stick, we could have taken it." He clubbed and stabbed the night air at his feet.

"Yes, perhaps if she just lay there quietly, as you're indicating. But I don't think we should find out. I'm sure a lot of dead guys in local papers say similar things. And by the way, I don't weigh twice that, or even close." Paul pulled the fish off the fire and handed one to his brother.

"I heard you and Z talking the other day and there are no grizzly bears around here, right?" David kicked a stone by his foot and it caromed off one of the rocks surrounding the fire.

Paul nodded slowly and stretched his broad jaw. "I looked at some maps of where grizzlies are today—at least are known to live—and there hasn't been any around here for the last thirty years. The hunters have driven them all north."

David laughed. "Sending them to Canada, I guess." Then he furrowed his brow, "We are totally jinxing ourselves. I feel like one is going to pop out of the woods as we're talking about this."

Paul pulled the tinfoil on his plate apart to expose the wrinkled skin of a cooked trout. "Though if I'm wrong," he said, "this would be what draws them here." As David grunted another nervous laugh, Paul examined the dead fish. The eye had cooked out. Paul hated when the eye stared back at him.

Above, the moon was only a white sliver in the sky as their campfire illuminated the Douglas firs around them. Rustles in their little meadow, untouched by light, kept them company. David took a sip of beer and popped the bottle away from his mouth. "I'll tell you," he said shaking his head and when he opened his eyes, the lids cut a little lower over the irises. "I love it here." The fire popped in response and an extra plume of smoke rose to the sky.

"Me too," Paul said evenly, and then winked. "A lady or two wouldn't hurt either."

David swallowed the bite and washed it down with beer. "No…not yet. I'm not dating anyone; you're not with Gretchen—for *now*," he said with playful provocation, but continued when Paul didn't react. "Let's bring back our friends next year. This meadow is perfect for camping and there is plenty of river."

"Make it an annual trip."

"No," David said with severity. "Make it a *real* place—for us, well, for fly fishermen." He cracked a new beer and the foam poured out. He covered it with his mouth and was quiet for a second, thinking about what he'd just said.

The night wind whipped into the sky and an eagle flew in front of the stars on its way home. Its sharp eyes looked down the dark, quiet valley. It could only see the sparkles of the Elizabeth bending in the moonlight and in a clearing by her side, curiously, a lone campfire with two men around it.

"This is pretty far out of the way," Paul remarked.

"So? Why would we want to go to a place already crawling with people? The Connecticut, the Platte, the Sacramento, the Green, any of those rivers?"

"I agree. I just think you'll have a tough time getting

people all the way out here."

"Why?" David asked. "Don't you think pictures and stories will be enough?"

Paul shrugged and opened another beer. "Doubt it. It took an act of god for me to get the time off work and I *really* wanted to. I don't know if other guys would do the same."

"Like who?" David asked. "Guys from home, your buddies from college—the ones that fish?"

"Yeah, I don't know how you'd convince them."

"Hold up a mirror," David said quietly.

"What?"

"Answer me this, Paul. Honestly. What is the best part of your week, outside of the weekend?" He leaned forward in his chair. "Best part."

Paul shrugged and picked at the label of his bottle. "Relaxing each night, probably."

"Exactly." David waved a hand; some fish flew from the end of his fork.

Paul furrowed his brow. "Exactly, what?"

David eased into his words slowly, "Look—a long time ago, I conceded that you...are smarter than me. That's the way it is. But, Paul, what are you doing? You can't put down books. You can't stop asking questions about stuff like insects with Latin names and why this river is healthier than any other—you take the time to understand things. And at the end of it all, you're willing to retreat to your little hovel under fluorescent lights in the corner of an office. Honestly—when I think about that, I'm disgusted with you."

Paul nodded evenly. "David, I agree it's not the way nature intended, but life is pretty different than the days of roaming the savannah, clubbing women and hunting with spears, or even from the days of Thoreau and his little experiment. We need jobs and offices and the rest of it."

"I don't buy that—or at least as wholeheartedly. I think that's what we're always told. Like when Mom used to tell us how bad alcohol was, that it would make us bad people, and we'd go to hell or whatever else she said. I feel that same way about '*The Modern Man*' story. That we're just told to suck it up because that's the way the world works. Screw that. For a guy that asks so many questions, Paul, you sure do miss the big ones. Don't be one of these people that walk through life with their mouth open."

The lid on Paul's anger jostled for a moment. "No offense—but you've never had a life like you're describing. You've bounced from job to job, bartending, construction, whatever, just squeezing by and working strange hours. I'd much rather have a real paycheck and know I can come home at seven each evening. It may be the best part of my week, but I'm comfortable."

David kept his eyes fixed in the fire. "Look, I don't deny that your life has *a nice comfort* or whatever. But you're the bolt that connects the tailgate on the truck—needed, but totally replaceable." Paul started to argue but David continued quickly. "But that's almost beside the point. That's why I want to have a trip—a *place*, a place like St George's to ourselves. Being here is living; that's what I care about. Pushing papers and filing reports…is not living."

Paul's anger flashed. He rose up in his chair. "You think this valley *cares* about *you*? That mountain lion sure as shit didn't."

David calmly waved him off. "That doesn't matter, Paul. It only matters if *we* care." He took another sip of beer and swirled it in his mouth, not swallowing. He spit into the fire; extra steam came from the hiss. He walked to the edge of the firelight. His shadow danced and jumped from tree to tree as he stared into the dark woods. He squinted into the black mirror of night for a long while.

Then looked around his feet. He stomped on a nearby branch, breaking it, picked up half, sat down and withdrew the bone handled knife from the case on his belt.

"Easy," Paul said slowly, having watched the theatrics. "I don't know how to sew fingers back on."

David looked up from the log, the bottom of his hair illuminated brown and blond by the fire, the top of his head fading into the darkness. "We're going to make this a tradition—coming here. We're not going to be scared of mountain lions. This is where I want to fish, where I want to be."

"We can come back next year. We almost—"

"We *are* going to come back next year, or I am, and we're going to bring some friends, anyone who wants to fly fish." David saw his brother flash worry and it heightened his intensity. "I'm just tired of living with *almost* hanging around everything. This world is so full of *almost*." It rolled off his inebriated tongue in a thick swaddle of disdain; he went back to carving.

The only noise was the crackling of the fire and the long blade of the knife against the wood. Paul stared at the fire and took a deep breath. The hot white coals under the logs pulsed into the night breeze; the orange embers heaved deeply. The smoke rose past the trees and disappeared. He stared for a long time.

"You ever really look at one of these?" Paul said after a while, standing to get another beer.

"One of what?"

"A fire."

"I'm not really sure." David hadn't looked up and wiped away a growing pile of wood fragments from his knees.

Paul continued, unconcerned with David's condescension. "They don't make sense. When you watch an avalanche, a waterfall, a mudslide, a hurricane or any of these other forces of nature, they make sense, right?" Paul cracked his beer and sat back down. "You can look at a hurricane and even though it's more powerful than we can comprehend, the winds and the rains and the debris make sense. They fly in circles and bounce off each other and accelerate in all the patterns that on some unconscious level, we get. But not fire. Nothing about it makes sense. The way it moves, dances, crackles. It all seems random. That's why we love gazing at it. It's energy that doesn't make sense." He took a sip and continued staring. "Maybe this is the real 'movement' of life Z mentioned."

"Maybe," David said aloofly and they were silent for a while.

When he finished carving, he looked at his handy work and fingered the grooves with his thumbs, smoothing the edges and picking out the remaining shards of wood. He cocked his head and gave one final brush with his palm. He exposed the white letters in the firelight to his brother: *The St George's Fly Fishing Club.*

Paul examined it from across the fire. "Let me see that."

"Why?"

"Check it out," Paul said walking around the flames.

"What?" David held the sign away.

"Just, trust me." Paul took the sign and laid it in the dirt next to the fire. He pushed back the big logs in the center of the pit with another stick, sending sparks into the swirling smoke. He grabbed a second stick to make tongs and picked up the white pulsing coals and set them in the grooved letters.

"Ah," David said.

The wood hissed and caught fire in spots. Paul blew out the flames as they slid up and down the rims of each letter. He let them sit for a minute as they smoked, then picked up the whole log and shook the coals back into the fire. Grey ash and sparks lifted into the smoke. The white grooves of each letter were now seared black and shown in the fire light. The beginning of the sign had burned longer and the letters faded as you read across the word *Fly Fishing.*

Paul felt the weight of the log and said, "There is heavy line in the truck." David followed him as the flames of the fire licked into the night sky.

They hung the sign by the old road.

~1~

I'M GOING TO MOSTLY SKIP over their second year in St George's, except a couple stories. It was simply pleasant, which, curiously, makes for a boring story overall. The Ambrose brothers returned and did what they had the year prior—fished, explored and took a breath of air—only they'd learned a little bit about life in the woods. David was more cautious around the Elizabeth. They hiked the valley walls and ridgelines with predator-specific mace and made noise to give animals ample time to vacate the area. (David swore he saw a mountain lion sauntering up a ridgeline, but it was so high that Paul, after referencing *The Hunter's Guide*, was fairly sure it was a bighorn sheep.) Paul, with enough time gone by, made his peace with The Grove—the massive trout certainly helped—and designed a rope swing over the Elizabeth so they could reach the other side without swimming. And they fished a lot, enjoying the cool waters of the Elizabeth every day and the warm confines of the campfire every night.

The only source of conflict—and it was mostly in his head—was that David could only round up two new guys for the St George's Fly Fishing Club. His fire and intensity about starting the club had not dissipated when they returned from their first summer in the valley. He had called his and Paul's friends individually and told them about the trip. He sent out emails with "Mandatory Attendance Next Year!" in the subject. When he'd meet friends for beers, he mentioned it to the point that people were nervous to bring up anything having to do with fishing or the outdoors when they'd see him. This is not to say there wasn't initial interest, but over the course of the year, one by one, each guy emailed him and said he didn't think he was going to make it. Reunions, weddings, money and the time off were the bulk of the excuses. David didn't respond to the emails and told Paul to do the same. He thought it was spineless for someone to bail on such a trip from behind the wall of a computer. They should have at least called.

There had even been a moment right before the trip where Paul almost bowed out. He had been asked to speak at a conference in Dallas and told David that it would probably conflict with the trip. "The dates of the conference are set...so I was thinking that we—"

"Paul, we're not changing the dates of the trip. And—" his voice rose "—I can't believe you'd pull such a *bullshit stunt* this close...."

For the next ten minutes, Paul listened to his brother yell on the other end of the phone. They'd hung up and he sat at his desk quietly for a while. He eventually sighed, shook his head and called the conference organizer and said he couldn't make it, that he couldn't put words to his regrets and that he'd put his name on the list of potential speakers for the following year. Then he called his brother back—the phone clicking to voicemail—and left a message.

He didn't hear back from him, but a week later, Paul got a call from a friend from college who'd been invited, but later cancelled. He wanted to know where David got off calling and reaming him out for not coming. Paul apologized for his brother and hung up, shaking his head and knowing his brother's anger loomed inside him like a shadow. He'd eventually need to feel whole about the slight.

So by early spring, a second cousin named Norton Tuttle, and Dr Steven "Stoss" Ross were the last names remaining on a long list of cross-outs. That was the first iteration of The St George's Fly Fishing Club and the anemic membership put a bit of a thorn in David's sock as he'd had visions of much grander participation.

~ 2 ~

THE CONCEPTS BEHIND FLY FISHING are not unique. A spider spins a web in front of lights to catch moths. The Venus flytrap displays vibrant colors and has a sugary smell to attract unsuspecting prey. Katydids reproduce the mating calls of the cicadas they hunt. The sparkling squid has illuminated tentacles that snatch prey too close to their light. The snapping turtle wiggles a tongue in the water that looks like a tiny fish, then slams its jaws around anything that comes to feed on it. Mimicry is a tool, a silent partner, a goal whose attainment betters the chance for survival.

These same principles are found in a fly fisherman's box, along with the human proclivity for labeling. The Woolly Bugger, the Muddler Minnow and the Clouser swim like leaches, large nymphs and fry. The Copper John, the Barr's Emerger, the Hare's ear and the Prince imitate the various stages of underwater life for a nymph. The Blue Winged Olive, the Pale Morning Dun, the Elk Hair Caddis, the Green Drake and the Parachute Trico alight on the water like various, but specific species of adult insects. The Adams, the Cahill, the Hendrickson, the Humpy and the Coachman mimic all the flies in between. All imitated species are part of the trout's diet and all are found in the complete fisherman's fly box.

A few days after their arrival to St George's, his box open in his lap, Norton Tuttle, a second cousin of the Ambrose brothers of about the same age, sat by the Elizabeth and looked at the contents of his seine and back to his flies. His thin, angular frame searching for balance on the slippery rocks and in the current, he had wandered downstream to try fishing alone. Being his first fly fishing trip, he'd required help with knots, fly patterns and reading water. But now he felt ready to cut out on his own, read the water on his own and cast on his own—though confidence in physical ability was something that had come and gone throughout Norton's life.

A lot of his problems with coordination were explained when he was five. His mother and father had been recalcitrant—mostly due to costs—to take him regularly to the doctor and in some odd manifestation of parental abandonment, were less motivated after they saw how awkwardly he moved and played with other kids. One day though, as everyone helped prepare lunch at his grandmother's house, he looked out her old windows. The glass had sagged and settled over the sixty-two years she'd lived there and was bent like a lens at the bottom. Norton saw blades of grass and the jagged edges of leaves and the thin, crooked knots of sticks and branches. He'd jumped back and ran to his mother, tugging at her arm and, in so many words, asked how the plants and grasses around grandma's house were *not* vague clouds of greens, grays and browns. Something suppressed clicked in Norton's mother and she rushed him to the eye doctor the next Tuesday where he was fitted with heavy glasses.

The now-clear world was a new movement in exploration for a young Norton Tuttle. To that point, he hadn't seen faces. Those that study these things will attest that when one is acquainted for the first time, they look exclusively at the face, their eyes flittering and darting imperceptibly between the new person's eyes, nose, lips, cheeks, forehead and jaw and create a sketch that equates to knowledge of a face, and thus, a being. But not Norton. He'd grown up learning people as shapes, as stances, as movements, as motions. He recognized classmates by the way they sat in a chair or raised their hand. He recognized adults as the way they bent down to him or wrote on the chalkboard. Until the moment he put on glasses, having never looked them in the eye, he'd learned people from the outside in.

As he grew, his revived vision gave him the confidence to speak, to raise his hand, to interact with people now that he saw their eyes and the dormant recognition centers of his brain had come to life. He graduated in the upper third of his high school class and paid his way through college, even playing a little second base during intramural sports. After college, he married sweetheart Karen Gilmore, moved to San Francisco and never looked east. They'd come across a small but significant sum of inheritance money from one of her grandfathers and decided to open a little deli near Golden Gate Park, forgoing their degrees, much to the chagrin of her family. Why they chose a deli was also a mystery to his family, but Karen often noted that Norton quietly relished migrating to the counter and looking people in the eye as they paid for their meal. For the next three years they poured every hour of their lives into the shop and a family — eventually rewarded with loyal customers and a healthy baby boy, named Adrian.

But the pendulum that swung in Norton's favor at his grandmother's, decided to take one back. On a morning in June, when the fog crept slowly off the Pacific, dissolving the city in a thick amalgam of steel, glass and cloud, a bad piece of soldering came lose in the walls behind the walk-in refrigeration unit. Norton had been getting around to replacing it. A fire quietly shrouded the cold grey box, as Karen Tuttle consulted her clipboard and organized crates inside. Three days of surgeries, waiting rooms and prayers passed in the same vagueness as his childhood and left Norton a soul-shattered widower and single father. Paul had flown out for the funeral and as he stood in the back row of black suits, made note that Norton was a guy who would need a hand after time had done enough to let him stand on his own.

The circumstances of being a single father, now working a day job, made it all the harder for Norton to get away for two weeks to St George's, but something about Paul and David's pictures, stories and his own strangely searing desire to learn a new art and science like fly fishing drove Norton to make it work. He got the time off work and scheduled family, friends and babysitters for Adrian—the first time he'd let him out of his sight for more than a day. That act of sacrifice and commitment alone was enough to keep David believing in the idea of a fishing club in St George's Valley. Especially since Norton had never held a fly rod.

Now he sat on the banks of the Elizabeth, rubbing his contact lenses and curly brown hair, sorting through his fly box and taking another run at self-sufficiency. He massaged and rolled his knobby, right shoulder; it was not accustomed to the constant motion of fly casting and he'd woken up fairly sore. He gave each prospective fly pattern rigorous examination. Paul had shown him how to match the thorax of the insect—the largest and most recognizable part of the fly, followed by the wings and tail—to what was in his box and a pheasant tail nymph called to him. The thin wrappings around the shank of the hook seemed to match a couple bugs on his seine.

"I would eat it," he grunted and laughed.

He tied it on and moved to the river's edge. He gauged the distance to his targeted pool and tried to recreate the Ambrose brothers' grace and fluidity, but he didn't compensate for a thick push of evening breeze from the west. As he brought the rod forward, the hook caught on his sleeve and the entire buildup came to a stop.

"Well, that was anticlimactic," he said trying to be cheerful but allowing sarcasm to seep through.

He removed the hook with a shake—a small hole tore in his new shirt—and cast again. Nothing. He cast again. Nothing. He checked his fly, took a few steps and aimed for a different part of the pool, and cast again. A big gust of wind rose up and smacked him in the face. "*Shit,*" he muttered as the green line draped itself over his head and arms. He peeled it off and cast again, but didn't load enough tension to give the line casting momentum and it flopped in a big wobbly mess, spreading over the river like a handful of noodles. Norton saw the strong shadows dart for the far bank and well out of range.

"Okay," he said aloud with a frustrated smile. He liked talking to the river. "Let us try this again—with less line."

He focused on a smooth swath of water above a protruding boulder and cast. The nymph plopped loudly and he watched it sink, disappearing as it swung under the rock. The line came to a stop in the current. Norton pulled, set the hook and the line pointed firmly under the rock in the current; he started to reel in excitement. The tip doubled over as he strained to keep it suspended in the air, a great weight pulling it under. He stepped away from the bank, like Paul had done, and slipped a little.

"Paul!" he shouted. "Paul, I have a fish on!" He kept the rod tip high and kept reeling. His line was fixed under that rock. "*Paul!*" he shouted.

A moment of realization passed over him. A cold feeling of adrenaline and embarrassment coursed through his arms and chest. He let his rod down and the line went slack, the end still pointing to the same window of water as before. He pulled the rod up again and the line tightened, still pointing to the same spot. Nothing swam away.

Paul appeared about a hundred yards upstream from around some bushes. Norton wasn't sure if he was asking "You all right?" or "Got a fish on?" but he waved him off and shook his head casually, not wanting to betray his embarrassment of being excited about hooking the earth. Paul nodded in understanding, gave him an encouraging thumbs-up and walked back around the bend. The quiet of the forest and the babbling of the river returned, and Norton was alone again.

His eyes drew to the woods.

They were deep and dark, and frustration and anger opened him to a twisting fright. The flicker of an unfamiliar instinct came alive in him. His eyes darted. His heart picked up pace and he wheeled around, tripping on a rock, stumbling forward and catching himself. His hand plunged into the cool waters of the Elizabeth. They were crisp, almost cutting, as they rushed over the back of his fingers and around his wrists. The shock calmed him.

"What is the matter with you?" he said scornfully. The shadow of fear dissipated into the breeze. "Everyone knows you are the rookie. You do not need to remind them by screaming and stumbling around like one of Adrian's little girlfriends."

He looked back to his line caught on the rock and continued yanking, but it wouldn't budge. He gave the rod a few sharp tugs and the line snapped, flying backwards in recoil over his shoulder and tangling in some brush behind him.

"*Damn* it," he hissed, walking over and shaking the rough branches it had enveloped. His mind wandered back to Adrian. He missed him. A simmer of sadness developed in his face but he fended it off by thinking how he'd coach his son in a similar situation. He'd tell Adrian to think logically about the way the line was wrapped in the bush, to not get frustrated and do his best—fatherly advice that he was having trouble following.

After fifteen minutes of patience and logic, he untangled the line. He tied on a new fly, walked a few paces upstream and cast. Nothing. He cast again. Nothing. He walked a few more and recast. This time a light tug and the vibrations of a fish came alive in his line. A trout jumped in the air and flopped back with a little splash. Norton let out a yelp. He played the fish around the pool for a minute and reached for his new net.

The line went limp.

He closed his eyes and brought the broken tip to his face.

It was frayed at the break point, rubbed and weakened by the bush's branches. "Damn it!" he yelled and threw his rod and kicked the water. "Damn it!"

The wind hummed around him; the mountains towered over him. The void of the forest absorbed his tirade with ancient apathy and he was alone again.

"Can I help?"

Norton jumped and almost slipped again; he turned. Stoss stood on the bank.

~

Doctor Steven "Stoss" Ross, now well into his sixties, had once examined a teenage Paul Ambrose for a displaced wrist while he was a visiting physician and professor at Massachusetts General Hospital. Stoss had made two notes during the treatment. First, Paul was tough. His face hadn't flinched during his palpations or after the surgery when the cast was set. Pain hadn't fazed him. And this made sense when his father had shown up. Stoss's second note was that the man was just mean—in stray animal sense—telling Paul through hot breaths of bourbon that he'd "caused a goddamn mess."

So in one of the curious moments where a doctor steps outside of his protective white coat, Stoss resolved to keep loose tabs on the teenager, just to make sure he grew up on the straight and narrow. To him, teaching was simply another branch of medicine. He also had no kids of his own.

A couple years later Paul told him of a friend on the football team that had just been paralyzed. Stoss well understood the conditions that led to the severing of the friend's spine. Though rare, patients grew up—usually unaware—with missing discs between their vertebrae. Without the spacing and the padding between the joint, the body naturally fuses the two vertebrae together with a brittle bridge of bone, but decreases the range of motion for the joint, in turn increasing the chances of a break during trauma. Paul's friend experienced that trauma in a football game when he crossed the middle of the field with his head down, caught a pass and a creeping safety leveled him.

Stoss took the opportunity to teach Paul about the anatomy of what had happened to his friend; but quietly hearing Paul's anguish lit a fire and five years later, Stoss developed a solution to the disorder. He created a hollow disc, inserted into the narrow space between the vertebrae. Over the course of six months, it was gradually filled with silicon and inflated, thus pushing the two vertebrae back to their correct distances while providing the cushioning for proper range of motion.

Stoss's new procedure and device was met with high praise and reviews throughout the medical community and within two years, his little company that had patented the device—Guardian Prosthetics—was distributing across the country and most of western Europe. Stoss retained a place on the board and the accompanying stock, but otherwise removed himself from the business, turning over operations to those that had studied the practice. Business, and even the potential of the stock, had never interested him. Only preventing future tragedies had been of any consequence. He just wanted to practice medicine and teach. But the motivations of medicine and business are never completely parallel.

Guardian was acquired by a device company in Brussels and eighteen months later, Stoss received a call from a reporter asking for a comment regarding accusations against Guardian for fraud and attempting to bribe insurance regulators and executives around the classification and coverage of the then "cosmetic" procedure. Stoss had said very little to the reporter and his testimony echoed the same—only able to tell the jury how and why he'd developed the device, and how it worked. The prosecutor had to cut him off a few times during questioning and objected other times that his testimony was *irrelevant*. The only admissible evidence he provided were a few character testimonials on the accused.

Since then his fire, his passion, his yearning to heal had

atrophied; something about having his work laid bare and hearing that what he'd done was *irrelevant* withered it. Medicine revealed an ugly face; healing was like a trick, rather than a trade. But the flame for teaching still burned. Now, he stood on the bank near a frustrated Norton Tuttle. "You should be more targeted with your approach. The big fish are holding tightly against the far bank," he said.

"How—how can you tell?" Norton asked putting a hand through his curly hair.

Stoss didn't notice Norton's nervousness or clunky speech; he was used to making a case around the hospital. "Because that's exactly where *I'd* be if I were a fish. That's how you must think. To be any good at this craft, or any craft among the wild, that is how you must *always* think. But do not think too hard! That is the cardinal sin. Think simply; animals are simple. They do not reason like us. They only think of survival. Fish do not like to move far for their food. If they had their way, they'd hold in the current with their big mouth open as the Elizabeth shoveled in meal after meal. But they aren't that lucky. So they hold in the spot where the current will bring the most food, but they will spend the least energy. That is why they are usually holding in the seams of the current, on the border of the fast and slow waters or on the outside bends of a stretch of current. A lot of food moves past and they can have their choice without fighting too much current. This is how a trout grows big and heavy. These are the fish you want to target."

"You said they do not use reason. If a fish searches out the seams of water with the most food and spend the least energy, is that not reason?"

A light flashed across Stoss's face. "Good question, but no. The game of reason is weighing options and choosing one. The fish sees no second option, or a third. There is only one—the best one they know of and they do not possess the faculties to hazard guesses that better options may be in store elsewhere, unless they find themselves in starvation or some other shock to their system. If they are content, they won't move until something makes them. If it were a human, curiosity, the reasoning that something else exists that they don't know about, would make them wander to other parts of the river."

"That is an interesting point, but I think you may be giving people too much credit."

Stoss smiled and nodded slightly. "I've never seen anything wrong with that. The world would be darker, but the shapes the same, if we didn't."

Norton's eyes came alive and their cautiousness vanished. "Adrian does not stop poking his head in places and asking questions. Sometimes I think he is too curious for his own good."

"Impossible. You can't ever be too curious. Oddly though, in most of us, curiosity dissipates with age. Perhaps if I'd been a father, I could have examined it more closely, but I've never understood why people, with all their great tools for thinking, seem to become less interested in their world as they become more able to live in it."

"Never had kids?"

"No," — he spoke with the insincere mechanics of rehearsal — "medicine is my child."

Norton looked at him for a second and then nodded back to the Elizabeth. "So I should cast before those branches and let my fly swing?"

Stoss snapped back to the moment. "Exactly. You'll need to wade upstream, where the current cuts hardest, and swing your line into that bank from the middle of the fast water. That's where you'll find your trophy."

"That's not what I'd do," a voice said.

Norton jumped and wheeled around; Stoss, with a surgeon's nerves, turned slowly.

David had talked about Z on their drive to the valley. From the stories, Norton had imagined Z with broad shoulders, an old rifle and a buckskin jacket, but he was just an old face with wind-hardened wrinkles, a thin beard, wearing a weathered shirt and jeans. He stood on the bank, rocking on his heels with his hands in his pockets, chewing a cigar and smiling at them. His bamboo rod leaned on a tree nearby.

"You must be Z," Stoss said calmly extending a hand.

Z shook his hand and continued as if they'd been talking all day. "There are fish under that far bank," he said. "But why would you wade out into the river, into the tough current, when you haven't fished closer to shore?"

"I wanted to show him how to locate where the bigger fish will hold," Stoss said testily.

"There are plenty of fish in the riffles and current right there, bouncing around looking for food."

Norton looked between the two men as Stoss straightened up and tried to reclaim his professorial tone. "But surely you'll reason with me that the largest fish in this run are lying under that far bank?"

Z nodded. "So?"

"That's the point—to catch big fish? That's what I wanted to show him." His tone had become pleading as he stood side by side with Norton.

Z turned his gaze on Stoss. To the old doctor, the sounds of the river and the shadows of the mountains disappeared. He stood in an endless room; Z stood before him with old eyes. "Every man fishes with reasons, Doc. Let him find his own."

"What do you mean by that?" Stoss asked trying to stand up straighter.

Z puffed on his cigar. "Well Doc," he said slowly pointing the coal at Stoss. "That's up to you."

Stoss stammered, "Well—well, you can take over the lesson. I'm going to fish upstream." He turned away. "I'm sure we'll see you around," he said over his shoulder.

Norton watched him go and then looked back at Z. He was walking in the other direction. "I want to show you something, Norton," he said over his shoulder.

Norton, though still wearing a look of confusion on his face from the interaction between Z and Stoss, found himself following. The birds swooped overhead in the evening air and shafts of sunlight cut across the branches, almost horizontal, as dusk approached. They crossed the road and came to a little stream that dropped and braided over rocks. Paul had named it Cougar Creek the year before.

"Where—where are we going?" Norton asked.

"A little further," Z said. "Just up ahead. I hope she's still there."

"Who?" Norton asked.

They passed some wildflowers and moss covered rocks. A couple squirrels sat on their back legs holding nuts, then scurried into the grass like tattling children. Z put up a hand and pointed to a spot in the creek as it braided towards the Elizabeth.

"Go check out that pool."

"That—that one, there?" The breeze blew and the line on Norton's rod rattled like brittle wind chimes.

Z nodded, then to the rod. "Don't need that."

Norton looked apprehensively at his rod, set it down and crept to a rock at the back of the pool. The roiling water bubbled below a couple rocks that poured from above and swirled in a wide oval. He didn't see anything. He squinted and looked for big shadows, but there was nothing. He turned back and shrugged.

Z pointed to the pool again.

Barely audible over the pattering din of the creek, Norton heard a light splash. He continued looking at the pool. He heard it again. The splashing came again but this time in rapid fire, like someone batting their hand in a bathtub. Norton looked closer. He saw a little trout holding still. Water fed in from a tall flat rock that towered above, but the little fish held off to the side, out of the turmoil. It was a baby rainbow, its pink stripe waved and shone through the top-water and Norton could just make out the spots. The little fish was the

length of his hand. Its wide, ready eyes seemed dispropor-
tionately large with the rest of its body. Its only movement
was long and heavy breaths, gills and belly expanding and
contracting rhythmically.

Norton watched the little trout for a moment and then
turned back to Z and nodded. Z pointed back to the pool.

The trout sat still under the tall rock, water pouring over
it. After a minute the breathing became subtle, more controlled, and it swam slowly in the shallows, gliding in lazy
circles like someone spun it by a string. Then, the fish darted
deep into the bubbling pool and disappeared. Norton shifted,
trying to find where it had gone, but as he focused, the trout
fired out of the pool and into the current flowing down the
flat rock.

The trout beat its tail, swimming and slapping water,
fighting upwards against the stone. It held on the rock for a
split second and flopped and shimmied through the rushing
water. It fell back a couple inches and slapped its tail in the
rushing current. Then, as if freed from the forces of gravity
for only a moment, the little fish shot over the top of the tall
rock and into the higher section of stream. And was gone.

Norton stood in the calm evening. The waters gurgled
around him unchanged. A slow grin eased across his face. He
started laughing. A warm, almost paternal triumph crept
through his chest and shook his head. "That was awesome,"
he said and looked at the pool and the tiny gravel bar where
the little rainbow had hovered. He laughed and turned
around.

"Okay?" Z said, now on the bank next to him and nodding to the pool. The stream around him disappeared and the
breeze stopped; the cigar in his hands left a plume of smoke
around his face.

Norton nodded slowly.

"Good."

The tree tops solemnly agreed as the wind wound
through and bounced them in the grey light. "Now it's get-

ting dark," Z said. "You better head back to your camp. Your friends have fresh fish waiting for you."

~ 3 ~

AFTER A LONG MORNING OF FISHING, Paul caught sight of David standing next to the river staring at a pool. They had been fishing The Giant Steps—the far end of the valley at the cascading drop offs, waterfalls and pools. He walked over to him and noticed his hand rested gingerly on the case for the bone handled-knife, snapping it open and shut furiously.

Paul stepped on a twig as he approached; David shuttered and jumped.

"*Whoa,*" Paul said calmly. "Just me."

David nodded and looked back to the pool.

"You alright?"

"Yeah, just thinking."

"David, I'm almost certain that wasn't a mountain lion we saw; it was a bighorn—"

"Not that—I was thinking about the club for next year." He paused and retreated his gaze to the pool. "I think I'm just hungry."

Paul gave him a long, skeptical glance. "Me too. Come on."

They climbed up some scattered boulders to an outcropping that channeled a waterfall. The sliver of water launched in a singular smooth pulse, but as air and gravity pulled it apart, the black water turned to a frothy white cable that plunged and fastened to the roiling pool below. Through the grey stone, peppered and speckled with sliver flecks of mica that had seen millennia vanish like a hot breath, layered veins and channels of browns and blacks waved, staying oddly parallel—petrified rivers compressed and stamped with the pressures of time. An ant watched the two brothers approach, picked up the nearest pheromone trail and scuttled along the invisible line towards the shadows. Paul saw the ant and stepped around it, sat down and handed a sandwich to his brother. David didn't see it and crushed it with the heel of his boot.

They took off their fishing gear and ate in the silent shade of the trees overlooking the pool. Soon, Paul finished his sandwich, leaned back and tipped his hat over his eyes. David tried to do the same, but a cool breeze carrying the cracks and scents and chatter of the woods kept him awake. He draped a shirt over his eyes to shield the sun, hoping that would help, but the shroud stressed him further.

"Paul," he said after a while, half whispering and sitting up.

"Mmm."

"We're going to get more guys back here next year. We have to."

Paul mumbled under his hat.

"I'm going to start hounding people as soon as we get home."

"I'm *sure* you will," Paul said.

"What does that mean?"

"It means…'let me sleep'."

"I'm serious."

"Me too: let me sleep."

"Get up. I want to talk to you," then he set bait in his words, "You'd do it for Gretchen."

Paul pulled his hat down farther over his face, the brim forming a seal against his chin; as he did, a middle finger flashed upward, alone.

"Get up, man. We're leaving soon. You can't sleep through these kinds of afternoons."

"David—I can do whatever the hell I want. Let me take a

goddamn nap."

"A nap—is this what happens when you're seeing thirty on the horizon?"

"I guess so; let me know in a couple years."

"A couple years?" David asked with mock dramatics. "I see the writing on the wall. I'm already finding weird hairs on my shoulder." His tone shifted into a firmer direction at his brother. "That's why we can't be taking *naps*."

"Save the speeches," Paul said with muffled but amused disdain.

David took a deep breath and stared at the top of his brother's hat. Not having to make eye contact made the words come more easily. "I am going to design the cabin when we get home. I know a couple guys from my construction days that can help me. How awesome will that be: a cabin in that meadow?" David picked up a rock and threw it, hitting him in the hip.

"Let me take a *nap*."

David rolled his eyes and stood, looking to the pool below them. "If you want to fish the pool below us again, I will move—*oh shit!*"

Amber fur flashed through a ribbon of light in the boulders about twenty paces away. David shouted and searched for a stick, finding none. He hurled a rock into the shadows.

"What is the matter with you?" Paul asked frantically, springing up and looking between his brother and the boulders. "*What?*"

"There!" David said. Adrenaline squirted through his tense muscles and accelerated his pounding heart. "*A MOUNTAIN LION*. In those boulders, I saw the top of its back"

Paul snatched a stone and hurled it; it thundered off the patch of light where David pointed. He and David began shouting at the shadows; they were too focused to hear the waterfall behind them or the breeze slide through the waving trees. Then, a head popped out from behind the rocks and cocked in curiosity. It was the face of a gopher, but much bigger and fatter, twitching side to side in interest. The little black drops for eyes vibrated in a warm engagement. Paul's shoulders relaxed.

"It's a marmot, you spaz—an oversized squirrel." He paused, startled by David's wide eyes. "It does have amber fur—an honest mistake if you only saw it quickly."

The marmot stood a little higher and peered intently; its tiny paws resting against the shadows. David watched the fuzzy head peer back at them from behind the rock, as the coolness in his veins dissipated and his breathing slowed. His eyes narrowed and his arm cocked to throw the rock anyway, but in the next instant the marmot was gone.

Paul continued, "Probably heard us talking. Marmots are attracted to voices and sounds. Though…" But David wasn't listening to his brother; he stared down at his hands. One of adrenaline's gifts is clarity for decisiveness and in him the hormone had been set free and ranged about his body looking for an undeveloped thought to devour and make lucid in his mind's eye: a lodge with distinct walls of pine and a towering chimney appeared before him. Fishermen moved in and out, ready to take on the Elizabeth as they walked with a confident peace towards her banks. David smiled; he tossed a small stone to the pool below their stony perch, following the gentle arc in the air as it moved down and along the waterfall. He saw the rock float freely, on its own, make a little splash and disappear in the whitewater. "…in fact," Paul continued, "that may have been what got into our food last year, when you left it out—*WHOA, David!*"

David jumped from their rocky outcropping.

Paul watched as his arms and hair waved in the air and splashed in the roiling water. He moved to the edge, eyes wide, watching the pool below. A moment passed. Then a head of shaggy hair appeared, waving carelessly in the current, and broke the surface. David drew a few strokes across the pool, looked back at his brother and waved him on.

Paul's neurons and muscles and emotions were still firing spastically; he had been ready to see his brother's body churning under the waterfall or dashed on a rock. "You all right?" he yelled with a strange, reflexive hollowness.

David was still treading water, his hair draped and matted over his face. There was a calm in his voice as he motioned to the center of the pool. "Land there."

Paul involuntarily put up a halting hand. He looked at the distance between him and his brother, the angle of the jump, the angle of the waterfall next to him. He figured he was about twenty feet off the pool and since he could only see the bank around the edges, that the center must be pretty deep, but when most people hit water, they go about eight to twelve feet deep if they put their arms out and —

He saw his brother treading water calmly.

Paul jumped. The weight of his body hung, then accelerated towards the earth. Every limb was caught in a thick tar. His feet and waving arms traveled along a singular line, a singular arc that plummeted towards the pool below. As the Elizabeth enveloped him, shattering the silence, that tension washed away. He held underwater and listened to the digestion of the river. The contrast of his heavy acceleration to the weightlessness in this large pool struck him through the heart.

He burst to the surface, opened his eyes and saw David on a rock staring back at him with a satisfied light in his eyes.

Paul swam to another rock and pulled himself up. He looked up at the ledge from which he'd just launched himself. The ledge seemed low now, like he could underhand a pebble to where he just stood. The mist from the waterfall rose back up along the arc he'd traveled into the pool, but it waved and bent in the air and seemed to do what it wanted in the breeze.

"I made a mistake," David said quietly to himself but enough for Paul to hear. "I was too obnoxious about trying to get our friends to come back here. I was too pushy." He kicked a little water across the pool and droplets pattered and disappeared. "I wanted it too much; I was shoving people by the neck when I should have let the valley grab them by the heart."

"Well put," Paul said with a little surprise in his voice.

David brushed off the compliment. "It turned them off. Maybe I let those 'invisible eyes' get away from me."

Paul turned away from the ledge and leaned onto one arm. "Curious psychology, huh?"

"Yeah. I don't really get it: the more passionate I was, the less interested everyone else was."

Paul spoke softly, "I meant *your* psychology but, yeah, personal discovery resonates pretty deeply." Then after a minute, more directly, "What are you going to do next year?"

"Just send pictures, and say everyone is invited, and keep them aware of the planning. I don't want people here that don't want to be here on their own," he laughed as he gazed at his reflection in the pool, "How profound." Paul turned the words over in his head, but didn't say anything. "And Paul," David continued, "I'm sorry I got so angry with you about the conference. I just—"

"Don't worry about it—I know," Paul said, casually waving him off. "It's in the rearview." He glanced to the waterfall and the ledge. "Certainly glad I came back."

"Yeah," David said letting the word hang. "Anyway, things will be different next year...." He trailed off and turned.

Paul followed his gaze. In and among the blanket of shadows, Z approached from the woods, a cigar burning in the side of his mouth under his wide-brimmed hat. He wore a brown and red pack, tight at the seams and his bamboo rod protruded from the side holster. David twisted his tone from thoughtful to friendly, and nodded. "Was wondering when we were going to see you."

"I've been around," Z said with a chuckle.

"Yeah, Norton mentioned you'd met." David glanced at his pack, "Where you going?"

Z shrugged. "Not sure yet—but I think I'll steer clear of St George's for a little while. Fishing's getting a little crowded."

David's face fell a little, but he tried to play it off. "Don't be intimidated by us, Z. I'd be happy to show you a thing or two on the river."

Z peered at him from under his hat, then looked back at the rock from which the two brothers had just jumped. He pointed the red coal of his cigar. "I get the sense you've got other plans for this valley," he said in his statement-of-fact manner. "Saw your rope swing. And the fishing has been kind to you." His cigar waved back and forth in his hand. Years later, Paul would swear he saw an apparition of a fish in the smoke. Z continued, "So I figure it's time for me to mosey on. Can't stay on the same stretch of river forever."

David's face tightened. "Z, I'm drawing up plans to build a lodge. I know there are only four of us this year, but next, we'll have more and we'd love to have you as our guide, to show everyone the best pockets of water, where there are good hikes, and lookouts, and....and everything else...you know?"

Z looked up at the stony outcropping and waterfall, and puffed on his cigar. "No thanks; been a pleasure though. You boys take care of yourselves. This is a big valley." The river and the rocks around them dimmed, "and remember to keep moving, no matter what."

They shook hands and Z walked into the trees. David watched him until the wisps of cigar smoke were gone. Then he sat back on his rock, staring at the deep pool in front of him and fidgeted with his knife case.

Paul lay back, looked at the blue sky and tried to finish his nap.

~1~

AS I'VE FISHED OVER THE YEARS, one of the phenomena that has always made me smile is the secrecy inherent to the sport. It straddles a peculiar border between ancient, animal territorialism and childishness. Not to say that there isn't logic to prevent a place from getting crowded, but it seems one of the requirements in doing so is a "hush-hush" reminiscent of tree houses and forts in the backyard. The following year, the Ambrose brothers kept two secrets from the new additions to the club, despite David's revised and calmer invitations. The first was The Grove. There was a lot of river to fish; it was a ways downstream from their camp and it was hard to reach because of the high rock wall on the north bank of the river to get there. Those were the practical reasons that created half a bridge of excuse to the idea that this was the brothers' spot and their spot only. They had agreed to not show Norton and Stoss the previous year, and this year, if someone eventually found it, so be it, but otherwise, they'd sneak there "since we started this club and built that rope swing by ourselves," David reasoned. Often times, I've noticed that a fisherman will share his best holes with his closest friends—making them a little better—but not the Ambrose brothers; they kept that one spot to themselves, at least for some time.

The second, however, had a different shade. David made Paul swear to secrecy about the run-in with the mountain lion. On the surface, as David organized everyone, Paul understood why he wouldn't want to tell people, but his practical nature thought about safety. He knew that mountain lions have little interest in tangling with people so after some thought, he let it alone. The flare of determination in David's eyes had touched off when they discussed it and Paul chose the path of least resistance. I think somewhere, probably, he knew that it couldn't last forever either.

Norton and Stoss both returned, in addition to four new members. Paul had roped in two of his old college roommates to attend—Ian Schumaker and Josh Diaz. Both of them had fished a decent amount after college and with David's invites (and Paul prodding from the background) they joined. David had also convinced a bartending buddy, Connor Maybin, to attend. In my recollection of this story, these guys are faded to the background and so I'll keep it that way. Sometimes the colors between the lines of a story fade on their own and there's no real reason to repaint them.

The last addition to the club, however, was a long haired fellow with a frame of trim cables and an explosive lupine grin. JP Francis had learned to spin fish while bouncing from home to home along the Mississippi, then later, the Chattahoochee River and the surrounding areas. He'd spent his sweltering summer days fending off snakes on the riversides as he fished for bass, crappies and bluegill. Even then, his big mouth got him into fights and competitions with varying degrees of friendliness, and wagers with varying degrees of severity.

And his work life mimicked his upbringing. He could claim employment at a gas station in Little Rock, a landscaper around the Outer Banks, and a mechanic at Graceland. But no matter where he was or what he was doing, he always had a spin rod kicking around the bed of whatever fourth-hand truck he was driving and a tackle box stuffed behind the seat.

When he met Paul in Atlanta, he was working as a maintenance man at a downtown convention center. The halls had been filled with a conference focused around the futures of the banking and finance markets and how to report and view them. Paul drifted from speaker to speaker, and from vendor booth to vendor booth, and gradually as the sales pitches and theories passed over him, his face drew into a numb mirror. Everyone was the leading supplier, the market leader or the authority on something, yet it all seemed to add up to nothing but his time.

He'd drifted to the edge of the hall and sat down, and from his briefcase, had withdrawn some pictures from St George's and began leafing through them, staring blankly, distantly. "*Hell* of a rainbow there," he'd heard in a twangy explosion of reverence. Before he could turn around, JP had set his tool belt aside and sat down with him, going on about a six pound largemouth he'd landed at Lake Lanier a month prior. An hour later they were still exchanging fishing stories. Paul had had obligations after the conference but he and JP exchanged emails. A few months later, the stringy extrovert received an invite from David. It took very little convincing for him to pick up and head west.

~ 2 ~

THE WINTER HAD ENCLOSED THE VALLEY in an icy casket. Great snowstorms moved through the Crescents, grey phalanxes marching over the mountains, leaving a glimmering aftermath in their wake. The tall trees that lined the valley floor bowed and sparkled. The grasses and bushes that filled the fields collapsed and flattened, smashed by the perpetual steps of the white boots. The rocks that slashed their way from the earth morphed to benign mounds, hints, suggestions that something laid beneath the snowfall. A piercing calm of crackling air remained over the sheath of winter. The valley was still.

When the first wave of storm trudged through, the bald rocks in the Elizabeth's shallows grew sashes of brittle water and wore thin white caps. After the second, the sashes turned to plates and their heads were covered completely. After the third, the plates extended to the current and the snow followed closely behind. By the fourth and beyond, the shallows, slow waters and pools of the Elizabeth shared the same white laminate as the trees and grasses. Only through her center was there any movement. The mainline of the current never stood still, always open, exposed, wavering, cascading, riffling downstream and out the end of the valley. The waters turned their darkest shades of black, a magma cutting and running under the shelves of ice that lay around her.

Then in late April, a bird chirped. Those that study these

things would claim her fragile tweet died in the air nearby, the wave of sound absorbed and destroyed in the frigid calm, the momentum and force not sufficient to carry. But others may disagree, saying that her chirp was absorbed — absorbed by the valley, and the clouds, and the sun, and the changing time. That chirp set off a small current of air, that grew to a breeze, that grew to a wind, that grew to a shift in the course of storms and seasons. That chirp was the final push, a shout masked as delicacy, and spring finally arrived, scraping away the casket's lid, pushing and draining it to the center of the valley.

That lone chirp hatched and soon its brethren filled the air, followed by the shapes and wings that made them. The fields shrugged their shoulders and emerged from under their blanket. The trees sloughed their sleeves of snow, their branches sighing in relief as the deer and rabbits and foxes moved among their shadows. The bushes and grasses stood taller; the rocks cracked a grey eye towards the sun.

And as each facet of the valley wriggled free, the Elizabeth took the melting jacket. The runoff tore through her bends and pools and riffles, wild horses charging for freedom. Frozen borders disintegrated and she swelled and burst at the banks. She scraped and clawed at anything brave enough to settle within her reach, snatching barks, branches, leaves, needles, gravel, rodents and even newborn game and swallowing them in her black torrent.

Then, with the same suddenness that had greeted the melting transition, she slowed — her excavation over, the load lifted and removed, sent to the ends and out the mouth of the valley. She slackened and returned to her quiet, steady and driving demeanor, weaving through the boulders, the trees and the fields as the only constant and smooth vessel of life, folding the heart and center of the valley in her depths. While the new sun rose in the eastern sky, the mountain lion crept to the river's corners looking for water. She bent her head and lapped up the sharp current. Her eyes closed and she rolled her neck and felt the life inside of her. The three cubs rolled in her womb and she could sense their excitement, their tiny tremors to be free and see the bright light of the world. The current ran and cascaded from each sip, filling, cooling the lines of her throat; they loved the crisp water as much as she did.

She opened her eyes.

She noticed strong shadows gliding in the current. They held and darted in the pools, into the riffles and back under the rocks, waving their tails with frantic abandon, hungry for a new summer.

~

A couple months later, the sun high above, breathing heat into the breeze, the mother lion perched on a rock overlooking the valley. The switchbacks of the old road bent back and forth below her on the northeastern wall of St George's. She drew in the dry mountain air and released it smoothly from her pink nose, twitched her whiskers and looked below her, near the road. Two rabbits emerged from the brush, sniffing and venturing to eat. They nibbled on grasses and thistles as they wiggled into the betraying sunlight, their own pink noses rubbing in the wind. With the breeze in her face, she picked up her ears and tipped her head down.

She slid off the back of her perch like molten gold and disappeared into the deep grasses. Each paw lay gently in front of the other. The long grass waved in the wind as they dissolved a pair of iron green eyes, easing down the slope towards their prey. The rabbits stopped eating, listening and sniffing with cocked heads. She stopped. They went back to eating. She slid closer. Again the rabbits stopped and listened for a moment. The mountain lion sank back into the deep grass.

As if set ablaze, the two rabbits bolted and jerked in erratic lines, back and forth on the road as they frantically dodged the tires of a swerving white pickup truck. Three more trucks followed. Dust plumed into the air and when it settled, and the first truck had stopped; one rabbit was into the grass on the far side of the road and gone; the other lay crushed in the dirt. The mountain lion looked from her spoiled prey to the white truck. The largest of the men got out and examined the dead rabbit. He picked up the empty vessel and set it off the road, covering it with a little loose dirt.

As he walked back to the truck, he took off his hat and whipped it against his thigh in anger and yelled something to the long haired driver. His aggression made her jump and the muscles of her shoulders loaded; then slackened when she saw he meant no real harm. She crept backwards in the tall grasses, slunk around her rock and dissolved into a grove of trees. She kept the trucks, dust clouds now billowing again, in the corner of her eye as she sauntered through the shadows.

They wrapped down the switchbacks into St George's Valley.

~ 3 ~

THAT EVENING, the light danced through the western trees as the sun set. It laid rails for the breeze carrying the sharp smell of waking pines and shouting wildflowers through the meadow. The tents shook and flapped and the branches and grasses nodded in approval. A new camp had grown in the grasses of the little meadow and the creatures nearby had heard the noise and taken notice, becoming used to the recurring presence of men—now eight of them. Two squirrels squabbled at each other in the trees, patiently waiting for them to open their coolers and begin dinner.

While sustenance was the only detail they cared about, an eye with broader focus would have noted some real changes in camp. The four trucks stood side by side at their edges like horses waiting in their stables. David had drawn up a plan for positionings around the fire. There were four tents and each was connected by a long table, creating an enclosed box around the ring of stones. The first table, farthest from the road, was for preparing food and doing dishes; all their coolers were in rows underneath; the ice was to be resupplied by a truck-powered ice maker Stoss had brought. The second table was adorned with fishing gear that, over the course of the coming days, would consume the surface with fly boxes, tippets, leaders, reels, nippers, vests, drying boots and waders, and countless other accessories to the sport; a rod holder that David had built stood at one end. The third and fourth tables were for eating, writing and reading. Paul had laid out a few books for everyone's use, but had kept *The Hunter's Guide* in the truck. All in all, this had become a very real fishing camp.

So now standing around the firering, the new club before him, David thumbed some notes. He had a speech planned for some time, but as he spoke each word came forward as if unconnected from the other, as if laying a row of cinder blocks. He was nervous. "Gentlemen, I am psyched to have you here. Norton, Stoss, welcome back. Connor, good to have an old bartending buddy with me. Ian and Josh, great to have two of my brother's oldest college friends. And JP, our friend from the south, I don't quite know you yet, but I'm sure we'll have a good time. Welcome to the second year of The St George's Fly Fishing Club. That sign hanging from the tree by the road is no joke. I want this to be a place where you can get away — like really away — and maybe some day, stay away. We all go through our daily routines and never stop to take a deep breath, and if we do — and live in a city — we probably cough when we take that breath." He paused for the punch line to settle but no one flinched. "So I really hope that you guys will see what I — and Paul — see in —"

"*Damn it*," Norton said abruptly with his palm pressed against his neck. A black, mashed mosquito lay in his hand, smothered in blood.

David ignored him and his dissolving ambit of attention. "Anyway, I really hope that —"

"Shit," Josh said slapping his elbow.

Then Ian batted his calf, then JP batted his ear. Mosquitoes hovered and hummed in the dusk air around them. They, like the rest of the creatures of the meadow, had found the new camp and the exposed skin. David watched as the new members swatted away the pests and dove to their tents to retrieve long sleeve shirts and changed from shorts into pants.

"I'll light a fire," Paul said calmly.

The Hunter's Guide had advised on always checking

snowfall before choosing an early summer campsite in the mountains. There were the logistical reasons, but melted and standing water is where mosquitoes breed and the two trappers had seen horses break a leg trying to get away from thick swarms wrought from a heavy winter. Paul had warned David, but since mosquitoes hadn't been a problem the previous two years, he'd brushed his brother off.

As the guys dove to their tents, Paul built and lit his log cabin of kindling. The flames licked the sides and the smoke drove away the nearby pests. Orange bursts sprung above the wood, popping and crackling with regularity, then a rhythm, ready to heat the evening, ready to cook dinner, ready to center camp.

They regrouped around the fire. David took a moment to relish that the group had expanded, but as he stood to speak, Connor interrupted him. "This is pretty sweet," he said sarcastically.

"I've never seen it like this," David said maintaining confidence in his voice. He and Connor had bartended together and David would often joke that Connor spoke quickly so he didn't have to hear himself talk.

"It won't be bad too long," Paul said, stoking the fire. David watched with his quick glances as the rest of the group turn their focus to his brother. "I checked the weather reports before we came. It should warm up even more and the standing water will evaporate. These little bastards will have nowhere to breed and should disappear after that."

"They better," Connor said quickly.

"Here will be the benefit," Paul said ignoring him. "The fishing will be better. The fish spent a long hard winter hunkered down in the river; now they'll slam anything to put the weight back on. These mosquitoes suck, but the fishing will make up for it."

Connor's voice shifted the short jump from sarcasm to condescension. "I hope so. Should I stand near the fire for a while to keep them away? I'd rather breathe smoke."

Before Paul or David could respond, Stoss spoke quietly. "They are a nuisance but you need to relax, if you want to make it out here." He was looking through a couple fly boxes and organizing patterns for the next day. A mosquito net draped over his face and neck, and the little pests bounced against it in frustration.

Connor turned and took in the old doctor who he'd only met a short while ago. "A net like you've got there, would put me at peace," he said.

"Take it."

"You don't want it?"

"I do, but I'm going to prove a point. You're surrendering the mental battle and that's what makes them seem so much worse. I am not saying don't swat, but don't let them break you down. That's where you lose." He took off his netting and tossed it onto Connor's lap.

He tried to hold his ground. "I don't think there is anything wrong with aggravation."

Stoss was ready for the counter. A professor's tone spread into his voice. "Not at its core. Aggravation or irritation is just anger, right? And anger, as much as we don't want to admit it, is one face for violence; defense is the other. Animals hurt for two reasons: they feel threatened or they are hunting. In nature, there is no other reason to be violent."

Paul threw another log on the fire and added, "From my experience, we are more prone to violence that falls out of those two categories—the meaningless kind—which always makes me wonder if humans are actually *less* evolved."

Stoss waggled two fingers. "I don't believe there are 'more or less evolved'. The idea is not binary; it's not an either-or proposition. We have just become different—though *not* as much as we'd like to believe—and deviated from the typical rules of the wild. For instance, our greatest crime is nature's greatest accomplishment. Killing an opponent in nature brings territory and food and mating. For us, it brings prison. That is a fascinating dichotomy; and a fascinating difference we've put between us and—" he waved towards the south wall of the valley "—here. Though, in that sense, one might argue that governments are 'less evolved' than people they govern—but that is a digression."

David popped his eyebrows and smiled to a few of the new guys at the lecture that had developed around the fire.

Stoss saw it but didn't care; he refocused. "But to say 'more or less evolved' is to imply a spectrum—that we are all moving along a line towards one goal: *most* evolved. Yet that implies nature has goals, and that couldn't be farther from the truth. Nature and evolution only move on the path of least resistance; and those movements spread from every point in infinite directions, yet only a few of them are sustainable and that's when we see ecological change or evolution. So there is *only* evolved—no more, no less. It is a relative idea. We consider ourselves more evolved than fish—we're so proud of our brains—but if the world flooded, they'd have the last laugh.

"So, Paul, to the question of anger and how it plays into the human psyche, we have to examine our most powerful gift: the ability to reason. This and all its complexities is the governor on our mind. So if all humans are granted the ability to reason—which may be an easy assumption to refute—then that implies that anger is a rational decision; that we make a choice to be angry and that we've weighed our options and anger has been deemed the best course." Stoss took a long sip from his drink and relished the silence that he left over the campfire. "How many times in your lives has anger seemed like a conscious decision and not an animal reaction?"

The silence persisted as he let the question hang. David's eyes narrowed in memory and he looked into the fire. Paul's gaze flickered between him and Stoss. A mosquito landed on his neck and it took a moment for him to brush it off.

Stoss continued, "Right. Never. It is not. Anger is animal in the purest sense and that's why we try so hard to subdue it, but why we feel relieved — though a little scared — when we let it out. So I will wind back around to you, Connor, and your mosquito problem. They make you angry. So I would say that if you can fight that instinct and keep it at bay, you'll satisfy the higher governors of your mind — your reason — for having made a conscious decision and not reverted to your most animal instincts. And you will become calm, born from a confidence in understanding."

David spoke, "But you said that releasing anger is relieving or calming?"

"Ah-ha! That is another clever trick played by reason in our minds. Because we have been given this tool to explore the world around us through the lens of rationality, there is no greater satisfaction than *understanding*, than grasping what is truly happening around us, being able to look at the forces at work and *see* them for what they really are, and *know* what is going on, what is truth and explainable. Why? Because in a beautiful coming of full circle, reason is born from survival. And nothing permits a wild creature to survive better on this violent planet than a complete knowledge of what's around him. And that generates the ultimate peace: understanding." The old doctor's eyes glinted in the waving light and he smiled at the pursed lips and slowly nodding heads around the fire. A mosquito landed on the back of his hand and he shook it away.

"Good campfire talk, Doc" JP said tossing a few sticks into the fire.

Stoss continued as if his train of thought was unbroken. Every word was a new burst of excitement. "Yes JP, campfire talk indeed. That gift Paul built between us — fire — is what allowed any of this to take place. There is a certain harbor man finds in fire, as he did many hundreds of thousands years ago. Fire brought safety to the dark woods — it brought light and heat, and a weapon if need be. The dark evolved from a time of fear and defense, to a time of peace and relaxation by the flames. Those that study these things would argue that this is in fact when we started to hone our skills of language, storytelling and finally, reason. We had the time. We could think about it, and we could try to understand it. Like many of the pieces of everyday life, it's easy to lose sight of how important a light in the darkness can be." He narrowed his gaze again at the dancing flames. "I do believe that is why a man can still look into a fire and draw a sense of peace: it's woven into his fabric."

Paul said, "I have another question: You mentioned using fire as a weapon was important to our development, but what about other weapons?"

"I don't follow."

Paul rubbed his face and sat up in his chair. "You got me thinking about weapons and tools for fighting or hunting. If fire was what gave us the peace to sit and think and develop these tools and pass on how to make them so they became engrained institutions in culture, well, haven't we let that hurt our own development as creatures? If we're depending on all these great tools and weapons that our mind has created using reason, have we started to hurt our core animal?"

Stoss nodded. "You mean: has the mind sabotaged its body by creating proxies for animal functions?"

"Exactly."

"Well," Stoss said with a glimmer in his eye. "Who here thinks they could win in a fight against, say, a fox?"

JP laughed. "Shit, Doc, I could handle a fox. I could get a good stomping on—"

"You're naked as the day you were delivered."

This put a pause of thought across JP's face and his hands drifted over his crotch.

Stoss continued with a wink. "He'd probably go right for those. You're not a small guy, JP, so you'd get him in the end, but not before those claws and jaws took a healthy piece. But a fox is thirty pounds, at most? Something a little bigger, like a coyote or a bobcat?"

"I bet the big guy could take that fox down." JP motioned to Paul, then flicked away a mosquito.

Paul looked back distantly, chewing his cheek in thought, as everyone waited for his response. A couple bugs hovered around his head unnoticed. His distance put a gap in the conversation and siphoned some of its momentum.

Stoss broke the silence with a nod to the dark woods. "Well anyway, enough lecturing. Now I have to utilize light's modern gift: allowing an old man to piss at night."

"Don't forget to be understanding when your dick gets bit!" JP yelled with a grin as the old doctor walked away.

Laughs evolved into smaller conversations around the fire. The thoughtfulness Stoss had injected turned over to visions of the coming days on the river.

~ 4 ~

LIKE MUSICAL INSTRUMENTS AND STAPLES OF CUISINE, the fishing rod—fly and spinning—exists as one of the institutions of culture whose history frays and winds so expansively that we just accept that it's always been there in some capacity, like roots of an oak tree, bending and writhing through the soils of time to countless indeterminable origins. Drawings of ancient civilizations, from the Egyptians to the Middle Kingdom to the Roman Empire, show their peasants casting some oblong stick or reed into the currents, a line fixed to the end. Hooks were made from wood, bone or even stone and covered in the remnants of a meal or slain animal as bait. Lines were fashioned from strips of leaves, plant fibers or woven hair from horsetails and later silk and catgut. The ancient fisherman stood on the bank and whipped his fixed-length line into the current or simply dangled the bait in the water.

Not until the 12th or 13th century in China did man take a look at his fishing rod and say, "I wish there was a way to keep more line on my rod, to cast farther, but not have it in a big mess everywhere around me," and invent the first iterations of the fishing reel. They started as just a simple place to coil line at the butt-end of the rod with no handle or crank. They were an onboard storage facility that gave no thought to mechanics. As in all inventions we now deem simple or mundane, like the pen, it took almost five hundred years before the reel evolved from a place to wind extra line, to what we know today—a crank governed by gears and knobs to control the give and take of line while targeting and fighting a fish.

As the realization that there was potential to reach those fish that had held out of range set in to the fishing community, a small fissure developed in how to put the bait in front of them. It was not a debate, just two schools of thinking. One thought that it was best to weight the bait and use its momentum to reach the farther pockets of the river. The other thought it best to keep the weight in the line and use its momentum to reach the farther pockets of river, in the same way a bull whip carries force along its unfurling wave.

This was the separation of spin and fly fishing: A spin fisherman casts a weighted lure, attached to almost-weightless line; a fly fisherman casts an almost-weightless lure, attached to weighted line.

Though as the two schools of thought developed their crafts, building rods—shorter for spin fishing, longer for fly fishing—and reels better suited for these principles, the fishermen on both sides took a closer look at their bait. To the spin fisherman, knowing he needed weight, the bait was a canvas to use heavy metals and plastics to design flashy and lifelike minnows, fry, frogs, fish and otherwise. To the fly fisherman, knowing he needed weightlessness, the bait became a minute canvas of artistry to mimic the delicate insects that caught the eye of hungry fish. He honed his craft, building and mimicking the intricate thoraxes and wings and tails on the shank of a hook less than half an inch long, activating the brain regions that exude a pride proportional to the intricacy of the task at hand. It is here, upon reconstructing the head and tail and wing casings of an insect, lighter than a whisper, that a fly fisherman derives the fuel of scorn for the spin fisherman that clunks and bounces his bait, abandoning the core principals of mimicry and dredging up whatever fish was dumb enough to slurp his clumsy lure.

And as is often man's proclivity, David had subscribed to

the reasoning of history without scrutiny and had climbed into the safe confines of the fly fishermen's point of view. It was the St George's Fly Fishing Club after all.

~

The next morning the sun was fierce and sent the mosquitoes buzzing to the shade. As the other guys wandered about camp getting ready for the day and a football was tossed to random receivers, and sometimes zipped at those that weren't paying attention, Connor and David settled at the table.

"Sorry I was giving you hell last night," Connor said quietly after a minute, "about the bugs. I think I was just fired up about fishing."

David stretched his arms and shrugged. "Don't worry about it. It's in the rearview."

JP emerged from his tent in his underwear, let out a rebel yell, and jogged down to the Elizabeth for a morning swim. David watched him make his way to the river and turned back to Connor. "That guy seem weird to you?"

Connor glanced up and thought for a moment. "Could be. Why?"

"I dunno," David said. "Just a feeling."

"Isn't he your brother's friend?"

"Not really—they just got to talking about fishing when he was down south for a conference, and eventually had me invite him here." David shook his head and stood, "Whatever, he's normal enough."

Soon Paul had the morning fire roaring and they cooked bacon, eggs and bagels, slopping them with cheese and pepper. No one seemed to notice Stoss and Norton had been up and left camp earlier, though separately. As the guys milled about packing lunches, piecing together rods, checking fly boxes, tying and building leaders, cleaning polarized lenses, putting on waders and applying sunscreen, David grabbed everyone's attention.

"Guys, to have a little fun and make things interesting, I was thinking we could split into two groups today." He paused briefly, scanning each set of eyes for dissention. "Half of us go to the large pool-water upstream and half of us head downstream. Paul and I will each captain a team. Whichever team catches the least fish *on average* loses, and has to do dishes tonight. Gotta be back in camp by five."

Everyone shrugged in agreement and soon, the spirit of competition took hold as they finished readying for the day.

"I can't wait to sit back after dinner tonight and relax," Connor said as he strung up his rod and checked his reel. He exaggerated his stretches.

Ian chimed in. "I haven't had anyone do my dishes since I lived with my parents."

"So, couple-three weeks ago?" JP fired back.

"I'm going to eat the messiest dinner of my life. I may even use my plate for a bedpan later on," Ian continued and tightened his wading belt.

"Oh really? That's hilarious," Josh said. "Maybe I'll do the dishes in your tent then. Or maybe I'll just go to the bathroom there anyway."

"That's a little over the line, fella," JP said sardonically, then nodded in Paul's direction. "We have the big guy on our team so you may as well start getting some suds going now...and get house broken."

"We are going to dominate you jackasses," David said with a layer of intensity. The talk slowed.

Connor spoke in his quick way. "Well—I mean—I'd hope you'd catch fish today since you've been here—"

"Don't make excuses," David interjected, heading him off. "Just fish like you always fish and you'll be fine."

"I ain't worried," JP said sitting in his chair. "I been fishing all my life and never met a piece of water I didn't conquer, just like I never met a lady I didn't neither!" He pointed to his crotch and then to his spinning rig. "This rod has seen it all, boys!"

David jolted to a stop. "You don't fly fish?"

"Naw," he said, still smiling. "Fly fishing's too much waving and slapping on the water. Why be a damn scientist when you just gotta get a fish worked up with something shiny—you know, like the ladies." He looked around for another laugh.

David peered back at JP, his eyes settling somewhere between his face and the spinning rod. "Not so sure about that, my friend—that's not real fishing." David tried to drape humor over the comments. The other guys slowed what they were doing.

JP's face tightened up. "What the hell you talking about, chief? Just because spin fishing doesn't use hair off a deer's ass, you're going to discount the way I catch fish? What—"

"Yeah," David interrupted. "Anyone can put a hook on a spoon and throw it in the water. It takes skill to match up your fly to the bug the fish are feeding on. I am discounting spin fishing. Absolutely. I—"

Paul put his big frame between the two. "Let this go." He looked straight at his brother. "Fishing is fishing." He turned back to the others. "I've been waiting for almost a year to fish the Elizabeth. It's why we're here—no matter how you want to catch fish. The only thought that excites me more than standing in her cool waters and hammering fish," he grinned, "is the thought of sipping a beer while half you goons clean my dishes."

David saw the way his brother spoke to the group, and how they reacted. The tension evaporated into the summer; they smiled and went back to gearing up. He scrambled for something to say. "Just fired up over here. I'll keep the final count for my team; Paul can do the same for his—use the honor system."

The obvious addition to the logistics met quick nods. In the distance, the victorious cry of a hawk signaled the start of the day. Paul watched everyone as they grouped into their teams and headed to the river, especially his brother.

~

Over the past year, Norton had occupied his time with three activities: working, caring for Adrian and studying fly fishing. Nothing else carried much weight in his life and really, the first was simply a means to make the other two possible. Starting his own deli, much less business again seemed a world away as a single father. So until a next step presented itself, he worked at a gourmet food shop in San Francisco, cutting meats, stocking shelves, packaging olives and recommending wines he'd never tried. He put in long hours stretched across short interactions that left him tired and glazed. But fatigue faded like salt in the ocean when he picked up Adrian. As soon as the front door opened and he'd jump down the babysitter's front stairs, Norton's young son would burst into a wobbly legged sprint, a vibrant smile cresting every corner of his face, a book bag and jacket tethered by his seven-year-old limbs—as much as Norton asked him to, he never wore either, preferring to have them haphazardly orbiting his body. To Norton, this is when the day really began.

When he'd send Adrian off to school the next morning, he usually had a few hours to himself before he needed to open the shop. He'd pack his fly rod and head to the concrete casting ponds in Golden Gate Park, practicing his roll cast, his false casts and the accuracy of his full casts. He'd spend hours locking in on the various targets in the pools— dreaming of them as a piece of remembered pocket water in the Elizabeth or a shallow riffle pregnant with a darting shadow. Of all the training, the best part was sitting on the benches with the old timers. He would listen as they imparted finely aged perspective on hatch patterns, trout habits, flies that work and flies that don't, wading techniques, fishing history, how to read a lake, how to read a river, watersheds, evolution and how to think about the overall concepts of the carefully balanced science and art of fly fishing. Norton loved it, and as the work hour approached, felt like a child that had to leave an extravagant birthday party.

That summer, Norton had quit his job. The meager insurance money from the fire still left a small cushion for him to make changes in life, but more importantly, there would be other jobs waiting for him when he returned. He set a rotating roster of babysitters for Adrian and returned to the valley. Norton had to smile to himself, if only to cover the small pang of sadness, that Adrian hadn't voiced a protesting word when he'd said goodbye; he's simply turned and began playing with his cousins. A child's independence has a strange way of being offensive to the parents.

Now the riffles and pocket waters of the Elizabeth stretched out before him; the sun-struck sides of fluttering mayflies danced and wove among the golden borders. The high peaks of the Crescents towered behind, their craggy stony teeth gnashing in contrast to the babbling and laughing waters. He stood on an oblong rock in the current shooting casts; his line zipped from the tip of his rod like a frog's tongue after a moth.

Paul found him at the riverside and watched him for a moment, taking in the change. Soon JP and Connor walked up and Paul called to Norton. "How you doing this morning?"

Norton jumped, put out a hand to balance, and turned. "Taken—taken five fish already and missed another six or seven." He wrangled his excitement.

"Damn, Norton!" JP howled and peered at the Elizabeth as if it were the first time he'd seen it. "Get me on this water!"

A look of surprise cracked Paul's cheeks for an instant then he remembered the long winter. "Want to join our team?" he asked. "We're playing for dish duty tonight; David took his team downstream."

Without missing a beat, Norton put one hand on his hip and pointed upriver. "I would space us about fifty yards apart," he said slowly at first, and then picked up speed. "I have fished out everything below us. From here we can leap-frog until the water thins out and can start over." Like waiting for the results of a very important exam, Norton looked sideways at Paul.

~

Downstream, and far from his brother, David led his team, scouting waters and marking spots where they should return. He walked a pace ahead of Ian and Josh, pointing to holes and runs and recapping how he and Paul had fished them the prior two years. They'd walked almost a half a mile when they found Stoss, fishing a silent black pool that eddied into a hovel of the Elizabeth's far bank. He was waist deep in rushing current and his tall, storkish frame looked like an old tan branch sticking out of the riffles.

David threw a small pebble and shouted over the din, "How goes it?"

Stoss turned slowly, careful of his footing, and gave the thumbs up and turned back around. David yelled again over the rush of river. "I've got us in a little friendly competition. Want in?"

Stoss turned again and put a finger to his ear.

"Competition!" David shouted. "You want to be on our team?"

The old doctor looked at him for a moment, sorting through what he'd heard, then waved away the offer and turned to fish.

"Well," David said to his team not making eye contact with anyone. "He's casting into a spot that doesn't hold a lot of fish so we're better off anyway. He'd have brought down the average." He waved them down the road a quarter mile to a long pool, leaving Stoss to himself.

He sought time that morning to think on his own. His recent retirement from medicine now felt impulsive, hot headed even, and he second-guessed himself. Shortly before leaving for St George's, he had gathered all the residents, head nurses and attending physicians around the oblong balsawood table in the top floor of his hospital and told them that he was retiring. It was a tough decision, the hardest he'd ever made, he'd said. He'd looked his colleagues in the eye, and thanked them one by one, reciting individual instances each had worked together on a particularly memorable case. The fire of healing had been extinguished and smoldering somewhere in the depths was a new challenge for his aging, but hopefully still, agile mind. He just had to find it. And with that, he walked past them.

Now, focused on the pool in front of him in motor coordination only, Stoss treated his second guessing of his decision as a symptom and worked clinically backwards to find the disease.

—What seems to be the problem?

—*I don't love medicine… anymore.*

—When did this start?

—*About three years ago, I think.*

—And it's gotten worse since, or about the same?

—*It was bad for the first two years and then it became progressively worse a little over a year ago.*

—Are there any particular events from a year ago that you think may be affecting this?

—*Only my fishing trip. Other than that, there have been no other changes in behavior.*

—I see. Well, these sorts of things do cause wandering hearts but to make you actually despise the craft you've practiced for so long seems to be slightly out of the ordinary. There are no other changes in your life, in your every day routine that you've made in the last year?

—*None that I can think of.*

—Hm. Well that may be part of the problem. Have you experienced any moments of panic or unexpected stress?

—*Well, I'm a trauma surgeon, but outside of that, not really except for a few tough losses of patients. But those happen every year.*

—What were the losses?

—*The usual. A couple were too overweight for their own good to withstand surgery, others too old. One mother didn't know about her child's antibiotic allergy and it killed him in recovery. A few other terminal cases that never had a chance. That's about it. The usual.*

—I see. What was the child's name?

—*Tucker Jensen. His friend convinced him to ride his bike down a flight of stairs. His wrist and elbow shattered in seven places, but he would have been fine. The anaphylaxis snuffed him so quickly; we barely had a nurse in the room. It was the first time that I couldn't really find the right words for a mother—she was single…and alone now, I guess.*

—You usually don't remember your patient's names—especially those you've lost. Let me ask you this: If you now hate it, why did you love medicine? Do you remember?

—*Well, I enjoyed the craft of healing.*

—I see. Do you still enjoy that craft?

—*Well, in theory, yes. I certainly enjoy walking into an examination room and talking a patient through their problems and then giving the proper treatment but I…I…*—

—That sounds a lot like medicine. You are here because you have said that you hate it. Is "hate" the right word?

—*Well, it's not that I "hate" it, per se. I don't think I said that. It's just that I don't want to do it, or no, I guess it's just that I would rather do other things. I don't walk in through the doors of the operating room with the same fight.*

—Do me a favor; try to answer the question in single words. List what makes you happy.

—*Well, teaching. Teaching is my other passion*—

A fish hit Stoss's fly. He snapped out of his trance and laughed as he recognized the trout. He absently stripped in line and it fell around his waist. He felt better about his decision. He'd dislodged something like a piece of food in a back molar. He couldn't see it or say what color it had been, but it was gone now—extricated and swallowed. He concentrated on the dancing trout in front of him, not seeing the winged shadow that passed behind him on the water.

~

An eagle flew in front of the sun and glided in the up-drafts and alighted on a high branch to watch the old man in the river. She'd seen his form before. He'd fished this pool the previous year and she'd watched him then too. Though he was old, to her, he looked stronger now. She rotated her cupped head and looked down across the currents. A fish appeared in the water before him, writhing in the bouncing waters. She was hungry, but decided he was too close to steal it.

Her long brown wings unfolded from her sides and she drew them downward, launching into flight. She glided up and down the river through the afternoon and saw more men. They shouted and laughed and fish appeared at their feet too. She didn't understand how fish were drawn to their feet. They seemed attached to that long stick they carried. When she swooped lower to see it all more clearly, the men would look up at her and point and sometimes shout, so she'd tip her wings and move higher. She'd wait until they were focused on the river and swoop lower again, but they always sensed her, pointed and shouted. Finally she lost interest and glided towards the setting sun.

~

David watched the eagle go. "That's right," he said to himself. "Don't need you losing this game for me because you're too lazy to catch one yourself." In front of him, two rocks stood like guards on either side of a long smooth flow of water. He cast to the head of it and mended his line so the faster current couldn't pull his fly off the window of water. He repeated a few more times and looked at his watch. It was four-thirty. He shouted downstream to Ian and Josh and waved towards the bank and pointed towards his wrist.

Looks of disappointment reached across their faces and David wished he hadn't said five o'clock. They trudged, heads down like children, towards the bank.

"How'd you guys do?" David asked as they met on the old road.

"Had to land them, a strike or hookup doesn't count, right?" Josh asked.

"Yeah."

"Sixteen."

"Twelve," Ian echoed sending his gaze downward.

David did the math. "Just over fifteen fish each. I had eighteen. Pull your weight, Ian," he said giving him a half-playful whack on the shoulder. "Fifteen fish is pretty good. The other guys had Norton so I'd imagine we've got a little advantage there."

However, when they returned to camp, David sensed that he was wrong immediately. Norton moved, almost jumped around the fire, holding up his hands like he was fighting a fish. Paul, JP and Connor had settled into chairs with beers glimmering in their hands as they let him go.

"How'd you do?" Norton asked excitedly as David approached through the field. Ian and Josh lagged behind talking.

"How'd *you* do, Norton?"

"Fifteen," he said confidently. "I had already taken five when I met up with these guys, but I will not count them because I started early."

"Connor?" David asked.

"Eleven. I suck."

David snorted and didn't make an effort to disagree. "And you two?" he said to JP and Paul.

"I also suck," Paul said. "I hooked a lot of fish but kept dropping them—only had thirteen in the net, probably dropped another fifteen." He tapped the black notebook in his lap. "But thirteen is my number."

A noticeable relief coursed through David's face. "JP?" he

asked without making eye contact.

"Well my friend, I *don't* suck. Me and my spin rig took down twenty-five fish—"

"Bullshit you did!"

Paul nodded slowly. "Every time I looked over, this joker was on another fish. I'd believe him if he said thirty."

David didn't acknowledge his brother. "We're not counting hookups: you have to have that fish in your hands."

"Chief, I don't know why you'd clarify: I would never count a hookup. Twenty-five fish were in these hands." He splayed out his fingers and locked them at the thumb. His grinning face appeared between the bind and he bugged his eyes so the whites dominated his grey irises. "*Boom*! Now I'm interested to hear what *you* had…but I get the sense I'm not cleaning dishes."

There was some muffled laughter from the other guys. David started to argue again, but Ian spoke before he could. "We're just short," he said tucking his wading boots under the table and sitting. "You guys beat us by a fish. I sucked too though, only landed twelve. Someone throw me a beer."

Before he'd finished the request, JP had a bottle arcing into his lap. Josh and Ian finished changing out of their gear and picked up the football again and the evening started to resemble a nice reflection of the morning. The only exception was David. It was a while before he changed out of his gear and later when Stoss came back and reported he'd taken twenty-two fish, David descended into an even deeper cave of frustration.

The mosquitoes were less of a nuisance and more of a bonding agent as guys started looking out for one another and slapping each other on the shoulder when one would alight. They tossed beers, traded shots of whiskey, laughed and set their hands at various lengths apart from in reference to the quality of their work on the Elizabeth. The momentum coalesced but the conversation took on an erratic rhythm of speakers and stories like the explosions from a burning warehouse of fireworks.

...yeah, that last brown I took was no shorter than eighteen inches. Fought like an absolute truck in four-wheel drive.

—I saw that fish...but Connor...eighteen...really?

—I measured: eighteen inches, asshole.

—You sure?

—Yes.

—An old girlfriend may have recalibrated your perception of "inches."

—Yeah, well JP, your mom set her straight.

—Actually, this one brown that I'd spotted hanging in a little pocket water behind a fallen tree had to have been at least twenty.

—Now, I will trust Paul's length vision. You raise him?

—No, couldn't get him to take for like an hour; I threw my whole box at him and he just sat there behind the branches. I could just make out his back and a little flash of mouth every now and again. Had to have been twenty-two.

—You mean down from here a few hundred yards, right near those three rotting firs stacked on each other?

—Yeah.

—Saw that.

—I saw that hulk too—couldn't raise it either.

—Yeah, I found a big rainbow, but she was coming up to the surface and sipping these little emergers. I tied on a big foam ant and then hung a tiny flash emerger behind it, just hanging it under the film. I put it a little short of her nose and—BAM! She came flying out of her lane and just CRUSHED it.

—Did you land her? Ian, need another beer?

—No. She ran me deep into some rocks and then wrapped me on a branch. I think the ant ended up getting caught.

—Lose your rig?

—Whole damn thing. But I had more of those little flash emergers and fished them for a while. Didn't get anything that big again, but they were on them.

—I had a couple of great fish on emergers and a couple

on duns, but noticed that they were really hitting the nymphs, even when a hatch was on full tilt. I think it takes them a while to key on the surface.

—*Well, I was squatting on this big hole way downstream for about an hour and saw them working on all phases. One 'bow was nosing the bottom; another was on the surface; another was just hanging in the column, moving up and down. I watched for a while and finally said, "Fuck it!" and threw on a little Parachute Adams*—POW! *Second drift, one took it.*

—I think I saw you fighting that actually; did it come into the top of that big hole with the rock that looks like a gravestone?

—*Epitaph Rock*—*I'm not talking about that time.*

—Oh because, that almost spooked out this nice rainbow I'd—

—*Hold on. Let me finish; I couldn't move that big rainbow most of the time because of the deep runs of current.*

—I almost got swept away a couple times myself.

—*Totally. So I was horsing this fish upstream, trying to work her back to my pool, and I just got her head out of the water and then she put on one last dance and then,* SNAP *goes the weasel.*

—That sucks.

—*That does. I don't know how many fish I broke off today.*

—More than you landed, I'm sure.

—*Eh, maybe not. If I got a good hook-set, she was done.*

—You fishing with barbs?

—*You're not?*

—Pinch those tomorrow, Norton. We don't need to rip lips.

—*Do all you guys pinch?*

—Yeah.

—*Yeah.*

—Most times.

—*Yeah, most times.*

—It'll increase your LDR's, but won't lay as much of a beatdown on the fish.

—*Paul, what's an LDR?*

—Long distance release.

—*Right.*

The pops and sparks continued until they'd exhausted every element of the river, fish, bugs and day that they could squeeze from their increasingly inebriated minds until the last bragging rocket had sailed and fatigue crept into the outer edges of the meadow like a long shadow. Empty bottles and almost-finished cups lay at their feet, as if their collective, as a whole, had frenzied to such a fury that the final release, the final details of their day, everything they could squeeze out and compare against one another from their experience on the Elizabeth, had been exercised and they now sat slackened and drunk around the campfire in a dreamy bliss and ready to sleep—to do it all again tomorrow.

Paul looked over at his brother who'd been almost silent the entire time. David had his chin and mouth buried in his fleece, his faded blue eyes just visible over the top of the zipper as he peered into the dancing fire. Paul stood. "Guys, like David said last night, we're happy to get everyone down here. Now if you'll excuse me, I'm drunk and want to fish just as hard tomorrow. I'm going to take a leak and crash." He nodded to a tree on the edge of the meadow and the jerk of his neck activated an ejection mechanism under each chair around the fire as they began heading for bed in bending lines. Only David stayed watching the flames as the tents opened and closed and the rustle of nylon signaled the end of the evening.

When a man sits alone with his thoughts, he can wander a great distance. He can take all that is on his mind and reorganize it and reshuffle it and form it how he likes. And that is usually a problem—especially if that man has alcohol on his breath. Whatever ills or wrongs he senses in the worlds will be dumped on the table in front of him and he'll sort through them until he finds the ugliest and easiest to turn about in his dumb hands. That lens of ethanol will stretch over his mind's eye and magnify the wrong and make it dirty and personal. But that ethanol membrane also plays a clever trick. It reverses. It melts from an outward lens to an inward lens and the man then uses it to find the solution to the exaggerated predicament.

As David sat by the fire and thought about the club he was trying to form, that lens turned back on itself after shedding a fisheye view on his meaningless loss from the day. The loss tasted acrid in his mouth. That the guys on his team had not cared only heightened his angst. He looked into the fire and tried to ignore the snores bubbling up in the meadow around him. Then he crawled off to bed.

~ 5 ~

THE NEXT MORNING everyone except David slithered out of their tent and encircled the smoldering firepit, flopping into their chair; Stoss had been up early and was already on the river. The sun glared back at them as they peered longingly into the woods and the cool caves of shade under the long branches. But soon, as the ethanol seeped out in their sweat, their pulsing headaches began to sync with the hot rays and a strange relief passed over. The rush of hungry fish was fresh; the alacrity of the Elizabeth's trout brought light into their eyes as they stared ahead in silence. The grasshoppers in the long grasses drew their legs together and sent tinny messages to one another.

The only two having a conversation were Ian and Josh, able to work through a hangover better than anyone. They were somewhat of a dynamic drinking duo in college, always up the latest and always showing it the least. They'd kept in touch with Paul since, but recently he had found himself wanting to hang out less; he always found himself restless around them.

"Hey Ambrose," Ian said as Paul walked over. "What was the name of that guy who used to get high every morning before class? He lived down the hall from you freshman year, I think."

"Stu Donovan?"

"Stu Donovan. Did you know that he's running his own accounting firm now?"

Paul sat down with them. "I heard — in Philly?"

"No outside DC."

"Right. Why do you ask?"

Josh jumped in. "I just can't believe he is doing so well. I'm not sure if I ever saw him go to class."

"Yeah," Paul said. "Good for him, right?"

"He was really good friends with the Barks brothers. I bet he tapped into some of that money." Josh was straining to remember something and his eyes were tense with a frenzy about them. "You know that Taylor Barks—"

"Their little sister?" Ian asked with a smile and pop of the eyebrows.

Paul shifted in his seat.

"Yeah," Josh continued, "she ended up marrying a hedge fund manager out of New York. Can't remember the name of the fund…A.L.R. Capital or something…."

Ian's smile deflated to a grimace. "That sounds right. Lucky bastard—all those guys. Can buy whatever they want."

Paul threw out, "I remember her—sweet girl," but the comment went unnoticed.

Ian continued, "You just have to be 'right place, right time' somewhere. That's all it is. I ran into Derrick Chen in the airport last month—he thinks he'll take in close to half a million this year. *Half a million* and he's turning thirty. Can you imagine?"

"How's Derrick doing?" Paul asked.

Ian stared at him and smiley coyly. "I just told you: he's rollin'." Then waved off the joke, but broke his gaze, "No, he seemed fine. Turning grey though."

"Ambrose," Josh said and his smile indicated he'd been waiting patiently to ask the question, "didn't you take down Taylor Barks?"

"Me? No. I only met her a couple times right after college, but I was dating Gretchen at the time."

"Ah," and "Right," the other two said at different, yet

skeptical paces.

"*Right*," Paul echoed with annoyance in his tone. He let the silence sit and shielded his eyes from the glaring sun.

"Damn," JP said loudly, tipping his head back. The southern extrovert sat slumped in a chair, drinking a glass of water and stretching his skinny white legs, but he straightened up. "I'm gonna fish hard...but then nap harder. Find me a rock, right in the middle of the Elizabeth, pull my hat down and pass the hell out."

"Sounds like a good idea," Paul said.

"*Great* idea," Norton said rubbing his temples. The tag end of his fly line was in his lap with a new leader but he had not started the task of tying them together yet. He looked at both ends warily.

"I tell you, man," JP said profoundly. "You'll never find peace like napping on a riverside."

"There—there is not much of *anything* that would not better by a riverside," Norton said.

"Damn right!" JP hollered and slapped his leg.

Norton grinned confidently and was about to continue, but a grumbling from David's tent made him stop. David opened the door and took in the slow moving camp. Wavering forces dictated his balance; he was still a bit drunk and sported only a pair of white boxers.

"Looky this guy," JP said with a laugh. "You going to make it on the water?"

David tripped on the bottom of his tent door as he stumbled out. "Ready if you are."

"You sure about that?"

"I am—JP—in fact I'm thinking about heading downstream to The Flats for some sight fishing if anyone wants to join me—" he glanced at JP "—fly fishing that is?"

JP spoke with a grin. "Hey now, looks like you had a rough night's sleep, chief. Maybe you'd prefer to nap and take a dip in river if fishing don't catch your fancy anymore. We'll have some dishes once breakfast is over. I *know* you're good at that."

David smiled the wry smile a drunk drapes over his face when being toyed with, but the faculties aren't clear enough to outwit the provocateur. The breeze blew and he side-stepped, overcompensating for balance. "Why don't you shove your spin rig up your ass?"

"Alright David—take it easy," Paul cut in. "Get your gear and let's go."

JP continued and the lightheartedness of his voice was twisting to frustration. "I didn't invent the sport. Just because fly fishing markets itself with thoughtful movies and preppy shirts don't mean it's any different at the core. I don't see why you're making a deal of this." He paused. "You guys used spinning rigs on Cape Cod didn't you?"

David didn't answer but his escaping eyes proved JP correct; he waved about sarcastically, "We could just throw some dynamite in the river too. That seems like fun. Then we'd have more fish—"

"You sound ridiculous. It's the same damn sport."

David took on a mock professorial tone, "Hmm, there are caddis coming off right now, what shall I use? *Oh*, a big red and white spoon with big hooks. Hmm, there are little *baetis* coming off, what shall I use? *Oh*, a big red and white spoon with big hooks. Hmm, there are tiny midges coming off, about a size 22, what shall I use? *Oh*, a big red and white—"

JP cut in, "Why don't we wager on who catches more fish today? Huh, *chief*?"

David swayed for a moment and squinted. A small blinking light in the ether of ethanol warned that he was getting in over his head, but the nickname put enough oxygen in his fire that he disregarded. "What are we betting?"

JP continued like he'd never broken his thought. Stoss had wandered back into camp to get a little breakfast and JP flicked a thumb at him. "In light of Doc's point about aggravation, loser has to stand in only his shorts, without moving for fifteen minutes after the sun goes down—and the mosquitoes are out."

Someone muttered, *"Whoa."* Stoss pretended he hadn't heard his name mentioned in these apish proceedings, but everyone else stopped what they were doing and looked at David. He wavered in the thick silence.

Occasionally a drunk will come across—like a vivid glimpse of an object on the bottom of a disrupted pool—a good idea. The nature of *good* is left to interpretation, but in this instance, David found one that afterward, everyone agreed actually was. "Let's do *this*," he said feeling the eyes upon him. "We'll play HORSE—like basketball, where I make a shot and you have to match it. If you match, we play another round and nothing happens. If you don't, you miss, you get a letter and then we trade turns, until one of us spells the word.

"But we'll play on the Elizabeth, fishing, not basketball. You find a hole and get one cast to catch and land a fish—get it in the net—and then I have to match what you've done." He picked up a water bottle and unscrewed the top, losing his train of thought and rewinding a little, "We'll trade off until one of us spells H-O-R-S-E, and loses." David took a pull of water and wiped his face as the drops fell off his chin and winked in the sunshine. "Same stakes—loser has to stand in the mosquitoes wearing only shorts."

JP nodded. "Make it P-I-G and you've got a game. I don't want to stand next to your smelly ass all day. Three is enough."

"Done," David said and his hand came forward for a shake; his face betrayed a little surprise. JP grinned and shook his hand. The tension broke and everyone prepared for the day, a smile at the corner of their lips—glad they could be a spectator, yet quietly squirming at the thought of being defenseless against the mosquitoes.

David stood dumbly for another moment and wiped the water off his face, some of it dripping down his chest and onto his white boxers, soaking the thin fabric.

Paul glanced over as he left the firering. "Invisible eyes," he mumbled.

"What?" David asked, the intensity returning to his face.

Paul spoke over his shoulder. "Just put on some pants."

~

With the sun rising in the eastern sky and the light still sharpening a new day, a grove of pines sent a dark duvet of shadows over a pool in the Elizabeth. A boulder sat at the head, centering the flow and turning the vacuum filled by the backwater into a wide curling eddy. Leaves, blades of grass, fragments of bark and flecks of indeterminate origin fluttered about the surface, and through all the detritus, peering with never closing eyes, was a shadow. This particular rainbow trout had been born two springs prior and through stealth and wariness grown to call this pool her own. After the winter run off, when she'd put her head in the canyons of the riverbed rocks and let the spring run over her back, she'd chased off invaders looking for new residence. Across the low pink border of her gill plate was a faint scar from a female brown's pointed teeth—but she'd sent that intruder down the current too.

So this rainbow held her seam of current that flowed from around the towering rock in front of her. She never wanted to move. She knew the world as a bubbling panorama that passed her on the right and often carried food. That was it—what she knew. Shadows would pass overhead now and again, and she'd scurry under the big rock and wait until an innate timer rang that it was safe to return to her post along the seam of water. In other instances, stunning vibrations and thuds would send her to the same place. But she always returned to her post, content and watching life rush past her. She was almost back to her normal weight after the long winter, having gorged herself since the sunlight returned, but she had a little more work to do.

If only as a faint plop, she saw a small fish appear ahead

of her in the current and sink for a moment, his sides glittering and fluttering reds and whites in the light. By now she was familiar with chasing off challengers and she eyed him to see what his next move was. The little fish started swimming towards her, weaving back and forth, bearing directly at her. Her defenses went up and she charged. But just as she was about to smack him with her jaws, she decided he was just too large to swallow. Simply scaring him would do. She arrested; he swam past, unconcerned, jerking erratically, not fleeing, but certainly leaving.

She watched him go out the back of her pool and returned to her post on the seam water. A small pupa swirled near her snout and she snatched it; another appeared who met the same fate—the protein and nutrients replacing the energy she'd burnt chasing the intruder. The current bubbled and passed by until a healthy stonefly nymph appeared and she wagged her head lazily to one side. She hadn't seen many stoneflies that year and it was larger than she'd expected. She opened wide to get around it, her throat contracting to keep the current flowing into her gullet and flush the unsuspecting prey. She closed her mouth and—

A blinding pain tore through her filament neurons and fizzed their synapses; her face involuntarily jerked to the left. The stonefly jumped from her mouth, fixing onto the side of her jaw with a claw she hadn't noticed. It pulled her towards the back of the pool and with an instinct the little rainbow couldn't identify, she turned her shoulder and ran in the opposite direction. She didn't know why she ran or where she was going. She didn't know why the stonefly tore her towards the back of the pool, but it was causing this searing pain. That's all she knew.

She plunged into the current, hoping that the roiling water would wash this pain and parasite from her face. It tore at her lip and she ran harder. She shook her head, hoping to come free from its claws. She ran again, leaning her shoulder down and away from where the stonefly dragged her, but in a feat of strength that violated every conceivable notion she knew about her prey, the stonefly yanked at her face and pulled her across the current and towards the end of her pool. She shook her head again and ran for the base of her rock. She saw its safe shadows in the distance, every muscle and fiber along her body vibrating and shaking to get there. The stonefly pulled her. She tried for her safe shadows again, but it pulled her with the same unseen strength. She jumped and splashed. She shook her head. She jumped again. She tried to run. Nothing worked. The stonefly held on, dragging her where the rocks were covered in algae and the water turned warm in a stagnant brown.

She was too tired to fight now. The running, the shaking, the turning, the jumping left her spent.

A huge creature loomed above her and extended a limb. She didn't have the energy to run. Her organs compressed and air came from her mouth as if through a cracked pipe of gas. Then she couldn't breathe at all. The river was gone—below her. She looked up at a strange creature with one eye, down at the river with the other. She didn't recognize her pool. She was suspended in a different stratum—one she could never imagine existed.

The creature made strange noises that vibrated and rattled her head. With another limb, it pointed at a creature nearby and the vibrations intensified. She saw a dark row of shadows beyond. They also generated cascades of vibration.

Then the creature brought the other limb to her face. It grabbed the stonefly, which had become quite calm, and freed her of its claw. The air rushed through the hole in her jaw, and she was relieved to be free of the treacherous insect. The jacket loosened and she watched the pool approach beneath her. Then the cool waters wrapped around her and the creature moved her back and forth. A deep rush went through her gills. She breathed again. The pain started to fade. But she was still so tired. She waved her tail slowly, feeling it work again, and the creature's limb pushed her away. She glided in the slow shallow water, slinking; then in the distance of her calm pool, she saw her old rock and the shadow beneath it. Safety.

She slithered under and rested in dark. When the oxygen returned to her brain, she cataloged the stonefly, its shape, its color, its size, its texture. She had been tricked by something that felt like life.

~

David watched the trout sulk under the rock and then turned back to the pool.

JP cast and retrieved his lure unsuccessfully.

"P to nothing," David said and shot a quick, triumphant glance to the row of guys on the bank.

Except Stoss, the rest of the guys shambled along in the nearby shade of the trees weaving murmuring discordant lines, unaware of the used barley and digested hops wafting into the summer breeze from their pores. Now winning by a letter, David read the angles and the riffles of another pool and cast, his line alighting on the water as he mended in the current. The choppier water would be less suited for JP's red and white metal spoon; it wouldn't behave naturally in the quick water like a stonefly nymph.

However, David watched his line drift past without a take.

JP walked around him, grinning. "Okay, chief. I'll play in waters for fly fishin'. I ain't gonna let you prove that point."

David's morning inebriation was starting to crest, giving way to a headache, if only as a pulse around the rims of his eyebrows. He watched casually, as if he were ready to move on after the mere formality of JP attempting to catch a fish in the riffles. "You do whatever makes you happy, JP."

JP cast and a moment later the audience erupted in whoops as his rod nodded at a fish. The support surprised him and he slipped, sending a huge splash as he plopped onto a rock. He kept his rod high in the air and reeled furiously. The water rushed around his chest, just threatening under the rim of his waders as he danced the trout to his open hand. It writhed in JP's skinny fingers. He rubbed one against the vibrant pink stripe, then as gently as he could, put the trout back in the Elizabeth, nursed oxygen into its gills and set it free. He took a moment to watch it swim back into the depths; then he took a bow to the bank and winked at David. "*That* makes me happy, chief."

David's eyes raced back and forth, and he shot quick glances to the bank and their recent applause; the cork handle of his fly rod compressed under his condensing knuckles. The unfocused movement betrayed him. He cast erratically, tried to reach a far riffle where he'd spotted a shadow and his line flapped onto the water, slurping like noodles dumped in water. He tried to yank out the slack, but the coils passed by in a disorganized mess, spooking any nearby fish.

JP put a hand on his shoulder. "Tie game at P's. As in, *p*-lease watch me catch another fish."

They made their way downstream. Dehydration and a lack of salts made their piercing case across David's forehead and burrowed in his temples. He took a sip of water and watched JP as he cast. He snapped his wrist like an angry copperhead on the Seneca, sending his treble-hooked plug to the vulnerable part of the Elizabeth's riffle like three fangs. He kept the tension just right; a fish took. Playing it cool this time, and making sure his footing was good, JP retrieved the little trout, and then casually released it. David rushed the rebuttal again, leaving JP ahead: P-I to P.

JP didn't hook a fish on his next cast and David took his turn, targeting a long submerged log. It was gnarled and grey, still not fully rotted, and as David tightened and loosened his line to give his nymph a correct drift, his mind wandered back to the gnarled black log at The Flats that had lured him with the prospect of a helluva brown trout. A pit rose in his stomach as he remembered the water pouring over his waders and the current sucking him under; the pit grew to an ache as he remembered trying to breathe—

—his rod shook with a fish.

"Lucky," JP said calmly, a sharp eye locked on him from under his stringy hair. "You were tracking that fly about as graceful as a fat chick on a bull." The guys on the bank burst out laughing.

"I saw it," David said quickly, retrieving the fish and snapping back to the moment, then, "Hey—touch this reel, JP. Does that feel hot to you?"

"I don't need to touch nothing you're advertising as hot. Just get the fish in the net."

"Be civilized, my spin fishing friend." David held the rod with one hand and made a dramatic wave with the other. He shot a quick glance to the guys in the shade. "The St George's *Fly Fishing* Club doesn't tolerate such language."

"Jackass Club is more like it."

David landed the fish and took a long bow as JP cast a rebuttal. As the red and white lure arced over the river, David harmonized the tone of the whizzing reel with "Gotta match *meeeee*," and used the finality of the lure's plop as the abrupt stop on his taunt. Faint chuckles murmured behind them.

JP bounced the lure over rocks in the bottom of the pool, giving terse jerks during his retrieval to add a degree of stress, like a spastic, fleeing fish. Soon, the spoon became visible in the water in front of him and he retrieved the rest of the line.

"P-I to P-I," David said as he walked away. He hummed in a high whine like a mosquito. "One *mmmmore* and you're done."

They reached a section of the Elizabeth that split around an island, layered in scattered rocks, drift wood, detritus and determined bushes. The land had been submerged during the spring runoff and now gasped for air and sunlight, the grass making up for lost time, peeking from any possible window in the refuse and hanging over the water at the bank. In their shadow was a long eddy of calm water, set up by a fallen tree, draped awkwardly across the front of the island as if the current had receded so quickly that it hadn't had time to properly set.

"*Mmmmaybe* right here?" David said. He drew a few false casts over the water and let his fly plop just behind the log. The line drifted lifelessly through the water and bank, bouncing and bubbling along; no real motion came to it. His shoulder slumped a little. He looked back to JP, keeping up the façade of confidence. "P-I to P-I."

JP looked at him coolly, "Let me show you," and cast behind the log. The red and white lure whipped close to the bank and disappeared in the shadows. He reeled slowly as the line swung under the bank. Then it tremored, a mess of water kicking around the angular log.

"I see you have a fish on, friend," David said winning the race to speak. "But can you land *himmmm*?"

JP had been calm with the other fish, but with a chance to put David away, his neck and shoulders stiffened. The fish plunged downstream and JP's rod doubled over; his reel screamed line as it sucked into the current. The guys on shore clapped and yelled; Paul blasted his looping whistle. JP stumbled and tightened the drag on his reel as the fish ran, unable to keep good footing or fight the fish back to shore. He kept his rod high as he stumbled; the group followed.

"This is the weirdest damn fish," he said with uncharacteristic seriousness. "Keeps running erratically."

"*Mmmmmaybe* you should stop whining," David said. "Or you could—"

Two tails splashed in the current, right next to each other.

"Holy shit!" Norton yelled.

David's headache exploded to life.

The two trout were side by side, a treble hook linking their jaws like two canoes at the bow. The group watched JP fight and bring them to his net as they descended from bank and crowded around. A moment of calm passed as the fish lay next to one another breathing in rhythm. Reverence washed over JP's face. He gently reached down and grabbed the two fish under their soft bellies, and with real care and precision removed the treble hook from either fish's mouth. He put one back in his net and nursed the other in the current. When it kicked away, JP grabbed the second and put her into the current, letting the water rush over her gills. Soon, she popped out of his hands and was gone into the current. JP stayed kneeling next to the water for a moment, watching the Elizabeth pass. He washed off his hands in her cool currents and dried them on his shirt. "Wow," Norton said and a heavy silence fell.

Everyone's eyes turned to David. He stood among them, alone. Seven mirrors had appeared before him. He shifted on his feet and his mind started to race; the adrenaline ranged about his vessels and mind. The fire of competition had returned to JP's face and he waited like a cat outside a mouse hole.

David started, "I don't need to match *both*—"

"Yeah you do!" JP erupted with a twinkle in his eye. "Your exact words were 'then I have to match what you've done.' You said those exact words when you were stumbling around like newborn calf this morning. Any of these guys can back me up." David searched but everyone averted their eyes. Only Paul kept his head up, looking at his brother with soft eyes and a set jaw, expressionless, letting him make his own decision; then he mouthed a word. David couldn't immediately make it out.

He looked back to JP; he would have rather swallowed every hook in his fly box than acquiesced, but he nodded. "I did say that—you know what I meant—but you're right: those were the rules I made." He paused for a second and looked at his lone stonefly and suddenly what Paul had been mouthing lit his face. "What I am going to do is tie on a *dropper* off the back of this stonefly."

JP looked at him sideways. "A wha'?"

"Add a second fly; it's a common fly fishing set-up, two flies at once." The joints of his voice started to rattle as he defended himself.

"Wait, you're going to add another fly?" JP said. "That's some bull—"

"*NO IT'S NOT!* It's a perfectly normal way to *fly* fish. Everyone knows that—there are books about it!"

The rest of the guys went silent and stepped away, never quite turning their backs. He tore into his vest and reached for a small box of nymphs; his fingers fumbled with the zipper. He pulled out a curved green glasshead with a little tail of elk hair and then went for a spool of tippet. JP watched his frantic behavior and a pang of compassion lobbed dull blows against a wall of competition, wearing away at the foundation slightly, but not enough. He grinned and pointed at the grassy island when David was done with his setup.

"You got your two little flies now. I won't rule out a comeback—stranger things have happened. But if not..." He repeated the high whine of the mosquitoes.

David looked back at the run of water that had just produced the two fish. He looked down at his two flies and checked his knots. He took his time in the hopes that nearby fish would repopulate the hole, or the two fish would have enough time to return and still be hungry. Those hopes were thin and pathetic, and he knew it. His headache pulsed. He pulled some line off his reel, and then turned back to the guys. Before he could say something heroic, Connor blurted out, "*Go.* I want to fish today." Everyone mumbled in agreement.

The apathy made David focus. He searched for a shadow or a tail. He adjusted the line in his hands. He cast. His two flies splashed like pennies and he held his rod high to keep the drag out of the current; he pulled out the slack; his vision tunneled to the end of his fly line. It jerked. He raised his rod high, and thick vibrations coursed down the line and into his hands. He set the hook and the pool swirled at the whim of a tail. He let out a faint yelp.

But it was only one tail; it swam downstream alone.

JP came up behind him and put a hand on his shoulder carefully. "There is no fish attached to that second fly: *P-I-G* for you, chief. Looks like a red and white spoon *was* a good idea. Let *mmmmme* know what *timmmme* you'll be back in *cammmmmmp*." He smacked extra emphasis on the "*p*" and walked away to fish with the rest of the group.

David's fists condensed into rocks and he started for JP. But a light breeze blew past; it cooled his pulsing headache. David stopped and took a deep breath. No one had seen the flash of intensity. He sat down by himself and watched the Elizabeth as she wove through the rocks and among the trees.

~

The mountain lion scampered up a drainage that still trickled faint run-off from the grey peaks around her. The boulders and scree through the fold of the mountains lay as if they'd been poured from a bucket and then smoothed with a run of the thumb to fit against the crevice. She cleared a small opening in the running water and moved off the seam onto the wall of the mountain, keeping her soft feet in the angles of the slope and traversing to the other side through the sparse trees and bushes. A boulder towered before her and she ducked under its shadow into her cave.

Her two newborn cubs waited inside, their cavernous brown eyes set in a permanent question. She carried a dead fox in her mouth and it didn't hit the ground before they had it in their own. Little chomps and squeals on the pine needles filled the cave with high pitched excitement. She nudged one of the cubs to the meatier shoulder, away from the boney feet and purred with the presence of a thunderhead. She circled them and lay down and watched them eat for a while. The memory of her lost third cub had finally left her.

As she watched her remaining two, she thought about the men she'd seen that day on the riverside. She remembered the largest of the men, but had been unable to see him; he'd stood to the back of the group and kept his head and eyes under the brim of a hat. She picked out the weakest of the men, the one who moved awkwardly on the rocks of the river and had curly hair. From behind her rock, she had caught his brown eyes.

She looked at her two feisty cubs and dozed off amid their swats and snarls with one another. The light outside their rock started to fade and the breeze brought the cool scent of pine. As the sun lowered, the breeze grew to the winds of dusk, rushing up the valley. Pushed by the heat in the west and pulled by the cool in the east, the current moved among the great peaks.

~

A gentle evening light sailed through camp. A couple of deer grazed in the far corner of the meadow, away from the tents and the trucks. They mowed through the grasses, their lips wavering above each bundle of blades and their hips shifted gently to re-center the body over the uncut patches. Their eyes remained up, and alert; soon they heard footsteps and jogged back into the woods.

Paul was the first back to camp. He put his gear away, turning his wading boots upside down under one of the tables. He let his feet dry in the cool air, then slipped on cotton socks. Cotton is often considered a dangerous fabric in the woods. It holds water better than most sponges and never makes the slightest effort to retain heat. If a cotton shirt, a set of blue jeans or even a pair of socks gets wet, you're essentially wearing a cold bucket of water.

But Paul allowed himself the pleasant reminder of home. The fabric, in its rough and gentle way, gripped his feet as he built his miniature log cabin in the firepit. The flames spread up the walls, and he threw on bigger logs, with the smoke carving into the air. As it reached higher and came level with the tree tops, the wind laid into it and sent the grey clouds up the seam of the valley towards the head. To the west, the sun dipped into the tall branches. He leaned back, closed his eyes, and after a while, heard voices and footsteps approaching.

With the exception of David, the guys trickled back to camp, cracked beers and started the evening with cheers to their second full day in St George's Valley. Fish sizzled in tinfoil and rice boiled in a big pot on the fire as the air cooled in the late breeze. Laughing could be heard through the woods as the joy of another good day numbed them. A strange denial also settled into camp in terms of discussing David's ridiculous punishment for losing the bet. When they'd slap at a mosquito, they'd look around for someone to acknowledge the connection, but each time the dead bug was met with a fleeing glance and continuation of whatever the topic of discussion had been.

Paul chatted and cracked a beer and meandered over to JP. Out of earshot from the rest of the group, but in the dying borders of the firelight, his large silhouette stood over JP's and spoke with measured movements and words. JP nodded and when Paul was done speaking, followed him back to the fire.

"Hey Paul, one more thing," JP said tentatively.

Paul turned. "What?"

JP motioned him closer. There was a wrinkle of insecurity in the corner of his face. "You agree with your brother?" he asked quietly.

Paul took in the gravity with which JP asked and there was a distant flicker of frustration at the entirety of the situation. "No," he said with finality. "You do your thing. Fishing is fishing."

"Cool," JP said quietly.

"And don't worry about David," Paul continued, "He picks the wrong battles sometimes. For whatever reason, he just needs to get them out of his system. Don't ask me why. When we were little he used to stay peeved until he could get something out with a fight or a bet or something, so I…" He trailed off.

JP saw that Paul was a little embarrassed by how much he was talking about his brother and waved it off. "No big deal. Was just wondering what you thought."

"Yeah," Paul said, then nodded. "Speak of the devil..."

David's silhouette approached from the road and the conversations slowed. There was overconfidence in his steps and he carried two thick rainbows. He landed them on the table with an intentional thud and looked around, then noticed the ample amount of fish already cooking on the fire.

He looked at the waiting group. Paul stood stoically like a tower and Stoss read a book, uninterested by the proceedings but unable to leave the scene all together because of the calm firelight. Everyone else looked at David with anticipation.

"Let's get this over with," David said with forced indifference.

"Atta boy," JP said.

"Down to my shorts?"

"Sounds about right."

Without another word, he stripped off his boots, waders, socks and vest and stopped. A vague cloud of mosquitoes started to sharpen about him. He slid his shirt over his head and at the first sign of his bare stomach the group erupted, the chord of anticipation severed. JP whooped and snapped a rag off a rock. The fire seemed crackle in response. "Looks like you've come full circle since this morning, chief," JP howled.

Stoss looked up from his book. Over his reading glasses he took in the scene and looked sideways. "Interesting," he said to Paul quietly.

"That this will end one of two ways," Paul responded stoically.

Stoss started back to his book and grunted. "I don't need practice sewing up split eyes and lips."

Paul eyed his brother, then glanced at JP still playing the

ringleader. "I don't think you'll need to."

Now Stoss looked to David, then eyed Paul more seriously, shaking his head. "You don't have to diffuse every bomb he sets," he said quietly, almost to himself.

Paul didn't respond.

David pressed his eyes shut. A moment passed where the only noise was everyone's uncomfortable laughter. A mosquito landed on his arm, and then his shoulder, and then another on his chest, and then on his calf. The call was out. The cloud around him began to darken. David looked like a pale magnet attracting filings. He squinted harder.

"This feels sort of gay," Connor murmured, wincing.

JP wheeled around on him, then grinned. "Grow up," he said with a twinkle in his eye, then smooched the air.

"At least they won't bother us for the next fifteen minutes," Ian joked, waving his hand in front of his face. His expression didn't match the attempt at irony, looking more like he was passing a car accident on the highway.

"And we appreciate that," JP said, turning back to David and grinning.

Paul stood quietly in the background, pacing a little. He watched the mosquitoes that had first arrived depart and red welts remain in their place. As he grimaced, he picked out one distinct hum from the swarm around his brother, near his shoulder. It wobbled around his neck, behind his ear, over his head and dropped in front of David's face like a spider lowering on a strand of web. It veered left and landed in the center of his cheek—the first to land on his face.

The laughter and cheers sucked into a vacuum. Paul elbowed JP.

"Okay, chief," he started. "You been up there for a minute taking this like a man—I will give you that—so to be a good guy I'll let you down to smother yourself on one condition."

The black bulls-eye vibrated on David's cheek. He kept wincing as others touched down and wobbled off. He started to flex his shoulders to suck up the shaking pain; small tremors jerked in his arms. JP stayed quiet, grinning expectantly. David cracked one eye. "WHAT'S YOUR FUCKING CONDITION, JP!?"

JP continued in a tone between sarcastic and dramatic, laced with southern drawl and his customary lupine grin. "As a spin fisherman, I have felt persecuted in this fly fishing-only establishment. I feel that my craft deserves the same level of respect as yours, but hasn't gotten it." He cleared his throat. "There is one way we can rectify this: I'll let you out of your debt if," he cleared his throat "we remove the sign by the road and replace it, and the name of this growing gathering of fishermen, with the St George's *Angling* Club. That word covers all kinds of fishing and, my friend, sounds far more *civilized*." He gave an overly dramatic flare and wave of the arm. "What do you say?"

David looked around the fire but found no sympathy. The seven mirrors had reappeared again. He could see how foolish he looked on their faces. He winced tighter and didn't utter a noise. His shoulders shook. His legs wobbled. His hands looked as if they were being harnessed by heavy iron shackles, screaming to swing and swat. His entire chest, shoulders and legs were littered with little dots that vibrated at their easy meal. David tried to hold still. But mosquitoes kept coming.

"*FINE!*"

He morphed to a frantic animal. He lost control. He smacked his cheeks, his face, his legs, his calves. Every inch of his body shook. Nothing was voluntary. With each swipe little black and red spots appeared over his white skin in bloody dirt. He stumbled, grabbing a flashlight off the table, stepped into his boots, sprinted across the road and plunged into the Elizabeth. A tremendous splash filled the night air as the guys broke into hysterics—David's relief supplanting their guilt.

A flame surged in Paul. He tore out of his seat and started to speak—those mocking paused with wide eyes—but a surgical voice cut through.

"A few nights ago," Stoss said, "I made the point that nature has no goals for evolution—she feels her way around in darkness for survivalist change. None of you made the leap to argue that this can't be true because if we, as humans, perceive goals, and we are from nature, then those are inherently nature's goals to begin with." he paused, "And you would have been right: I'm not sure how to deal with that contradiction." He looked up at the group, shook his head and squinted; a regal set of wrinkles came to the rims of his cheeks. "On another note, and perhaps this is because I never had any children, much less sons of my own, but until this very evening, as I've sat watching you silverbacks and your ridiculous theatrics, I never realized that estrogen is the best remedy for overactive testosterone. If it were possible, I'd prescribe all of you a full course of female." The old doctor looked up at Paul. "Invite some women. Stat—or at least next year."

"Hell yeah!" JP howled, then cracked another beer. A murmur of agreement bubbled from the rest of the guys. The normal proceedings of the campfire resumed.

But after a while, Paul walked over to Stoss's first aide kit, grabbed a towel and some of David's clothes and walked past the worn sign that named their club to the river. The air had become chilly. David was on a rock, his legs dangling in the waters. His hands splayed on the stone behind him as he looked at the stars with his hair hanging wet. Each star pulsed lucidly in its far off home. Paul set down the clothes and medicine, and threw his brother the towel. David wrapped it around his shoulders but didn't look up. Paul stood over him in the dark, the moonlight casting a halo over the rocks and waters. He looked at the stars, then turned to leave, but hesitated, his boot rubbing to a stop on the rocks.

"I'm fine," David said quickly.

Paul nodded then left.

David stayed by the Elizabeth watching the reaching night sky and cooling his wounds. A couple bats fluttered and hunted and dove for mosquitoes between him and the moon. He watched them bounce and dart after the bugs that had just laid him bare. He smiled inwardly and thought back to the day he'd churned in the current down from the black log with the gnarled branch. He thought back to the eagle. He thought back to the mountain lion. He met the gaze of the invisible eyes. And he stared them down.

~ 6 ~

LIKE THE SHIFTING OF THE CONTINENTS, changes will come over a man—often simple, quiet, subtle and only detectable by those who know him. Sometimes they start as a smoldering fuse, petering out to a small pop and appear in choice instances: a new favorite word during argument, a different tick, a lost or gained interest in something mundane, or a grin when a grimace is expected. This creeping alteration will stop, doused with the complexity of his being and the crimp is so slight that those who know him have little to discuss in its reference.

Other times that change is simply considered part of the natural progression and everyone chalks up the differences to life. A child will discover the benefits of precociousness. A teenager will suffer the humbling epiphany that rudeness carries less mileage than manners. A young man will have the shocking realization that his parents, however tall and mighty their pedestal, are simply people with strange habits and insecurities like the rest of humanity. Even an old man, after scores of alienating acts of self-righteousness, will sometimes learn to say he's sorry. They all occur over great arcs, grounding the end of the curve and completing a turn in his life.

But other times that slow-burning fuse can explode in a shower of white fire and detonate a real change in a man's malleable mental landscape over a short period of time. The arc comes to rest quickly and after a seismic event. The change is manifested in a real, palpable, outward difference in his being, beyond the smoother contours of personality and into a shift in focus and values and thought. But since this change only occurs in him, it is jarring to the people around him. We humans do not appreciate sudden change, especially in others. It scares us. We need to time to calibrate for the burning fuse.

~

In the grey dawn, with snores still coming in fits and spurts from the other tents, Paul shook David's tent. "Hey," he whispered. "Get up."

The tent was still.

Paul took off his hat and batted the tent lightly. He unzipped the door a few inches and in the thin light could make out the lifeless form of an empty sleeping bag. He zipped the tent, then grabbed his pack and headed out of camp, noting that the sign by the road had been removed.

When he got to the end of the long rock wall that ended at The Grove on the north bank, the rope swing was on the other side. He yanked the small retriever line; the rope came to him, dancing across the top of the current; he caught it and swung back across. The river passed silently below him as the big wraps and half-hitches creaked on the tree branch high above. The sun had already haloed the eastern peaks and shreds of light stretched down the valley, barely peeking through the thick woods. Paul landed lightly on the south bank of the river and after a short walk, could see his brother sitting on a rock. His back was to the river and his hair draped over his concentrated face; he added a blood knot and new section of tippet to his leader. Paul could just make out the tops of his irises as they darted back and forth while he approached. "How you doing?" he asked cautiously as he approached.

"Fine," was the quick response.

"Those bites heal up?"

"They never last too long."

"I know." Paul shifted on his feet and scratched his chin. He hadn't shaved in a few days and his nails scraped in the silence of The Grove. "You fished yet?"

"No. Been sitting and thinking for a bit."

Paul checked over his tone to be sure he wasn't being sarcastic, then took off his hat and rubbed his forehead. He fanned his face and cleared his throat. "Hate the new name, huh?"

David grabbed the tag end of his line with his teeth, pulled the knot tight and gave both ends a few sharp tugs. "It's fine, sounds a little nicer," he said through gritted teeth.

"Yeah, it's not—"

"I mean, I do want this to be a club for guys who fly fish though. We can teach guys who don't."

Paul hesitated for a second and put his hat back on. "That sounds like a huge pain in the ass, to be honest. Why don't we just let people do what they want?"

"People can do what they want, but I think our common bond should be fly fishing. Spin fishing doesn't match insects or anything that the fish really feed on." David looked up for confirmation but Paul met his gaze with a flash of intensity.

"*Honestly*—cut that shit out. If you don't like the way he fishes, don't fish with him. Everyone's tired of your hang up and you know something? I don't think *you* believe it. I hear it in your voice: you just don't want to give up."

David looked back down and didn't say anything. A little shrug rippled over the tops of his shoulders.

"Right?" Paul demanded.

David's hands fell to his lap and he met Paul's stare. In his eyes, he agreed.

Paul continued, "So let it go. I get how important it is for you to get this club going—I do—but you need to take it easy. I saw how pissed you were when you lost and had to do dishes. You need to let that shit go—"

David cut him off. "I try to," he said quietly. "I try to but sometimes, I can't. I don't know why. I just can't."

Paul held his hat in his big hands and sat down, resting his elbows on his knees.

David toed some moss on a rotting branch and continued, "It feeds on stuff like losing. I try to push past, but sometimes it's too much." He rubbed the back of his neck and kicked the branch away. "I can always justify it in my head...but after it's out, I see what I'm doing, how I'm acting, and it just makes me angrier."

Paul nodded slowly.

A tired pleading sighed in David's voice. "Know what I mean?"

A few seconds passed. Paul said softly, "Of course."

"Well, what do *you* do then?"

"I push it away—with all my strength, I push it away."

A look of hopelessness passed over David's face.

Paul continued, "That's all you can do, David. Stoss was right: we have the tools to be in control. We just have to use them."

David's eyes narrowed; his jaw tightened. "I think that's easy to say for a rich old doctor or—" he examined his words "—people who didn't have a dad like—"

Paul put up a heavy hand and David stopped short. The only noise was the Elizabeth's gurgle as she flowed past them. They sat in silence for a minute, then Paul spoke, kindly. "We were dealt a tough hand. Both of us. That stuff infects you and it'd be easy for us to sit by the river and cry on each other's shoulders that Dad used to whack us around and now we've got problems with anger and we don't know how to express it and all the rest. But that wouldn't be taking responsibility. You're your own man and so am I. If I get angry, it's *me* getting angry. The past is a reason, not an excuse."

David blinked and nodded slowly. "Yeah," he said quietly. The breeze meandered through the tops of the thick trees; the light at their feet wavered and winked away. Soon a playfully devious grin cracked David's face as he tried to lighten the silence between them, "You remember that time Aunt Dee and Aunt Aubrey got us out of the house and took us to the shore when we were little."

"Sure," Paul said quickly.

David continued, "And we got in all that trouble for going out on the jetty with those Korean—"

"Vietnamese."

"—Vietnamese fishermen?"

"Of course," Paul said as his face went ablaze in a distant memory.

"What do you remember about it?"

"*What* do I remember about it? I don't know—I caught a striper and then we got in a whole bunch of trouble."

David laughed to himself and nodded.

"What's so funny?"

"Just seeing how you remembered our first fishing story. That's all," David said, setting bait in his voice.

"Why—how do you remember it?"

"It was *not* a striper. It was a dinky little porgie."

"No—it was a striped bass about this long." Paul set his fingers about twelve inches apart. "And it flopped around; then you wanted to catch one; I wouldn't give you the rod; then Dee and Aubrey showed up and we had to sit near them for the rest of the time at the beach."

"Yup," David said. "All except the twelve inch striper part. It was a porgie, shorter than my dick."

"Porgies don't run that small; and neither do stripers—David, it was my first fish. How are you going to argue with me about this?"

"Because it scared me shitless. The picture of it flopping on the rocks is still stuck in my brain. Even when we live-lined them on our charter trips in high school porgies gave me the creeps. That first one scarred me."

Paul chuckled a little. "You sure? I *do* remember how scared you were."

"Positive." David shuddered and gagged over-dramatically.

"Alright, you win," Paul said shaking his head and leaning back, smiling. "I still remember holding the rod away from you, and how mad you were that I wouldn't give it to you."

A hawk passed over the treetops and its silhouette blinked out a little puddle of light by Paul's feet. He shifted on his rock and a light beamed across his face at a chance for him now to lighten the moment. "Remember how we were going to start our charter company—"

"Ambrose Brothers Charters—of course," David said and his eyes turned stony.

Paul drew back at the cold face; then chewed the side of his cheek and nodded. "You're mad that we never did it," he said slowly and his tone drifted between a question and a statement.

David shrugged.

"Are you?" Now it was a question.

"It's not worth talking about, Paul, it's in the past—like you said."

"Everything's in the past. It doesn't mean it's not important."

"That *was* a long time ago. I don't think about it now."

"No?"

"No."

"You got pretty serious when I just brought it up," Paul said with a coaxing in his voice.

David's face was set. "Of course it was something I counted on, but again, that was forever ago. It doesn't matter now. We've got…this." He waved his hand towards the trees, indicating the peaks of the valley beyond.

Paul started to speak, but tripped on his words. "You sure?" he said weakly.

David nodded.

"Okay…." Paul let the idea trail and there was a hope on his face like maybe David would continue the thought.

But he evaded Paul's gaze and peered into the waters of the river, speaking with the same wistfulness. "I'm going to try harder." Paul cocked his head curiously and David continued, "I'm going to try harder with the anger stuff."

Paul sat forward. "Good," he said quietly, then with a twinkle, "Is it okay if I still keep an eye on you, tell you to pipe down now and again?"

David laughed, "That's your job."

"Well," Paul said slowly, "yours too." He reached over and smacked his brother on the shoulder, then grabbed his fly rod. "And now, for our *other* job: showing The St George's Angling Club how to fish—who needs Z guiding us anyway?" he said playfully.

"You think he'll ever be back here," David asked, rising with him and looking through a vest pocket.

"I don't know," Paul said looking to the river. "Maybe."

"Where do you think he goes?"

"Maybe to Boston,"—Paul let his joke trail off; his voice took on an aloofness—"and works in a cubicle." He gazed at a point in the passing waters of the Elizabeth, and stalked slowly to the bank.

David laughed to himself as he removed a fly box from his vest, not seeing or sensing his brother's change in demeanor. "I don't know either," he said and glanced around the shady confines of The Grove. He drew a breath, held and released; the air almost hid his words, "So...I *have* drawn up plans for a lodge."

Paul continued to peer at the river. He spoke more distantly, "I'd like to see the sketches."

"No—they are *plans* with measurements and everything. Blueprints, I guess."

"When we get back to camp."

"Okay," David said with a slight scowl. "What are you looking at?"

Two big jays cawed in the tree above him, breaking The Grove's silence and David jumped. He shot them a dirty look, then glanced back at Paul.

The jays hadn't fazed him. He stripped line from his reel and stepped slowly, like a stalking cat, towards the river. He dropped onto his right knee by the bank, tugged off a little more line and cast a Hare's ear nymph with a red glasshead as a dropper. The line uncurled without a sound over the still waters of The Grove; the two plops echoed in the stillness. They sank out of sight and the rest of the line continued to flow gently along the surface. Before it came perpendicular to Paul, he shook his head and recast—this time farther upstream. The rig made its delicate plops and drifted again.

This time it stopped. Paul lifted his rod and the line flexed. Normally a fisherman can set the hook and feel the fish's head twitch, but a subterranean tremor came into Paul's hands. The fish eased upstream with menacing deliberateness. Paul stood and adjusted his hat, holding the rod high with his right hand. The dark waters were still, but the tip of the rod began to curl like a question mark; he stabilized the butt against his hip; the knuckles of his right hand were red and white around the cork handle. The green fly line was pointed straight into the depths of The Grove.

"What size tippet do you have on?" David asked.

"4X."

"The good stuff though, right?"

As if provoked, the fish bolted; Paul's line left a small wake on the surface of the calm waters; without thinking, he rotated the drag free; his reel hummed in a smooth whir. The green moss on the rocks, the leaves, the branches, the bushes, the trees watched Paul move past them along the bank, careful to keep his rod at the right tension. Tremors ran down to his hands from the dark parts of the river. Despite the shakes, the fish ran in a constant line, as if it tracked along an underwater I-beam.

Then the line went slack; Paul hoisted the rod upward to keep tension and it came taught again; a huge pink stripe flashed under the green veneer and David stuttered in his steps.

"Holy shit," he said quietly.

Paul's line doubled over and they saw the full length of the fish.

"*HOLY SHIT!*" David yelled and followed his brother.

A wind blew over the river. It snuffed his words but kept moving. It meandered through the trees and over them as it flowed up the valley away from The Grove, carrying dust and seeds and bugs and the wings of birds, until it settled and blew through a lonesome bend in the Elizabeth.

Norton fished alone.

~

The mountain lion watched the smaller man fish. She peered at his odd curly hair and his soft eyes. She watched how he moved; she took in his sounds and caught his scent. Somewhere, it was cataloged. She saw his meek hesitations. Two more men approached from the far trees and talked to him. He waved to the river and the new men walked excitedly downstream a ways; they waded into the water and began casting.

The sun shifted to the western sky. She looked up and twitched her long white whiskers, jumped down from her rock and sauntered up the valley.

Her cubs were waiting. She knew a small meadow that held deer. As she jogged through the shadows, she spooked two jays from their branches. They squawked and rose away.

~

The two jays caught the breeze and glided in and among the dense forest, down the valley until the flora dissipated into a meadow with the Elizabeth winding through it. They alighted on a branch and squawked at two men by the river, the largest one kneeling in the water with a massive trout in his hands. A child's excitement had come over him and the great beam that seemed to run through his shoulders trembled.

"Look at this beast!" Paul shouted.

David paced behind him. "Yeah, that—"

Paul spoke breathlessly. "Ones this big usually cruise the bottoms of reservoirs. I can't believe this little Hare's Ear/glasshead dropper combo." He held up the two flies. Both were battered, frayed and coming apart by the thread.

"Well, do you—"

"Have you ever seen color like that?" David started to speak but Paul kept going. "The stripe looks like it came off a fire truck. Do you think—"

"*Paul*," David said, careful not to yell but making sure he cut his brother off.

Paul deflated a little and shrugged. "Well it's an amazing fish."

The breeze blew through the long grasses around them and pushed down the moose willows interspersed on the banks. Paul held the fish; the girth making his hands look small and boyish. He lifted it into the air and looked down the lateral line and the wide pink stripe. He dissected it with his eyes and then rested it on his bent knee. The mucus of the fish's skin left strings and films on his vest and shirt sleeves. Its white stomach heaved and expanded. The muscles of its shoulders and back were soft, weathered, tired from their long battle. Paul had chased it over a mile, never applying too much pressure on the line, just letting the fish exhaust itself in the currents of the Elizabeth until he could ease it to shore.

Still pacing, David tried to fill the silence he'd left. "Are you going to hang that over the fireplace—get it stuffed?"

Paul looked back at the tired eyes of the great trout, then said, "I'm going to release it."

"*What?* Let's have it for dinner! Can you imagine the look on the other guys' face when we bring that back?"

"I don't care. They can see the picture. We don't need it for dinner, nor does it belong on a wall." Paul set the fish back into the shallow water and began rocking it back and forth, coaxing water through the gills. His hands came around the fish's back, barely, as he tried to nurse energy into the muscles, gills and heart. The stomach sagged between his fingers.

"Paul, we have to bring it back. It's pushing twenty pounds, at least."

Love left Paul's eyes and he examined objectively: "Too high."

"Well whatever—it's a monster. We can have a feast with it."

"We have plenty of food, David. I'm going to let this old guy live his life out in the river. He deserves it."

"Don't give me that crap. Besides, it's not reviving anyway."

It was true. The wavering tail had stopped. The fish started to turn sideways in Paul's hands. He stepped farther into the river, getting away from the muddy bank and lowered the fish deeper into the water. He grasped its tail and moved the fish faster, with franticness. A mantra evolved under his breath. "Come on…come on…" Dull movement pulsed in his hands. A slow, lumbering shake. A vague tremor of life. He released the soft sides and watched the tail move in one long wave and disappear into the current.

The river flowed around him, gurgling and laughing in the light confluence where it came back together on the other side of his hips. Paul gazed up at the north wall of the valley, the tops of the peaks colored with the light of the setting sun; the shadows ensconced at the bottom. The blond grasses in the meadow around them rustled and whispered to themselves.

"Gone?" David asked as Paul walked back to the bank.

"Yup. Thought she was a goner."

"I can't believe you would—*nope, shit.* Paul, grab it."

David pointed. The great white stomach flashed against the surface, the fish bouncing lifelessly in the rhythm of the river. Paul jerked around and splashed towards it, grabbed the fish in his arms and fumbled to turn it upright; he centered the fish's stomach in his hands and began to move it back and forth again.

"Come on...shit...come on...come on...."

He held only a vessel. He picked up the lifeless fish and looked into its eye. A fire of anger flashed in Paul's face then dissipated. "Damn...I'm sorry," he said dolefully to the vessel. He peered at it closely, then trudged out of the water holding the great fish with both hands the way a fireman holds a hose. He stepped onto the bank and began to walk upstream. David followed silently.

After a couple hundred yards, Paul stopped and shifted the fish, sliding his fingers under its gill plate and letting the lifeless body hang from his massive hand. Its mouth came open from the pressure on its jaws; the eyes stayed wide. Paul peered closely for another moment then continued walking along the Elizabeth. "I shouldn't have acted so childish," he said after a while.

David looked up, startled. "What?"

"You were right: I was acting childish."

"Oh—I was just jealous. I would have been the same; that's the fish of a lifetime."

"Yeah, but that's the problem—or what's bothering me. I'm going to get back to camp and the other guys are going to be fired up, and tell me what a hero I am, and high five me and all the rest of it. But all I did was kill a fish."

"Don't be dramatic, Paul. We're going to eat it for dinner—"

"That's not my point." Frustration cracked through his voice. "I don't see why killing a big fish makes me a hero. Size is a stupid currency."

David laughed a little.

"I'm serious—who cares? It's just a fish like any other in this river. We're so...*beholden* to stuff like that."

"But ten minutes ago you were saying that you wanted

to let it go because it was so big and old. That's the same thing."

Paul turned and a little light beamed through his frustrated face. "No. That was a reason to let it live or die." He jerked his thumb upriver towards camp. "They will use it as reasons to praise me. One is important; the other is about something material and ethereal. It's like the other day when Ian and Josh were talking about our friends from college: they weren't looking for ways to rate them—rate them by their job, rate them by their salary, who they hooked up with—anything but *them*. They were gauging," he nodded to the fish, "*size*. I kept thinking the stats on a baseball card as they talked. And we'll make one about this fish. But I didn't create it or do anything other than catch and kill it—so why praise me?"

"It'll feed everyone."

This put a pause in Paul and he shifted the fish to his other hand. "I guess that's what it comes back to," he said after a minute, then spoke in mock dramatics. "*The great warrior-hunters must provideth*."

David shook his head. A little jealousy enveloped his words as he spoke to himself. "And you'll be him."

The rest of the walk was quiet, but when they reached camp Paul was greeted like a returning Spartan. JP howled, slapped his knee and whacked him on the shoulder, "You're a beast!" he cried. Stoss, like Paul, inspected the fish closely and shook his head, "A relic of the dinosaurs." The other guys took pictures. Then, quietly, after the excitement died, Norton asked Paul if he could clean and prepare the trout for dinner.

"You know how?" Paul asked quietly.

"I have—I've watched you and Stoss." He paused and shuffled his feet. "This is a special fish—sorry—you have honors of course."

Paul put a hand over Norton's knobby shoulder. "Let me know if you need help."

He didn't, and later, they feasted with full compliments to the chef, and of course, the hunter. David agreed and raised his beer in congratulations with everyone else.

~ 7 ~

A FAWN GRAZED IN A MEADOW not far from their camp. He was a little older than the other fawns. His mother and father had mated in the middle of the rut the previous fall, but some trigger in nature decided that he would be born before the usual two hundred days were over. Most young deer cling to their mother's side during their first summer, learning the ways of the woods and fields and trying to strengthen and make it through their first winter. But this fawn was oddly independent. He never ran from his mother or the herd—his mother wouldn't allow that—but he drifted to the periphery of whatever meadow they grazed and ate there, preferring solitude and separation. The herd was crowded and he started to learn that the grasses were longer when there were fewer of them around. He didn't mind grazing at the edge of the meadow near the woods. He wasn't old enough to know how the herd, the buck's tall points and the open meadows afforded safety.

Though even if he did, he may not have changed his ways. An animal makes a certain compromise when quartering and existing in close contact with others. A certain strand of their innate fibers is crimped and altered in such a way as to feel a light rope between the shoulder blades. The benefit afforded by the herd can be forgotten as the animal shakes, trying to come free, looking to the fields beyond with a longing to call them their own. But sometimes, like that fawn, an animal will show that courage to break free and graze alone.

~

Camp settled into an easy rhythm. A few days of fishing and exploring the valley passed in a panorama of cool water, crisp air and sunshine. Their campsite turned into a sort of incipient alpine agora with everyone milling in and out and about with their days. One afternoon Paul returned to their meadow early to write in his notebook before the evening commenced. He passed the now-missing sign for the club and remembered David saying he was going to hang around camp that day; like Pavlov's dog, he involuntarily started counting how many fish he'd taken. But before he reached an answer, he stopped suddenly, and stared out at their meadow.

David sat sipping a beer with a peculiar smile across his face. Around him were piles of glistening dirt, the smooth casts of a shovel still clear in the mounds, interspersed with rocks and overturned sections of grass and mud. But what stopped Paul was around them: four long trenches cut the earth at right angles. Just in looking at the corners and perpendicular lines, an innate sense of symmetry came alive in Paul. It was a perfect rectangle.

"You're going to do this," Paul said quietly.

David raised his beer. "The foundation."

"You dug this all today? You...you must be exhausted."

He shrugged lightly. "Easy work when you care."

"Why didn't you ask for help?"

David didn't say anything for a moment. "I didn't want it for this part—wanted to do it on my own." He kicked a rock and it sailed over the sharp ledge and disappeared. Occasionally, we are blessed with being able to see people, as if we are *seeing* them for the first time. The newness gives us pause.

Paul blinked at the trenches and surrounding meadow. "The St George's Angling Club, huh?"

"The St George's Angling Club," David echoed.

Before he was done speaking, a cabin appeared before

Paul. He could see it. The vision was simple. The walls were crimson, white and orange of fresh pine. A few stairs ran to a thin porch. The roof was slanted. One wall was divided by the spine of a fireplace. He bent his head back, gazing at the top of the chimney and imagined smoke. The grays and whites and blacks wove and rose into the evening sky. Paul etched more detail in the flat walls; they started to fold and dimple and separate and ruffle into rows of stacked timber with surfaces of stripped bark. The windows reflected a little sunlight. The breeze shifted the smoke. His mind raced and the little porch now had shade under it. The flat grey chimney rippled, and individual stones appeared. He spoke, still in his dream, "I mean, we could live here for a few months." Suddenly, the summer light dampened and turned grey and the cabin, still smoking from the chimney, was surrounded by snow. "We could stay here through the winter."

David jumped up, spilling a little of his beer. He stood next to his brother and looked back at the trenches. The setting sun cast long shadows of grass and put a twinkling in the dust and seeds swirling around them. He looked up at his brother. "We could do it—survive a winter in a cabin *we've* built." He laughed to himself. "I'm single; you're single," then under his breath, "until Gretchen calls you again."

Paul nodded and a thin crack in his reverie appeared. "We can't build it on our own though."

"No," David said, snapping back to business. "Of course not. I'm going to talk to the club tonight. We'll call a 'real' meeting and talk about what needs to be done, and how we're going to do it."

Paul's image of the cabin vanished. He had almost chewed his cheek raw; he rubbed his tongue against the inside of his mouth. "A meeting?"

"Yeah, when everyone gets back, and let them know what needs to happen. I've drawn up plans, and teams, and tasks so we can get this done in the next two weeks."

"Build the whole cabin in two weeks?"

"No. Just cut trees. We'll build the cabin next year—"David froze. A loud crash burst from the woods.

A fawn rushed into the clearing. Wasting no effort with noise, terror shrieked from its wide brown eyes. Its head was tossed back; its neck fought to maintain the role of supporting conduit, but the hips are always stronger. The fawn veered left, kicking dirt and dust into the air.

The mountain lion burst into the clearing behind, cutting down the angle. David didn't have time to move. He just stared at the charging cat, back legs exploding and extending away from the amber hips; its head was low and straight; its spine was a sleeve on an infinite wire. Grass spat into the air as prey and predator adjusted in the meadow. The fawn slipped and the mountain lion closed. Then, they disappeared into the trees and were gone.

There was some light patter and then, the woods were silent.

David stood in the long grasses, staring into every corner of the meadow; his glance fired into every shadow like rifle shots, searching and absorbing; his breathing was labored and harsh; he didn't notice the tweets of a couple birds. He didn't notice the breeze in the tree tops or a couple warblers swoop into the meadow and alight on a branch and fidget around one another carelessly. He did notice something rest on his shoulder; he whirled around, throwing one arm about his neck, with the other snapping a fist like a bullwhip.

Paul batted David's assault away with a recalled experience, letting the blow pass harmlessly beside him, yelling, "*It's me*—it's just me," sharply, then less so.

David glanced with quick embarrassment at his errant fist, but turned away. "Just give me a minute," he said, still breathing heavily, and dove into the confines of thought. His face searched, replaying the chase again. And again. Adrenaline ranged about his body. Finally, a moment of recognition passed over his face and he turned to his brother. He released a large exhale and faked a confident grin. "That was *intense*."

A bat fluttered overhead and headed for the river. Paul let David walk past him and trailed a step behind as he hurried to the firering. "The eyes," Paul said slowly after a second. David wheeled around. "Pretty different," Paul continued.

David's neck gave way in a slow nod. "I can't believe it," he said carefully.

When he and Paul had encountered the mountain lion on the ridgeline, there had been a fierce defense laid in their edges, as if they had disturbed a ghost that spat venom in protection of its realm; its eyes were the central, *outward* flowing conduit of rage. But as the mountain lion chased the fawn, the eyes were soft and calculating. They steered a predator that adjusted and reevaluated every step, turn, rock and blade of grass in pursuit of a prey whose capture existed as a foregone conclusion. There was no malice. The conduit flowed *inward*, absorbing, processing and reacting to every, single, infinitesimal detail.

David's pace of breath was still rapid; gallantry came to his face. "I'm going to tell the others."

Paul nodded.

David continued, "It was selfish not to have before. I don't know what was the matter with me."

"Scared it would deter people from coming," Paul said slowly, and his tone was neither question nor statement, then reflectively, "Yeah, I'm not sure what was wrong with us. There was no reason to keep that secret."

"No," and David's tone was incomplete, "We still have The Grove."

Paul nodded and echoed quietly, "We still have The Grove."

David looked back to the two trees that the fawn and mountain lion had run between. "You think it made it?"

Paul followed his gaze. "I don't know. Doubtful—though I didn't hear anything."

"Me neither."

"Doesn't mean anything though."

"They cry out when they kill something don't they?" David asked. He sat down at the table and took up a few stacks of notes and shuffled them without intention.

Paul continued peering at the dark gate between the two trees. "We would have heard the fawn, not the lion," he said finally. "They don't hoot and holler when they do something to be proud of. That would attract attention. She has no interest in sharing meat with anyone—except cubs, if she has them." He broke his trance on the woods and turned back to David, "Anyway, I'm trying to think what to say—"

"I said I'd tell everyone," David cut in. His hands fidgeted with two diagrams that indicated which nearby trees should be felled, he continued quickly. "I'm just going to tell them that we saw one close to camp, but up on the mountainside. No reason to say it ran through. 'Close' is good enough." He absently rubbed the plans between his thumb and forefinger. Some of the ink marking the edge of their meadow smeared.

Paul watched his brother fidget for a beat then walked towards the woods.

"Where are you going?" David asked quickly.

"Collecting more firewood," Paul said coolly over his shoulder. He peered into the shadows for a moment, took a deep breath and stepped under the gateway of branches.

The sun soon blinked out from behind the trees; the gold grasses dimmed. The breeze picked up in the coolness; the meadow waved and bounced like a ghost pond. Nervous chatter began to simmer and pop from the shadows and low branches. Paul returned with a handful of kindling and stack of wood in the other arm. He knelt by the firering, built his log cabin among the dead coals and set the new structure ablaze.

"Where do you think everyone is?" David asked after a while.

Paul billowed and kindled the base of the crackling logs.

"A lot of *baetis* were bouncing around when I left the river. Probably a good hatch coming off." He gave a look of satisfaction to his fire, then sat down at the table across from his brother and looked at the notes. A few lined pieces of paper were covered in disorganized markings and groupings of names, tools, tasks and goals.

David glanced at him. "By the way, where is *The Hunter's Guide*?"

"In the truck — why?"

"I wanted to see what they said about hunting deer and the meat. They talk about that?"

Paul put up a finger, silencing him. A murmur carried through the dark woods and over the fire. "You hear that?"

David's face contorted and he turned his head. In the distance were familiar voices, popping and cracking. Then, flashlights waved through a haloed row of fishing rods. The group walked into camp and there was tension in each of them. A long-haired specter spoke with a southern twang. "You aren't going to believe what happened."

"What?" Paul and David said in unison.

"Saw a *mountain lion*," JP said.

"Where?" David said not allowing a beat in the conversation.

"Downstream. There is a huge flat pool that —"

"The Flats. We know it."

"Well just above there, she came out from behind a mess of rocks and tried to give ol' Norton hell." In a seemingly rehearsed choreography, the group split in two and Norton was left standing between them.

"I didn't see her coming until she was charging," he said. "I had just waded into the water, but after a few steps, I turned," he shook his head, "she was coming *right* at me." The dim light accentuated his still-ashen face. He absorbed the palpable tension, but waited too long.

JP continued, "So I see this big cat running across the field and I start shouting, '*Hey, you bastard. Hey!*' while Norton is doing all he can and wades—or runs—into the current."

Norton took back the spotlight. "The water almost poured over the top and sunk me, but I did this—" He put a thumb behind the rim of his waders and lifted into the air. "She ran right to the bank, stopped and *screamed* at me. It sounded like a thousand shattered glasses. Then I hear this guy yelling from downstream." He thumbed at JP, and he took over.

"So as I'm running, I reach onto my hat and pull off this spoon—same one I used during our game of PIG—and hurl it." As he spoke, he made an exaggerated throwing motion and finished with his elbows on his knees like a pitcher praying for a called third strike. He rose slowly, timing his words so the last syllable came when he stood completely upright.

Paul and David stared blankly. The eyes of the group were on them and Paul gave the obligatory, "And?"

"I hit that mountain lion right in the goddamn eye!" JP burst out. "It took off running and howling and pawing at her face!" He caught Paul's shocked eyes, retreated a little, then gravely nodded to Norton. "But man she wanted a piece of *him*. Five seconds earlier and this story would'a been *different*."

Norton shrugged, not sure if he should be embarrassed or proud. "I was having a good day fishing; maybe it was jealous."

"Maybe," JP said. "But I think it was more interested in *you*."

Paul put up a hand. "Wait—back up—you hit the cat in the eye?"

JP flexed his biceps, rose up on his toes and kissed his right shoulder. "Yup."

"And it stuck?"

"Hell yeah—batted at the plug with its big ole' paws, but that little spoon didn't move. Guess it's always worth it to pay for good hooks!"

"And it just ran off?"

"Gone. Into the woods and gone," JP said triumphantly. "Won't see her again—*guarantee* that."

Paul shook his head. "*Wow*," he said, sighing, his disbelief braided with compassion. He turned back to the fire, interlaced his fingers and made a big fist and leaned his mouth against them in thought. The group followed the cue and slackened, making their way around and preparing dinner. The encounter's energy simmered at the tops of their minds and while conversation occasionally dipped to fishing or small talk between bites of pasta, for the most part, it hovered around, or in relation to the subject of the mountain lion. Regalement is the quickest path to serenity.

"What about grizzly bears; you ever see those around here?" Josh asked after a while.

"No," Paul said quickly. "They've driven them all north."

"Well—I had a friend backpacking up in Alaska and someone in their group was almost killed by one," he said gravely. "It charged out of the woods while she was taking pictures in a meadow. The guide saw it coming and actually had to shoot it—though they don't think they killed it. It ran off and they saw it, or some bear, a couple days later. Apparently it was following slowly on their trail a couple ridgelines away."

"Damnation," JP said laughing and slapping his knee. "If you think *that's* spooky, I knew a fella who fished the Boundary Waters, up on the Great Lakes, and a big ol' wolf came around their camp while they were cooking dinner, staying just on the border of the firelight and watching them grill the fish they'd caught. My buddy said that they'd be eating, and then catch a flash of two eyes way back in the woods—then they'd disappear. I'll tell you, he did *not* get up and take a piss in the middle of the night!"

"My sister," Connor started, "was scuba diving in the Florida keys once and a barracuda swam up next to her...it didn't do anything but it was really close. She could see the teeth and everything."

Norton started, "This is not—this isn't as much about an animal as it is just danger in the outdoors; but I had a friend in college whose brother was fishing off the coast of Newport. They anchored their boat near some rocks, but somehow, they didn't time the waves right—or something—and one big one flipped their boat into the rocks. Killed him."

David cleared his throat. "We saw that a few times when we were younger," he said bouncing an index finger between him and Paul. "People that don't know what they're doing will set an anchorline too tight in low tides, especially in close to rocks going for stripers. If the anchor catches or the craft is small enough, and they get sideswiped with a big swell, they'll get swallowed, pulled under before they know what's happened."

Paul finished solemnly, "Called a 'widow-maker'."

A couple guys shifted in their seats. David surveyed the descent into severity, then pulled some notes from his pocket. "Hey, so—I'd like to call a meeting." He glanced around at their faces, still reflecting on their own mortality; Norton gave a courtesy, "Okay," and he continued, "Did anyone notice the trenches over there—that way," David said, correcting their gaze from the firering into the dark meadow.

"In case we go to war with the mountain lions?" JP asked and David patiently waited out the nervous, alcohol-aided laughter.

"No. These are real trenches, for pouring a foundation. I've set the initial footprint of a lodge—a lodge for The St George's Angling Club." The group was silent and their attention put a nervous confidence in David's words. "I've also drawn up a plan for building it. There are—"

"You mean *us building the lodge*?" JP said.

With a quiet, honest pleading David said, "Can you let me talk for a minute? Please?"

JP put up a hand in light apology.

"But yeah, *us*," David continued, "I see this happening in

two phases. This summer: pour the foundation and cut trees. You may have noticed the bags from my truck that I'd stacked in the back corner of the meadow. Those are concrete; and combined with rocks and sand and gravel from the Elizabeth, it should be enough to give us a real foundation." He paused and bounced from each pair of eyes looking back at him. "I've divided us into teams and tasks to get that done."

He let that settle for a moment and no one said anything. He shifted on his feet and stood a little taller.

"For the second phase I've mapped out what trees we need to cut, how to fell them and what to do with them. Basically, we need to cut about thirty, strip their bark and let them dry through the winter. You can't build—just like you can't light a fire—with fresh wood. It has to be good and dead so it doesn't shift or move after you set it. We've got saws, winches and of course the trucks to move them. We'll cover what we cut for the winter to keep the snow off, and then come back next year for phase two: when we'll actually…" he involuntarily waved to the field, "build this damn thing."

For the first time during the entire evening, David smiled. Genuine pride beamed in the corners of his eyes. He turned away and looked out at the dark field. He could see his cabin. There was a light on in the window. He and Paul were sharing a beer on the porch, looking at the flat shadows of the trees against the sky, just crowned by the pulsing stars through their branches.

David began to speak. "So let's talk about this and—"

"I'll be back next year with Adrian," Norton said before David had turned back. "He'll be eight, but he'll help, and, of course, I'll bust my ass." His eyes were taught and focused on David. He leaned to the fire and threw on a small branch.

Stoss pursed his lips and nodded slowly and light came to his eyes. "Sounds like fun," was all he said.

The glaze had gone from David's eyes and they were a fuller blue in the firelight. He tried to lock with Connor, but he fiddled with the buttons of his shirt. He tried to lock with Josh, but his head tipped back enjoying the stars. He tried to lock with Ian, but he stared into the fire. They all passively deflected David's gaze to JP. His head was tipped back slightly, long hair dangling behind, holding up his lupine grin. He started to speak and the papers in David's hands folded together under the pressure of his knuckles.

"David, if you think, for a minute, even one goddamn *second* that I'd miss a day fishing, and drinking beers, to build a goddamn cabin, having never seen your plans, or the idea, or anything; and putting my faith in that stupid folded piece of paper in your tense hands," he winked as David drew in an angry breath, "well then you know me a little better than I thought you did. I love me a little poorly-organized chaos. That's where this redneck is at *home*. Shit, you need someone to protect you from that one-eyed mountain lion anyway." He burst out laughing.

David gulped a response, the angry air coming out awkwardly. "Thanks—sounds good," he said lamely and shifted his gaze to the other guys; and JP followed it.

Josh started to speak but pretended like he thought Ian was going to speak and nodded for him to continue. Ian shook his head and nodded for him to go on with what he was going to say. Connor didn't make eye contact with anyone.

Paul filled the strange silence. His head was tipped back a little and his wide jaw threw a stubbled shadow up the contours of his face; his eyes were hidden. "Why were you excited to come here?"

"What do you mean?" Josh asked quickly, turning from David.

"What I said: why were you excited to come out here?"

"Is this is a trick question?"

"No, but I don't understand why you wouldn't want to make it perpetual. Do you have that same excitement about going back?"

A dancing wind blew through camp, pushing the silence into the trees.

"Exactly," Paul continued and leaned forward. His eyes came alive in the fire. "Ask yourself why, if you love fishing and being here so much, you wouldn't bust your balls to make sure you were doing it every day?" He took a sip of beer and no one said anything. "Yes, cutting trees, trimming branches, debarking, clearing, splitting and stacking the wood is going to suck—*really* suck. It's going to be sweaty, shitty, back breaking work. But you know what? It will be totally worth it. Then we have a place here—if we want it."

Connor looked at him with a distant curiosity. "We all have lives, Paul."

"We do," and Paul let his silence settle.

Josh shifted in his seat and though he spoke challengingly, a light grew in his eyes. "So—what? You are going to leave your job next summer?"

"Yes."

David turned towards his brother, mouth slightly agape. A look of surprise hung on Paul's face for having said it, like a strange food had been shoved in his mouth that he realized tasted quite good.

"I thought you were going to get promoted to director soon," Ian said.

"I'll have my own team, an office and everything I ever dreamed of." He stood and threw another log on the fire. Sparks and smoke crackled and shouted into the air.

"And you're going to quit?"

"I'm quitting *because* I'm being promoted."

"What do you do again?" Connor asked.

"It doesn't matter." A confluence of sparks plumed and sucked together and Paul's words came smoothly. "It doesn't matter. Being promoted just pulls me farther in. I don't want that; I don't want any of it. I can put a smile on my face about it, but I quietly wince when people ask me what I do. When I get home each night, I look back and have trouble being truly proud about anything I've accomplished. I finished *this*; I did *that*—so what? It doesn't matter. None of it does. But we act like it does with each other, like children playing pretend. I'll give you an example: I didn't get into business school last year. You know what part I hated the most? The thought of telling *you*." He took another sip of beer and pointed the bottle at his friends.

Ian started back at him and stammered, "So we all leave our paychecks and bum around in the woods, exercise our right to be *one* with nature—"

"Not a right; rights are things you shouldn't have to work for. We'll work for this without a doubt. We've just been tricked to think that working for others is how life was intended. Somewhere, we know that's wrong. We know that, at some point during the quest to laminate the world in concrete the desire for *true* independence died because we don't *need* it; we can get by with our lives as is. 'The average day' became our greatest form of denial. And now? People don't take the hard road to happiness, because there is an easy road to complacency." His eyes calmed and he scratched his chin, then continued with an air of freedom as the breeze blew across the humming flames. "So we forget what life is: our own, free movement about the world. Life is movement. That's all. If you're not moving, you're the same as dead. That much I've learned here."

He sat back in his chair and waved at the dark ridgeline above them. "You guys had a run-in with a mountain lion and you're sitting around the campfire getting drunk—not scared. You're already moving more than you realize." Paul finished his beer and signaled to his brother, giving him back the floor.

David tapped his folded paper against his knee. In the firelight, he looked around at the eyes. And they looked back.

IV

~ 1 ~

A BOY STOOD ON THE BANK OF THE ELIZABETH on an early morning, in early summer. Light danced and hugged his silhouette as the sun rose over the peaks and scattered golden smiles on the water around him. His thin, little frame descended from a brown bucket hat as he cast. He casted well, though not far. His tight loops shot, crisp as lasers, and uncoiled just above the water. The riffles bounced and laughed and swirled in front of him, moving between him and his fish. He was careful not to venture into the current, heeding instructions from his father, and staying close to the bank.

Norton appeared downstream. He stepped through the rips of the current like he was barefoot on a rug, unfazed by the loose stones under his boots. He walked to his son slowly. He knelt and watched the river with him. He pointed downstream. Adrian looked at his dad and nodded. He let his fly drift farther and soon he found his rod dancing. He played the small trout across the current, holding the handle like it tethered a kite in a strong wind, and to the bank where his dad took the little fish in his hands. Norton motioned for Adrian to kneel next to him. He gave the fish to his son.

"Remember what I've told you. Keep her in the river," he said. "The gills should always be covered with water so she can breathe." The fish lay in Adrian's boyish hands, making them seem older and worn. "Get your hemostat in there and twist firmly. The hook will come out." Adrian did as his father said and the hook released as promised. "Now move her back and forth in the current like I've shown you. Hold her gently, but don't let go until she shakes her tail. That's when you know she's revived, and ready to swim."

Adrian carefully moved the trout back and forth a few times, her mica scales glimmering in the sun. Adrian watched the trout intently, only stealing quick glances at his dad with sideways flicks of his big brown eyes. Soon, it kicked out of his hands and back to the aqua current of the Elizabeth.

"Put 'er here," Norton said, beaming.

Adrian smiled and high-fived his dad.

Norton looked back to the woods and sighed. "We need to get back now, bud. David is probably wondering where we are."

"Dad?"

"Yeah."

"I like building; it's fun."

"It is, isn't it? I'm having a good time too. What's your favorite part?"

This sent Adrian into thought and he turned his head to the river and hooked a small finger onto his lower lip, rocking a little back and forth. Norton brushed his hand away from his mouth. "You were just holding a fish."

The swipe and correction didn't faze Adrian. "Dad?" he said slowly, as if confessing. "I like building...but my favorite part is still fishing."

Norton laughed and nodded. "Yeah, me too. We'll be done with the cabin soon, then we can fish all day. How does that sound?"

"*Great—*" Adrian's smile twisted into thought. "*—but* Dad?"

"Yeah?"

"Can we still sleep in the tent sometimes, even after the cabin is done?"

"Of course we can."

"I like being outside."

"Me too, bud." Norton looked into the taut blue sky, then

to the rising sun as it tucked behind layered clouds. "But we have to get back. David will wonder where we snuck off to."

~ 2 ~

THE GRASSHOPPERS CHATTERED IN THEIR TINNY SYMPHONY as the breeze blew across a rabbit's face. It was a cloudy day and she nibbled in a field with the shadows of the trees smearing about her. A rotting basin of a dead pine wrapped around her, its insides deteriorating at the hands of termites, fungus, grasses and flowers. She picked and ate at the buds and leaves that birthed from the crevices and cracked wood.

Though the meal was bountiful, it was stressful. She was cornered and her olfactory bulbs were saturated with pine and wildflowers, unable to detect a predator. She ate quickly, her small heart starting to race as she continued her confined meal. She heard an extra pop through the hoppers and looked up, her brown eyes vibrating at the sides of her head in every direction, her nose rummaging through the air. She went back to eating. She looked up again, to be sure, and saw nothing. She climbed to the upper rim of the fallen pine and looked into the trees. There were only shadows and pine needles and a couple large rocks. The clouds rolled softly overhead. She climbed down and continued eating. The jays in the tree above her squawked and flew away.

The rabbit felt the firm thunder of the mountain lion before she saw it over the top of the log; the cat's ears were folded back and tight like an arrowhead. She bolted and felt the swoop of a paw crash behind her, chips of wood spraying in the air and into her eyes. She ran sideways and another paw smashed near her back legs. She sprung from the log and out into the open field, the pounding of paws in the earth behind her. She tore straight ahead, shaking her face to clear the debris, her back legs pumping through the tall grasses. She veered left at a rock with loose gravel at its base; she heard the pounding of paws behind her and then a sliding of rocks.

She kept running. She saw the wall of trees in front of her, the shadows behind them, and they drew her in, to safety. Her legs continued to pump. The draft of a swinging paw breezed against her tail. She turned again and heard sliding.

Her back legs complained for the first time. They were tiring. The trees still seemed so far away. She heard the paws again. She kept running. The trees were closer; then they were almost above her. She came beneath their reach, their branches high overhead, casting weak shadows. She felt a breeze of paws and was into the shadows. She turned one more time at the base of a pine, never slowing, and saw from the edge of her wide brown eyes, a mountain lion slowing in the field behind her, thin and panting and peering at her with one empty eye. The rabbit ran until an ancient voice told her she was safe.

She hid under a rock for a very long time.

~

The mountain lion lay down, her tongue dangling from the side of her mouth, her ribs visible under her molting coat. She'd wasted too much energy trying to catch rabbits recently. They were too quick. She could keep up with them, but she couldn't catch them. The surgical swipes of her paws always came up empty, short. She'd lost a perception of depth when that lure fell out.

She lay in the grass and the wind blew over her.

She had finally forgotten about the loss of her cubs. She'd cried into the hollow air of winter when they'd stopped moving as the question in their eyes was extinguished one by one. She'd paced around her cave frantically and nuzzled their starving bodies in the hopes they'd play and fight with one another again. Now, that hope was gone, a memory flushed in the current of perseverance by her body's silent decision that she would never be in heat again. She just needed to eat and live out her days.

She watched a couple warblers fly overhead; they braided towards the trees and the field where the men were. The tools and noise had kept her away, but she'd watched them from a distance when they seemed tired and unaware. There were more of them, twice as many, though she focused on only one. She'd caught the largest man's eyes—a brilliant green, radiating droplets eclipsing the sun. Eyes of fire.

~ 3 ~

PAUL CLICKED OFF HIS WATCH before it could chirp a second time. He lay in bed, setting his bearings, and clawed
through the fog of sleep. He sat up and put on pants and his
hat, laying his feet on the firm wooden floor. It was rough
and unsanded and still carried the fresh scent of pine.

He walked to the other side of the lodge, lit a propane
burner on a folding table and heated some water in a thin tin
pot; the bottom crackled in the sudden intensity of energy.
He stretched out his back, grabbing his feet with his worn,
calloused hands, then stood and loosened his shoulders, his
big arms making audible whooshes in the air as he swung
them. He rolled his neck, filled his lungs, released the air,
then walked to David's bunk and shook him lightly. David
opened an eye and ran both his hands over his face, his
messy hair filtering back onto his pillow. He could just make
out his brother's huge silhouette against the flame from the
stove in the dark cabin. He tried to focus his eyes in the darkness.

But if Paul had closed the propane and killed the blue
heat, David would still be able to see each feature of the
modest lodge he'd designed, along with the crew that built
them. Without a single ray, he could point to the front doorway with its thin fir frame that Norton had fitted so carefully.
He could point to where Stoss, with steady surgical hands
and dedication, had cut, fitted and jointed each column of
pine flooring. He could point to the porch and the exact spac-

ing between columns for the tin, visor-like awning that Ian and Josh had constructed. Around him, he could point to each heavy fir bunk frame and flat pine platform, and even in the dark, bounce a pebble off the rivets and dowels that Paul had measured, glued and clamped together until they appeared as one piece of wood. He could still see the supplies in the back of the trucks and in the trailers start to disappear and dwindle in the exact cadence he'd calculated, vindication rising in his tired chest as the lodge rose in front of him over the weeks.

But most importantly he could see and point to his pride and joy: the fireplace, the one feature that every returning and new member of the club had built together. As Paul walked silently back to the table to fill his daypack, David thought about the work he'd done to design it. He had adjusted for the added weight of concrete on the soil of the glen. He and Paul had searched the Elizabeth and collected the smooth and flat stones to fill her walls and stacked them like china plates. He measured and remeasured her mouth's dimensions being sure she was wide enough to heat the cabin, but small enough that she wouldn't distort the wall. In the end it had come together, somehow, exactly as he had hoped. Like every fireplace for a great lodge he'd ever imagined, a monolithic rocky tower now ran the spine to breathe life into the cabin. Few thoughts pleased him more than looking at the foreground of the hearth and imagining everyone sitting around, sipping and telling stories into the night.

Only about two weeks earlier, did he realize that he hadn't hoped and dreamed about the fireplace hard enough. He had swore out loud at a revelation, as the hum of tools and hammering came to an abrupt stop, everyone looking up, expecting to see blood spurting from an appendage. Instead, he stood shaking his head; he hadn't thought of, or designed a mantle over the hearth. The guys had said it wasn't a big deal, not to sweat it, but David hadn't heard a word. He went to his plans, made some quick but accurate adjustments in the long timbers and saved a space, an empty hyphen, over the rocky mouth for a plank of aspen. To him, it was the keystone in the arch.

He and Paul just needed to cut it.

"Let's go," Paul said. "I've got the saws."

"Coffee ready?"

"Yeah."

"We forgetting anything?"

"No," Paul said. "Just wish that aspen grove was a little closer."

As David pushed him toward the door, a delicate voice sounded from the corner bunk. "Where are you going?"

Paul walked over to Adrian and put a big hand on a messy head of hair. "David and I are going for an early hike, bud, to get the last piece for this cabin. You're fishing with your dad today."

Adrian rubbed his eyes and yawned. "Can I hike with you guys sometime?" Norton stirred in the bed next to him, opening and shutting one eye.

"Sure, Ade. Not today though. Go back to bed; I want you to get a little more shut eye."

"Okay." And he put his head back down and closed his eyes.

When they stepped into the crisp, pre-dawn air, David told Paul to wait and ran over to one of the trucks. Paul looked up at the stars still shining and the pockmarks in the moon. He breathed deeply, taking in the early morning of a mountain summer.

David returned with a plank of wood with two rings, two nails and a hammer. "I wanted them to find this when they got up," he said. He gently hammered the nails above the door and hung the sign. Even in the dark, the letters of *The St George's Angling Club* gleamed, crisp, heavily lacquered like an expensive car's dashboard and stained black. The little possessive "s" hung higher and slightly resembled an exclamation point. The two brothers gazed at the sign, then stepped back and took in the whole cabin and the dark meadow. Finally, David extracted them from the moment with an authoritative wave. "Okay," he said with a curt command from the past month.

They went into the woods, away from the river. They moved along a path towards the northern wall of the valley, both clearing the cobwebs of sleep and staying alert. As they walked, they could hear rustling and scratching in the trees and the shrubs. After a while, with help from the moon and stars, they could see beyond the beam of their flashlights into the forest. On cue, a grey owl hooted in the distance. Like arms with severed hands reaching from the earth, they saw frayed stumps scattered throughout the woods, moonlit through the gap in the canopy once filled by the boughs and branches that had risen and stretched above. Scars remained where they had landed in a rickety crash, been trimmed and dragged back to camp. Some of the gashes triggered memories, but for the most part, they blended into the previous summer's weeks of cutting and hauling logs.

Paul stopped as they reached the end of the site and the path melted into the trees; the ground sloped upwards. It was still night above them, though the eastern sky had a hint of grey at its base.

"Let's get a pull of that coffee before we start climbing," David said.

"How did you sleep?" Paul asked as he poured a cup.

"Fine. Good bunks—you built them well. They may be the sturdiest piece in the lodge besides the fireplace."

Paul casually shrugged away the compliment. "First night in the lodge, what do you think?"

"I think we're badasses." The reminiscence in David's eyes vanished. He knocked back the rest of his coffee and handed the cup to Paul. "Let's go."

Paul laughed a little. "Not sure if I've ever seen you this fired up to catch a sunrise."

They had been up this way a few times before. It was

built like most of the valley walls: dirt, rocks and scree fields with a dissipating forest as elevation increased. They hiked for a while. The eastern sky lightened and the stars began to disappear. They came to a large rock overhang. It towered above them, its face descending in a long dour frown. They climbed around the formation until they were behind it and could step on its back. The breeze picked up. They moved into the open and sat down, taking in the dying night sky and the sharpening contours of the valley.

"How long, you think?" David asked.

"About twenty minutes, give or take."

"How can you tell?"

"Only Vega and a few constellations are still visible."

They sat in silence for a while, watching the sky absorb stars as the moon set in the west. Structures in the valley took hold, the Elizabeth first, her black waters unchanging with the growing illumination. Then the little meadows and clearings came forward and the trees shifted back and grew branches and tops and trunks.

Paul cleared his throat. "David, I am impressed by what you put together over the last month. Very impressed."

David didn't say anything but his head nodded lightly.

Paul continued, "That was a well oiled machine: the plans, the groupings by abilities and skills, the jobs and their timings with one another. As soon as a piece was cut by one group, another had its space ready, and a third fastened it in place. It looked better organized than a racetrack pit crew— only stretched over a month. You even had little Adrian running around delivering tools and doing odd jobs." Paul laughed and flicked at the small rocks around his boots. "You don't see that kind of organization much anymore. I was really impressed."

David grunted. "Yeah, it worked. We still need to finish it with the mantle—"

"Quit trying to poop the party with modesty," Paul said smiling and putting up a hand. "Toasters and tables *work.*

You had everything planned out to the last rivet. It didn't just work; it came *alive*. We were like one breathing organism making our nest—"

"Paul—"

"I'm serious, David. There was never a moment where something wasn't being done to move forward and build that cabin. It was spectacular and now we get to spend the rest of the summer in it." A thought caught Paul by the ear. "Hey, let's get down to The Grove tomorrow. We've been here for a month and haven't gone near that place. Well," he cracked a smile at his brother, "since we weren't exactly allowed to fish that much either."

David's face darkened in the shadow of insecurity. "Do you think I was too demanding?"

Paul leaned back on his elbows and looked out over the valley. "David, I think you did it the only way you know how. And it worked. That's all that matters. Let's focus on the rest of the summer now."

"Yeah—well—thanks," David said quickly and then gazed towards the head of the valley.

"I don't even think of it as a compliment," Paul said. "Just a statement of fact. It was impressive." He followed his brother's eyes. "Anyway, looks like it's time to start the day."

Behind the eastern peaks, a whitening sky gave way to blue and yellow and the towering ghosts assumed their shapes. Small shafts of light broke through against the rocky faces until each held a halo of radiance. And then the entrance. The first morning beam blasted over and through the tallest peak as the blacks and grays hid in the far corners of the valley like draining ink. Everything came to attention. A second blast fired over the peak and the orb morphed off the stone tapestries, the white raging cornea now exposed, sending rays across the cosmos, through space and time, into the ozone, through the morning air and into their eyes, at a pleasant sixty degrees Fahrenheit.

"It never gets old," Paul said as the shadows rolled up

the valley floor. He extended his knees and sat back as the newly-warmed breeze swept across mountains. "What should we call this rock? It needs a name."

David thought for a moment. "I dunno. Sunrise Rock."

"Needs to be more original than that. The Perch?"

"No. We already have *The* Grove and *The* Flats."

"How about Morning Rock?" Paul said with an expectant grin.

David laughed after a second. They poured coffee again and toasted their stony outcropping. "To a healthy Morning Rock."

"To sporting a solid Morning Rock."

"To walking through the Morning Woods to get to Morning Rock."

"To…I don't know. That's probably enough," Paul said smiling. "But also, to The St George's Angling Club. There are ten of us now, plus Adrian, a cabin and the sense that something awesome is coming together. It came alive in me last year and now I'm ready to let it breathe. We'll have our time to fish and be with just our friends, then Gretchen and the girls will be here, then we're going to see what that cabin is made of through the winter. You said it earlier: We *are* badasses."

David nodded and let his brother's words settle. "You still think Gretchen will want to stay with us through the winter?"

Paul averted his eyes. "Of course."

"You sure?"

"Yes."

"I need you to vouch for her."

"This isn't the mafia, David." Paul saw the resoluteness in his brother's face. "Fine, I *vouch* for her. Why are you acting like you've never met her? You know she'd love being here."

"I knew her at the end of high school and I've gotten to know her again since you guys have tried to make it work for the—what, fifth time? I just need you to promise that she'll be okay out here."

"I'm not worried."

David winced and gauged his next statement. "I have to say it, Paul: you two still have your blowups. We don't need one out here."

Paul started to get upset, but pulled back. "Fair enough. You're right."

David leaned on his arm and gazed down the eastern wall of the valley as the sun crept higher. "Alright," he said. "I've said my bit."

"You have...until the next time." Paul tried to inject some light sarcasm.

The sun had dissolved the long shadows. David watched a hawk carve menacing arcs over a meadow on the south side of the river. "You know what I'm proud of, maybe the most outside of the cabin?" he asked.

"What?" Paul threw out the remainder of his coffee and screwed the cap back on the thermos.

"That *you* quit your job and are committing to this summer and winter."

Paul looked at his pack and pretended to fit the long thermos around his windbreaker. He turned over his brother's words, unable to tell if David was proud of him for taking the plunge to leave his job, or was proud of himself for playing a part in it. He shook his head, moving on and zipped up his pack.

"Okay," David said taking authority into his voice. "We need to go get that mantle. That grove of aspens is just one or two gaps over, I think."

"It is," Paul said as they stood and walked off Morning Rock. "Though there may be some improv. This ridge doesn't get us all the way there." He looked to the east, trying to remember hikes he'd taken before.

As he did, David looked at his boot and laughed. "Did you step in shit?"

Paul broke from his concentration. "What, oh"—he looked at the treads—"I did."

The sun glistened off a flattened pile behind them and Paul turned to examine it. "Some critter must have been enjoying the view from up here," he said bending down. But David was off the rock, into the woods and out of earshot. Paul's eyes widened for a moment, then he spoke solemnly to himself. "She must have been surveying her territory too."

He looked back at the haloed peaks and exhaled the entire contents of his lungs into the wind. The air blew and hummed and dove to the west, down the corners and center of the valley as the heat birthed from the east. It carried over the Elizabeth, over the old road and into their meadow where it rattled the new windows of the cabin, and pulled Adrian's eyes open.

~

He had not really gone back to sleep after the Ambrose brothers had left. His sponging mind would not allow it. As the morning light crept into the lodge, he sprang up and nudged his dad.

"Dad, Dad," he whispered putting on his bucket hat, conscious of not waking the other guys who snored in nearby bunks. "Dad, get up."

Norton rolled over and looked at his eager child rocking on his heels. "Good man," he said, and lay back in his pillow for a moment, rubbing his eyes. "Grab a couple of apples and a jar of peanut butter and put them in your backpack. And get your waders on. I'll meet you outside in a second."

Adrian was gone from his bedside before he'd finished speaking.

Stoss stirred in another bunk and rolled onto one elbow. "I thought you may be sleeping in after the way you carried on last night with that bourbon."

Norton smiled sheepishly and rubbed his temples. He nodded towards the large plastic bins and metal coolers where his son was extracting supplies. "Not with this guy around."

Stoss grunted. "Would you mind if I joined you two? Now that the fishing is less rushed, it would be nice to enjoy a piece of water with you and Adrian."

"Sure, I'll wait for you outside—er—we'll wait for you outside."

"Wonderful. Do you mind if I teach Adrian a couple things on the river?"

"Of course not."

JP was a couple bunks away and woke during their conversation. He got out of bed, waved through a yawn, walked to the porch, high-fived Adrian and jogged to the Elizabeth with a towel. A few minutes later they heard his rebel howl and "*DAMNATION THAT IS COLD!*"

Adrian glanced at his dad and giggled.

~

"There she goes!" Paul cried as the aspen teetered and fell with a flourish and rattle, the leaves pluming into the air like confetti. The creak echoed off the other trees and into the forest around them, fading like rolling thunder. They walked to the base and examined where it had been severed. "How long does it have to be?" Paul asked.

"Four feet, four inches." David withdrew a measuring tape from his backpack.

"We're not going to split it here, right?" Paul asked.

"No. We'll cut it back at the cabin with one of the Alaskan sawmills."

"Why didn't we think of this? We have to carry twice as much weight now." Paul started loosening his shoulders and cracking his knuckles.

David waved him off. "Stop being a baby. You're twice as big as me."

"Whatever. I'm just realizing what a lug this is going to be. We're doing all this for a damn mantle over a fireplace."

A fire glanced across David's eyes. "It will be worth it. It'll look good, especially if we keep the bark from getting dinged as we carry it."

They set about cutting the aspen trunk with their handsaws, white bark and sawdust spraying in the air. When finished, they tied the ends of the log with two lengths of rope as makeshift handles for carrying, not looking unlike two henchmen disposing of a body off a pier. They left the rest of the tree behind in the shade of the still-standing aspens, and set off back to camp. As they walked along the ridgeline, the sun moved towards the western mouth of the valley, flipping the shadows. The clouds were sparse, thin wisps and puffs against an expansive blue ocean. They moved through a small high mountain meadow; red and yellow wildflowers peppered the tall grasses.

They could see down the length of the St George's Valley. David had fought the feeling for so long. He had always turned his head when it smiled at him and pushed it away when it set a hand on his shoulder. But now, with his view down the valley, his hands taut under the final addition to the cabin—the section of aspen that would slide above the fireplace like a lynchpin in a hinge—it coalesced into a thick vibrancy in his chest. He tipped his head back and let out a howl.

Paul chuckled to himself.

They walked for a while, sweat building on their shoulders and above their ears, until they reached a low point on the crest. A drainage ran steeply to the valley floor to their left. Flows of gravel and scree funneled into the trees. They came to its edge and set the log down and stretched their hands.

"Let's cut down here," David said. "I don't want to carry this on any more uphill than I have to. We can get down to the valley floor and walk the road back to camp."

Paul took off his hat, wiping his brow. "Have you hiked down that way—looks steep? We don't need to take a spill with this thing." He rubbed the joints of his fingers, massaging the blood in his swollen fingers.

"I haven't, but someone did last year and said it was okay." David said but avoided eye contact with his brother.

"Yeah…you made that up," Paul said evenly.

David focused on the pitch. "I may have. It'll be fine, Paul. I want to get back for some late afternoon fishing."

Paul closed his eyes and shook his head. "Fine. This is stupid though."

~

In the trees, on the other side of the high mountain meadow, beyond the red and yellow wildflowers, the mountain lion watched them pass with her one eye. She didn't move.

The shadows stretched around the meadow. Their dark fingers bridged over the ridgeline and covered the drainage that Paul and David started to descend. They slithered onto the steep slopes and spread into the valley. They ran through the trees and the brush, hiding foxes and rabbits and squirrels and setting a border between the cool and the warm air. They extended, and reached, and smothered, and protected until they came to the river.

~

"And it was here," Stoss said to Norton with his faux-dramatics as they approached the Elizabeth. Adrian was well ahead of them, and already peering at her sparkling waters.

"Hemmingway?" Norton asked.

"Of course," Stoss said and called to the eager boy. "Adrian, where are the fish hiding this fine morning?"

Adrian gave Stoss a hard stare, grabbed the corner of his hat with one hand and shrugged coyly. "Have to find them yourself."

Stoss clapped in laughter. "Well trained," he said.

"Ade, you can tell us this time," Norton said gently.

The boy looked back at the water. A gravel bar wrapped widely around them. In the middle of the river sat a small island. The bank was undercut and dark. Adrian put one hand on his hip. "There," he said pointing and standing on as much authority as he could find. He peered at he waters rushing past him.

"Prove it," Norton said and then turned to Stoss. "He's lucky to have his mother's eyesight."

Stoss shifted on his feet. This was the first time Norton had brought up his late wife with only him. "Well, he certainly has your interest and love of fly fishing." Stoss paused and took in Norton staring at his son. "She would have been very proud."

Norton nodded in a dream as he watched his boy. "I know." Then after a minute of Adrian casting, he turned. "Can I ask you something, Stoss?"

"Sure."

"You ever regret not having kids?"

Stoss sighed. "Not long ago I would have vehemently said I *didn't*. I would have said I'd made a choice and that I would never have had time to be a good father. 'Medicine is my child' was my usual line." His voice trailed. "But that's bullshit. We're put on this planet to have children—plain and simple—and I missed that. I don't regret my years of medicine, but I do wish I'd been selfish enough to take the time to be a father."

"I don't think that would have been selfish," Norton said. "Caring for a child is about the most unselfish job in the world."

"I'm sure it is—I don't see 'selfish' as an insulting word; there is nothing wrong with doing something for one's self. People have children because it's in their core to do so, but also because the joy of a child is addicting. There are reasons upon reasons why I forwent that joy, but they are all quite boring...and selfish, in more of the sense you were just implying." He nodded at the river. "Let's get this boy some fish though. He seems frustrated."

The current moved swiftly in the extended track of water and around the wide bend. On each cast, Adrian's nymph came up short of the island with the undercut bank.

"Raise your arm a little higher," Stoss said as he walked over.

The cast fell a few feet shy again. Adrian's shoulder slumped.

"If I may," Stoss said trading nods with Norton. "Adrian, step out to this rock."

"Wait, which rock?" Norton asked putting out a hand. "What's our rule, Adrian?"

"That the water is never above our knees when we're wearing waders," he said in a sing-song response.

"That's right."

"Let me help you then." Stoss lifted Adrian out and onto a rock high in the current, away from shore. "There you go. Now you are keeping with the rules but a little higher and closer."

The current rushed under his knees and into the dark water around him. Norton watched for a moment, then walked downstream from his son and casually took a few steps into the current.

"Cast again," Stoss said.

The nymph plopped next to the bank of the island and disappeared. A few seconds later, Adrian's rod stuttered and a little trout jumped on the end of his line. The fish bent in the water, flashing its white belly; light splashes laughed into the air.

The motion attracted an eagle that shifted her flight and moved towards the river. She glided past the old man, the small man and the boy. She glided up the valley, throwing her shadow over the treetops and scree fields as she looked for food.

She examined a drainage on the north side of the valley. Two men appeared. One lay against a rock injured; the other, larger man looked to the first from the top of the slope. She veered away to find another section of the valley where she could hunt without disruption.

~

David lay against a rock, blood trickling down his pants into the dust. He looked back up the slope at his brother. "My ankle's broken. And I think the log smacked me in the head," he shouted weakly.

They had made it about twenty yards down the pitch when, due to the incalculable forces of nature, the sloping gravel beneath David gave way like a cartoon banana peel. He'd slid down the drainage slope until a boulder field, caromed off a few rocks and then plopped at their base, on a small, flat landing surrounded by bushes.

"Hold on, I'm coming," Paul yelled back and put out his arms to balance.

As he began his descent, his heart jumped. His chest went cold. A sleek, brown shape dissolved in the shadows on the other side of the drainage. He yelled savagely and leaned over for rocks and handfuls of dirt, while fighting to maintain balance. He looked again, but couldn't find the form. He picked up his downward speed, shouting until he cleared the rocks near his brother.

"What are you yelling at?" David asked but knowledge of the answer was in his tone.

"Can you stand? We need to get out of here. Give me your knife." Without waiting for an answer, Paul unsnapped the knife from David's belt and unfolded the blade from the bone handle. It glinted in the sun and for a split second, Paul stared distantly at it.

David winced at his swollen ankle. "My whole leg is pretty jacked; also I feel like puking."

Paul looked around again. "We gotta get out of here." He pulled his wind breaker from his daypack and started to cut it into strips. "I'm going to wrap your leg. I need to find a branch to splint it. Can you—"

David convulsed and his good leg shoved him against the rock. His eyes focused and bulged.

"*Paul.*"

Behind him, the mountain lion lay in a crouch, her one eye cut to a slit, ears tucked back and her long teeth hissing. Her hind legs were loaded, but boney knobs jutted from what had once been rippling sheets of muscle. The amber fur was haggard. But a rusty knife can still kill.

Paul moved first, slowly, sidestepping away from his brother and tossing his hat aside. David yelled and threw a rock, but her one-eyed gaze stayed focused on Paul. The cat screamed and hissed in a harmony with her twitching tail. Paul began to wrap his wind breaker around his left forearm, never unlocking his eyes. The cat hissed and snarled again and followed him. David threw another rock, but she didn't flinch. She lowered into a deep crouch exposing long fangs. Paul had finished wrapping his forearm, still locked in with the lion. David threw another errant rock.

Those that study these things will agree that when the eyes and brain observe motion, fast motion, they take mental pictures, then drawing from reasonable memories, fill in the connections between the frames on their own. When a batter watches a fastball leave the pitcher's hand, he only "sees" the ball about three times. The white line of the spinning baseball is filled in by the mind. Over the years that David retold the story of the mountain lion attacking his brother, the filler had faded. He only saw the event in four snapshots, like a short comic.

[The first is the cat suspended in a broad spring towards Paul. Its paws are outstretched and the muscular back is uncoiled like an overextended piston.]

[In the second, the cat's jaws are clamped on Paul's wrapped arm. Its hindquarters are hinging downward. Its claws are laid against his shoulder. Paul's head is turned like someone just hit him in the face with sand.]

[In the third, the cat's stomach is suspended by Paul's right hand driving into its gut, like a support beam of a bridge. His thick thighs have extended towards the sun. There is an incision along the cat's belly, but no blood.]

[In the final image the cat lies on its back in a violent spray of dust. Its belly and legs flail, separated by a dark, bleeding chasm. The head is strangely foreign to the body, as if the deepest survival instincts are trying to disassociate from the mortal wound.]

For years David would recount those four images and tell the story as he had *seen*: It rolled its head wildly in circles, its eyes wide, blood pulsing onto the ground, as it staggered back and forth; it wobbled away, thick crimson semicircles carved the dirt, and leaned on a rock, tipped its head, rolled its neck and screamed once more, filling the valley. And then it slumped over.

David would tell that story—but that was only what he saw. He kept what he'd felt wrapped in secret. He'd felt the mountain lion wanting to die. He felt that she'd sought this fight in a day of reckoning. He could see it in that one eye. He couldn't put it to words, but it resonated in his core. And about the same time he stumbled upon that realization, many years later, he gave the mountain lion her gender. "It" fell away and "she" took the place: *she* rolled *her* head wildly in circles, her eyes wide, blood pulsing onto the ground, as she staggered back and forth; she wobbled away, thick crimson semicircles carved the dirt, and leaned on a rock, tipped her head, rolled her neck and screamed once more, filling the valley. And then she slumped over.

When she had made that final cry, Paul took a few steps backward, his right hand wrapped around the bone handle of the knife like gnarled oak roots, and slumped to his knees in the dust. The wind had died too. There were no bird calls or humming insects. Even the trees bowed in silence. He looked at the body of the cat against the rock—now a molted and bloody heap. His shoulders relaxed and his eyes reddened, softened and glazed. David lay still against his rock, looking between the dead cat and his kneeling brother.

"Are you—" the words didn't leave his mouth before tears appeared in his eyes too. "Are you okay, Paul?"

Paul didn't say anything, his face hidden in shadow. His head began to rock back and forth, and a tear fell off his thick cheekbones into the dirt. He stood up slowly, never taking his eyes off the cat, his torn shirt hanging about him and blowing in the breeze, stains of crimson in the frayed edges. David could see through the tatters that his brother's chest had a set of bloody tracks, and a second on his back. Though battered, the great beam that seemed to run through Paul's shoulders had not bent. "I'm okay," he said. The words came smooth and gentle like the breeze. He unwrapped his forearm and turned it over to expose two bleeding divots. He looked them over carefully and then stared back at the cat. He flexed his fingers and a thin pulse of blood bubbled through each hole. He wiped it away and rewrapped his arm, his head haloed by the sun, his shoulders cutting a broad outline from the acid blue sky.

"You sure—you're okay?" David asked. His face was still fragmented in the aftermath of fear.

Paul turned from the mountain lion to his little brother in the dirt, blood around his ankle, slumped against a rock. The vision startled him and a beam of compassion burst through his stone face. "Let's get you home," he said quickly and bent down to stabilize the leg.

The shadow of an eagle passed over them. She dipped low and saw the carcass of a mountain lion slumped over, but flew higher, away from the men. She noticed them leaving, slowly. She circled above patiently, letting them vacate and preparing for her meal against the rock.

~

Stoss netted Adrian's fifth fish of the morning and held it high for the boy. It was a little brown trout. "Well done, sir! Want to keep this one?" Adrian looked to his dad, who looked back at Stoss.

"I've been teaching him that we don't keep fish unless we're having it for dinner. He's also never seen me clean one—not sure he's ready for that."

The word "clean" triggered a little thought on Adrian's face. He had already been comfortable with one definition. He figured Dad cleaned the fish before he served them, just like fruit and veggies. That process was pretty boring, so why watch him clean a fish? But the way he heard his dad say it now made him wonder if he was going to learn something new.

"I thought I might give an anatomy lesson," Stoss said.

Norton thought for a moment. "Okay, we'll eat it later."

Stoss withdrew his knife and sat down on the bank. Adrian sat down too, cross-legged and put his elbows on his knees, his chin in his hands, watching intently. "First, to be humane, we must kill this little fellow quickly." Stoss held the fish tightly and whacked its head against a rock at the base of the skull. The eyes widened; the trout shook and then was still.

Adrian now knew he was learning something he didn't know.

"Now you place your blade below his belly," Stoss pushed the knife into the fish's soft white stomach "and draw it up to his neck." He sawed the blade upwards until he was just under the fish's chin. Adrian squinted and turned his head sideways slightly. He rubbed his nose and looked back, but didn't say anything.

"You okay?" Norton asked.

Adrian nodded, his chin back in his hands.

"Now here is the interesting part," Stoss said and reached his index finger into the open abdomen. "This is his stomach right here, with the veins running around it." His index finger wrapped a peach colored sack, pulled it forth and let it lay in his palm. "And if you look, it goes all the way down here to where he takes a poop." Stoss looked up to see if this made the boy laugh, but was met with serious eyes. He continued quickly. "Now, see these? These are the gills. That's where the fish breathes. We have lungs—where are they? Good—but fish have gills because they get air from the water." He spread the neck and the red tissue splayed apart. "Now here is the most interesting part. Do you know where your heart is?"

The boy pointed to his chest.

"Correct. Well here is the fish's heart." Stoss held out the little crimson cube that was beating only moments before. "Do you want to touch it?"

Adrian hesitated. He hadn't been scared to touch it and only examined the idea because of the question. Stoss had been touching it; why should it be a problem if he wanted to? He touched the heart cautiously.

Stoss continued, "Now, to clean a trout is very easy. You just take your fingers right here," he put his index and middle finger into the cavity above the anus, "and pull upwards like this." He yanked two surgical fingers, shoveling the vital organs from the incision in the cavity, as coagulated blood and roe splattered onto the rocks. At first, Adrian did not shutter, but the hollow moan of the ripped tissue and torn sheaths filled his ears. The touch of destroyed life brushed against him and he winced and covered his ears, then buried his face into his dad's chest.

Stoss looked on helplessly, "Oh, I—"

"It's okay," Norton said to Adrian, "it's okay," he said a second time, looking at Stoss.

~

Back at the cabin, JP laid a ringer with a loud clang ending the game of horseshoes. He whooped, and high-fived his partner, Bruce. JP and Bruce had spin fished in the foothills of the Smokey Mountains together for many years and JP had roped him into coming this year. Their bond of friendship was mostly based on JP's loud and extroverted nature as a foil to Bruce's quieter, dimmer demeanor. They were quite a pair standing next to one another; JP tall and thin and Bruce doughy and rounder.

JP stuck out a hand to the losing team. "Sorry to keep beating up on you new guys. Better luck next time—though I've said that enough that I'm starting to think my powers are wearing off!"

Drew and Miles, two new members, shook their heads with beers loosely held in their hands. They looked at the cabin, standing tall in their golden meadow. A moment of silence came between the four men and they looked back at their work.

"Good cabin," JP said, the brown wood gleaming in the afternoon sun.

Drew laughed and raised his beer. "I still am in disbelief that it came together like that. That whole month went by in a blur and then here it is. It pained me sometimes—but I'm glad I listened to David."

"We could build another cabin if we wanted," JP said. "There is enough room in this clearing. Hell, we could build a few more." He picked up a rock and threw it to the back corner of the meadow and watched it bounce into the trees. "I know David wants to get more guys next year. But either way, we are going to outgrow this lodge quickly. It's already tight with the ten of us and Adrian."

"You think they'll invite that guy from last year back— David's bartending buddy?" Miles asked.

"Connor? No. David didn't want anything to do with him after that. He only wanted people who'd bust their ass to get this done," he said and nodded reverently. "David and I don't always get along, but he respected that I fell trees and busted my ass with him."

Bruce nodded and took a sip of beer. "You think he'll invite us back?"

"Hell yeah, dummy. Like I said, you busted your ass on this thing, how could he not?"

"Speaking of which," Drew said. "It might still be a day before I feel like casting a fly rod. My friggin' back and shoulders are sore as all hell."

JP cocked his head and nodded back to the horseshoe that still lay wrapped around the metal spike. "That why we've taken four games in a row?" His toothy grin broadened. "Don't try your excuses with me, boy. I'll sniff those out a mile away."

Drew laughed. "I'm not making excuses. I just think I'd hurt myself if I started stumbling about in the streams trying to catch fish."

"Well," JP said with some finality. "We'll fish tomorrow then—hey! Looks like our eight-year-old friend has more balls than you do." They turned and looked across the road at the boy, the father and the old doctor approaching from the river. "Adrian! How goes it my man?" JP put out a hand for a high-five.

"Good," he said quietly and reciprocated half-heartedly. By his own dedication and the endearing manner in which he counted on his hands, Adrian had become the official scorekeeper for horseshoe games, and in many ways, the mascot, of sorts, for the group. The young dedication to each of his tasks during the construction put wings in their steps.

"Okay, okay," JP said, a little confused by the boy's quiet mood. "How'd you guys do this morning? Fish not cooperating?"

Stoss walked up to the group and his voice was proud. "Not too bad. I think Adrian took eight or nine fish this morning—"

"I had five," he said. His voice lacked disappointment or

frustration or embarrassment. He was correcting; it was a fact.

Stoss nodded quickly. "Well, Adrian, you learned some anatomy, right?"

JP turned to Adrian. "Hey buddy, do you want to keep score during our next game? Bruce and I are probably going to give another lesson to Drew and Miles soon—*holy shit*."

The Ambrose brothers limped towards the cabin from the road. Blood soaked David's ankle and shin; blood soaked Paul's arm and shoulder.

~

Stoss, anticipating the construction for the summer, had brought a good first aid kit that year, complete with sutures, painkillers, stethoscope, splints and a variety of other remedies. His usual kit—the dimensions of a couple stacked books—had ballooned into a wide rubber suitcase, filled with elastic pockets for bottles, hemostats, scissors, scalpels and sealable compartments for storage. Next to the canisters of propane, packs of batteries, fresh globes for the lanterns, multiple stacks of Paul's tattered books—*The Hunter's Guide* still the foundation of the library—and a litany of other outdoor accessories, the huge first aid kit had occupied half a shelf and had been the butt of a number of jokes, usually inquiring if there was a nurse inside. But now with both brothers battered at the table in the lodge, Stoss seemed to have the last laugh.

He examined David's ankle and determined it wasn't broken, just badly sprained. Paul had done a good job splinting it for their walk back, keeping the joint straight. In addition to the sprain, David had also suffered a mild concussion and a few bad scrapes, though nothing requiring stitches. He'd need to lay low for a few weeks with tape on the ankle. No fishing or walking on the slippery rocks of the Elizabeth. He would be fine, Stoss said and noticed strangely that the unheroic prognosis disappointed the patient. Stoss then closed the two holes in Paul's arm and put him on a strong course of antibiotics against whatever infection lined the cat's mouth. He had lost some blood but had kept his arm high as he walked, minimizing the hemorrhaging. The tracks on his chest and back were cleaned and sutured too. Paul just needed a couple days off his feet and to eat well.

While Stoss sewed his shoulder, the crew gathered in the lodge and Paul told the story. He described David's fall and then the actual run in with the mountain lion and the group's eyes widened as he told of pulling the knife up the cat's suspended chest, its jaws clamped around his arm, and its final cries of life, how the screams still rung in his ears like the toll of a shattering bell.

When he was done, everyone was quiet. The dim light drifted in through the cabin windows and exposed the dust in swirling clouds. They could hear the bouncing chatter of birds and the grasshoppers in the meadow. They could hear Adrian playing on the porch—this had been a grownup discussion—narrating a survey of his dad's fly box.

Norton spoke finally with an eye locked out the window on his son. "So you're positive it's dead?"

Paul breathed slowly, "Yes."

~ 4 ~

IT IS IN THE FABRIC OF MEN to know the hero among them. Their ancient need for the title sniffs him out before they acknowledge him consciously. If they were able to stand outside their body and watch themselves for a while, they'd recognize the changes in the way they deal with him. Their eyes cut lower. They agree faster. They shy from competition with him or drift towards his side when teams are formed. They think an extra moment about his words.

And the hero is unchanged through it all. Nothing happens to his ego when men won't meet his gaze. Nothing swells his confidence when they choose his team. Nothing alters his thinking when others nod their heads too early. He does what comes naturally to his being and for that reason, sees no reason for change when people react in accordance. The world exists in his expected rhythm.

But that need for being the hero never dies in the men around him—especially those who have spent lifetimes wanting to stand in his footsteps.

~

Now with its stout wooden capitol building, the meadow had blossomed from a campsite for fishing, into a Camp. David's sign beamed over the doorway. The alpine agora pulsed as everyone set their face to the sky and made their way through days in the valley; an ease and adventure settled in them, knowing that their fort in the woods would be resolute and waiting when they returned.

In building it, the work had not stopped at cutting trees or the construction. To clean off after a long day, a stagnant alcove of the Elizabeth just across the road had been reconstructed into a calm, but circulating pool of water. They had spaced black rocks—selected to heat the water that ran by them—enough so that current flowed into the pool to drain suds, but left enough shielding to create back current that let the water continue to warm in the sunlight. The rock-bottomed floor that had caused the tenderfoots to move gingerly had been cleared and smooth sand remained. Around the pool were branches lashed on trees for drying towels and clothes.

Inside the cabin, coolers for perishables were kept on the northern wall, away from the windows, in a fitted holder of extra planks and insulation. The ice they'd brought, if the lids were only cracked in times of quick use, would last days, but when it would finally melt, Stoss's little truck powered ice maker whirred to life. Next to the coolers were two large containers of dirty and drinking water, one with a red X, the other with a green O. It became habit, if you were returning from the river, to bring back a bucket of water that was poured into the vat with the red X, boiled, treated or filtered and then repoured into the vat with the green O.

Managing refuse took a little time to harness. A pee was simple but finishing the digestive process was a little more complex. The previous practice had been to wander off with a roll of toilet paper into the deeper woods, but after enough time that summer and over the years, it was not uncommon to go for a walk and come across a sign or smell that someone had taken that same walk. This was obviously unacceptable and—after Adrian came back with tears and dirty little hands, while exploring the dark wood—construction of the lodge halted for two days as all ten guys staked out and built an extremely deep pit latrine, about a hundred yards into the woods, in a tiny clearing that received just enough sun and wind to catalyze all things natural. The rest of the waste, usually just cooking byproducts from what had become very simple but exactly nutritious meals, was either burned or if a heavy organic, carried far away from camp and chucked. If you walked back to where you'd thrown it a few days later, it'd be gone. Other garbage was minimal, except for the occasional plastics, which were put into a bag and sent with the next truck out on a supply run.

A week after the Ambrose brothers' run-in with the mountain lion, the late morning sun cut angular sections of warmth and coolness across the meadow through the eastern trees. Stoss had noted a caddis hatch coming off, so everyone had a quick breakfast of granola bars and heading out before the direct sunlight hit the river. With camp cleared, David hobbled to the river on a pair of make-shift crutches and put his ankle in the cool water. The edge of his foot was purple and the ball of his ankle tender to the touch. The water raced around and the pain swept away and the pulsing subsided. He looked back up the valley, to the east. Birds dashed over the Elizabeth and the brush chattered. He leaned back on the rock, keeping his ankle in the water. He looked to the south rim of the valley and the mountains seemed taller, almost trapping like the top of a tank. He looked back to the north rim and scanned the peaks. He saw the ridgeline where the mountain lion had turned them back a few years ago. He moved his eyes farther east and saw the ridgeline where the mountain lion had met her end.

"Guess we had the last laugh," he said aloud, closed his eyes and dozed off. But his words were hollow

In the amber ether of a nap's dream, when the deepness of sleep has not usurped reality but the mind still wanders to strange places, Z appeared. He stood across the river but his face was without feature. He puffed his cigar and the smoke drifted into oblivion, into David's eyes. He waved the burning coal in the air and his words were laced with acid.

Why don't you get it? Your brother does.

David wanted to reply but his mouth was trapped and empty and dry, like he'd swallowed ashes.

Why don't you get it, chief?

A high whine came to the back of his throat. A yell covered, sealed and sectioned off.

Why don't you get it, Dave? Or do I have to smack you around?

Z's figure melted into the brush and the bushes and the trees and the walls of the valley in a tapestry of dreamy cigar smoke.

Why don't you get it?

A breeze blew across and David shuddered and sat up; the sun had shifted and was lower in the west. He'd napped a while. He blinked and looked at the peach sky and the long strokes of clouds. The birds flew with purpose, picking mayflies from the air and settling back onto their branches. He sat up and looked down at his ankle. It was red from the cold submersion. He rubbed it gently and looked back at the setting sun and then back at the mountains that had loomed above him as he dozed off. They seemed calm and stoic now, like they always had been. The dream only remained in his mind as an imprint without specifics or contours. He rubbed his face and eyes. A truck grumbled on the road behind him and the doors opened and shut. David paid it no attention, then a voice called to him.

"Howdy! On the rock!"

David twisted around. Two men in cowboy hats stood at the edge of the trees looking at him.

"Howdy!" the tall one said again. He was skinny and pale like an aspen tree in a t-shirt and fading blue jeans. The other guy was short and fat, five feet tall and almost as wide. He stood by the aspen with his hands on his hip and severity on his face, like a scowling bowling ball. He had a pistol holstered on his belt and wasn't wearing any kind of uniform.

"Hey," David said flatly. He realized this was the first time he'd talked to someone he didn't recognize in St

George's besides Z.

"This your lodge?" The aspen pointed back into the woods towards the cabin with a spindly finger.

"Yeah."

"Well, we're here to do a little fishing and are going to settle up the river on the other side."

"Okay. There isn't a bridge," David said and condescension crept into his voice.

"We scouted a place where our rigs could ford—don't need a bridge with these big tires," the aspen said casually. "There's a big meadow on the other side where we'll set camp."

The bowling ball spoke up. The buttons that tracked over his belly flexed under duress from the bulging mass behind them. "Would be nice if you came over and introduced yourself there, partner. It's a bit rude to look at us all cockeyed from the river with your feet dangling in the water."

David held up his purple foot.

"What the hell you doing out here then? Shouldn't you be at home nursing and gettin' kisses on it?" the bowling balls said with a laugh.

David allowed a few beats to pass before responding to the question. "Maybe."

"Okay partner, we'll see you around," said the aspen tipping his hat. "Just wanted to check in with you." The bowling ball had already turned and was walking away. David gave a short wave and watched the two cowboys disappear into the woods.

He tried to relax on his rock but he couldn't sit still. As he put his good foot on the ground and began to stand, he heard an extra splash upstream and shifted on his rock. Paul was kneeling in the water, unmoving. He didn't have any fishing gear with him—he hadn't fished since the injuries—and had taken off his shirt in the hot afternoon and turned his hat around. His back was to David and even from the distance, he could see the claw marks running over the tan mounds of his brother's shoulder. Stoss had removed the sutures the previous night and the scars looked like railroad lines that mysteriously started and disappeared. Paul remained motionless, focused on the water, as still as the tree trunks on the bank. Then he shifted to the balls of his feet and moved upriver staying low to the water. He put his left hand down to balance and David could see the two divots, staring like cat's eyes, in the top of his forearm. Paul took a few more steps and stopped behind a rock. He lowered himself onto his elbow, wincing, and looked into the water. In a flash, he plunged his big hand into the Elizabeth and withdrew a trout, writhing in his grip. The fish shook like a loose fire hose but Paul held it tightly with calm but intent eyes. The fish eventually acquiesced, bending rhythmically side to side, succumbing to lack of oxygen, surrounded by air.

Paul knocked the back of its head on a sharp rock and drew the trout to his face. He stared at it for a while, then pulled his notebook from his back pocket and jotted down a few quick bullets. When finished, he nodded to his brother, like he'd known he was watching all along.

"Nice work," David said as he approached.

"Had to wait. She hung low in the current for quite some time," Paul said, setting the fish down and putting on his shirt.

"So now that you've killed a mountain lion with your bare hands, you're taking on the rest of the valley like that?"

Paul laughed. "Only seeing if I could do it. I read about bare handing and wanted to try; that was probably my thirtieth attempt today. I was going to make a spear soon." He paused. "And it wasn't my bare hands with the mountain lion. I had a knife."

"So you've been reviewing the *Guide*?"

"No, those old trappers used sharpened branches as spears. Have you been reading now that you've got more time?"

"Trying to. Stoss had a couple good books from Colorado

about winter fishing."

"Yeah, we'll need to plan food like we're not going to be able to leave."

"Why?"

"Because…the pass will snow over at some points."

David was quiet for a second. "Right," he said slowly. "Does Gretchen know that?"

"She does."

"You sure?"

"*Yes*," Paul said staring his brother down but continuing as if it didn't hear the loaded words. "We'll have to fish a fair amount and keep everything. Winter fishing is a different game. The water is low so they spook more easily—but they can be hungrier as well. Either way, it'll be a challenge when it's freezing."

"Maybe I need to kill a deer with *my* bare hands. Then we'll have the meat we'd need."

"Would be far more impressive than just a fish."

"It would," David said abruptly, "By the way, speaking of rifles and guns, did you see that truck of guys roll by?"

"Yeah but they didn't see me," Paul said and looked back to the road. He shifted the dead fish in his hand from one to the other. "And who said anything about guns?"

"One of them—fat guy—had a pistol. I talked to him and his skinny friend. Morons."

"What did they say?"

"Just that they were staying up river, on the other side."

"They going to ford at the headwaters?"

"Yeah."

"That's shitty; that's going to tear apart those gravel beds. Fish spawn there." He paused. "Idiocy and kindness are not mutually exclusive though—did they seem like good guys?"

"The skinny guy did; his fat friend seemed like an ass."

Paul thought for a moment. "Well…we'll see what happens. Let's head back."

David turned, then stopped. "Can I ask you something?"

His eyes met Paul's.

"Sure."

"Why do you look so intensely at the fish you kill?"

The flash of intensity came to Paul's face and then re-treated. He held the trout up again and looked at its lifeless body between his fingers. The limp vessel sagged in his big palms. "I'm trying to see when it dies."

David smiled a little. "Pretty sure it died...when you smashed it on a rock."

"No—I mean, what exactly happens when it dies."

David shot his quick glance to the vessel again. "Really?"

"You have to take something from tragedies, even if it's nothing more than understanding."

"It's just a fish."

"Well, I'm just a human."

A little smile crept onto the corner of David's mouth and he shook his head. "Sometimes, I find you really strange."

"I know."

"So, have you seen it?"

"The moment? I don't know, maybe."

"And?"

"Sunlight stops reflecting in the eyes. That's the only dif-ference I've noticed."

"Sunlight," David said trailing off, and they were quiet.

Paul put out a hand to help his brother as they turned away from the river, went up the bank and into the woods towards their cabin.

~ 5 ~

EARLY ON AN OVERCAST MORNING, a thick sash of mountain fog breathed down the valley. A mother fox shepherded her pups to the river. They waddled onto a gravel bar, careful to step around the sharper stones, and stuck their snouts in a shallow pool, their little tongues lapping up the icy water in pink, rhythmic slurps. While they drank, she kept her nose in the informative air and her eyes alert in the grey light. She smelled two men and saw them across the river, moving down the dark road. One of the silhouettes moved with briskness, excitement, almost in a trot; the other was slower; and neither carried gear or wore packs. She watched them intently, but didn't feel threatened. There was no menace in the way they moved, maybe some mischief though.

"I thought you would have trimmed up by now after all the work we've done—*let's go*," JP said like he was coaxing his favorite lazy dog.

"Shut up. I'm trying," Bruce huffed.

"I know man, I know." JP rubbed his hands together and clapped them softly. The grey morning melted into the grey mountains around them. It started to drizzle and droplets collected on their arms like glistening goosebumps.

Bruce slid his hands across the back of his soft triceps and the skin turned red, searching for warmth. "I knew I shouldn't have listened to you, not bringing a breaker or anything," he said dourly.

"Aw, quite your bitchin'. This'll burn off."

They walked another mile until they were near the head of the valley. The forest had thinned and the long grass fields were braided with the beginnings of the Elizabeth. "Here," JP said as he pointed to a couple sets of huge tire tracks that veered off the road and into the shallower water. They walked down to the bank and JP started trudging through the lighter currents. Bruce stayed on shore.

"You're not going to take your boots off?"

JP turned around, "Naw man, let's go. God damn, you baby, your feet'll dry later."

Bruce shook his head and waded into the water. His feet stayed dry for an instant until the river reached into his socks and wrapped his feet in cold embrace. They stepped through a few stony islands and reached the far bank. They moved quietly through the grass and trees on the south side, following the tire tracks until two trucks appeared in a clearing against some dense trees with three tents nearby. JP crouched and pulled Bruce down and he fell sideways trying to balance on his knees.

"Hold steady, ya goof," JP pushed away and then looked back at the camp. "Doesn't look like anyone's awake yet."

"So what the hell do we do now—wait? I thought you wanted to catch them at breakfast and talk to them."

"I might have stretched the truth a little." JP flashed his long grin. "What we're going to do is let them know that this is our damn valley and they're not wanted."

"What the heck does that mean?"

"I may be a redneck, but I know bad news when I see it. Even if it's another redneck. You heard David last night at dinner: these guys are *trouble*. And I tend to agree. Plus, you said it yourself when we were fishing: they smell like a bummer. Now you *know* that I hate nothing more than a bummer. And while I don't mind trouble, I don't necessarily like it directed at me—especially if it'll affect my fishing. So we're going to send these cowboys a message."

Bruce stared blankly.

JP spoke like he was explaining a simple joke. "We're gonna let the air out of their tires."

"*Wait*—what? Didn't David say one of them had a gun?"

"He ain't gonna shoot us, besides, I'm quieter than a cat. You stay here, we don't need them hearin' you pant. Actually, creep over to those bushes."

"No!" Bruce said in raspy whisper. "We should talk to them and—"

"David did talk to them, yesterday. You heard him: a couple of morons. You saw what they did to the gravel beds back there. They're killing our fish and we can't have that."

"They're going to flip out on us."

"They won't know it was us; they'll think they just got a couple of bum tires and—"

"Not *them*," Bruce said pointing at the tents, then he thumbed back towards the road. "David and Paul."

This put a quick pause in JP, then he pushed past. "David will think it's funny and'll be glad we did it." His tone grew distant and he dropped eye contact. "He'll appreciate it."

"And Paul?"

JP didn't say anything for a moment, then he shrugged. "It's just air in the tires. It's not like we're setting their camp on fire."

"How the hell are they going to fill back up? We're in the middle of nowhere."

JP's face gained the confident grin of a man playing trump. "You see those round things on the back of each truck, big boy? Those are called *spares*. I'm only going to get two tires—so they'll be fine."

The rain came harder. "This is stupid," Bruce said quietly, shifted onto all fours and crawled through the bent grass into a thicket of bushes, just peering from behind a low clump of leaves.

JP crept low to the ground, almost slithering until he reached the rear of the first truck. He kept the vehicle between him and the tents as he unscrewed the cap on the tire.

A knife appeared from his pocket and he poked the tip into the nipple, releasing a violent rush of air.

SHHHHHHHT!

JP yanked the blade away, looked over to Bruce's hiding spot and bugged his eyes in jest. He kept eye contact as he slowly — like he was pouring something very precious down a small tube — applied the tip of the blade to the nipple of the tire. As the valve depressed he turned his head, winced and closed his eyes.

sssssssssss...

Bruce could hear the faint rush as he watched the truck lean to the side, and then onto one haunch. It started to rain harder.

JP screwed the cap back on and crept to the front by the passenger cabin. He unscrewed the cap and did the same, the big beast now slumping fully to one side. He looked back and another grin burst across his face. Bruce sat, unmoving in the bushes, and whispered, *"Paul is going to kill us,"* to himself.

As JP screwed the cap back onto the tire, the smooth hum of a zipper sounded in the wet morning air. JP froze. Bruce held his breath. A fat head poked from one of the tent's openings and looked up at the dark sky and shook in disgust.

"Son of a bitch," they heard the bowling ball say, then more zipping.

One spindly leg made its way out of the tent, covered only in a cowboy boot, followed by the other, and a pair of red boxer shorts. They backed out and the half-naked cowboy emerged and waddled urgently to the trees. He turned his back to the saboteurs, applied both hands to his midsection and tipped his head back in relief. A steamy cloud rose in front of him.

Bruce looked back at JP who'd shifted onto his stomach and was watching from under the cab. The cowboy jiggled and jogged back to his tent, then stopped, trying to sort out what he saw through the grey light. The truck leaned lamely to one side. He started to walk over but the wind picked up and whipped the droplets against his fat breasts. He wrapped his arms around his chest and dove back into the tent. The zipper closed with finality.

JP held still for a second, then jogged back to Bruce, keeping the truck between him and the tents. They headed back to camp.

~

The rain did burn off and by afternoon the sun sat heavy above the lodge, drying the damp earth and filling the air with a thick musk of warm water and soil. With dark clouds still scattered through the big sky and knowing the fickle nature of mountain weather, the rest of the guys had decided to stay close to the cabin that day. Paul and Norton organized and traded from their boxes of nymph patterns at one of the tables. David sipped on a beer just off the corner and kept his leg propped.

At first, he had been extremely tight-lipped about his injury, not letting anyone help him get around. When he'd wince because of unintended weight or a tweak, he'd wave off anyone asking if he was all right. Yet as the days went along and he noticed everyone's equal interest in Paul's wounds—how they were healing, what the scars were going to look like, how heroic they were—David started to allow for a hand on the cabin's stairs or valiantly acknowledged the pain when someone caught a grimace. The inalterable difference was that his wound would heal completely. Once the prognosis had run its course, David would walk and wade in the river as he always had, having nothing to show for the day he lay battered at the feet of a leaping mountain lion. But his brother would. He would always have those heroic scars across his shoulder and two violent bolt marks inverted on his left forearm.

David took a sip of his beer and watched Paul organize a pile of Copper Johns. "Hey, when this ankle finally heals up, you want to get that aspen mantle again?"

"Sure," Paul said.

A pause settled until Norton spoke. "How is the ankle, David?" he asked.

"I'll be back on it soon—Paul, when are the girls getting here?"

"About a week," he said absently, still focused.

David looked back to Norton and winked. "In about a week."

JP and Bruce walked back into camp. The sun had stared to dry their heads and shoulders, but otherwise, they were soaked.

"Looks like it was a nice hike," David said with a sarcastic sneer.

"Aw, it wasn't bad enough to send us back until we got a ways out," JP said.

"Where did you go?" Norton asked. He didn't notice Bruce trying to pull himself away.

"Aww, just upstream a bit," JP said casually.

"Did you see those cowboys?" David asked directly. "If not, we should probably go talk to them—"

Paul spoke, not looking up. "Let them be. They can do their own thing as long as they don't bother us." He squinted in the sunlight and peered into one of his fly boxes, and then back at his notebook.

"I dunno," David said. "It may not be a bad idea to go check out what's going on up there. I'd go, if I could."

"Let it be. They're a couple miles up the road."

JP looked at Paul for a long second and then walked up to the lodge, almost trotting. When he caught up, Bruce asked, "Why didn't you tell 'em?" and JP put a finger to his lips and winked, "Around the campfire." They stepped onto the porch and removed their shirts, hanging them on the railing to dry.

Norton continued to David, "I saw one of them fishing the other day and he wouldn't say anything to me, even when I waved to him from across the river."

"I get that bad vibe as well."

"Let's focus on something else," Paul said with finality. "We don't need to—oh, speaking of…"

Two trucks rolled down the road, wet gear packed in the back. Bruce shot a quick glance at JP, who smiled and let his tongue hang out. The trucks stopped. The aspen and the bowling ball got out and walked over to Paul and David, leaving a couple friends still in the cabs. Norton drifted, in a subconscious move of parental protection, to the horseshoe pit where Adrian was keeping score.

Paul nodded to the two cowboys as they approached.

"Just wanted to say sayonara. We're heading out," the aspen said as he ambled over to the two brothers. The bowling ball narrowed his eyes and looked around camp intensely. He crossed his arms across his cauldron-sized belly and one hand came close to resting on the handle of his revolver.

"Okay," David said. "Take care." Silence settled until one of the horseshoes clanged off the post. "Five-seven," Adrian chirped happily from the background.

Paul stood, took off his ratty hat and set it on the table, wiping his brow with the back of his forearm. "You guys enjoy your time here?" he asked kindly.

The bowling ball furrowed his brow. "Parts of it," he said and nodded at the cabin. "I see you've been hard at work."

"Yeah, this guy designed it." Paul lightly whacked David on the shoulder. "You should have seen us out here, busting our asses. Even that little guy was running around doing his part. Now we're fishing—"

"Great fishing," the bowling ball interrupted, leaving a hard stop.

"Yeah, great fishing…" Paul trailed off and met his dark gaze. He held it for a moment and then betrayed an honest confusion at the bowling ball's tenseness.

He nodded to David's ankle. "None of your friends are giving you those kisses?"

"No," David said and stiffened in his chair.

The bowling ball continued, now looking around camp, "Looks like two of you boys got pretty wet this morning." He nodded at Bruce and JP, drying their clothes.

"Yeah," David said coolly. "It was raining."

The bowling ball looked at David and squinted. "It sure was...partner."

"Well," said the aspen as if he were continuing a more friendly conversation. "We had some problems with the trucks, a couple of bum tires. So we're going to get them taken care of, and then be back *later*." The smile dropped off his face like a trapdoor had opened in his chin.

Paul looked down at the aspen, eclipsing him with his shadow. "Sounds good there—"he turned to the bowling ball "—partner."

The bowling ball looked back at him, the top of his cowboy hat coming just above Paul's shoulder and then glanced at his forearm. The two marks glistened in the damp light. A flicker of genuine interest flashed away the bowling ball's scowl. Paul caught the wider eyes and crossed his hand over the marks.

"Looks like you took a bad fall there, big fella. You boys seem pretty accident prone," the bowling ball said with a dark smile.

David bolted upright, but Paul put a hand on his shoulder. "Is there anything we can help you guys with?" he said calmly.

"No, we'll be on our way," the aspen said.

"See you later then."

"Okay, sayonara," said the aspen.

"We'll see you around though," the bowling ball said as they turned and got back in their truck. The doors slammed shut and Paul and David watched them drive up the road in silence. The truck curled around the corner of the pines and its grumble blew into the wind. They heard the clink of a horseshoe and Adrian excitedly declare a winner.

"Jesus, those guys really are a bunch of jackasses," Paul said finally. "What was their deal?"

"I told you. That fatass was in my face last time too," David said.

"Who needs that?" Paul said shaking his head, walking back to the lodge and rubbing his forearm. He passed Bruce and JP who'd been watching and listening. They averted their gazes. From the corner of Paul's eye, he noticed.

~

People that study these things will usually agree that everything in the universe, at some level, is attracted to everything else. However faint the charge, the book in your hand is attracted to your fingers; your body is attracted to a mountain. But if two objects get a like-charge in them, they can repel one another—sometimes in a violent explosion of sparks and energy. We've all experienced that in one way or another. Well, as those cowboys drove away on that rainy day, a charge was put into the St George's Angling Club. At first, it would move around quietly and discreetly like a mouse in the far corner of a room. It would soon become bolder and palpable, like a burr in their socks. Finally it would venture out into the light and cause a real reaction. Though, like most events of cosmic origin, it took a while for the various conditions around that charge to come to a head. And then an instant to explode.

Hunting hadn't been much of a discussion point in the previous years because no one had much interest and the meat wasn't needed. But after the run in with the mountain lion, a couple guys had offered to pick up a rifle on their run for supplies. "Just get more bear mace so everyone can carry one," Paul had said with his brother sitting nearby. They had picked up a few canisters of the predator specific pepper spray and that was the end of that, for a while.

Now, with the image of that fat cowboy resting his breakfast link fingers on the butt of his pistol and his belittling of their injuries fresh in David's mind, he thought about that conversation. But before he could get his brother's attention to discuss, Paul came out the door of the cabin carrying a half dozen fly boxes and looked right at JP and Bruce as they dealt a hand of cards on the porch.

"Did you guys mess with those cowboys this morning?" he asked with the calmness of a breeze ahead of black clouds. He filled the doorframe, palming four boxes in one hand, but didn't need an answer. JP's poor poker face gave them away. "What did you do?" he asked and the black clouds drew closer.

"Aw, we just messed with their trucks, let some air outta their tires. That's all," JP said casually glancing up from his cards.

"*WHY WOULD YOU DO THAT?*" Paul thundered.

"Hey—easy! Just having a little fun. I was just trying to send a message, you know?"

"What message was that?"

"That this is our spot, our river and we don't need their trouble..." he trailed off, "you know?"

"No, I don't *know*. The only message you sent was 'I'm an idiot.' Now we've got hothead cowboys thinking we're down here to fuck with them. This isn't some roadside bar in the Ozarks, JP—we've got an old doctor and a kid, in addition to some girls on the way in a few days. And I won't attempt to understand the logic of making someone leave by letting the air out of their tires."

Paul stormed away, not allowing a reply, and sat back down at the table with his brother. JP rolled his eyes and shrugged it off, pretending not to care, and turned back to his hand. The other guys were out of earshot or had lost interest after Paul's initial thunder.

But David had been listening. "How'd you know they'd done something?" he asked after a minute of watching his brother attempt to refocus on organizing the four boxes he'd gathered.

Paul looked up from his notebook and leaned forward on his thick arms. "No one acts like that big of a dick for no reason: something pissed them off. The fat one nodded at JP and Bruce when they were hanging out their clothes, like he thought they were guilty of something—they did look it—and as they drove away I noticed they had on two spares." He shifted his accent to an exaggerated twang. "And I made me a heck'uva guess."

"Nice work, Sherlock."

Paul shook his head and dropped his hands in exasperation. "Why would they do that?"

David shrugged and then spoke casually. "We should buy a rifle soon."

Paul looked at his brother like he'd chewed the head off a fish. "*What—why?* To *shoot* them if they come back? Is everyone losing their damn minds around here?!"

"No—*relax*. I've been thinking about our plans to stay here through the winter," David said half lying. "We need to be able to hunt. We won't be able to fish all winter and even if we can, it's going to be freezing at—"

"I know how cold it's going to get, David. I probably know better than you. Can we just not talk about this right now? I just want to organize my goddamn fly boxes and not think about guns, or the freezing winter, or angry rednecks, or stupid rednecks that provoke other rednecks into being angry." He put up a hand for himself, stopping. "Let's just talk about this later. I've thought about the rifle aspect too—for hunting, not some weird old west score settling—and it probably isn't a bad idea. You can do the shooting, whenever your ankle gets better. Maybe I'll learn how to clean a deer."

David nodded contently.

That night, Paul's frustration had dissipated, but his resolve to prevent further idiocy had not. As camp gathered around the fire with plates of fish and potatoes, he quieted everyone to talk.

"Gents, a quick moment of your time. As you know,

Gretchen and a few ladies are making their way to the valley in a few days—I think in a little red jeep—and I have no doubt that we'll all keep living as we are, and I have no desire for anyone to change their habits. Scratch yourself, burp, fart—like that Adrian?—and do whatever.

"The reason I'm being dramatic is that these are ladies, and will need the occasional moment of privacy. That's just the way females are, as we all know, but we should use this occasion as an opportunity to establish that when there is a decision to be made, with this club—say, to give up bunks and sleep in tents outside, or build a makeshift changing area—that we vote on them, so everyone is on the same page. That seem fair? So no one does anything we're not in agreement on."

JP's smile faded as he took in what was happening. He stared into the fire, a little crease of irritation at the corner of his eye. Paul didn't notice, but did catch his brother's eye. David had a mild look of shock at his brother holding court over the St George's Angling Club.

Paul looked away. "Okay," he said slowly. "Two things to vote on. First, that we use a couple spare tarps, and those sun showers that we never use, to build a little shower room towards the back of the meadow." He waved into the darkness. "They may want to use the bathing pool, but I'm inclined to think they'd rather have a private shower." He took a sip of his drink, darted his eyes to his brother, and then scratched the back of his neck. "The other is less of a vote, and more of a request for a volunteer. There are twelve bunks and eleven of us. I will pitch a tent—"

"Yeah you will," Ian joked.

"Yes I will, and sleep with Gretchen. But that will leave us with two bunks for three girls. I know they won't mind sleeping in there with you all, but I'm asking one of you to sleep out—"

"We will!" Adrian chimed before he could finish.

"Good man, Adrian. Okay, so that leaves an extra bunk

inside anyway. Good enough. Probably not a bad idea to put a little distance between them and you clowns."

"I'll sleep outside too," Stoss said. "I've found the cabin a bit stifling, to be honest." He finished his drink and didn't notice David grimace a little.

Paul continued, "Okay, well, now with the shower—"

"Christ, of course, we'll build the shower. It'll take ten minutes to string up," David said icily. "You don't need to *vote* on it."

"Well, let's just vote anyway, as a club," Paul said.

David rolled his eyes and stuck his hand mockingly in the air. "Okay, who votes in favor of building a shower for the ladies?"

Everyone put a hand up casually. Adrian put his whole arm straight up in the air, like he knew the answer.

"Whew, glad we established that," David said.

"Alright, alright. I was just establishing some procedure."

"What if there had been a tie?" Norton asked. "We might as well have a president, or someone to break the ties."

"Oh my goodness," David said, exasperated. "A president?"

The eyes around the fire gravitated towards Paul.

"Yeah, it should be Paul," Bruce said.

"Cougar hunter," someone echoed.

"El Presidente."

JP said with his grin, "You could be The Master-baiter!" He howled and slapped his leg. The crease of irritation had left his eye; it had moved to David's.

Paul laughed with everyone else. "That's one name, I guess," he said. Adrian looked on curiously.

JP pointed at Paul's scars, just visible under his rolled up sleeves. "Paul, you gotta be first president."

"No kidding. Teddy Roosevelt's got nothing on those," Norton joked, but not loudly.

Paul looked down at his wounds, a little startled. "Doesn't matter to me, but we should rotate the position. I nominate David to take it next, after me."

David's eyes darted around the group. "Jesus, I don't know if I'd want to be in a debate with this bunch, much less have to deal with breaking ties." He sat upright, pretending that he was joking, but his acerbic words burnt through the thin varnish of humor. "What are we really 'voting on' any-way?" The heads shifted his way slowly. "We just need to get up and fish or do what floats our boat? We didn't need to *vote* on building a shower out of tarps and plastic bags. Seems like we're breaking our 'life is movement' rule."

"It's just for club matters and stuff," Norton said a little helplessly and looked back to Paul.

Paul nodded. "This isn't a big deal. Might as well have a little order to it, right?"

David shifted in his chair. "I guess so," he said and fin-ished his glass. He sat back. The joints of the chair made an audible creak and the fire cracked in response. "*Voting*," he said under his breath.

Norton clapped his hands and pulled Adrian up to his lap. "Well, there we go. Paul's president."

"Master-baiter!" Adrian exclaimed.

Laughs exploded around the firering, mostly from JP, and the regular evening resumed. Adrian grinned, though not entirely sure why his joke was funny. David seemed to be the only one having trouble smiling back.

The charge in St George's shifted a little.

~ 6 ~

A FEW DAYS LATER, Adrian was up early and looked over to his dad through the flat light of their tent. He knew that he'd want to sleep longer; any time Dad put him to bed earlier than usual, he wanted to sleep in a little later than usual.

But he also knew the rules and tapped him on the shoulder. Norton opened his customary one eye, "Yeah?"

"I need to explore." His voice came out in a hoarse whisper and he bent his head down, looking at his dad from the tops of his eyes.

Norton rubbed his curly hair, thinking it through, his headache not helping. He looked back at The Explorer, still with creases from the pillow on his thin, red cheeks and his hair a ruffled mess. "Okay. Tell me the three rules for exploring by yourself."

Before Norton had finished the word *rules*, Adrian had chirped, "Carry the bear spray, always be able to see the road and never go near the river."

"And how long before you have to check in with me?"

"Half hour." He tapped his little wristwatch.

"Get out of here."

Adrian unzipped the tent door and crawled out into the meadow, past two more tents staked a comfortable distance away. The cool summer morning was just getting started and the grass was covered in dew. He waded through the dampness, touching each blade and thinking about why they could be wet. It hadn't rained. That seemed strange. He'd ask his dad later.

He walked onto the porch of the lodge and grabbed a can of spray and thought through how to use it. In vivid detail, he could remember his dad holding it at arms length and firing one of the canisters, with a strong breeze at their back, and showing him how to pull the trigger. He looked down at the nozzle; his mouth watered and he felt a little nauseous. The breeze had shifted after Norton had pulled the trigger and he remembered how that miniscule whiff of spray had tasted. He clipped it onto his belt and walked past the red jeep—he had heard it arrive the night before after he'd been sent to bed—and a rope tethering something on the other side.

"Percy!" he cried.

The black lab popped her ears, like car doors coming open, cocked her head and let out a nervous whine. Adrian hugged her and she licked his face. "I thought I heard you last night, but Dad said I had to stay in bed," he said in a delicate lilt as her tongue lapped over his smiling face. "Okay, okay," he said scrunching and laughing. He pushed her down. "I'll be back. Now go back to bed; I want you to get a little more shut eye." She let out another little whine. Adrian scratched her behind the ears and then waved good-bye. She perked her head back up as he walked past the red jeep and whined again.

Adrian began exploring a morning that would lead to many wonders. He wandered east on the old service road, remembering the rules and eventually spotted an old dead branch, just in the shadows. He knelt down and saw the ants and termites and bugs that crawled and ate at the crevices. He kept walking into the woods, the sight of the road tethering his course, keeping him parallel. Though he was a relatively well traveled explorer, the woods continued to reveal new layers and nuances along its floor as the dark trees watched overhead. He found mushrooms that looked like they'd been colored with orange markers, covered in salt and then given fish gills. He found an insect that looked like a piece of black licorice with a bunch of creepy legs that looked like the hair from his teacher's nose. He found a patch of purple flowers that were so bright he thought they weren't real or maybe—using a blunt intuition of unclear origin—poisonous. He found a frog the color of wet cement; though it could hop way farther than he could reach, making it uncatchable. He found some big tracks, but they looked like Percy's or some other dog's. He even found a discarded cigar.

Then he came across an old bone, half buried in the ground, near a tree. He knew it was an animal bone, but a moment went by where he sorted through the idea of digging it out. There was something bigger to it, he felt, and he gave the white fin a hard squint before kneeling down. He thought it smelled like his friend's basement as he brushed aside the pine needles and the bits of soil. Lined black and green, fuzzy in every crevice and crack, the bone lay before him. It looked like a boomerang. He picked it up and turned it over carefully. He was never afraid to get his hands filthy, but something about the smell made him think he'd better hold it lightly. Then a breeze blew through the trees and the smell intensified. He set the bone down and covered it again, standing and, for reasons he didn't consciously detect, looked into the tree.

Violent ripples of fear tore through his mind—an electric machete slicing through synapses. First he yelped and screamed as cool adrenaline surged through his chest; then he cowered and cried out almost in pain, stumbling backwards; then a strangely different fear and he turned and stumbled to run. But then, suddenly and rather unexpectedly, he had a lucid awareness, a calmness, to recognize what stared back at him, hanging from the low branch of the tree. He stopped and looked again.

It was a deer carcass. It hung, lifeless, mouth agape, with the remains of two legs dangling to the side. The back, the hindquarters, the hips were gone and the eyes had long since rotted out, leaving only a dry vessel of hair, skin and bones. At this point, the flies had lost interest. He knew it had once been a deer, somehow. Then he stepped away, not turning his back, and trotted to the road.

Adrian understood death but only as an abstract concept spread throughout a vague cosmos of slowly sharpening facts in his life. To him, death was almost a person, like a deliveryman or the guy who fixed the dishwasher—a some-one or some*thing* that came and took things away, made them not here anymore. Death was why he didn't have a mom—Dad had talked about that a lot—but he didn't blame this death character or even get the sense that he should blame him, or even have any feelings towards him at all. He didn't understand why Dad cried when he talked about death. That's just what death did. That's how it worked.

But he realized now, as he walked down the old road, that he didn't really understand death. There was more to learn, just like there had been more to learn with the word *clean*. That deer was dead. He knew that. The deer looked like it might have been very sad and hurt, even though it was dead. Death was probably not that nice, he guessed. This all seemed like something to ask Dad about.

If he'd had more time to think about it, he'd have worried that death hadn't been nice to his mom either. But he never got that far. His little wristwatch chirped indicating the hour. He kicked up to a trot and was almost back, when he heard the Elizabeth laugh.

He stopped.

Then he heard it again. He knew the rule, but looking in-to the deer's hollow sockets had clawed a small trench somewhere inside of him and he, without thinking about it, went to explore where this laugh came from. He had to. He stepped off the road and crept to the bank. He stayed low, not wanting anyone to see him breaking the rules and looked through the branches and leaves of a little bush at the river.

A woman lay naked on a long rock. Her blond hair was

wet and fell around her shoulders gently. Her head was tipped back in a smile. Under the shoulders were delicate breasts. Her flat stomach gave way to a little patch of hair, nestled lightly between her two tan legs that scissored around each other as she shifted onto her side and put an arm under her head. She scratched her nose and looked at the pool, biting her lower lip gently. A large man treaded water, looking back at her, wearing only his hat, carelessly turned backwards. Adrian couldn't hear what they were saying over the din of the Elizabeth, but he could tell Paul and Gretchen were happy and enjoying a bath together. Gretchen smiled again and pointed a finger at Paul, and shook it with no real intention. He shrugged, flicking a little water at her. She scrunched her nose and wiped the drops away with deliberate theatrics and pointed again. Before he dunked under water, he threw his hat onto the rock next to her. She picked it up and put it on backwards, in the same careless manner he'd worn it, and waited for him to surface.

Adrian didn't know why, but the interaction put a warmth in his chest. He watched their happiness for a moment longer and then crept back to the road. He looked at his watch and then jogged past the lodge, past Percy, through the drying field to his tent, thirty two minutes since he'd left it.

"You're late, Ade," the tent mumbled before he shook it.

"Sorry, can I go back out?"

"Yes. Thirty minutes. I mean that."

"Okay."

~

Nearby, hearing the father-son discussion, David opened his heavy eyelids too. He rubbed his face with one hand and looked at his other arm, trapped under a sleeping, blond head of hair. She had arrived with Gretchen the night before and her name was Anna. He listened to the sounds of the waking hoppers in the grasses around the tent and to Adrian's footsteps fading back into the woods. He surgically dislodged his arm out from under Anna's head, and crept gingerly out of the tent to start some breakfast. He'd given up the crutches the day before and was making his best efforts to walk normally; he'd gone back to waving off help. He hobbled over to one of the new coolers and a memory made him lightly pump his fist and in gratitude.

After the red jeep had pulled into camp, the guys had watched with a strange mix of wariness and competitiveness in their hearts as Paul had greeted Gretchen. After pleasantries with the other three women, Paul lifted down the coolers from the roof of the red jeep and, obeying an unconscious animal command, opened them. He let out a whoop and held up salsa, olives, cheeses, garlic, lemons and limes, vinegar, salad fixings, fresh coffee, maple syrup, meats, and fruits. In some sort of unspoken animal reversion, each of the guys had become content to eat simple meals of starch and fish over their time in the valley. This act of kindness and generosity filled a small void they weren't aware of and instantly made everything about the arrival of these unknown females wonderful—other than the stirring of their innate drives. As is the natural course, that gratitude had blossomed into full celebration that carried well into the night.

David now sifted through his headache and the coolers, and began preparing breakfast and the gratitude he would receive for having done so. He rubbed his face and pushed back his hair and organized some bacon, pancake mix and fruit on the cooking table as Paul and Gretchen walked into camp, swaying back and forth with each step—Paul in jeans and a t-shirt, Gretchen in jeans and a grey hoodie with Paul's hat turned backwards carelessly over her long blond hair.

"Morning. Where'd you two run off to?" David asked.

"Just a little early, balls-cold bath. Nothing better after a late night," Paul said.

"Not bad, eh, Gretch?

"Best bath I've ever had," she said and handed Paul's ratty hat back to him, looking at it like it was the first time she'd seen it. She giggled. "I can't believe I had that on my head. I may need to bathe again." She winked at David.

David nodded to Paul's arm as he took the hat. "Those are some pretty impressive wounds on your boy there, huh?"

The question sucked the smile off her lips. She pursed them to the side. Her eyes glistened. She shrugged lightly and shifted her weight to one foot, the other knee bending gingerly. "I'm just glad you two are standing here. That's all." Paul put his arm around her; the two gnarled markings draped next to her beautiful face. She clasped his wrist and pressed her cheek against the wounds softly.

"Sorry," David said sincerely. "Didn't mean to bring up something touchy."

"It's alright. Sorry myself—you guys aren't in your back-yard." She looked around the tree tops and the mountains beyond.

"So, you ready to take on this winter with us?" David said. Paul furrowed his brow at his brother.

Gretchen looked up at David and wiped her eyes firmly. "Yes, though—" she straightened and put one hand on her hip, "—I have been talking with Paul and am a little nervous that we're not thinking about food through the winter cor-rectly. I agree with you David: we should be hunting for deer."

He gave her a long gaze and then nodded, "Paul and I will probably get a rifle together soon."

"Great," she said continuing her tone of authority. "Then we can decide when, and how much meat to take." A shadow of self-consciousness passed over her face and she took her hand from her hip and twirled the ends of her hair. "But ei-ther way, I'm excited for this...this adventure with you guys."

"Me too," Paul said.

"Me three, guys," David echoed in a high pitched, self-mocking voice.

Neither of them caught David's sarcasm as Gretchen

looked up at Paul and made playful cat claws at his big chest. He smiled down at her and kissed the top of her head. "I'm going to get a fire going for that bacon," he said and gave Gretchen a squeeze.

As the late moon set in the west, and Paul teased the flames from the firepit in one match, and David pulled food from the coolers, everyone seeped out of camp's pores in that pathetic, asynchronous matriculation to nourishment that follows a night of heavy drinking. The ladies were up first, circling by the fire in sweatshirts and jeans. Soon the lodge door swung open and JP rubbed his head and walked onto the front porch with his boxers blowing in the early breeze; then he remembered the ladies, and waved to them. Bruce walked out a moment later, not paying attention to anyone, and went down to the river to soak his head. Stoss strolled up to the group around the fire, having quietly prepared coffee for everyone on a stove inside. A few guys looked sideways at one another about the gesture, but the ladies thanked him profusely. David took a cup and managed the skillet, sizzling cakes and bacon into the warming summer air.

Perhaps the happiest member of camp that morning was Percy, who after enough whining and barking was released from her tether and bolted into the woods. She didn't return for almost half an hour, finally trotting into camp on the opposite side of the meadow from where she left with a flat bone in her mouth.

Adrian watched her approach him as she set it down at The Explorer's feet and wagged her tail. He looked at her quizzically and scratched her ears. While The Explorer was eating his pancakes, he held court and answered questions from four inquisitive and adoring female reporters.

"No. They were short," Adrian said, clarifying the height of two foxes he'd seen by the riverside the second time out.

"How cute! Will you take me to where you saw them?" Gretchen asked.

"Sure. But they probably won't be there."

Adrian picked up a bite of pancake and stuffed it in his mouth. A thin hair of syrup, connecting the fork to the plate, transferred itself to his chin. He raised his other hand, arming his sleeve for cleanup.

"Use your napkin, Ade," Paige said, flicking an ant off her jeans.

Paige Franco still considered herself Adrian's mom's best friend. She had organized Karen Tuttle's sixteenth birthday, her bachelorette party and her funeral. On her dresser still sat a picture of her and Karen, skinny and in throws of puberty, each with a mouthful of smiling braces as they walked off the soccer field. So in the months after Karen's death, it had been impossible for her to talk to Norton. The thought of his name, much less Karen's, brought back a torrent of memory, not least of which, was a baby boy cradled in his father's arms during a foggy funeral by the ocean.

But the second-hand pictures and stories about Adrian rattled a dormant instinct that grew and waged war on her grief, until finally she couldn't stay away any longer, and swung by Norton's apartment one afternoon. It didn't take long before she swung by more often, sometimes bringing Percy, her black lab, sometimes bringing lunch or staying for dinner, until she finally inserted herself into the rotating roster of caretakers for Adrian. She had assumed the position of a friend to both of them, and remained excruciatingly vigilant in maintaining that role—and that role only. So upon hearing that her favorite guy in the whole world was going to be gone for the entire summer, she searched—sometimes with a self reflective laugh at her franticness—for a way to get her fix. Norton sensed it and through Paul, connected Paige with Gretchen and her two friends, Anna and Denise.

Now she sat to the background and just smiled at The Explorer, while the other three women passively fought for airtime to exercise their own unused, but ever waking, maternal ways.

Adrian paused, caught, and used his napkin to clean the

syrup.

"Thanks," Paige said. Her brilliant light blue eyes, sprinkled with small flecks of yellows like a sunflower sparkled in the morning light. The athleticism she developed on the soccer field had never faded, she'd kept it going through yoga and now she uncrossed and recrossed a pair of thighs tight enough to hold a tune.

David walked to the fire and asked for everyone's attention. "Ladies, again, welcome. I hope your headaches are going away faster than mine. As advertised, there is no structure and nowhere to be while you're here. Do what you'd like. I thought a fun activity for today would be to pack up lunches and go to the end of the valley where the river splits apart and there are some pretty cool waterfalls. We named them The Giant Steps and we can swim, bring cocktails, etcetera. That train will probably leave in about an hour. The rest of you should enjoy the river around here, the hammocks or the woods for a hike. I know a few guys are planning on fishing, of course. Paul and I built you a shower in the far corner of the meadow if you need it and there is a latrine about two hundred yards back that way. Also...."

"He's quite the organizer," Paige said quietly to the other girls when he was done.

Gretchen rolled her eyes. "He may be—" she poked Anna "—is he *quite the* anything else?"

She pursed her lips but couldn't suppress a grin, then jumped up with the rest of the group and got ready for the day.

A soft lid of clouds settled over the summer heat—dark and threatening with rain, but with pillowy edges that quelled their intimidation. Fleeting afternoon storms were common this time of year, and for better or for worse, signified the start of summer's home stretch.

~ 7 ~

AS THE SUN STARTED TO MELT into the tops of the western pines a few days later, JP pulled into camp in one of the trucks. He'd drawn the short straw the previous night and had made the day run for supplies. When others had offered to keep him company he'd waved them off. "No reason for anyone else to burn a day off the water," he'd said nobly.

Now, he stepped out of the truck quietly and grabbed two massive bags from the bed and walked to the cabin. Paul and Gretchen sat at a table playing rummy and watched him saunter past, not making eye contact. He'd been gone for a while, almost the whole day and as Paul watched him pass, he took notice of the way JP averted his eyes. Paul had seen a distant relative of that guilt before when he cornered him on the porch about the cowboys. As JP walked back to the truck, Paul slid out of his chair and walked up behind him.

"How's it going?"

JP jumped and half turned around. "Fine, fine," he didn't look Paul in the eye. Paul looked at his face closely and realized it wasn't guilt; it was nervousness. Close but different. JP continued, "I bought a couple gifts for the club—well, I guess one is for you and your brother. The other is for—well, for me. I wanted to make it a surprise, but I suck at this kind of thing."

Paul took a step back, a little ashamed of his intention. "Sorry man, I was just checking on you—or—seeing if you needed help unloading."

"It's okay. I probably looked like a creep."

Paul laughed. "I can leave it alone if you want to give your gifts when everyone is around."

JP looked up at Paul and an honest relief came over his face. "No, I'll show you."

Paul saw two black cases in the bed of the truck, recognizing one as a guitar, but squinting at the other. It was long, slender and triangular like it encased a skinny horn. Paul looked at it for a moment, trying to figure out what instrument it was until JP explained, "Got you a nice rifle for the winter."

Paul unconsciously stepped back from the truck. "Wow," he said stuttering a little. "Um—thank you. David and I have been talking about—or—meaning to buy one, so this is great."

JP's face refilled with confidence. "No problem. I heard you talking about getting one that day I was a real dumbshit and messed with those cowboys. Anyway, I respect that you guys are going to do something like gut it out here for the winter."

"Yeah, man. Thank you." Paul stared at the long black triangular case and realized that he stared at an apology.

"The last part is that I'd like to show you or David how to use it. I did a little hunting when I was younger and have a good sense about guns."

"That'd be great. I'm on the hook for taking care of her," he deftly jerked his thumb at Gretchen watching intently from the table. "We would love a lesson. I probably couldn't hit that mountain over there, so that'd be great."

"Great. I got a couple boxes of rounds in the cab as well. But for now," he popped his eyebrows and pushed his hair back, "I'm going to get out this guitar and play, so you better hold onto Gretchen nice and tight there, big fella. Don't let 'er outta your sight." He slapped Paul right between his shoulder blades and his grin cut a V-shaped canyon across his face.

"Why didn't you tell us you could play guitar? That would have been really fun."

He shrugged and Paul noted a quick glance to Gretchen at the table. "Dunno. Just didn't feel right before."

"Well…glad you are now." Paul turned and walked back to the table of cards.

"What was all that about?" Gretchen asked sardonically as he sat down. "He bring back a body or something?"

"Got us a rifle for hunting this winter—and a guitar to woo your friends."

She focused on the half of the statement that resonated. "Well, he better woo fast, and stop being such a goof. Anna's already into David; Denise isn't in to him, not her type. I'm not sure about Paige, but I don't get the sense she is either." She paused and waved her hand by Paul's eye. "You listening?"

He looked up at her but his gaze was still elsewhere. "David and I should have bought that gun together."

Gretchen glanced back at JP unloading the truck. "Oh," she said softly.

Paul continued to himself, "I don't mind killing a deer for meat, but I had it in my head that David and I would pick the gun out and buy it together."

"You can still learn together."

"I know," he looked her in the eye, "You don't need to learn to use it if you don't want to."

"Well, I *should*—right? In case you and David can't hunt."

"I guess," he said absently.

"I *should*," she repeated, then continued with pain in her voice, "I'm going to hold my own."

Paul engaged her eyes and forced a friendly smile. "I know," he said. "Anyway—sorry—enough of that. Whose turn is it?"

She locked in with his gaze. "What's the matter?"

"Nothing—I think it's your turn."

"You sure?"

He opened his eyes wide, like he was turning out his pockets, and shrugged his shoulders. "I'm sure—it's your turn."

"Okay, okay. Just give me a sec, cow*boy*." She forced a smile back, finishing with a mock twang.

As she discarded, and the sun started to filter through the low boughs, the faint but delicate strum of a guitar emanated from the porch—a light brushstroke of color on the evening. Then there was silence. A songbird filled in the void with a little chirp, getting close to resonating with one of the tones she had just heard. Then another strum, more slowly, as each of the six strings were plucked individually, in succession. The increasing tones resonated off the cabin and into the meadow; then another, a different, higher chord. And then a foot started patting, then tapping, as JP gained his confidence and was stomping his feet, smiling and playing tunes into the sunset.

Over the next hour of music and cards, folks started appearing back in camp. Paige found herself drifting towards the southern extrovert and soon she and JP were searching for songs to play together. Adrian and Norton returned with a couple fish between them, but when Adrian saw a game of horseshoes going, he quickly handed his catch to his dad and ran over to keep score.

At last, David returned.

"This is my last hand," Paul said to Gretchen when he saw him arriving. She nodded in agreement. JP finished his song with Paige, and ducked into the cabin. David caught his brother's beckoning glance as he entered camp; they talked quietly for a moment, and then went inside.

JP had opened the canvas case and held the gun gingerly, like it was hot. Paul started forward to take a hold of it, but stopped and looked it over from a distance away in JP's shifting hands—the black barrel, the brown body, the heavy bolt, the dangling finger of the trigger and the thin hourglass scope all had an indifference about them in the dim, evening light.

"Wow," Paul said. "A fly rod has more pieces."

"Well, there is a pretty little firing mechanism in here," JP said coolly, tapping the body.

"This is really nice," David said slowly. "We would have bought it anyway…so this saved us a purchase."

"Well guys, we've had our ups and downs but when it's all said and done, you invited me here, twice, and now I feel a part of, well, *something*. Here—give her a feel."

David held the rifle and in his hands it seemed to become imbalanced and shaky. He shifted the body and the barrel from one to the other, but with each motion, the instrument assaulted his grip, like it could push him aside and free itself from him at any moment. A darkening came over his eyes.

"What?" Paul asked.

"Nothing. Just need to learn to use this. Feels awkward," David said putting a finger on the round knob of the bolt.

"Well," Paul said with a laugh. "Figure it out. That's our other meal ticket now. Let me see." He took the rifle, his big hand covering the neck, his thick index finger resting on the side of the trigger guard, his thumb wresting on the back. "Heavier than I'd guessed," he said. But it moved smoothly in the air, balanced perfectly. He fingered the bolt with his other hand and took it in his palm and gave the black handle a smooth pull, locking the chamber with a resounding click. He lifted the barrel and brought the handle to his chin, tipping his head and putting one eye into the scope.

Through the lens, through the window of the cabin, and through the crosshairs, he focused on a tree. He could make out the grooves and fissures between the bark and even catch the glint of sap or a little fungus in one of the corners. The black lines and hashes of the crosshairs, imprinted next to his eye, moved with him as he scanned the bark. A squirrel poked her head around the corner of the tree and twitched. She cocked her head to one side and then the other, unaware of the man pointing the rifle at her face from inside the cabin.

Paul shoved it away and looked at the scope sideways; the blood seemed to drain from his tanned face and veins crept in the long ridge of his jaw and right under his eyes.

"You alright?" David asked cautiously.

"This will be your thing," he said quickly and extended the gun to his brother.

David didn't take it immediately and peered at the little tremor in Paul's hand. "Okay, I'll do the hunting," he said and some excitement was edited from his words.

JP glanced between the two brothers.

Paul's face relaxed as he came out of his head and the color went back through his cheeks. "It'll be good for you two," he said winking at them both. He handed the stock to David again and looked back out the window at the tree, now far away and across the meadow.

The squirrel was gone.

~ 8 ~

GRETCHEN RALLIED FOR A GIRLS-ONLY AFTERNOON the next day. They'd hidden away a couple bottles of wine and she wanted to lead a little hike where they could sit down and enjoy the afternoon and talk. She knew Paul wanted to fish. Paige, thankful for the invitation, declined to go.

As they took off, Norton and Adrian walked back into camp, their hair wet from a morning bath. Norton, for the first time, had noticed that Adrian resisted bathing just a little less. Usually getting him to soapy water was a chore, but just recently his responses had evolved from running and hiding, to shrugging and absently going through the motions. He never volunteered to bathe, but it wasn't an assault on his soul anymore either.

"Hi Paige," he said as they ambled up to the dying morning fire. He may have washed his hair but he certainly hadn't combed it, and his cheeks were pink as a rainbow's stripe.

"Hey there, you look clean."

"I caught a frog near the pool."

"You did, huh? Was it slimy?"

"No, dry."

"Okay—so what are you going to do today?"

"Fish."

Paige didn't fish; her face dropped a little, but she was growing used to this answer.

"Why—why don't you come with us?" Norton asked quickly. "Adrian can show you how he casts; maybe he'll catch dinner." He winked at his son, whose eyes widened at the idea.

"Yeah?" she said looking at Adrian, now nodding vigorously.

"Good," Norton said mentally running through the camp. "Paul and Stoss are coming too." His tone became skeptical. "David and JP were going to shoot that new gun. The other guys are already out for the day."

A half hour later, with the sun smiling overhead, a crew of five walked out of camp to fish. A short ways up the road, a finch tussled with a pair of squirrels over territory in a tree. Paige and Stoss stopped with Adrian to watch; he pointed and giggled as they ran and swooped around the branches, and chattered or squawked. Norton and Paul continued walking.

"He loves it out here," Paul said.

Norton looked over his shoulder and drew out his glance. "I couldn't think of a better way for him to spend his summer," he said reverently. "When I was his age, I was still practically blind."

"Yeah—I remember hearing when your parents figured that out."

Norton shook his head disdainfully. "Would have helped if they'd taken me to the doctor once or twice." Then lighter, "I think Ade's grown about up five years since we got here. It's hard to articulate, but he's changed so much. He asks questions with different angles. Like, the other day, he really wanted to know about the dew on the grass; he'd reasoned that the water couldn't have come from the clouds because the top of our tent wasn't wet. It seems simple, but it's a little thing like that that makes me so happy I brought him here."

"Learning not to take the world at face value."

"Yeah—asking 'why' in smarter ways."

"That's awesome," Paul said putting a hand on Norton's shoulder. "You deserve that. So does he."

Norton didn't say anything and a silence grew between

them. Paul tried to lighten the moment and spoke playfully. "So, I'm not sure when the last time I heard *you* unsure about something on the water. Feel like a 'true *fisherman*' now?" Paul made mock quotes around the words.

"I do," Norton said without hesitation, then his tone turned thoughtful. He made quotes with his fingers. "You know you '*are*' something when you can teach it. It's strange…to remember thinking I had it figured out—that I was a fisherman—when I learned to cast. That was the easy part." He made exhaustive, back and forth gestures with his arm in a mock cast. "The hard part is the science: when to fish nymphs even though there are mayflies on the water; when to fish a streamer, and then when to fish it on the swing rather than the strip; when to cast away from a stack of fish because you know one will come out of its lane and you don't have to spook the rest with the fight—all that, I'm still learning."—he laughed—"And I *really* learn that I don't know much when I try to teach Adrian; he always finds a question that throws me off."

"And you can't just say, 'I don't know'. Then you feel like you're letting him down."

"Exactly. You feel like you owe it to him to have something. So I try to come up with an answer, but he's gotten so good at sniffing out when I start talking from my ass, even a little. I can see the moment he tunes me out."

Paul shifted his rod to the other hand and rolled his broad shoulders lightly, nodding. "Interesting. His sponging brain is learning how to absorb, or triage, good and bad water. I've always thought of 'I don't know' was one of the most telling answers a person can give, shows a lot of confidence, but I guess that doesn't work—or translate—with a kid."

"Nope. They just want the answer and they want it now. But you can buy a little time and say that you'll 'figure it out together' or—"

"*Dad!*"

Norton wheeled around reactively, but his son approached smiling and pointing towards the river; Stoss and Paige walked closely behind.

"Can we fish here?" he said excitedly. "I saw a twenty incher last time."

"And you *didn't* catch it?" Paul asked, poking his side as he ran up.

Adrian's lips hardened and drew a serious line across his face as he rocked on his heels. "I couldn't cast that far," he said.

"Sure, we can fish here." Norton turned to the others. "You guys can go upstream—"

"I want to fish with Paul!" Adrian said taking one of his big hands. The father looked to the newly assigned babysitter and raised his eyebrows. Paul shrugged carelessly.

"I'll stay in case Paul wants to fish on his own," Paige said.

Norton looked between the two babysitters, gave the requisite *"just let me know"* in his eyes, then turned back to his son. "See ya, bud. Dr Ross and I are going to go upstream and fish." But Adrian had already started towards the river. Paul signed off with a quick wave and jogged up behind the boy, putting a hand over his collar as he waded into the Elizabeth. The current swarmed and bubbled around his legs as Paul loomed over the boy in the bucket hat. After a dozen fearless steps, Adrian slipped; the water rushed towards the top of his waders; Paul's hand closed.

"Careful," he said calmly. Adrian shrugged out of the grip and kept moving towards a gravel bar.

Paige shuddered and caught her breath; she noticed Norton still watching his son. He shook his head with a mix of relief and pride, then turned and walked upstream with the old doctor. She sat down cross-legged on the grass above the riverbank and watched Adrian and Paul. He bent down in front of the boy—facing him rather than standing next to him like his father—and opened his fly box. He moved a big finger through the rows of flies as they spoke. Adrian finally nodded, pinched a marabou minnow and handed it to Paul. He tied it on for him and they started to fish. When they turned back to the river, Paul's hand drifted over the boy's collar again.

Paige closed her eyes and inhaled. The dry mountain air coursed through the small spaces of her lungs, swollen with heat and life. She exhaled. Two warblers swooped overhead. The breeze picked up their wings and they shot over the trees and looked down the valley at an inviting field in the distance. They relaxed their muscles and tucked their wings on their sides, turning to bullets and dipped above the branches; then they opened their wings and glided, alighting in the trees above the field. A shadow moved slowly below them, slithering between the trees.

A fox jogged into the light.

~

The mother fox stopped and peered into the tree, looking back at the two birds and turning her head and sniffing the air. She sauntered out into a field near the base of the northern valley wall. The image of her two pups in their little den, forged between a long flat rock and the earth, flashed to her mind; they whimpered and crawled over each other. She nosed the loose earth and peered through the tall grasses and could vaguely make out the scent of a rabbit, perhaps two, but continued to sniff the ground and air. As she moved through the loose branches, the scent disappeared into the wind. She backtracked and lost it again. She sat on her hind legs and washed one of her paws, peering around the woods and at the mountains above the tree tops; their jagged grey peaks stood so high. She rarely ever looked up and their tops seemed strange points of stone.

Then she caught another scent, one she didn't recognize. As she sniffed, something glinted off a fallen tree. She looked closer and saw shiny objects in a row. She cocked her head and took a cautious step.

An explosion rang through the valley, an ominous gong.

"Nice shot!" JP hollered. David looked up from the scope and squinted, satisfied. "That can didn't stand a chance!" David bolted in another round and hastened into his second shot. He missed and the gunshot settled into the valley like a lead blanket.

"Now slow down. Those cans aren't going to run," JP said with an uncommon level of seriousness.

"I need to adjust the scope," David said, a little defense in voice.

"Well, do it then. You gotta be on-site for any deer you're lookin' to take down." JP tapped his heart lightly with a knuckle.

"Can you show me how again?"

As JP explained, David rubbed his hands; the vibrations of the recoil still shook within his tissue, then he looked through the scope—as if he were heeding advice—and imagined a big deer at the end of the crosshairs. He squeezed the trigger just to hear it click. The deer morphed into cans on a log.

"You paying attention?" JP said, the seriousness back in his tone.

David looked at him with his cheek against the scope. "Yeah."

JP grinned wryly and patted David on the shoulder. "You got a little something on your mind—a little cat on the brain?"

"What?"

"All your bird-doggin', chief," JP said loudly, then when David still didn't register: "Anna?"

"*Oh*—no. I—"

"Don't lie; I know when a man's thinkin' about a little *movement*."

"No, I wasn't. I—"

"Your brother too, with Ms Gretchen America." JP whistled through his snaggled teeth and the notes drifted high and down again in a light dance. "Lucky bastard."

David rolled his eyes and nodded to the rifle. "Gretchen? Trust me, she may not be worth the hunt."

"Chief, a girl like that is worth a whole hunting *party*. Don't you be jealous now — Anna's puttin' on her own smokeshow. Don't get your brother rivalry going on that."

"Yeah," David said trailing off and shrugging, leaving a purposeful void in the discussion.

JP gave his a long, searching gaze, then nodded. "You don't think she can hack it through the winter with you guys." He allowed for David's silence to confirm the thought. "I'll tell you — I got an eye for that sort of thing and I can guarantee she's strong enough to hold up. I have a sense about this stuff — "

"It's not that, JP. She and Paul will get in a fight and it'll be awkward and weird."

"That shit happens, man. Just do your own thing for a while if it does."

"No, you don't get it. Right now, you're getting just one of their many phases." David set down the rifle.

JP moved his hands to his pelvis and grinned. "You mean like doggy style, missionary, catcher and so on?"

David didn't acknowledge the joke. "In their relationship. This is about the millionth time they've tried to make it work. You are looking at the famed 'core proclivity' of Paul Ambrose and Gretchen Wilde."

"You make that up?"

"I did. I — "

"Then why use those funny quotation marks?"

"I just do. Let me finish. The 'core proclivity' — " he made big quotation marks " — is when their relationship is based only on passion and not much else."

"You mean they like banging?"

"Exactly. But their 'cyclical dysfunctionality' is always sure to follow."

"Stop with the quote marks. It's weird."

David continued, "Usually they are vacillating from 'temperate dating', to 'Gretch and Paul' and then, predictably, to the final 'Big Bang'—when they find a locking point and grind the machine to a sudden, and usually theatric, halt."

"Wow, chief, how come you never speak-so-smart? You're a regular fraud."

"Freud."

"I know, man. A joke. You know your stuff though."

"We're not done. Then we wait until 'the other Big Bang' when some cosmic spark causes one of them to pick up the phone and before you know it, they're cooking breakfast together." David shook his head and coughed a little.

"You ever call him out on it?"

"Of course, but he never listens—always so sure of himself. I've got my own problems with women, commitment and all the rest—I would never say otherwise—but I've told him, the problem with him and Gretch is that they know each other *too well*. It is too easy for them to slip in and out of fights, not examining them the way new couples do. If they were still in the crotch sniffing phase, they would be cautious about arguing. They would want to tease out why one was acting one way before charging in, guns blazing." He looked through the scope at the beer cans.

JP thought, then spoke quickly. "But isn't that everyone's deal with people they've know forever? It's easy to fight, but easier to forgive. That's the 'core proclivity'—right? Let stuff *go*." The moment of discovery snuck a tremble into his voice.

David took his eye away from the glass window. "Yeah…maybe."

JP continued hurriedly, "I think it is, chief. I've lived a life moving all over the damn place and had very few people I'd call my own. But you know something, forgiving the ones I do have is probably the only reason they're still around and answer my call. I mean, hell, if we don't do that we're just going to be mad all the time—and unhappy. No one wants that."

"Yeah, but the key is remembering to do it."

JP clapped his hands and let the grin hang on his face. "No *shit*, man."

David lowered his gaze into the lens and put the barcode of a can in the crosshairs. His lungs contracted smoothly and he pulled the trigger in the same rhythm. Wood shards and bark exploded off the log in abrupt concert, but the can only wobbled. "*Damn*," he hissed and shoved the gun at JP. "Show me how to use those sites. I'll listen this time."

JP pushed the barrel back. "Just take a little more practice. Relax, chief."

David met JP's eyes coldly. "Stop calling me *chief*."

JP put up his hands lightly. "Sorry, man. If your brother was *prez*, you could still be *chief*."

"I don't like it."

JP smiled. "See? Now we forgive each other. It's that easy."

"Right," David said distantly. For a brief instant, an idea lit behind the curtain of his eyes, then he shuffled it away.

JP gave him a second look and his drawl slowed. "What else you got on your mind, *David*?"

David met his eyes, then flickered away. "What are you talking about?"

"Something else is on your mind. I can see it on your face."

"Yeah—trying to hit these cans."

"That ain't it. You got some mischief on the brain; I can see it. I know that sort of thing when it passes by."

"I'm just frustrated. That's all."

JP gave him a long, unconvinced look and turned his gaze to the rifle, "Alright, let me see the gun then. But this time, listen." A dark cloud unsheathed the sun and the wind whipped between them; the cans blew off the log. "Shit," he said somberly. "We need to put a little water in those."

~

The breeze blew over Gretchen, Anna and Denise sitting cross-legged and talking. They had hiked the valley floor and spread out by the headwaters of the Elizabeth, basking in the sun and letting the waters trickle and laugh past them in the field. Gretchen sat at the head of the blanket.

"I *am* excited to stay through the winter," she said to the women on the blanket around her. "But I just can't shake the feeling from David that he's pissed that I'm here."

"He just seems like the tough-guy type when it comes to that kind of thing," Denise said quickly. Their eyes searched towards Anna.

"I think that's right," she said with pitiful conviction. "I haven't known him that long, but I can tell he's a good guy underneath."

"Trust me—he meddles; I know he does. It's hard to explain. It's just one of those things I can't put to words but I know he doesn't want me here, and if I'm going to stay," her eyes welled up a little, "I can't have this feeling that he's out to get me."

Both of the other girls nodded their heads solemnly. In their minds they wanted to ask her what the hell she was doing, but she was too far along. The river babbled past in the meadow. They were just far enough from the road for it to drown the grinding of a stopping truck.

Gretchen continued and smacked her thigh lightly. "I signed up for this rodeo, I shouldn't be crying about it. I've been dealing with David chirping in Paul's ear for years now. This won't be any different."

"Who knows," Denise said, "maybe you'll spend enough time with him and you'll make peace."

Anna looked down and then drew in her confidence. "Can I ask you something else, Gretchen?"

"Sure."

"Would you ever do something like this on your own—without Paul?"

Gretchen set down her glass and thought for a moment; before she could answer, a voice sounded from across a braid of the Elizabeth, "Howdy."

A fat cowboy stood about twenty yards away, smiling.

Gretchen looked at him cautiously and stood between him and the other two. "Hi," she said evenly.

"How you lovely ladies doing on this warm afternoon?"

"Fine," they each said coldly.

"Good. Don't mean to disturb you but we're just passing through here."

"Okay…." Gretchen let the word trail off.

"I mean *here,*" the bowling ball said with a gentle flick of his finger. "We're going to drive our trucks through the river and camp on the other side. This is the shallowest point. She gets too deep downstream and there are too many bushes upstream." He took his hat off and exposed strands of wispy, sweaty hair. "Sorry to make you move."

The aspen walked up behind him. "Howdy ladies."

Gretchen moved her hand towards the bear mace strapped on a daypack.

He put up his hands gently. "No need. We just want to pass through. We're nice guys, I promise."

Gretchen turned to the other two and started lifting the corners of the blanket. "Come on," she said quietly to the others.

The thin cowboy continued, "That bear mace stuff is great. You could take down a grizz with it, no problem."

"That's the idea," Gretchen said not looking up.

"Me?" said the fat cowboy, now with a dark smile. "I figure it's much easier to just pop them a couple." He turned his planetary waist and for the first time the women noticed he carried a gun on his long belt. He looked at the mountains. "Not to worry. We haven't seen one yet."

Gretchen nodded and they shuffled their blanket and backpacks to the side. "Is this enough room to get through?"

"Yeah. Thanks," the skinny one said with a tip of his hat.

The fat one adjusted his chalice-shaped jeans. "Say, where you camping?"

"We're not camping. My boyfriend and about ten of his friends built a lodge downriver and we're staying there."

Both cowboy hats nodded and the skin around their eyes tightened for an instant. "Nice cabin," the bowling ball said as he turned away. "See you ladies around."

The three women stood back from the water as the black tires of the big trucks plowed through the shallow current and trudged up the grasses on the far banks. The bowling ball tipped his hat as they passed.

~

When Gretchen and the girls returned to camp, the rest of the crew had already started to settle in for the evening. The late light laid its long shadows against the boughs and grasses of the valley as they walked up to the fire circle. She wasted no time telling everyone the story, complete with creepy descriptions of the bowling ball's fat fingers. She also played up how the fat cowboy had flashed his revolver in jest.

Paul nodded during the last detail. "They're just some bozos with their buddies. We'll leave them alone," he said.

As the conversation moved on and Adrian explained fish he'd caught and horseshoes clanked in the background, Paul motioned Gretchen into the cabin. She smiled as he opened the door. Under lantern light, Paul had laid out the basic rig of a fly rod, reel and line on the table inside. He'd prepared his thoughts for this discussion, practicing with Adrian that day, wanting to give Gretchen a lesson that resonated not only in content, but in interest. He had very honest fantasies about them sitting by the river and talking at great depth about all of the various nuances of each cast; though these fantasies always evolved into them naked at some point.

"I'll start with the basics. First the rod," he said as they sat down.

"Mmmm, I like this already," she said playfully and poked his side. The lantern made a white halo behind his head and shoulders.

"Oh yeah," he said in return, covering her knee with his hand and giving it a squeeze. "This is where you hold my rod—excuse me—*the* rod, right here on the cork handle. Now, that seems obvious, but the key is that this cork handle is where the power of your cast transfers from your shoulder and arm to the rod and line. In other words, this is where the magic happens, baby."

He winked and went on to explain how the pieces of the rod fit together, the line guides, the butt and where you hook your fly when it's not in use. Then he moved to the various types of line and grains, explaining the different tapers and weight distributions and what they'd mean for casting on different types of water with different types of flies. He got out his leaders and spools of tippet and showed her the different sizes and pound-tests and the knots to connect them when the line was broken back far enough. After that, he took apart one of his reels and showed her the various mechanisms for drag and how to spool a new reel with backing line.

This lecture went on for some time. While Gretchen was at first very interested and keen on asking questions, she started drifting into her own thoughts or shooting glances around the room as Paul talked. She tried to refocus but found herself tuning out his words when he wasn't making eye contact. At one point she asked if she could try casting, (to show interest, but also to wake herself up) but he said that would be for the next lesson. Finally, they had covered, as far as she could tell, all of the gear that lay on the table and she quietly prayed he would not pull his classic move of quizzing her. She hated it; it was vaguely insulting, though he did because he really wanted her to learn.

He didn't ask her anything and instead, reached under his chair and grabbed a handful of black fly boxes. "So now, I want to show you the various patterns we use," he said and cracked the first open. Rows of hackle, hair and hooks spread before her.

She gently put out a hand and spoke carefully. "Sweetheart, can we take a break? I do want to learn, but I need to do something else for a little while." She knew he'd be a little hurt and annoyed by the question, and it would bother her.

"Can I just show you a few patterns, the really common ones?"

"Well—can we just take a half hour break or something?"

"Sure, I guess."

"Don't be annoyed. I just need a break."

"I'm not annoyed. I just want to show you this last bit."

"Not now." Her timbre was hardening. "I need to do something else for a while."

"Okay." Paul clapped a fly box shut, a little too hard.

Gretchen leaned back to get a better look at him. "Why are you acting like that? I appreciate the lesson; I just need a *break*."

"I just wanted to show you this last bit." He waved the box lamely in his hand.

The fact he'd repeated himself bugged her. "Don't be a baby," she snapped.

"I'm not being a baby. This is important. If you're going to be here through the winter, then you need to know how to fish. If David and I are off doing other stuff, cutting firewood or fixing something on the cabin, and we need fish for dinner, you'll have to pull your weight."

"I'm going to learn, Paul. We have a few months before it could snow. I'll pick it up just fine."

"It's not as easy as you think," he said defensively.

With the energy void left by his retreat, Gretchen moved in a little more. "And also, don't do that. Don't try to scare me into learning with dangerous talk about the winter."

"I'm not," Paul said rolling his eyes a little.

"I know something like that could happen, but we can take care of ourselves—again, I don't appreciate you making it seem like I'll be the weak link."

"*You are,*" Paul hissed.

She stepped back, hurt, and he saw it on her face. Paul stammered to continue turning his palms outwards. "You have the least experience is all. I want you to learn."

The hurt did not leave her face. "Well, I asked if I could try casting earlier and you said *no*. Look—don't talk down to me, Paul."

"I'm not, I just think you have a lot to learn."

"I know I do!" she yelled, then looked out the window a little embarrassed and repeated softly but with seething force, "I *know* I do. I just want to take a goddamn break from your lecture." Paul looked a little hurt and annoyed again and she slapped her hand against her leg. "Stop being offended. I understand how important this is. I quit my job to come here—"

"Thank me later," he said coldly.

She turned her hands outward, her voice rising. "What is the matter with you?"

Paul put up a hand, stopping himself. "I'm sorry—fine. We'll do this later. I don't want to fight. Let's just go hang out with everyone and continue this later." He stood slowly and opened the door.

She shot a quick dagger with her eyes as she walked past and said, "Try apologizing like you actually mean it next time," over her shoulder. They walked separately to the rest of camp; everyone was well on their way to enjoying the evening.

At the firering, sipping a beer, David was talking with Anna. He glanced up, looked between Gretchen and Paul. Then he caught JP's eye from across the fire.

JP looked up, but when he saw dark exasperation still hanging on their faces, vindication was not reflected in his eyes. He shook his head lightly in bewilderment and went back to his conversation with Stoss.

"What?" Anna said to David, vaguely catching on to the

tacit discussion.

David smiled and waved dismissively. "Nothing. Inside joke."

~ 9 ~

A FEW DEER SCATTERED as Paul swung on their rope swing across the Elizabeth and into The Grove. His boots made a dull thump under the jangle of his fishing vest as he landed on the soft ground. He adjusted his hat and looked around. Still calm and quiet as it always had been.

David barked from across the river, "Hey, asshole, throw me the rope. You forget how this works?"

Paul absently tossed the rope back to his brother as he looked around. He heard David struggle to reach the swing as it came back. A moment later he alighted next to him. He looked around and spoke with a mix of excitement and reverence, "Been a while," he said. He coughed and the sound died in the air around them. He looked up at his big brother. "Just the two of us."

Paul gazed around the treetops, chewing his cheek, and not listening to his brother. The argument with Gretchen still lingered in his mind like stale milk on the back of the tongue.

"You know what the word *crepuscular* means?" David asked loosely.

The silence between them eventually brought Paul to attention; he turned. "What?"

"You are retarded. Do you know the word crepuscular?"

"Yeah."

"And it means?"

"Like, evening or morning activity. Animals that are active at those times are crepuscular creatures," Paul said, the words coming dully and reflexively.

"How do you know that?"

"How do you know the word *asshole*?"

"I need it a lot."

Paul looked at his brother finally. "David—why are you asking me this?"

"I heard Stoss use it, to set the scene for when he came across the cowboys on the river a couple days ago, and I thought it was a cool word. It made me think of The Grove. Everything in The Grove seems *crepuscular*, at all times of the day."

"Gotcha. Can you stop using it? It doesn't sound like a word anymore." Paul started walking downstream, his fishing rod bouncing like a metronome in front of him.

"Crepuscular," David said with a smile, following.

"Enough. Where did Stoss run into the cowboys?"

"Near The Flats, I think. Not too far from here."

They walked downstream for a little while. There were some small evening duns bouncing on the water and the occasional rise of a trout. Each dun disappeared with a faint click on the surface. Paul turned to his brother and grinned. "You know what matutinal and vespertine mean?"

David hesitated. "No."

"Do you want to know?"

"I guess," David said.

"They are more specific forms of crepuscular. Matutinal refers to the morning and vespertine refers to the evening. Now you can break down your Grove descriptions even further."

"You're so smart," David said sarcastically, whacking a little caddis out of the air.

"I thought we were playing vocabulary games."

"One was enough. Speaking of all of this, you starting to notice that the matutinal and verpres—"

"*Ves-per-tine*," Paul corrected.

"Exactly. You noticing those two times of day drawing a

little closer to one another?"

"Yup. Our big rock rotates away from the sun every year, no matter how much we all want to stop it."

"Deep, Paul. Deep."

"Thanks." Paul stopped and looked out at the river, taking it in; David pushed past him and Paul followed, speaking wistfully, "I have to say, I am excited to see fall. I bet it's beautiful—winter too, despite the cold."

Now without having to make eye contact, David's voice became more direct. "So with that in mind, let me ask you: how does Gretchen seem? You get the sense that she's ready for things to become more *crepuscular*?"

"Stop using the word. And yes."

"You didn't convince me," David said not turning around.

"Well—she's a little nervous. The whole proposition is daunting, you know?"

"Have you guys talked about it much?"

"Sure. I've talked her through the needed stuff: layers and staying warm, first aid, how to handle an axe, use the stoves, change the globes on the lanterns. That kind of stuff."

"What about fishing?"

"Yeah, fishing too. She needs to work on casting, but she'll be a good fisherman—or fisherwoman, I guess." A little annoyance brought Paul's tone tight.

David stopped and turned around. He looked at his brother and popped his eyebrows. "Yeah?"

"Yeah." Paul pushed him lightly to keep walking.

But David maintained eye contact. "Okay. Just checking."

Paul quickly rolled his eyes. "You ready to do some fishing here, and not around my personal life?"

"Well, it's going to be my personal life for a while too...which should be *great*."

Paul slapped his hand against his thigh. "*Damn it*, David. This is important—for both me and Gretch." He searched for his brother's eyes.

Now David looked away. "I get that...I get that. Anyway—JP's been showing me how to use that rifle and once he and these other jokers clear out, we'll have the valley to ourselves. We can come here and fish and not have to feel secretive about it."

After a beat, Paul said, "We can do that anyway."

"Yeah. I'm just getting a little sick of the huge crowd. Maybe we should have kept the St George's Angling Club a little smaller." David kicked some of the mud from his heels.

"Would have been a lot harder to build that cabin with any fewer guys."

David shrugged. "Rather have the valley more to ourselves. Now those cowboys are here too."

"I don't think it's that big of a deal," Paul said quietly.

"Don't get me wrong, I'm having a good time too. I mean—I've had an *especially* good time with Anna these past few nights. Check this out." He pulled up his shirt and showed off a set of claw marks along his waist. "See, Mr. Badass? I'm not the only one who can take down a cat?"

"Nice. But seriously, are you really psyched for everyone to bug out?"

"Well, you are their president," David said sarcastically.

"No one's mentioned it since."

"So—when do I get to take over?"

"Quit being a cocksucker."

"I was just joking."

"Kind of like how you were 'just checking' on Gretchen?"

"That...I was a little more serious about. Let me ask you this, Paul. What do we do if we're knee deep in snow and you guys have one of your blowouts? Are we going to build her a separate wing of the cabin?"

"That won't happen. And if it does, I'll deal with it. She's not naïve about this either."

"Okay. We'll need to see if she can shoot a gun too."

"That's your job—and your job only," Paul said quickly and wiped his brow, flicking away some sweat. "I don't want her doing that."

"Why not?"

"I'm not going to make her shoot a gun."

"I feel like she'd want to know."

"Fine, David—I'll ask her. We should talk about when you're going to do that anyway."

"Do what?"

"Take down a deer."

David looked at his brother and shrugged casually, "I was thinking about going soon."

"Wait until everyone's gone." Paul squinted at the river.

"Why?"

"Just don't," he said distantly. "Let everyone clear out before we start dragging carcasses around."

"Well, I'd like to go with JP."

"Do you mind waiting? Just go in a couple weeks." Paul dipped his hat in the water, shook it out and put it on. "You know—this conversation is making me tired. I'd like to just fish for now and not think about it." He looked at the handle of his rod, the hook of his fly buried in its side. "I'm going with a pale evening dun; that's what these last few fish have sipped on."

A light of vindication flicked on and off in David's eyes, then he shifted gears with his brother. "You mean a pale *vespertine* dun?"

"Exactly."

"Well, I'm using a Hare's ear, like the one you used to catch that hog last year, but dropping an egg pattern underneath."

"Have at it," Paul said and nodded to the section of river next to them.

"Don't mind if I do…" David trailed off. He pointed to a pocket in the current behind a couple fallen branches. "What is that?" he demanded with incipient rage in his voice. Where the water caught and held, it frothed and turned yellow, stacked with dirty bubbles surrounded by plastics, bottles, aluminum cans and wrappers. A film of oil coated made a shiny veneer.

They stared at it for a moment. "It's a pile of trash," Paul said but it was almost a question. He could hear his words above his heart pounding in his ears. "It's a pile of trash," he repeated.

David took a slow step towards the alcove. "Who left trash in the *river*?"

Paul nodded; he tipped his hat as if it had a wide cowboy brim.

~

That night JP was the lucky man to have Paige next to him at the fire. When he grabbed his guitar and started playing, she couldn't help but saddle up and see what kind of music they could make. They had found a few songs they both knew and tried to work out the kinks.

"No, the chord changes in the middle there." She pointed her finger, making a U in the air to mark the change when she sang over it, a capella, "'running everywhere at such a speed, 'til they find, that there's no need.' Right at 'find,' there is a quick chord change."

JP listened intently, inserted the chord and they kept singing. The guys enjoyed the music as they milled about helping prepare dinner, sipping on drinks, talking, playing horseshoes and cards. Adrian wandered over to the newly formed duo. They were in the middle of song but she drew him onto her lap without missing a beat. He leaned back against her chest and turned over a rock in his hands, half aware of the song that resonated under the breasts behind his head. Soon, dinner was served.

"You guys sounded great," Paul said. "I'd forgotten about most of those songs."

Gretchen watched his compliment from the corner of her eye and her face darkened a little.

"Thanks," Paige said blushing. "Couldn't have done it

without my one-man-band though."

JP dismissed the compliment with a wave, "Naw, you could do any of those without me. I was just here so you didn't sound *too* good." His face tightened and became heartfelt. "You sounded great."

"Thanks," she said and took a bite of fish. "What kind of trout is this?"

"Rainbow. Best kind."

"Is that the only kind of trout in this river?"

"Naw, there are brown trout and brook trout. But rainbows are the king. Biggest rainbow I ever caught was about twenty six — took me almost an hour to get her in the net."

Paige looked at the fish on her plate. "That is *huge*. How much does this one weigh?"

JP tried to laugh off the confusion. "No, twenty six inches," he said.

"How long is twenty six inches?" Adrian asked. He stretched his arms as wide as they would go and glanced back and forth between his hands. "Longer than this?"

"No Ade, less than half of that." Paige looked down at him and tapped his chest, signaling a midpoint.

"Well, maybe not *less*. Maybe about half," JP said, doing his best to seem as if he didn't care.

Paige shrugged. "Maybe."

"Hey everyone, can I get your attention," Paul said moving towards the firelight. "President here." He said it as sarcastically as possible. David looked up. Percy barked twice from the corner and they were all quiet. "Thanks Percy. Just a quick question: did anyone lose the handle on a bag of trash recently?" He scanned everyone's faces quickly, but thoroughly. "Maybe lost it eating by the river?" He looked around again but everyone was casually shaking his or her head. "Okay, didn't think so."

"Why?" Norton asked.

"We found a bunch of garbage in a little eddy and were wondering if someone accidently let it go or the wind blew it into the river or something." Paul looked around again, especially at JP but he seemed even. "Not trying to accuse; I just think this may be the work of our friendly neighborhood cowboys."

"Where did you find it?"

"Near The Flats," David said quickly.

"Near where you fell in?" Norton said with a provoking smile.

David's face darkened a bit. "Near where I fell in, smartass."

"Anyway," Paul said. "I've got a little plan to deal with them."

"What?" David asked with mock excitement. "What, *Prez*?"

"I haven't thought it all the way through, but I'll let you know, *bro*." He sat back down and that ended the discussion. David looked at him for an extra second; the conversations around the campfire resumed.

Paige turned back to JP. "So I heard you were going to go deer hunting soon—when? I've never had deer meat before."

"I don't know, let me ask the man. Hey—Davey Crockett, when you want to take your first deer?" JP added a little extra volume to his voice. A hush fell again.

"Tomorrow," he said coolly.

"Really?" Paul interjected quickly, but trying to sound offhanded. "We have coolers *full* of food."

"I think everyone would enjoy a venison steak. We've been eating so well recently, we may as well keep the cooking interesting."

"We should finish all this great food first," Paul said motioning at the plates around him. Gretchen began looking back and forth between them intently. She started to say something, but David's words rolled over her.

"We're going to need to hunt for the winter soon—why not sooner?"

"And we'll—" Gretchen started, but Paul cut her off. She

glared at him but he didn't notice. David did though.

"Why don't we sort this out in the morning," Paul said waving away the discussion calmly. "This isn't a huge deal."

David spoke matter-of-factly, "We only have *two* fishermen for the winter. We might as well get started storing food early." Uncomfortable glances bounced Gretchen's direction and she looked down at her dinner. David saw them and looked back to his brother. "But, *Prez*, I don't mean to break procedure: we should *vote* on it, right? That was your rule."

A subtle smile drew across Paul's face. He knew his little brother had caught him in a little trap. He didn't notice Gretchen shift nervously in her seat. "I suppose we should," he said.

"Okay," David's voice took on a mock official tone and he stood up. "Members of the St George's Angling Club: raise your hand if you are in favor of JP and me hunting and shooting a deer for food?"

The guys' hands went up. But the girls kept their arms crossed, not in a vote of NO but in abstention as visitors—save Gretchen. Her hand shot in the air and stayed there. Paul looked at her and, for a flash, betrayed skepticism about her voting at all. Gretchen caught the look and glanced at the other three girls with their arms crossed and flashed mortification, then anger.

David had watched it all. "Does her vote *count*?"

"Well, it—" Paul stammered.

"We need to vote on new members, right?" David asked innocently but it wasn't a question.

Again, Paul hesitated for an instant as he remembered his words a week earlier.

"Why are you *thinking* about this?" Gretchen demanded. Her voice rose, but her eyes were sad; they darted to the shocked faces around the fire. Then she looked back to David and suddenly the focus of her gaze was lost. She cast it at a funny angle between Paul and the fire.

"Yeah, of course her vote counts," Paul said quickly. "Of

course—"

"What's the matter with you two?" she demanded and there was a strange calm of perspective in her voice. A sad glaze smothered her eyes. "I just wanted be here with you"—she looked to Paul—"and *here*, a part of your stupid little boys club...have some fun—" her words faltered. Her eyes flicked to the shocked faces and pushed the glaze around so it built in the corners.

Paul's gaze bounced between Gretchen and his brother, and since his eyes were undirected, the sharpness of his words dulled, "David—she is staying through the winter and of course—hold on, *Gretch*—"

David came alive from his trance at the scene he'd created. "I was just kidding, Gretchen. I didn't..."

She covered her face and walked away from the fire. Everyone was silent as Paul followed her out of camp and down to the Elizabeth. David stared through the flickering flames as they went—a little scared of what his little trick had just done.

~

"What the fuck did you do that for?" Paul shouted as he stood next to the Elizabeth amidst theatrics for the second time that night. Gretchen had gone to bed, leaving him by the river, looking into the night sky. David approached in the darkness. "You're lucky you didn't walk down here a half hour ago or I would have socked your fucking lights out. I swear to God, if you say one thing about me and Gretchen, and how we...how we...." The great beam that ran through Paul's broad shoulders cracked. A calm cloud set over the moment. "She wants to leave tomorrow." He looked at his brother and shook his head.

For a moment, David prepared to launch a counter argument for why it wasn't his fault and it was just a joke, but found it impossible. The Elizabeth flowed and laughed around them. She twinkled back at the night sky. David had seen his brother sad and he'd seen him cry; he'd seen him fight and break up with Gretchen too, but he'd never seen his brother look like this. He looked at Paul's massive, bent frame in the moonlight and realized that he had hurt his big brother. For as long as he could remember, that had been an impossibility. Paul was too big. But this time, he'd shifted him.

"Just let me be," Paul said quietly.

David started to speak but he put up his hands and walked back through the woods to a quiet camp. Everyone had turned in early.

If he'd stayed he would have seen Paul kick a little water off the top of the Elizabeth and watch the droplets patter across the current in the ivory spots of moonlight. He'd have seen Paul do it again, and again, until he was simply kicking the long, winding river in anger. He'd then have seen him stop, breathless, and fall back on the rock with his wide hands over his face.

The charge in St George's began to move around.

~ 10 ~

PAUL PACKED THE JEEP IN SILENCE. The rest of the guys watched from the corner of their eyes, pretending to focus on gear or a game of horseshoes. There were winces as Paul lifted two heavy coolers back onto the roof of the truck and sideways glances to Stoss, cooking a breakfast of unseasoned eggs and toast. Anna and Denise quietly loaded their bags and got in. Paige and Percy were going to stay behind and leave with Norton and Adrian. As Gretchen approached, Paul went for a hug but she waved him away gently and shut the door. The engine stuttered and they left in a cloud of dust.

Paul walked out to the Elizabeth and sat on a rock to watch them work their way up the switchbacks. As they crested around the last peak, a tightness came to his chest. He took a knee on his rock in the current and coughed and pounded over his heart. Tears almost came, but he shoved them back. He looked up to the ridge as the dust drew into the wind and disappeared. The tightness was almost unbearable.

A few minutes later, his footsteps thundered the ground as he returned to camp alone; his entrance from the road had the presence of a train leaving a tunnel. Adrian looked up and gave Paul a big wave; he ignored him. He put two fingers in his teeth and crushed them in a piercing whistle. There was no looping note in the end. He indicated Norton, Bruce and JP should follow him into the lodge with a curt nod of the head. The other guys noted the intensity, but went back to their horseshoe game. David had left that morning to fish by himself.

Norton eased in the door first and looked at Paul sitting behind a table in the shadowy cabin. "You all right?"

Paul gave a curt nod. "We'll talk later—need to take care of something."

JP entered and shot a quick glance to Norton, then to Paul. "What's up big fella?"

Bruce tripped as he followed through the door.

Paul gave them a quick nod. "You jokers remember where the cowboy's camp is, right?"

JP rocked uneasily and looked at Bruce.

Paul raised his voice a little. "You remember, right?"

"Yeah, a ways up river, on the south side."

"Okay. Good." Paul motioned them around the table.

"Why?" Bruce asked his mouth slightly agape.

"We're going to send those bastards a message. Just pay attention."

"This is for the trash?" JP asked warily.

"Yeah, this is for the trash. I don't care what you two did to their trucks a while back, that's no excuse for them to take a dump in the Elizabeth."

"Is your brother in on this?"

Paul ignored the question and looked to Norton. "Paige is watching Ade today, right?"

"I was going to fish with him—but she was going to tag along so I don't think she'd mind taking him on her own."

"Good. And ask her if we can take Percy."

"Okay. She does like to keep her when she is by herself since she barks away animals, but I'll ask."

Paul turned to Bruce. "I need you to go around camp and collect three or four cans of bear mace and bring them here. JP, I need you to locate David's bone-handle knife. It should be around here or in the truck."

"Okay. Why?"

"And then I need you to get the rifle and a box of shells."

Norton put up a hand. "Hey—I'm all for pulling a prank, but what the hell is your idea?" He glanced out the window at the horseshoe pit. Adrian was dutifully keeping score, rocking on his heels.

"Don't worry: no one—or no person—is going to get hurt. I'll tell you when we're on our way. Just get all the stuff I asked for and meet me a few hundred yards up the road in a half an hour. I'll explain then. Don't say a word to anyone. Make it seem like I'm heartbroken or something and we're going to talk—actually, that reminds me: gear up for fishing, rods, vest, waders, the whole thing."

The three nodded and filed out of the cabin. Paul sat alone at the table chewing the inside of his worn-out cheek.

~

A smattering of pillowed clouds filled the sky and the shade moved in waves over the valley as the sun lowered in the western sky. Four men walked in pairs through the woods just off the south bank of the Elizabeth, stepping and stumbling over branches and making their way up river. They wore full fishing gear but one carried a backpack, another carried a gun. The fattest of them carried a few dead trout, a stick running through their agape mouths. The fish were big—abnormally big. While they pushed branches out of the way and moved around rocks, there was a spring in their step as they laughed and talked on their way back to camp.

"Jesus, Don. I can't believe this hog," the fat cowboy said and looked down at the longest trout. Its tail started where the other two ended. He gave a baiting smirk. "It must have taken you half an hour to land."

"Hush. I had that big boy on the bank in under fifteen." Don, the aspen, made pistols with his thin fingers and fired off a couple celebratory rounds. The two men walking behind smiled at the theatrics.

Pete, the bowling ball, continued, "How'd you find that stretch of river? Felt like an enchanted forest. I've never seen a riparian environment like that, especially in the mountains."

Don ducked a low branch and adjusted his wide brimmed cowboy hat. "Just lucky. I spotted one of these mondo trout and that was it—the same day I'd spotted that older guy from the cabin fishing that wide flat pool by himself."

"Well, nice work partner—not sure if I've had a better day of fishing in my life. Next time we come back we'll use that rope swing on the other bank to fish that side of the river."

"Hey Pete," one of the guys in back said. "You sure you don't want to stay a few extra days or so."

"I'd love to, but school starts on the first and I gotta get my classroom ready. Hey—" Pete turned around, his belly shaking as he rotated. "—you got that bag of trash, right?"

"Yeah, in the bottom of my pack."

"Good. I can't believe those sons of bitches would leave a bag of garbage like that. If we were staying longer I'd have a talk with them. When we go on fieldtrips, I'm always teaching my kids: take care of these kinds of places. It's a shame those boys never learned that—"

A gunshot sounded ahead, then another. They heard men yelling and a loud hissing. They glanced at one another and began running through the woods back to their camp. They heard more yelling and then caught a faint, noxious whiff. The fat cowboy began coughing and covered his face with his hat. They burst into their clearing and found four men in their camp. One carried a rifle, two had bear spray and the fourth was a big guy with a hand wrapped around a bone-handled knife with a long blade.

"What the hell is going on here?" Pete yelled. He still had his hat over his mouth, but could see that his camp had been torn apart. Over the long grasses of their little meadow, their tents were shredded and mashed. Food from one of their coolers was strewn around their fire circle. What was left of their meat was mangled and spread on the grass. As he continued absorbing the wreckage of their camp, his eyes widened. The driver side window of his truck was smashed and there were three long lacerations in the door.

"A grizzly bear was in your camp," the big guy with the knife said. He hacked some spit and sat down, wiping his brow. His green eyes pulsed and burnt with intensity.

"A grizz?!"

"We were fishing down on the river and Percy," he nodded towards the dog, "started barking her ass off. She took off in the woods so we followed." He paused dramatically and shook his head. "We had seen the bear before—that's why we fish with the rifle and the mace now—so we had an idea that the dog may be after it. Damn dog has no fear. We got here and a big sow was tearing through your stuff. We fired off shots—didn't faze her—and then drowned her in the mace." He coughed. "That got her going; we chased her until she jumped on some rocks and was gone up the mountain wall." He nodded to a stoic peak above them littered in scree. "It was a mess. Bruce took some mace to the face and ended up yakking." He nodded to a pile of vomit and let out a deep sigh. "My name is Paul, by the way. We met once, when you guys were pulling out after some car problems." He tapped the markings on his forearm.

The fat cowboy nodded to him in acknowledgement and continued surveying the scene. The others walked over to their tents and kicked through the remains.

"Hopefully that's the last we'll see of her," JP said through his thick twang.

"Well—shit," Pete said, shaking his head and looking around his camp again. "I could have sworn I'd heard there were no grizzes around here," he chuckled and shrugged, "but I'll be damned if we aren't the unluckiest bastards alive."

The aspen laughed, "Not you—now your wife will let you replace that old piece of junk you called a tent." He waved a ribbon of his own tent in the wind and laughed, "I'll just get in trouble for being careless!"

The fat cowboy turned to Paul. "Nice to meet you. My name is Pete Rollins. We appreciate you doing what you did." He and Paul shook hands and everyone introduced one another. "I may have had the wrong idea about you boys," he said quietly to himself.

"Hey," JP said, "let us help you clean this up."

"Naw, you don't have to do that. We can get it," Pete said and waved him away.

"Don't worry, Pete. Many hands make little work." Paul smiled kindly and started picking up the scraps, throwing them towards the bin in the bed of the pickup truck.

~

"You're a damn beast, Paul!" JP slapped Paul on the shoulder and skipped one step ahead of them. They'd just crossed the Elizabeth and walked down the old road. "That'll show those sons of bitches."

"Keep it down," Paul said solemnly.

"That was amazing, a well-oiled machine," Bruce said, then turned to Norton. "I though for sure that they'd see you keeping watch in the woods."

"No way. Fish in a river, fish in the woods: same kind of stalking. You just have to worry about your lines of sight."

"And Paul," JP said putting a hand on his shoulder and bowing his head in laughter, "remind me never to get in a fist fight with you—not that I'd need it—but I don't think I've seen a pair of hams land as hard as yours did on that truck door and tear a hole with that knife. Hell, you could have slammed your big fingers through instead." Paul nodded vaguely and JP continued, "And also," he started laughing uncontrollably and turned. "I'm sorry Bruce, but when Paul sprayed you with the mace, even from thirty yards, to get you to puke and make it all seem more real, shit, I almost lost it. I've never seen your fat ass move like that before."

"Yeah, sorry Bruce," Paul said absently.

"It's okay," he said. "Didn't get me that bad. I just had one little whiff."

"Well, did you hear them?" JP said. "They are heading out tomorrow. So it did the trick."

Paul adjusted his hat, ignoring the comment, and looked at Norton. "How's the one casualty?"

He looked down at a little tear in his waders. "That was my fault: walked too close to that shredded door and it caught me."

Paul mumbled, "That sucks. We'll patch it up."

JP looked up at him. "Hey Paul, why are you down?"

"I'm not...just decompressing." He stopped and locked in with their gazes, one by one, deliberately. "Look," he said slowly. "This stays between the four of us. No campfire talk, no talking while fishing, none of that. This just exists between the four of us and ends there. Okay?"

They shifted on their heels and agreed in a smattering of mumbles, exchanging quick, confused glances.

"I'm serious, guys. Not a word. Okay?"

"Yeah," JP said disappointedly.

Bruce nodded.

"Right," Norton said trailing off and looking at Paul's still far-off demeanor.

As the four of them had gone through the motions of helping clean up, Paul had seen one cowboy unpack the trash from the bottom of his pack. It was wet and had an oily coating. He had put the dripping refuse in a lockable bin in one of the truck beds, on top of other bags of trash.

A deep hangover was setting in Paul's temple, worse than any morning he'd had in St George's. Pain of guilt has no equal in the body. He'd let his anger lose. It had slithered out of the inky corners and performed a dark symphony of clever destruction on men who didn't deserve punishment;

and its face had been masked to everyone—every party believed that good, or a favor had been done. Paul was the only one who saw its sharp teeth. It had only been anger, no matter how dressed up or decorated everyone else believed it to be.

The tightness came back to his chest—far worse than before. He rolled his shoulders, his breastbone cracking at the ribs as he walked in silence with the others. He glanced side to side and Paul, using all of his strength, took the cables and the sheaths and the tightness of his chest and wrapped them in his thick hands and pushed them into the farthest corners, shoving guilt and self pity with them, and slammed the door shut. That was all he could do.

"You sure you're alright, Paul?" Norton asked again. One hand fiddled with the tear in his waders.

"Fine," Paul said speaking reflexively, "got to keep moving."

~ 11 ~

SOMEWHERE ALONG THE LINE, people decided that life's waves travel in threes. For some reason, never wholly explained, the events in the world around us pack themselves in trios released in succession and holding a common theme of good, bad or something in between. This conventional wisdom is unfounded, living in close relation to old ideas like a bird defecating on your head is good luck and rain on a wedding indicates a successful marriage. They're constructs to make us feel better when we've just taken a shot to the stomach—our way of explaining inexplicable tragedy and turning it for the better.

The problem is that in the backs of our minds, with that ever-restless voice that can only speak truth, we know what we're doing. We know that the good and the bad are discarded from a hand of which we'll never sneak a peak, and there isn't much we can do about it other than take the play in stride. But we don't behave that way, and strangely enough, this is what makes the third member of the wave the most pronounced.

For the next few days, there was a blank aftermath in camp. The guys were still shell-shocked at the abrupt departure of the red jeep and evenings around the fire were courteous but brief. No one blamed Paul or David, but now that three of the four girls had left, the meals lost their color and the small void returned; and the two brothers, who'd been the solution that dissolved camp, had turned oily. They glided past one another in a strange indifference; there was no palpable malice and that made it all the worse. Contourless fights are the most uncomfortable—there is nothing to hold onto. So the other guys focused on the river and fishing, and the changing quality in the air that told them summer was winding down. It would be time to head home anyway.

Paige, however, existed on a slightly different plane. Being the only woman in camp had made life a little better. Not because she had a dozen men to herself, but because she had Adrian's undiluted attention. He would be her guide for her remaining time in St George's Valley. Adrian picked up on this, in whatever way his eight-year-old mind could. One morning he took her to some of the areas that he'd explored, showing off the orange mushrooms and the purple wildflowers. He showed her the gravel bars where the foxes came and the pools where the trout held. He showed her a little island with an undercut bank and a large pool with a long rock where he liked to fish.

"How many fish have you caught here?" she asked.

He shrugged. "Dad knows."

"What was the biggest?"

He thought for a moment and spread his arms wide and extended his fingers, crimping the digits at the end to indicate boundaries. He giggled.

Paige smiled. "Are you pulling my leg?"

"Maybe."

He led her back to camp and did his very best to organize his thoughts and explain the game of horseshoes (which she knew, but let him continue anyway). And by the time the sun was high in the sky, her feet ached in her new hiking boots and she asked Adrian if they could sit at the table near the firering for a while and play Go Fish or just read.

"Sure," he said and set his hat on the table like Paul did. "Do you mind if when my dad comes back, I go fishing with him?"

"Well, I don't think your dad is going to be back until

much later, Ade," she said fighting to keep the whiff of defensiveness out of her voice. "He and Paul went way downriver to fish and I don't think they're going to be back until evening."

"Dad will be back," he said not looking up from his book. "I know it."

Paige recognized statements of finality from Adrian and knew it was best to move past them without engaging. She cracked her water bottle, rubbed her feet, and looked at the boy. He sat, his head slightly cocked, reading a book about dinosaurs, a towering well-drawn brontosaurus on the cover. A sky full of pounding thunderheads wouldn't have broken his concentration. She looked past him, to the waving fields of the meadow, the stout cabin, the bowing trees and the towering mountains that rose above their tops. The breeze blew summer's final heat and it swaddled her in crisp air.

She sat upright and slipped her boots back on her sore feet. "*Adrian,*" she said and the excitement in her voice gave her pause. "Are there other areas of this valley you haven't explored that we could go look at together?"

"Well," he said and dove into thought. This struck him as a new kind of question: being asked to describe what he *didn't* know. He was used to describing what he did know. "Well, I don't think I've ever"—he burst into a beaming grin—"*see,* told you Dad would be back."

Paige turned and Paul and Norton walked into camp, laughing. Norton was carrying his waders rolled up in his arms and his pants were soaked. Adrian looked at his father with a sly, knowing grin that slowly grew into a bubbling laugh, and then finally into an outburst. "Dad! Did you pee your pants?"

Paul burst out laughing: "Can you believe it?!"

Adrian never took his eyes off his dad, who shook his head. "My wader sprung a leak and the water got in. See?" He showed Adrian a small opening, near the top of one leg. "Can you believe that one little tear let in all this water?"

Adrian didn't answer and looked at the small opening, thinking it through, validating his dad's story. A part of him really wanted to believe he'd peed his pants.

Paul whacked Norton's shoulder playfully. "Okay, I'll grab the patch—do the job right this time will you?" He winked at Paige and headed to the lodge.

A wave of fatigue crashed through Paige, as if the air had been knocked from her. She watched Paul go and then turned to Norton. "Your accuser was wondering if he could fish with you this afternoon."

He glanced at Paul, then gave her a sideways look. Before he could ask Adrian if he was sure he didn't want to explore with Paige some more, Adrian looked up and smiled hopefully.

"You sure?" Norton asked.

"Yeah, I want to fish with *you*, Dad."

"Okay, okay."

"Alright," Paige said. "I'm going to lay down and read, maybe do a little yoga. This one ran me ragged this morning." She looked quickly at Norton and then ruffled Adrian's hair but he didn't seem to notice. He'd taken an interest in one of Paul's fly boxes.

As she walked away, she barely heard, "Namaste."

She turned around. "What was that, bud?"

Adrian was looking up at her with the self second-guessing of a boy. His eyes flickered away when she met them. "I heard you say that once," he said quietly.

"Oh." She smiled and her eyes glazed over. She put her hands together. "Namaste, Adrian." She gave him a wink and walked away with a new lightness in her steps. Percy caught onto her happiness and skipped at her heels as they went over to the hammocks.

Norton had no idea what was going on and figured the interaction was one of the many affections and jokes between them of which he sat on the outside. As she walked away, he leaned back in a chair and took in the afternoon. The brush had its usual chatter, the air had its usual chirps and everywhere else there was life. He filled his lungs and held it.

"Dad," he heard Adrian say, now investigating the fly box again.

Norton exhaled. He had come to recognize the tone of this intro and unconsciously left his mountain air mindset to prepare for a fatherly distillation of one of life's complexities.

"Does dying hurt?"

But he hadn't been ready for that one. For all the obvious reasons, Norton had trouble discussing death. In the times he'd spoken about it with Adrian, it had been when he was ready and he'd deliberated at great length on how to present the facts of death itself. He had never told his son how his mom had died either. It never seemed relevant and to Norton, explaining death by fire to a child seemed impossible if not sadistic. So he'd just said that Mom was dead and that was it. Death had taken her and she was gone. He wasn't going to make anything up and Adrian hadn't asked any real follow ups, so it was left alone.

So now, successfully fending off a surge of moisture around his eyes, he looked at his son. He was still exploring Paul's fly box, investigating the sizes, colors, materials, beads, hackles, tails and patterns that mimicked insects. The question had come plainly, so Norton tried to answer with the same lightness.

"It *depends*—" as the words left his mouth, he knew he'd left a door slightly ajar and there was no way to close it. Adrian knew that "depends" meant no singular answer. Norton hurried to speak. "But *most* of the time it doesn't. People die in their sleep, just going to heaven from their beds. They—"

"Did Mom get hurt when she died?"

Norton paused. "Yeah bud," he said quietly. "She did."

Adrian didn't look up but nodded a little. He pushed a tiny elk hair caddis with the tip of his finger, thinking. "I feel bad for her."

"Yeah?" Norton's eyes were watering again.

"Yeah, well, I saw a deer…"

Norton didn't hear much of what he said after that and quietly prepared for the moment in the not-to-distant future when Adrian would realize that death is not just like a deliveryman, but can be very cruel and take people away in the worst possible ways. Then he'd finally have to answer the question of *how*. But for now he watched, and listened, as his boy told a story about a bone he'd found in the earth and a dead deer hanging in a tree.

Soon Paul came out of the lodge, carrying a patch kit and threw it to Norton. "There you go. Double the tape this time."

"Thanks," Norton said and set to work on his waders.

Paul sat down next to Adrian and looked through the fly boxes with him. He began with a deliberate explanation of the Royal Coachman Adrian had been examining, but after a few sentences, Adrian's percolating mind took over and he interrupted. "How big a fish will it catch?"

"Well," Paul said slowly. "It depends on where you are fishing. If you are in a river with large bugs, then this will work pretty well because they'll think—"

"But it has an orange tail; what bugs have orange tails?"

Paul stammered a little, "The orange is to excite them; fish like bright colors."

Adrian thought about this for a moment. "So how many fish have you caught with it?"

"Let's see…a bunch, but—"

"What about this one?" He put his finger on another Royal Coachman. "It's smaller. Does it catch smaller fish?"

"Well not necessarily. It could—but—sometimes big fish want smaller flies—and…"

"If they're big, wouldn't they want bigger food?"

"Usually that's the case, but sometimes—" Paul put up a hand and continued more evenly. "All of these will catch fish. You just have to use each fly in the right conditions, and use your seine or eyes to figure out what they are."

"Have you used all of these flies before?"

"No way. Well sort of—I have—"

"Then how do you know when to use them?" Adrian asked cocking his head at Paul.

"Well," Paul said trying to organize his thoughts again. "There are patterns or things you recognize about the water, the weather and the stream, and the bugs and the time of day—"

"You just have to fish a lot, Adrian," Stoss said with his surgical calm. He had quietly walked up behind them. "Then you'll know."

Adrian looked up at him. This was a different way of thinking about it. Maybe that's why Paul's answers were so confusing: he didn't know either.

"Exactly," Paul said. "That's what I was trying to say. Thank you." He exhaled and turned. "Norton, you almost done or should we get you a new pair?"

"Almost done, and like hell I'd get new waders. These cost me a fortune; I'm going to send them back when we get home."

A stone sank in Adrian's face. "I don't want to go home, Dad," he said. It wasn't in a whine or cry; it was a direct statement.

Norton was putting the finishing touches on the fix and missed the tone, hearing only the words. "I know, bud. I don't either. But you need to get back to school—which I know you love. We'll be back next summer."

Paul grinned. "Hey Ade, what do you think about going somewhere you've never been to fish? We'll go to The Flats. I haven't been there in a while, and then if you're lucky, Ade, we'll go to a secret fishing hole that not even your dad has been to, back in the woods." Norton looked at Paul quizzically; Paul winked at him. "How's that sound, Ade?"

Adrian turned to his dad without answering. He'd forgotten about leaving the valley—one of the tenets in his universe had cracked a little. "Dad, there are fishing places *you* haven't been to?"

"Sure there are. Answer Paul though, bud."

Adrian wheeled back around. "That sounds *great*," he said in his high-pitched squeal.

Paul tipped his finger off the frayed brim of his hat. "And maybe if you catch fish, I'll think about giving you my hat for the day too."

Adrian crinkled his nose. "I'd rather wear mine."

~

Far from the promises at the picnic table, but not far from where they were heading, two men walked side by side away from a pickup truck. One carried a gun. They walked with purpose, upright, at attention, and one squinted intently as he listened to the other.

"Okay, I'm going to remind you of a few things we've talked about—no more practice. This is the real deal," JP said. His loose southern speak and court jester demeanor had vanished. David shifted the rifle nervously. "First, when you aim at an animal, you shoot to kill. Now, I know that seems obvious, but you'd be surprised how many guys get something in their sites and just pull the trigger. Otherwise you're going to send the poor beast into the woods, all wide-eyed, with a flesh wound and you'll never find it and it'll die a lonesome death somewhere as it bleeds out. And that ain't right." He allowed himself a little twang for effect. "Gotta see that heart."

David nodded and beer cans on a log entered his mind.

"Second, you must be sure you're firing with something solid in the background. My cousin once missed a deer and shot a guy in the arm that was shooting at the same deer from the other side of the meadow. No joke. He's lucky he got off that shot first or the guy probably would have nailed *him*. Anyway, you have to be shooting with one of these mountains in the background or some dense trees where you know there aren't people but don't shoot if there are big rocks or you're liable to get a ricochet."

David took all this in with an edgy excitement. JP's words, however direct and instructive, took on a kind, fatherly quality and David found himself nodding.

"And third, and probably the most important: Keep that barrel up. Forget about those pictures where guys are walking down the road holding their guns near the dirt, posing for a magazine or something. That's bullshit stuff. You get some dirt, or a pebble, or anything down the gullet of that rifle and pull that trigger? That thing'll backfire and blow your damn face off with a hot mess of iron. No joke. That same cousin I was talking about saw a kid who'd fired a backed-up gun." He paused and rubbed his cheek. "No eyes, no nose and a ragged little hole for a mouth, no left hand either. So keep that barrel out of the dirt. If you think there's any chance that something's in there, we'll completely unload the chamber, leave it unbolted, put on the safety and have a look—always better to be safe."

David gave a sharp nod. "Got it," he said quietly. A tenseness had come to the joints of his wrist and fingers and his hands shook a little. He flexed them open and closed, and looked ahead to the waving grasses of the field where they'd hunt. He could make out the shifting brown shapes of deer.

~

A short while later, a large man, a small man, an old man and a boy walked down that same road and made their way to The Flats. The sun was sinking lower and the clouds moved in, just a little. The breeze had a hinting undercurrent of a chill. The large pockets and flat pools spread out around them as they fished. Paul fished at the head of the pool by himself. Stoss fished to a submerged black log with a gnarled branch and raised nothing. Adrian watched Stoss from the corner of his eye and saw the frustration; he saw that black log with a gnarled branch defeating the old doctor.

They fished like that for a while, until Norton's waders

leaked again. Paul walked over to help him patch it up correctly, once and for all as Stoss drifted over, taking a break from the submerged log.

As he stepped to shore, he startled a doe that ran into the woods. Her fawn leapt and bounded to catch up as they disappeared into the shadows of the tall trees.

~

They slowed after the old man was out of sight and drifted through the woods, across the road, and eventually into a field. The fawn bent down to feed on the grasses; the mother followed close behind, then drifted away, unaware of the danger that lurked in the shadows of the trees.

JP's tone was sorrowful. "Damn, this is a little too easy. These things are so damn dumb. Aim for that doe on the edge there, to the right. She's about the perfect size and doesn't have a fawn with her." They kneeled in a grove of trees in the shadows of the Crescents. The meadow held about a dozen deer, grazing and unworried about the day. A little trickle of a stream bisected the grass as it ran to the Elizabeth, between the deer and the men, and quenched the thirst of the doe. As the wall of the valley loomed behind the animals, dark clouds loomed behind them.

David looked out at the field, trying to bottle his emotions and keep his hands steady. He bolted a round with a heavy thud and click, and raised the rifle. He balanced it in his hand, which balanced on his knee, looking through the scope with one eye. Then he set down the gun and turned.

"Is it better to aim at the front or the side?" He pointed to his breastbone and then to his shoulder.

"Where would you shoot yourself?" JP asked.

David nodded like he should have known that. He tapped his heart and raised the rifle again, peering through the scope at the doe. She grazed with her head down and her back legs shifting in a light back and forth dance. He could just make out the top of her lips as they bounced and wavered, mowing the grasses around her.

He set the crosshairs on her heart; his hands shook a lit-tle. The tenseness blurred to a strange and uncomfortable giddiness. A freedom came over him. The instrument he held afforded a distance not only between him and the task, but between him and the emotion of the task. He'd always held fish, feeling it shake and pulse and swallow for a final gasp in his grip. When he'd crack it over a rock, the spirit left through the spaces of his fingers, and a cloaked guilt that had been peering over his shoulder sneered and climbed into the back of his mind. Now he could spy through an oblong window and squeeze a lever and that same end would come; his prey would die but that guilt would be too far away to touch him. The rifle afforded distance between him and the moment of death. Now he understood why Paul had been so hesitant to use the gun, why he'd come up sallow after he'd peered through the scope. Paul knew he might like it, too.

David put the doe's chest back in the crosshairs. His hands shook again.

~

A gunshot rang through the valley, caroming off the peaks and shoulders of the jagged mountains, aided by the thick moisture in the summer air, and bounced off the grow-ing clouds overhead; it rippled to the eastern wall, bounded and tore down the currents of the Elizabeth, and swept across The Flats.

Paul looked up from the hole in Norton's waders and grunted. "Guess we'll find out whether I can dress a deer," he said to himself.

The word *dress* charged a little framework of thought in Adrian as he looked up at Paul. Not the word itself, but the way it was used even though he already knew what it meant. His eyes narrowed a bit as he thought about it. He didn't notice the second shot ring through the valley.

"What a treat: venison steaks," Stoss said. "Anyway

gents, if Norton's wader is fixed, I'm going to meander up-stream a bit. I've frustrated myself enough here." Before he turned to leave, he looked at the black log, then at the boy next to his father and kneeled and lifted his sunglasses, staring at Adrian with soft grey eyes.

He nodded to the river. "Show us how it's done, Adrian."

Adrian smiled back at the old doctor and nodded with a sense of understanding at the task at hand. Stoss patted him on the shoulder, but the gesture didn't knock the boy from thought.

"I'll tag along with you, if these two are going to stay here," Paul said as he caught up to him Stoss. They made their way along the riverside as the glittering water dulled under the sheet of passing clouds. A breeze snapped over the Elizabeth with a chill in its underbelly.

As the large man and old doctor walked away, Norton kneeled down to his boy. "Okay buddy, where are we fishing?"

Adrian's eyes were still thinking under his bucket hat. He looked up at his dad and then out at the water. "There." He pointed to Stoss' submerged log and before his father could speak, he picked up his rod and trudged into the river.

"Hold up, hold up. If you're going to fish there, I'm going to stand with you. The current is strong."

"Dad," a beat passed, "can I please fish on my own?"

Adrian looked his father in the eye. He'd asked this question, in many forms, many times prior, but now there was a difference. Before, his high-pitched emphasis had been on the words *please* as he elongated the vowels in endearing child-ishness, having learned that this word held the key to some fickle lock on permission. Now his son's subtle emphasis was on the singular "I" and was quick. The whole question was even, each word individually polished and well examined, and for the first time Norton felt as if he was speaking with the early incarnations of a young man.

He sighed. "Remember the rule—"

"I know, Dad."

"Okay, okay. Would you mind if I stood here and watched you?" Norton motioned to the ground.

"Just don't get in the way of my back cast."

The brown bucket hat with the boy underneath waded into the river, the light current tugging gently at his calves, gurgling around them. He crossed the gravel bar and stopped. The water was at his knees. He turned to his dad, in the small chance he wasn't watching. Norton smiled back and raised a halting hand.

Adrian turned unemotionally and cast, the line uncurling in a little U over the water toward the black log. He thought about his father, standing on the bank behind him and for the first time in his eight years, Adrian could consciously detect his own ambition. It was only a distant star, but he recognized it. He was determined to find and catch a fish. On his own. And the determination was amazing. It meant something to him. He needed to. He needed to catch a fish with his father watching from the bank.

The Elizabeth flowed and gurgled and laughed around him. It laughed loud enough that he couldn't hear the crashing in the woods around his dad.

Norton jumped, as a wounded, wild-eyed doe spilled from the brush next to him and fell into the river in a great crash, startling every nearby creature. As Norton turned to the hemorrhaging animal—a gunshot in its haunches—he only heard Adrian's startled cry, then just making out *"Dad!"* as his son slipped and the Elizabeth swallowed and swept him away in her black currents.

~

Through good listening and sharp perception, Paige had noted that Adrian did not have his own box of flies. He always fished next to his dad, Paul or someone else, so any time he needed to replace a fly someone had to make the change for him, from their own boxes. To her, it was time to fix this.

So after her day on the water with Paul and Adrian, she had bashfully asked Paul if he had any old, empty boxes he didn't want anymore. "Yeah, in the truck. What do you need—" His face exploded in a grin. "*Great* idea. I'll show you which flies would be best for him."

So with camp empty on that cloudy afternoon, she rolled out of the hammock with a long stretch, hugged her limber legs and walked over to Percy and scratched her ears. She looked up at the gathering thunderheads and through the grasses and into the lodge. She rifled through her bag and pulled out two black boxes. She found a spool and wrapped them in fishing line making a delicate, ironic bow. Then on a short, flat piece of kindling that would function as a rugged card, she wrote:

> *To Adrian,*
> *For all the fish you'll catch.*
> *Love,*
> *Paige*

She walked outside and set the gift on a table by the firering. The charred wood still smoldered softly. She stretched, picked up a book and waited for him to return. The shadow of an eagle's broad wings sailed over the black scab of coals nearby, and continued down the valley.

~

Carving through the winds, the eagle glided; her piercing eyes scanned the clearings, skies and waters, hunting for movement. Though air currents flowed around her wings, the unyielding fire to provide for her two chicks propelled her. She could see their hungry mouths extending helplessly from their fuzzy heads in a treetop nest.

Dark clouds were moving through, dimming the light. She swooped lower. She veered away from the river and hugged the north rim of the valley, bending side to side, until she came to a larger field with deer dispersing into the trees. She beat her wings a few times and glided back towards the river. She sailed on until she reached a wide pool. There were three abandoned fishing rods thrown in the bushes and a little farther along, three men running along the tight rock wall, keeping their balance, but moving frantically. One man was large, one was old and one was small with curly hair.

She saw the small one's eyes. Something awful tore at his insides.

She glided on. The forest thickened and she could make out a dense floor of moist pine needles. The trees extended their branches over the dark river and covered the waters. A healthy mist rose from the flora and dense shadows.

Then something caught her eye.

Through a small hole in the treetops she noticed a boy draped over a log in the river. His cheeks were red but he didn't move. A brown bucket hat lay washed on the bank next to him and the black waters wrapped around his thin waist. For a moment, the mother eagle thought he slept, but an instinct that she called on every day, an instinct that had spent generations honing the dissection of movement, told her the boy was dead.

A thunderclap rolled in the distance and it started to rain lightly. She alighted on a branch and cocked her yellow, arrow-tip eyes in curiosity. She watched the three men appear from the woods; she watched them see the boy. The small man covered his face and the awful thing that had been tearing at his insides came forth and struck him down; he fell onto the soft earth. The large man stumbled into the river. He lifted the boy off the log and brought him to the small man on his knees. The old man knelt beside them, a command on his calm waging war with grief. He put his ear to the boy's mouth, then pushed against his little chest, over and over. He breathed into the boy's mouth and pushed against his chest again.

The boy did not move. The smaller man cried out, pushed the old man away and collapsed across the boy's body, hugging him and bringing him to his heart. He rocked back and forth. The old man and the large man stood by helplessly with their hands on their heads. Their tears cascaded from their cheeks and disappeared in the rain.

The rain came harder. Under the rumbling clouds, the mother eagle ascended from her branch, above the trees and glided in the great currents over the valley. In the dim light she could see the tall peaks and the long river that wound between them. The rain poured down the stony faces, through their crags, into the fields, among the trees and into the winding ribbon of division.

She caught an updraft and turned into the currents of the wind, heading for her nest. She would be without food. But she knew that tomorrow, after the rains had passed, life would re-emerge and she would hunt again.

V

~ 1 ~

I WON'T DESCRIBE NORTON'S SORROW except to say that it was terrible and complete. The light in a child's eyes is nothing but our hope. When it's extinguished, the grief is imbedded in such a way that we wither and disintegrate into helpless, trembling pieces. From afar, we have a tendency to quietly lick our teeth and want to know how the grief played out, maybe on account of natural curiosity, maybe on account of it making us feel whole, but I've never thought it was right—whatever the reason. Every word I'd write would patronize a piece of Norton's completely broken heart. So I won't. But this story does need to end with a light in the tunnel. I wouldn't have written it if it didn't.

As is often the case in cataclysm, some knew things and others didn't. At first, no one knew that the deer David had shot and allowed to run away had been the one that startled Adrian. Norton knew that a deer had startled him, but he didn't know why and never cared to think about it. As he watched the Elizabeth swallow his son, he blocked out the details around him; his brain sealed the centers that built memory. Norton only recognized the animal's form; in the way one recognizes trees on a country highway— background. He could only focus on Adrian.

For the second time in his life, Paul had heard a scream from The Flats and had come running with Stoss in tow. The deer had stumbled back into the woods and was gone at that point. He caught sight of Norton bounding along the bank, caught up and took him to The Grove for the first time.

Later when the three men returned, Stoss organized a truck to leave the valley, consisting of himself, Paige, the father and the lifeless sleeping bag. There was no room in their brains for a jump of reason that tied together the tragedy and David and JP's hunting trip. And when David returned, he didn't either. He had seen the bleeding doe run off, but in a different direction than the river, so he listened intently for any details of a gunshot wound on the animal— and heard none. No one would leave a detail like that out, right? He just kept hearing that a deer stumbled out of the woods, startled Adrian and ran off. Deer were everywhere. He did leave out his hunting story; there was enough death around that it would have been weird. But when Paul had asked David, "I heard your shots; where's the deer?" after the truck drove over the ridge, he only responded, "Missed her. Both times," and averted his gaze and wandered away. He didn't feel like he was lying, he just didn't want to be anywhere near the events on the Elizabeth, even figuratively.

But even in grief, Paul was sharp. Somewhere in the subconscious, he registered his brother's tone and evasiveness. He recognized the tone that had claimed a self-perceived innocence many times before. But it would take a while for the realization to clarify. So everyone agreed that it had just been a bumbling deer.

Except JP. But to him it was a detail that was not his responsibility. If David wanted to come clean, own up to it, he could, but on his own terms. That was up to him. It was such a cosmically linked accident that to even bring up the possibility of them being the same deer felt sadistic. It wasn't provable; it wouldn't change anything if it were. So the introvert that lay so hidden in JP convinced him to move on and he quietly loaded the trucks and trailers, being as helpful as possible.

Only later as he pulled up the stakes of the horseshoe pit with a reminiscent glaze on his eyes did Paul look at him and recognize a wave of guilt through the tide of sadness. Paul knew what he saw; he'd seen guilt on JP's face before, and it echoed his brother's tone from earlier. The connection wasn't intuitive immediately, but as the remaining guys packed their trucks and headed out, Paul linked the two events.

Caged by words, he turned inward. He stood next to his brother on the rocks in the Elizabeth and watched the last truck's clouds of dust carry their friends away, and when David asked, "You okay?" Paul didn't answer.

From there, over their following weeks in the valley as they plowed ahead to stay through the winter, Paul allowed the two of them to drift apart, and did so in the most powerful way that those with great strength can affect change: he didn't use it. He let their bonds lie fallow; he let them atrophy. He set a tent in the meadow and slept there alone. He went on walks by himself. He didn't go to The Grove. He didn't make attempts to engage David on any level and when they'd pass, he simply nodded or responded to David's questions shortly.

And with a subconscious sense, like a nighttime face in the growing flames of a bonfire, the reason for Paul's brooding slowly came clear to David. It became an unspoken thing between them.

Now, one may hear of these dreadful conditions and ask why the Ambrose brothers didn't pack up with everyone else and head back to the city and resume life again. I don't know. As much as we humans have been gifted with reason, we can never escape the occasional moments where the tool abandons us and we revert to our animal.

~

A while ago, people agreed that a passage of time has healing powers. However the simple notion often robs the true catalysts and conditions of credit for their work. Wounds don't disappear on time's whim alone. Time employs agents.

And so it passed.

In the fall, when the rains began to sweep with regularity, Paul ambled darkly into their meadow from the Elizabeth. A dense drizzle was thick through the valley, laying a fine mist over the damp leaves and soil. David stood on the porch of the cabin as Paul walked past, his finger gaffing a trout's jaws. Percy clipped at his heels and eyed the trout warily.

"I've got a fire going if you want to cook in here," David said as casually as he could.

Paul continued and spoke without tone, "I'm fine."

"You sure?"

"Yes."

Then David said quickly, "I'm going for a hike down by the Giant Steps tomorrow, you want to come?"

"I'm good."

And that was that.

A few weeks later, the first snow dusted the valley and the chatter in the woods took on a tone of shock and planning. The winds blew crisply through the trees and the clouds of snow swirled and collected in the corners and waited for reinforcements. Paul was chopping wood behind the cabin. David came around the corner with two thick rainbows dangling from a piece of rope threaded through their gills. He had given up hooking his fingers through their gills as the icy coating turned the digits red, then blue.

"Want one of these?" he asked casually.

"No thanks," Paul said, moving a block to the chopping stump and splitting it.

"You sure?" David asked, injecting lightness in his tone. "I'll cook...and do dishes."

"I've got the venison you left me."

"Come on...these are meaty Grove fish."

Paul shot him an iron glance. "*I'm good.*"

The casualness faded, and there was a note of pleading, "Want to go for a hike then—soon, before the snows are too deep?" David asked.

"Not really."

Defeat finally passed though David's face and he turned. "I'll cook both in case you change your mind," he said over his shoulder.

Paul went back to chopping wood. That night he cooked his remaining venison and kept his hands near the flames. A frozen mist blew off the reaching boughs around the meadow and it laid a sparkling veneer on the backs of his hands, then it melted.

The reinforcements arrived and the snows began to layer the valley for winter. Early one morning, before any light had crept into the treetops, David awoke and heard a rustling and shifting on the deck of the cabin. He picked up his head and could just make out Paul's specter moving back and forth in the moonlight. Percy watched, curled by the fireplace and then lay back down. Shortly, Paul came inside, his sleeping bag in hand, and laid down on one of the bunks; flecks of snow drifted in the dark air and caught the reflection of the dying fire. After a minute he said, "My tent collapsed" and there was a pregnant pause. Then he laughed to himself. David allowed himself a chuckling echo and they laughed softly together in the dark.

The storms and white phalanxes continued moving through and marched silently into the New Year. One morning, a biting cold cleaved the valley. They huddled in the great cabin by the fire and were quiet; Percy was wrapped over Paul's feet, her head on her paws and her eyes shifted back and forth, silently asking man's ingenuity to invent more heat. David's gaze began to wander, and soon he looked to the far wall where the bunks lay, then he looked to the high ceiling with the drafty ribcage of rafters. "We need to tear up the bunks—all but two," he said solemnly.

Paul glanced up from the flames, confused. "There's plenty of wood."

"No—we need to build a wall, to keep the heat closer to the fire. I designed this cabin big enough for twelve people in the summer, but not small for two in the winter. If we take apart those planks and bisect the cabin with a wall, and hang a few reflecting planks in the rafters, and drape a few extra blankets, the area by the fire will stay way warmer."

Paul nodded, impressed with the idea, and the next day they set to work, hacking and tearing the bunks to their elements and reconstructing a haphazard wall, leaving a wooden womb around the fire. The hard work and construction put warmth in their chests and the synergy of creation teased out light conversation. As the last planks were laid and the remaining two bunks moved next to the fire, David abruptly stopped. He looked up at his brother, "I shouldn't have done that."

"What?" Paul said uneasily and his shoulders came taught.

"I shouldn't have pulled that bullshit with Gretchen."

Oh," — a relief washed over Paul's face — "*that*. Yeah, well" — he looked around at their dreary setup — "probably for the best."

David took on the gravity of the still unspoken and it manifested as a nervous laugh. "Well, either way, I shouldn't have done that. It was mean."

Paul wiped his brow with a gloved hand and shifted onto his other foot. "I've thought a lot about it — had the time," he said with a faint smile, "and it really was for the best. She and I were trying to force something based on immature love, for whatever reasons. I was pissed at the time, but I'm past it. It's in the rearview."

David nodded and the silence resettled. They went back to work.

The cleaving cold eventually left the valley. The venison ran out and David took another deer; Paul dressed it down. And as the days wore on, the snows, which had layered into sheets of grey-blue faces that gave record to how they came to pass, began to soften. The sun peeked more regularly and winked off the corners of the drifts; and drops began to form and fall to the wet earth.

~ 2 ~

DAVID AWOKE ONE MORNING to the sound of a lone bird chirping outside the cabin window. He pulled down the lip of his sleeping bag, glanced at his brother's empty bunk. The wall of reconstructed bunks stood tall next to him. He rubbed his eyes and rolled out of bed. Paul had left some coffee on the stove, now cool, and David turned on the burner and let the heat crackle against the tin pot. The morning fire had reduced to pulsing embers and he threw on a few logs and rekindled the base. He stretched and stepped outside.

The cold air pricked goose bumps over his skin, yet there was an auspicious quality; it lacked aggression. There had been times, usually a day or two after a bad storm, when David had found himself running and covering his ears to get inside the warmth of the cabin. He hazarded that it was a little warmer now, not much, yet there was far less menace in the grip of his skin, like a mother's cold hand on his neck. He went back inside; a few birds harmonized in song as the door clicked shut.

Paul had made a recent custom, as the road thawed, to take early walks alone; David did not expect him back until lunchtime. As he poured a cup of coffee however, he heard heavy chopping behind the cabin and the plink-plink of wood falling onto itself. He sipped his cup in the dim light. The goose bumps dissolved and the veneer of his winter-hardened skin returned. Another *thwack!* and plink-plink came from outside as he sat down at the table.

The Hunter's Guide lay open, or half of it did at least. At some point in the late fall, the spine had completely deteriorated and now all that remained was a stack of pages. Some had been lost, others had also dissolved into the elements, but the book still repeated the old advice it had spoken since the trappers penned their thoughts many years before. David noticed that it was open to the short section about fishing. He chewed on a piece of venison jerky, sipped his coffee and read.

"Trapping a fish relies on the same core principle as any other: patience. As we've said, the Woods never show the way, you do. We'll start with the Stream. [Skip ahead to Lake Fishing or Netting if relevant] Use Stalking Principles (pp. 9-18) to approach a streamside—managing Wind and Scent are unnecessary. Observe the Stream. You'll see signs of fish you didn't know were there, sometimes, right by you. (Fig. 12.3) Stay hidden. Watch for a head rising to the surface, an unnatural swirl and lurking shadows. Begin to visualize your Hunting Path through the stream. Working downstream to upstream, mental-mark the Pockets and Riffles that will yield the best catch, then the next, the next and so on. (Fig 12.4) Fish spend most of their time facing upstream. Be conscious of the likely direction one would run, should you miss, and how it would affect the others. Review your Hunting Path until it is committed to memory, and then return to the Woods.

[Skip ahead to the Hand Line section, if relevant.]

To make your spear, find a tree branch between one and two fingers thick and cut from the tree. Use live wood as it is less likely to break during spearing and will not unbalance when submerged..."

Outside, Percy barked. The top of Paul's head bounced in front of the window; the white trees drooped in the distance, their branches dripping. David moved away from the table quickly, as if caught, and sat on his bunk as Paul pushed open the door with two loads of wood. Percy trotted at his heels.

"Morning," David said watching him closely as he walked past.

Paul murmured affirmation as he stacked logs by the fire. He uncurled either arm carefully so that the contents fell together in a fitted wall. He shot a sideways glance to his brother, looking patiently in his direction. "What?"

"I was thinking about something," David said after a moment. "You ever wonder how many fish we've caught here...like ever?"

This put a pause in Paul. "Ever?"

"In St George's—but yeah, ever."

Paul stood quietly for a long moment. His breath was still labored from carrying the logs and his cheeks were the color of a rainbow's stripe. He took off his gloves, wiped his face and stepped behind the wall of bunks. After a few minutes of rummaging noises, he returned with a stack of notebooks.

David was a little startled at the relic from the summer. "You know?"

"Hold on," Paul said quietly, then looked at the fire distantly. "I'll know what we've done until the end of last summer."

David looked down at his hands. Paul began marking and copying numbers to one page of the last notebook. Percy came over and put her nuzzle under his arm as he worked, and he scratched her with one hand. Eventually, after about twenty minutes, Paul circled a figure towards the bottom of the page.

"Guess," he said calmly.

"Both—" David started to ask, sitting up quickly, then edited excitement from his voice, "Both of us or each of us?"

"Both. There are a handful of days where I didn't separate our totals."

"This goes all the way back to our first year here?"

"Yes."

"Did you count the ones during JP and my game of PIG?"

"Yes."

"Even the one at the end, when I was going for the win?"

"Yup."

"There were days when I fished on my own. How did you get those numbers?"

"I asked you, but if you were with someone else, I'd ask them too, then take the average. If you'd fished on your own, I'd casually ask you and multiply the answer by a percentage, depending on how you looked me in the eye."

David scratched his cheek with his middle finger standing alone. "Well aren't you just a smart bastard."

Paul shrugged.

"What about the fish that eagle stole?"

"Only counts if you put the fish in the net. You know that." Paul put up a hand as David readied his counter and continued, "I'm asking you to guess how many fish we've caught over the last four years." He looked down at the page of the notebook and made another careless arc. "One fish isn't going to make a difference."

"Fine. Give me a second." David squinted and closed his eyes, mouthing numbers and occasionally looking at the rafters and bouncing a finger as he added. Percy watched too. "Okay," he said finally. "Between the two of us, since we've started coming to St George's valley, we've combined to— actually…" The flicker of competition passed through David's face. "How about this," he said playfully, "if I guess within a hundred fish, we go on a hike of my choice?"

Paul didn't look back at his brother. "And if you lose?"

"I'll swim in the Elizabeth." David's eyes searched with a little panic trying to corral the words, but as they did, he owned them.

Paul nodded slowly. "Okay. Guess then."

"Give me a minute," and David went back through his math. After a few more bouncing fingers and mouthing of numbers, David looked up at his brother and stamped the answer with confidence. "1,992—just shy of two thousand."

Paul clicked his tongue and looked back at the notebook. A faint whistle drifted through his teeth. "How'd you arrive at that number?" A shade of genuine curiosity lined his voice.

"Well, we were here for about a week the first and second year, then a month and then about two months last summer—" he flushed a little "—that's a little over a hundred days. Figure about nine or ten fish per day each since we didn't fish every day...I don't know, part of it's just gut— what's the answer?"

Paul looked at the figure and started shaking his head.

David couldn't tell if it was in disbelief or disdain. "Am I right?" he demanded, his voice rising in excitement.

Paul began to speak, but stopped. He ripped the page from the notebook. In a broad step, he cast it into the popping flames of the fire. At first stunned by his suddenness, David leapt and tried to stop him; Percy barked at the commotion. But Paul gently held his brother at bay with one arm until only a bouquet of ash remained.

"What was the number?" David asked after a moment of stunned silence, looking at the charred record.

A disconcerting calm twinkled in Paul's voice. "You win."

David looked confused at his brother. "Tell me the number."

Paul pursed his lips in mock thought. "Nope. You win."

"What's wrong with you?" David hissed and snatched one of the other notebooks off the chair, leafed through it, then threw it back. "Fucking chicken scratch."

"Yup."

"Tell me the number."

"You win, David. That's all that matters." Paul grabbed his hat off the table, flipped *The Hunter's Guide* closed and walked to the door, Percy trotting at his feet. "Let me know where we're hiking," he said as the door clicked behind him.

David watched him go, then looked back to the fire and the coals that pulsed underneath. He reopened the book and, outside, could just make out the sound of his brother laughing to himself as he took up the axe. The *thwack!* and plink-

plink of wood followed shortly thereafter.

~

If David had looked out the window, he'd have seen Paul chopping wood with smooth blows of the axe as both new pieces fell to the side as if pulled gently apart by a string. He may have heard the laughter fade into the breeze as his brother set a second piece of wood faster and split it. He'd have seen Paul take a third even faster, and a fourth, until he was a machine moving in a hastened set-chop-set-chop whir while perspiration coated his forehead. Then he would have seen Paul lose footing, slump to one knee, and tears of a tired frustration come to his eyes.

After a moment, he would have seen Paul regain his feet and resume chopping at a normal pace as Percy cocked her head in curiosity from a short distance away.

~ 3 ~

WITH A PANE OF DARKNESS still pressed against the windows, David shook his brother awake. "What are you doing?" Paul asked, too sleepy to muster aggravation.

"You said I'd won," David responded coolly. "So I'm cashing in. Come on; we're going for our hike. I checked the cloud cover, temperature and pressure last night; the weather will be nice today."

"I'm going back to bed. There wasn't anything in the bet about waking before sunrise." Paul rolled over in his sleeping bag under the protests of his creaking bunk.

"The bet was *of my choice.*"

"Go to hell."

"Get up." David's even tone made Paul look back at him; his silhouette was only highlighted by the faint gas burner heating coffee.

"We'll go on your hike when there is light." Paul rolled over.

"Get up," David said and whacked his shoulder.

"Don't."

"Get up." He whacked him again.

"David, *don't.*"

"Come on." He whacked him again, harder.

"If you do that one more time—"

"You said it yourself: life is movement." He smacked him as hard as he could.

"*DAMN IT*—" Paul burst from his sleeping bag, fists

clenched, but David stood his ground.

"It was a hike of my choice…you said, I'd won. We're going to Morning Rock." The cold calm in David's voice was softened by the faint tones of pleading. Paul lost the violence in his face and fists, started to say something, then sat back, rubbing his eyes.

About twenty minutes later, they made their way down the steps of the cabin in the moonlight. Paul carried a daypack. Percy trotted nearby at their heels, weaving in and out of the pearly grasses and the shadows. The stumps from the previous summer pierced the patches of snow. They walked among them and the scars of the fallen trees. It was still—without even the hoot of an owl. They pressed on. The pitch began to steepen at the north rim of the valley and the stars, one by one, were stepping to the background of dawn. Soon the trees began to thin and in the distance, they could make out the face of Morning Rock.

Through the winter the great stony face had acted like a great seine for the snowstorms, catching the flakes and blizzards as they'd passed and collecting the contents at the base. The drift extended down the slope from the tall rock like a long, thick ghost tongue. Paul patted the snow while Percy lapped up the edges. It was still light and fluffy. Soon, they made their way onto Morning Rock and sat. They looked at what they could make out of the valley under the low ceiling of thick clouds, which was almost nothing, as if they sat on the inside wall of a long sock. The Elizabeth was the only feature with clear edges; she was still the black ribbon of division; she sighed a thin white mist at her edges. The wind was still. They sat for a while.

"A little different than the last time we did this," David said with false cheer.

Paul pawed through the gravel next to him with a funny smile in the corner of his mouth that made David uncomfortable.

"How long you think?" David asked after a few minutes,

distracting himself.

Paul shrugged absently and didn't say anything. Percy, now sleeping, had nestled under his big, coated arm, her black ears flopping on his jacket. He looked down and his eyes flickered around strangely at points on the dog and the ground.

"What's so funny?" The hackles on David's neck began to stand.

"Cute dog."

Paul looked at the lightening eastern sky again and sighed as a breeze slid past. He let the vapors pour from his mouth into the mountain air. They folded and dissipated above him. He gently shifted Percy's head to the tops of her paws and stood. He set his daypack aside and stretched, swirling his big arms, the whooshes even louder with the creaking of his jacket. He rocked his head from side to side and rolled his neck. He touched his boots and rubbed his shoulders and back.

"What are you doing?" David asked but Paul didn't look at him.

"Wait for it....wait." Paul started rolling his arms faster and faster as the whooshes got louder and louder. "And there it is."

A single strand of light appeared over the mountaintops to the east through the ceiling of clouds—the sunrise.

David turned in time to see Paul take two long steps and jump from the end of the buttress. The last image he had was Paul's huge, jacketed frame spread eagle, before he disappeared over the edge. The tops of the pines were a little ways in the distance calmly waving in the cold breeze.

David heard himself cry out, then mutter his brother's name, and turn it to a mantra, one continuous word. He sprang to his feet, but was frozen in thought and action. He didn't hear Percy bark and howl. Did he go to the edge and look, or did he go around and down to him? He stood awkwardly. He took a step towards the edge, then the other way, then he watched his footing so he didn't slip. The grey clouds had descended into his brain. As he attempted to clear them away, he just barely made out the sound, in the background, of Paul laughing.

He stopped and cocked his head.

David thought, through the clearing fog, that he'd just witnessed his brother's suicide and promptly gone insane. He stopped. He listened. It was laughing; it was real. He stepped carefully to the edge and looked over.

At the end of a long smooth track in the drift was his brother, waving for him to jump too. David looked again and could see where Paul's hips had detonated the snow and how a confluence of the snowfall's height and density, the slope of the pitch and his brother's outward, X-axis movement, had allowed him to land and slide safely after seemingly jumping to his lonesome death.

"Jump!" Paul shouted.

David looked back at Percy, whining with her ears out and her head shifting from side to the side. She barked at him. David looked back to the valley spread before him and its dark beauty smacked him across the face.

"Jump!" Paul shouted again.

He jumped. He defeated every fiber of self-preservation in his body. David jumped as far from the rocky outcropping and the wall of St George's Valley as he could. As he fell, he heard his brother yell, "Life *is* movement… asshole." He hit the drift and the crackle of sliding snow filled his ears. His hips and back hurt dully as the crunching rumbled beneath him. Then noise ceased and all was still while he gazed at the bottom of a tree branch.

Two hands closed around the shoulders of his jacket and he came free of the snowy cast he'd created. A fire was burning in Paul's face as he motioned to the peaks. "Come on! We're going to keep on going." David looked his brother over carefully, noting that the disconcerting abandon hadn't vacated his voice. Rubbing his neck and hips, he jogged to catch him; Percy trotted effortlessly between them.

They resumed their hike upwards. Paul moved with an energy that popped in fits and spurts, like an engine rearing to start. They reached lower ridge, near where they had walked with the aspen plank almost a year before, and continued up another pitch, going higher. The sweat came to both of their faces; their breathing was thick and labored as their lungs searched for sustenance. Paul continued charging without turning around, then, as the final rim drew closer, he broke into a run; Percy bounded at his heels. David began to run too. Finally, they reached the top, and Paul still did not turn around to face the valley. He walked forward, his eyes transfixed ahead of them. They had not reached the highest peak.

Before them, laid out like a black mirror, was an alpine lake. It nestled at the base of two looming spires—both reflected in the flat waters. The water body was shaped like a teardrop and the point funneled back to the Elizabeth. Percy ran to the still banks and sniffed the water's edge; Paul began walking around the lake in the opposite direction, then stopped and took off his pack. He withdrew his water bottle and drank, then to David's surprise, withdrew a short rod holder.

"Did you know this was here?" David asked, still taking in the entirety of what was before him.

"Had a feeling," Paul said wiping his mouth and slowing his wheezes.

"Why'd you wait so long to come up here?"

Paul cocked his head in honest thought. "Don't know," he said then continued like it was any other conversation. "Did you bring a rod?"

"Why would I?" David asked a little frustrated.

Paul shrugged and took another sip of water.

"You okay?" David asked carefully.

Paul gazed at David, surprised. "Of course. You?"

"Fine. You seem to have a lot of—I don't know—fire, all

of a sudden."

Paul watched Percy jog off and explore the neighboring woods. "Let's fish," he said turning back to the lake.

Paul assembled his rod and procured a reel and a few boxes of flies from the bottom of his pack and was soon casting to the flat waters of the lake. David stood a few paces away and watched as his brother hauled, released and stripped his line in smooth fury over the water. He could see the energy flaring in his brother's movements. Every snap of the wrist and stop of the shoulder exploded the line, until after a minute, the fishing seemed secondary to the casting, and Paul stood as if alone, a lone figure trying to release a coiled energy on the banks of a black lake in the middle of the Crescent Range.

David waited for his turn patiently on the rod, but moved closer for conversation as he watched. "Didn't see what you tied on," he said.

"Woolly bugger."

"You think a fast strip is best right now? Seems like the fish would be getting their energy back from the winter freeze still."

"No," Paul said with resolution. "If there are any fish in this lake, it'll be a fevered competition for anything to eat. Might as well attract the most attention."

"Right," David said slowly. He didn't agree. "It'll be cool to have a secret lake this summer." Paul's neck and arms tightened; his cast and retrieval slowed. David continued, "We should name it too. Maybe…Twin Peak Lake? Or Summit Lake? What do you think?"

Paul shrugged.

David continued, "You know—I've been thinking about how we could route some power to the cabin. If we put up a half dozen solar voltaic panels on the roof, we could probably draw enough power during the day for lights and maybe a little heat each night. In the summer we could use it for that icemaker instead of gas. Also—and we'd need the whole crew for this—but we could set a pipe running from one of the big pools in the Elizabeth to the cabin so we didn't have to traipse down for water. I don't think we could pipe it *into* the cabin but we could at least have a well for everyone or a—"

Percy came jogging back from the nearby woods and Paul nodded to her as she approached. "Hey," he said with patronizing casualness, "do you remember when Paige left with Stoss and Norton, how she left Percy behind?"

A gate slammed shut in David's face and he shifted on his feet. "No," he said cautiously.

"It was something. It was like she couldn't handle the thought of taking care of someone, or anything, like some sort of emotional sloughing of weight...you know?"

"That sounds terrible," David said not letting down his guard.

"Yeah, it was," Paul said keeping his tone. "Did you happen to see—"

"What are you doing?" David asked cutting through with acid-laced words.

Paul faced him. "What makes you think people will be back next year?" His voice was toneless and even like a gray wire.

This put pause in David and his eyes flared a little. "I think people will be back," he said quietly.

"Do you?"

"Look—I get that what happened last summer was terrible. But I think enough time will have passed that the other guys will come fish again. That's all." David noticed Paul's hands were shaking slightly and his tone tightened. "Don't guilt me because I'm being optimistic."

Paul's hands trembled further. "I just think you need a little perspective on what happened. You don't seem to have *learned*."

"Learned? I learned, Paul. Don't tell me I didn't *learn*."

"You think you have—but you haven't."

David's voice turned to dark ice. "Don't lecture me—don't think of lecturing me. Paul, did you ever think *why* Adrian was at The Flats in the first place?"

Paul squinted and seemed to catch his balance.

"Norton's waders had a tear; you went back to fix them; and that's when he tagged along. Do you remember why they had that tear?"

Paul's throat closed as he drew the line off the water. He released the cast.

David continued, "Of course JP wasn't going to keep his mouth shut about that stunt you pulled with the cowboys. So Paul—*don't* lecture me about *learning*."

Paul looked out at the thin crooked division of his fly line on the black lake. Around it, a few bugs were popping and hatching, though he couldn't tell what they were. He squinted; they looked like midges, but he wasn't sure. A calm passed through him.

"David," he said slowly, "its not my fault when you screw up."

~

We fish because it allows us to think. When we have success we are flooded with a concurrent calm of recognition and fire of exhilaration at our integration with the wild. For, that is all we truly are.

The bugs continued popping to the surface and drifting away on the dark lake in front of the Ambrose brothers. As he continued with his eyes in a trance on their fluttery paths in the wind, Paul's calm betrayed him: he didn't notice David charge. He only heard a quick patter on the gravel and then felt a shoulder drive into his hip. The fly rod sailed from his hand as they slid on the beach in a cloud of dust and sand.

Paul, snapping to childhood instincts, got an arm around his brother in a reverse headlock, but not before David raised his fist and punched him in the side, then again. Paul tried to stop the blows with his free hand and in shifting focus loosened his grip on the headlock. David wriggled his head free and dug his knees into Paul's arm and pinned them. Paul tried to free his arm but David bore into him. He punched Paul in the chest, then reached for Paul's free arm with his non-swinging hand. Paul stretched it away and avoided capture. David lunged and as he did, Paul shot it back into his chest, palm open, with a resounding thump.

The broad surface of Paul's hand depressed into his brother's chest as the ribs bent and the air rushed out his mouth like a soul. And for a moment, an instant, a blink that would outpace lightning, Paul looked at his brother and he seemed lifeless; his eyes were empty. Then in the next instant, the life returned and Paul saw a sadness, a longing in David's face—a hurt. He saw a frightened little boy that draped anger over his fear.

The grind of mountain pebbles reappeared in his ear and Paul watched David's anger storm across his face as he drew his breath. The shock of clarity settled Paul. He focused. He fastened his big hand to David's chest and in one rocking motion, rolled him and pinned him.

"*GET OFF ME,*" David roared as his brother's huge weight smothered him. Only one of David's arms was free. He punched Paul across the face. The blow landed flush above the cheekbone, cutting below his left eye; air rushed through and cooled the tissue and some blood burped to the surface.

David raised his fist to strike again, but his eyes glanced forward and widened in shock; he put out his hands to defend himself. As he did, Paul's jacket and shirt constricted around his neck and yanked him backward by the throat, then upward; his larynx bent under the pressure and he flailed his arms as he rose in the air.

"Stop," a voice said softly, yet matter-of-factly.

Each brother, eyes wide, found himself tethered to the extended arms of a man with a white beard, keeping them at bay by their collars. He was the same size, but the old strength with which he kept them apart expanded his being in the mind's eye. Their struggles began to subside. "If I let you boys go, you going to quit?" Z asked.

For a moment, both brothers stood in a savage trance, then their shoulders slackened and the tension drained their faces. David shrugged away the grip; Z let Paul go. They stood in silence by the black lake with the wind snapping across the mountains. Paul's eye began to bleed down his cheek and he wiped it onto his sleeve. David saw the blood and turned away, toward the water.

"Alright," Z said finally. "You got that out of your systems." He flicked his glance toward the valley and began walking down the pitch, "The dog'll stay here," he said over his shoulder. And like little boys, Paul and David followed.

They came off the plateau and made their way across the slope. Life pulsed. The deep patches of snow scattered about them in shady puddles as the high mountain brush coughed and gasped for the sun and melting spring water. The trees began to thicken and their shadows draped over the fallen ones and the large discarded stones of the rising peaks. Paul and David looked about wide-eyed as the adrenaline diffused, not noticing their sore necks or the bruises they'd stamped on one another, but taking it all in. The shouting new grasses, the red and yellow wildflowers, the quivering brush and the bowing trees, with the banter of chatter and chirps in the shadows was suddenly new, a rebirth and they absorbed it as they followed the old mountain man down the slender neck of a game trail in the arms of the forest.

After a slight bend around the low shoulder of a peak, he put up a hand and stopped them, a finger over pursed lips. He crept quietly to a large pile of rocks embedded in the mountainside and peered into a gaping fissure, then waved them over and put the finger back to his lips. Paul stepped first; David followed quietly. They crawled up behind Z and peered into the darkness.

"Wha—?" David started, but cut himself off.

In the remnants of light gleamed three small pairs of

eyes, set in a permanent question. They huddled to the back, frightened, and looked out at the three men. Little ivory claws blinked as they shredded the air in incipient aggression. One cub purred deeply.

A hand came to Paul and David's shoulders and pulled them away; Z nodded back the way they'd come. "She'll be back soon—out hunting." They began following him back up the game trail, their pace at a light run. The woods re-enveloped them.

After a few hundred yards, David stammered, "That mountain lion died." He looked over his shoulder at the darkness of the forest that followed close behind, then to his brother for confirmation. But Paul was jogging in a trance and looking into the opening light ahead, chewing his cheek.

"It's a big valley," Z said.

They retraced their steps, back up the pitch until they reached the lake again. The fly rod still leaned against the rocks on shore; its line pointed and vanished into the depths. The clouds were lifting and patches of blue blinked on the water when the wind died. Z lit a cigar and let the smoke puff around the brim of his hat. He scratched his beard and looked at the two brothers.

"Okay?"

"Okay, what?" David asked indignantly, but as he did, he saw his brother nodding solemnly.

Z looked at Paul and tipped his hat. "Good. Now finish fishing, and I'll catch you boys later. I need to set camp before dark."

"You're welcome to stay at our cabin," David said quickly.

Z laughed a little, "Naw, that's your place—would be a little cramped." He turned on his heel, "I'll see you on the Elizabeth soon, after the last bits of ice are gone," he said over his shoulder. The brothers watched him grab a discarded pack—a rod holder on the side—and throw it over his shoulder. The cigar smoke sifted up through the shadows and spread among the boughs as he disappeared into St George's Valley.

"That old man..." David said and trailed off. "What was his 'okay?' about?"

Paul turned to his brother and said quietly, "We had no right to spend the winter the way we did. That was selfish."

"What was?"

"Us. The way we...I acted." Paul walked over to a rock and sat down; he looked out at the lake with his elbows on his knees. "Maybe I did it with my bare hands and a knife, but on some level, life itself took that mountain lion. But it kept moving. And on some level," he swallowed and a tear squeezed from the corner of his eye, "life took Adrian...but it'll keep moving. And that's where we were selfish this winter. The only way we stay moving is if we recognize that once-in-a-sad-while a piece will stop and when it does, we have the right to be sad, but an obligation to keep going. That's how it has to work, because the whole picture will *never* stop. It's the only way to keep up, and I guess...be happy."

David followed his brother's gaze onto the lake and, after a moment, nodded—gently with solemn conviction. They sat in silence for a while. The sun peeked through the clouds and warmed their backs. With the color in the sky they could see the contours of the lake under the breeze and the way it gently leaned against the shore. They had not seen water hold that still in a very long time.

"I didn't mean what I said earlier," Paul said after a while. He rubbed his shoulders and looked at his brother. "I'm sorry." The breeze cracked the black waters again. "You all right?" he asked after it was gone.

"Fine...you?"

"You socked me a couple of good ones," Paul said with a hint of humor. His eye was swelling, but the bleeding had stopped. "But yeah, I'm fine."

After a minute David took a sharp inhale. "I'm sorry too.

I'm really...very sorry." A block fell from his shoulders, turned to dust and dissipated in the air; it caught the wind and swirled and mixed with the currents and rushed down the ridgeline into the valley below. And though he fought to keep his breathing even in front of his older brother, his eyes had turned a sorrowful glaze and a few tears dripped down his cheek and fell onto the shore of the lake. Paul put a hand on his shoulder and squeezed; they continued looking out at the reflection of the two peaks while time passed between them peacefully.

Finally, David coughed, rubbed his face and stood up; a smile whispered at the corners of his mouth. "What do you weigh these days? You really fattened up over the winter." He rubbed his chest and rocked his head from side to side stretching his neck.

Paul grunted a laugh.

There were more bugs on the water; a hatch was on, though there weren't rises yet. David coughed again and looked at the discarded rod thrown between two rocks. Line creaked off the reel. "Holy shit..."

"Well, reel her in," Paul said, standing.

"My wrists kill. Put your big mitts to good use."

Paul bent down and took the rod. The added resistance incited the fish and it took off, the reel whizzing as line disappeared into the depths. David took a knee and dipped his hands in the water, and ran it over his face. He rubbed his wrists a little more and then looked up at his brother with a sly grin, as Paul tried to dampen the whirling reel.

"You, ah, need some help?"

Paul put a lonesome middle finger to his ear and grinned. "Sorry—what was that?"

David grinned back. "Just checking."

"She's running weird, too smooth—may be foul hooked or something. I'm not feeling any headshakes." Paul kept the rod high and took the fish on the reel, slowly gaining line.

"I can't get a good look at her," David said, craning his

neck.

"Me neither."

The fish breached on cue, a dark torpedo splashing in the water.

"*Whoa!* What the hell was that?" David yelled.

Paul stepped back from the bank and gained more ground. The fish breached again. He continued reeling, keeping the rod high, and soon the fish was near to shore; swirls bent the reflections of the two peaks, and then the dark torpedo shattering them with another jump.

"Get away. I can land my own damn fish," Paul said trying, but failing, to push his brother out of the way.

"I'll—what the hell is that thing?" David scooped the fish from the water as it writhed in his grip. He held it up and they both looked closely. It was average size for a trout, but with iridescent scales that burst purple, not the patterns of a rainbow or brown. Bulging eyes in an off-shade of green and brown sat above a downward turned mouth with puffed lips, pursed, like for a kiss. But the most striking feature was her dorsal fin. David stretched it in his hand as it extended a spiny sail, taller than the body itself.

"Grayling," Paul said. "Arctic Grayling."

David nodded. "Grayling." He turned the word over in his mouth and said it again. "Cool. It looks like a whitefish." He handed the fish to his brother who looked at it closely like he had many fish, many times before.

"A Salmonid, stocked at high altitudes. *Thymallus arcticus.*"

David suppressed a smile. "Cool, Paul."

"Shut up," he laughed, and moved the grayling back and forth in the shallow water. The dark sparkling fin luffed gently as the fish undulated in his thick fingers; then it crept away, disappearing into the reflection of the two peaks, just bending them with a gentle ripple from its tail.

David gazed back at the lake, then looked his brother in the eye, "You ready to head back?"

"No," Paul said slowly, then waved his arm to the still waters, "I'd rather stay and catch a bunch more of those. Here, on Bucket Hat Lake."

David took the rod. "Good call," he said after a moment. He pulled off a length of line to cast, then stopped. The fly dangled from the tip of the rod, swaying in the breeze. He turned to his big brother. "What was the number?"

Through green eyes, Paul looked at his little brother and smiled. "It's your turn, David," he said and nodded towards the water.